Sleeping With An Angel

A Rock Novel

with Music

Frank,
Thank you for your friendship, leadership, and all the good will you provide to your community.
Best personal regards,
Roger

by Roger A. Campos

music by Jon Campos

St. John's Press
Washington • Baltimore

Although based on a true story, this book is written as a fiction novel. The names, characters, places, events and incidents protrayed have been created, changed or used fictitiously and are the the product of the author's imagination. Any similarities to a person either living or dead is unintentional or coincidence.

The purpose of this book is to entertain and therefore, the author, songwriter, publisher, record company or individuals and entities associated with publication shall have neither liability nor responsibility to any person or entity with respect to any loss or damage caused, or alleged to be caused, directly or indirectly by the story contained in this work.

Published by St. John's Press
P.O. Box 61362
Potomac, Maryland 20854
1-888-605-4808 (toll-free)
http://www.sleepingwithanangel.com

First Printing

Cover Design by Craig Herron
Photography by Michael Defilippi

ISBN: 0-9676067-5-6
Library of Congress Catalog Card Number 99-097009

A Note from the Editor

Roger A. Campos has written an engrossing modern parable about a man's spiritual descent into hell and ultimate redemption. The writing style is excellent with prose, crisp and poetic. The story moves at a rapid pace to an emotional conclusion.

This Rock Novel approach, with father writing and son singing, is the first of its kind in the publishing industry. Readers will be enchanted and absorbed in both the words and the music.

Robert Broomall
Editor

A Note from the Record Label

Roger and Jon Campos have created a whole new dimension with the addition of pop/rock music to the scenes of the story. By playing the appropriate track of the CD when it appears in the text, the reader will actually hear the music when the characters do in the novel.

Jon's sensitive style of music and inspirational lyrics bring Rogers words to life.

Gary G. Waitt
Inca Gold Records

About the Author

Roger A. Campos, grew up in Modesto, California and then moved to Washington D.C. after graduating from law school. He has worked for several federal agencies including the White House's Office of Management & Budget. After leaving Government service, he now specializes in governmental relations. He graduated from the University of California at Santa Barbara and earned his law degree from United States International University School of Law (California Western campus) in San Diego, California. He is the father of singer and songwriter, Jon Campos. He is divorced and living in the Washington-Baltimore area.

About the Songwriter

Jon Campos, a singer and songwriter composed, arranged, and performed all musical selections on the thirteen tracks of the CD which accompanies the book ***Sleeping With An Angel.*** He has performed and toured throughout the United States, Hawaii and Japan. He attended the Cincinnati Conservatory School of Music, the Guitar Institute of Atlanta, and the Grove School of Music in Los Angeles. He is the son of Roger A. Campos and lives in the Washington-Baltimore area.

For bookings contact:
1-888-605-4808 (toll-free)

Acknowledgment

This book would not have been possible without the unwavering, tireless support of Christina Montana. She guided this work and shaped it through many rewrites. She listened and transformed my thoughts into words. No writer could have been blessed with such a creative talent and Literary Agent.

I would also like to thank the editor, Robert Broomall, for his encouragement, and especially Craig and Barbara Herron for meeting tight deadline schedules in order to fine-tune the artwork, graphics and layout.

This new multimedia approach of a book accompanied with a pop/rock CD required the musical talents of my son, Jon Campos and many other people. The CD took over one year to produce. I would like to thank the musicians and team at Inca Gold Records for believing in this project and especially Gary Charles at MS PRO Productions for his music guidance.

Many people have shared and touched my life in so many ways. I want to thank them all especially my family - my brother, Stephen and my sister, Cecilia and her husband, Don for their support throughout the years.

Several people really made a difference and their contributions are deeply appreciated. My special appreciation goes out to Barbara Slomoff who shared her poetry and nurtured my original writing at the beginning.

...Then, there is a Zen proverb which states-when the student is ready, a teacher will appear. I would like to thank my friend and teacher, Jane Ross for her patience, caring, understanding, and guidance. She has made a significant contribution in my journey.

Sleeping With An Angel took four years to write and would not have been written without the occurrence of several unforeseen events. After my father's death, I received an invitation to an experiential encounter weekend led by Peter Bloch who said the experience would be better than going out on a date. After that November, 1995, weekend, I began to write while snowed-in for several days during the blizzard of January, 1996, with only pen and paper.

Finally, I would like to thank you, the readers, for supporting us in this effort by purchasing a copy of the book and CD. We hope that you enjoy the story and the music.

Dedication

This book is dedicated to two people that I love very much, my Mother who has always given her unconditional love and wonderful sense of humor, and my son who collaborated with me on this project.

In remembrance of my father, Arthur R. Campos

"In the story of women is the life of all men."

Zeptha

I am a warrior from an ancient land. My victories have been many, the battles hard fought; but now I lay on the ground, my shield next to me, my sword far from my hand. It is my father's sword, passed on to me at his death, and it has never lain so far from my side. I am not alone here. There are others not as fortunate. Their eyes gaze vacantly upward, but I, I can still see a bird soaring through a sky of blue with white clouds drifting across it. Somewhere close by I hear the labored, wheezing breath of a dying warhorse. When I try to move, I find that I can not. Some force pins me to earth, holding me against my will. I struggle to remove my armor, to tug at the leather thongs lacing it together, but I can only move the fingers of one hand and open and close my eyes.

Why was I struck down? I pray to the Gods. I made the sacrifices they asked. I brought them the offerings, the spoils of war to win their favor. Why have they abandoned me? I think of my father, who died gloriously in battle, a warrior of the first rank. I remember him telling me how at death the Gods weigh men's souls. "Truth and justice must balance one's life," he said. Were the Wise Ones weighing my soul? I did not want to die.

"Father, help me!" I cry aloud to the silent sky.

"Speak to the Gods for me. I have tried to honor you on the battlefield. I have worn your armor with pride and wielded your sword skillfully, but I am fallen before my enemies. Help me to rise."

In answer, the ground vibrates under me with the thunder of approaching chariots. I know their wheels could crush me like a small desert scorpion. My enemies are here, surrounding me, speaking in a tongue I cannot understand. They are coming closer, and I am afraid, and my fear is the fear of every man who has fallen by my hand. It smothers me, pushing down on my chest, slowing my breath to long, shallow sighs.

My enemies pass close by, like the shades of death, bringing darkness with them. They prod the bodies of my fellow warriors, plunging their swords into those still breathing, but me they pass over, and I am filled with despair. So then it is true. I am dead. The night sky above me is the vault of heaven, and I am doomed to lie beneath it for all time, and I weep for all I have never seen and all I will never see again.

In my grief I do not hear her coming, nor do I know from whence she came. I wonder who she is, this woman wandering alone among the dead, gliding from man to man, corpse to corpse. Who is this vision, glowing in white silken robes?

"Zeptha," she answers, yet I hear no word spoken. "I have been sent to warn you that there are those who wish you great harm." She kneels and leans over me, her long golden hair like the wing of a bird falling across her face. Two sea green eyes look deeply into mine.

But am I not dead now?

"No. Not unless you choose it."

So this is not the end. I will live! I will survive! "How will I know them?" I ask her eagerly. "I will need your help. I will need someone to help me."

"A woman comes," is Zeptha's reply, "but it is only you who can save yourself."

"But I cannot move!" I cry, not believing she would ask the impossible of me.

"There is nothing that holds you," Zeptha says. Then she rises and walks from me, vanishing into the night.

"No! Don't leave me!"

But no one answers my cries for help. Only the night wind blows hot and dry across the plain. I struggle to reach the leather thongs of my armor, and through my tears, the stars tremble and flicker.

Play CD Track 1
"Zeptha's Theme"
instrumental

Celinda

A voice penetrated the thick fog of my unconscious, pulling me back from the very edge of death.

"Sir, do you need some help?"

"You're back!" I mumbled. I knew she wouldn't abandon me.

"Your seatbelt, sir," the voice said. "Do you need help getting it unfastened?"

I forced my eyes open and found, bending over me, a young woman. I looked into her worried face, but I didn't know her. My eyes traveled down to her striped blouse and the pair of golden wings pinned above the pocket.

She repeated each word slowly, pointing to my headphones to make sure I understood. I removed the headset from around my head. "You were trying to unfasten your seatbelt, sir."

"Where am I?"

The woman smiled uncertainly at me. "You're 29,000 feet above Texas, on Flight 208 to Albuquerque. Is there anything I can get you?"

The man seated next to me interrupted. "Get him a Jack Daniels, on me. Seems like he could use a drink."

"Jack Daniels, sir?" asked the flight attendant. I nodded my head.

"Roy," the man said, extending his hand.

"Tony," I replied, and I noticed my hand shook as I took his hand in mine.

The flight attendant brought our drinks and set them on the trays in front of us.

"Thanks for the drink, Roy."

He waved it off. "My pleasure. You've been out since we left Dulles Airport."

"I've been working pretty hard," I said, rubbing my eyes with the palms of my hands. "Guess I was more tired than I thought,"

My fellow passenger sighed. "I know what you mean. I've been on the road for a long time. Almost three months." He shifted uneasily in his seat. "Damn seats keep gettin' smaller, or maybe I'm just gettin' bigger."

He had the broad shoulders of a football player, and a square head sitting on a thick neck. By the size of his stomach, I guessed he liked a few beers too many. I smiled to myself, pleased by the great shape I was still in. My stomach was flat and hard as a board.

He grinned and raised his glass. "But I'm on my way home now. I've got a couple of weeks to be with the family. Wanna see pictures of my kids?" He brought out a worn wallet, bulging with credit cards.

"That's my son Chip, and that's Mandy, and the tall one's Lisbeth," he said, pointing a thick finger at each one in turn. Poor Lisbeth was wall-eyed, and Mandy was missing her two front teeth. I found it hard to believe that little girls like this, all arms and legs and teeth, could turn into beautiful women.

"Nice looking kids," I replied politely.

"Chip's goin' to be a great little baseball player. I played baseball in high school, you know. Almost got a scholarship for it." He flipped to another photo. "This here's my wife Nora. Nora and me lived next door to each other. We were both little tykes when we first met."

I looked down at the plain, blank-faced woman staring out of the photo. She looked pleasant and was probably a good mother. I found myself thinking of my own mom, and I wondered if Nora ever drank.

"You have any kids?" he asked as he put his wallet away.

"No. I never had any kids," I lied.

"That's a shame."

"Yeah. It's too bad."

I swirled the ice around in my drink and watched the cubes float back up to the top. I thought of Julie and my son David, whom I'd not seen since he was eight. "Marry her. It's the honorable thing to do," my dad had said, and I did as I was told. I always did what my dad told me. Julie and I met during our junior year of high school. She had just transferred from Albuquerque. We started going together right away. During our senior year, we were voted "best looking couple" in the school. One early spring night, we took a ride in my grandfather's 1956 Plymouth with an automatic transmission. It was in that front seat, behind an abandoned farm house in a peach orchard, that we both lost our virginity. I was too young to be a dad. I didn't know what to do, so I kept on doing what I knew best, and that was being a big man on campus, while my wife and son lived with my folks. Julie eventually left and took David with her. Can't say I blame her, but I did love her and regret that I never told her how much she meant to me. Since then, it's been a string of women. Maybe one good woman is what I need.

"Where are you from?" I asked, to stop the thoughts.

"Brownsville, Texas, originally, but I'm from Albuquerque now. What about you?"

"Washington, D.C., but I grew up in New Mexico, in Sanibel."

"Never heard of it. Where's it at?"

"Down by the Mexican border."

"Don't get down that way much."

"It's a pretty small town."

"Is that where you're headed?"

"Yeah. I'm going home for a visit, and the first thing I'm going to do when I get there is go to Rosita's."

"What's 'Rosita's'?"

"It's a diner that's been in Sanibel for thirty years. Rosita's still the cook. It's the best breakfast in town."

"There's a place like that in Brownsville. I wonder if it's still there. Haven't thought about it in years. Biscuits big as your fist. Say, what do you do in Washington?"

"I put people together who need each other," I said.

"What kind of people?" Roy asked, puzzled. "Like people in Congress?"

"In Congress. In the White House. I'm a lobbyist."

"Have you met the President?" he asked excitedly.

"Yes, I have."

"Wait 'til I tell Nora I met someone who's met the President. When you shook his hand, did he have a good, strong grip? My father always said you could tell a man's worth by his grip."

"I don't remember."

He seemed disappointed.

"Who else do you know?" he asked.

"I really couldn't say," I replied coolly. In my business, you don't give out information, and when you receive it, you don't reveal your source. You don't commit to anything, or anyone, unless they're paying you. That's the way it works in Washington.

"Sorry," Roy said, backing off. "I didn't mean to pry."

"It's not a problem," I said. I reached for the headphones in my lap and put them on. I closed my eyes, pretending to listen to the music.

There was a bump, then another, as the wheels touched the runway. Roy and I parted at the airport with a handshake and the usual "It's been great meeting you." He started to walk away, but before he did, he turned and said, "Work on that grip, Tony."

I stood there by myself, watching him disappear into the crowd, and I shivered as if someone had just "walked across my grave." *Tocando el hombro de un muerto.* "Touching the shoulder of a dead man" — that's what my grandfather used to say when something spooked him.

I picked up my suitcase and headed home.

How I love driving this old truck of Dad's. 350,000 miles on her, and she keeps on going. No matter how many Cadillacs he has, he can't bear to part with her. The hand-painted tortillas on the side doors are just about worn off; the shocks are long gone; and the bench seat is cracked and split; but it still smells of all the dusty, desert roads we traveled, me and my dad. We'd load up the back with freshly-made tortillas when it was still dark. The sun coming up would find us making our way to all the little town stores from one end of this valley to the other, delivering the best tortillas in the world. Now he pays drivers in fancy, painted trucks to deliver Tortilla King tortillas in the neighboring counties. My dad is a big success. When he crossed the Rio Grande in 1919, he couldn't even speak English; and me, I can't speak Spanish worth a damn anymore, but then, I don't need to.

Old downtown Sanibel had changed a little since I left. There were a few new buildings, and gaping holes where buildings used to be. I was sad to see that the old jewelry store was gone. Mom had Dad's diamond ring made there. That ring had really been a big deal when I was a kid, and he still wears it every day. I think it was the only time my mom ever won anything. Actually, it wasn't the ring, but the diamond that she won, by answering a question on the radio. We've all heard the story so many times about how she was standing in the kitchen, doing the dishes and listening to the radio, when the announcer asked the listeners to call in if they knew the answer to today's question. At this point in the story, Mom would pretend she was the announcer and repeat the question, "What airport is named after a New York politician? Well, I knew that," she'd say in her own voice. "La Guardia. So I just called up the radio station and told them, and that's how I got your daddy's diamond." The station probably thought no one in New Mexico would know the answer, but Mom grew up in the Fort Hamilton section of Brooklyn. She picked up the diamond at the jewelry store the very next day, and had them set it in the center of a square of black onyx. It's still a real handsome ring.

Anyway, the jewelry store is gone, and a lot of the old businesses have moved over closer to the interstate. A whole new downtown runs on either side of the big, four-lane highway. There's a lot of new restaurants, too, and they're all buying Tortilla King tortillas. As I drove slowly by, looking at all the old store fronts, I noticed the shoe store only had a few styles of cowboy boots. The whole window had been filled with them when I was growing up. Now there was a display of running shoes in all stripes and colors. Rosita's was still there, though. She even had her name in neon, hanging in the front window now. I wondered if her pancakes still tasted as good as I remembered.

I pulled up in front, parked, and slid across the seat to get out on the passenger side. The door handle on the driver's side had broken off years ago. There were a few customers eating at the counter, and I noticed the walls had been painted a new color. I sat down in a booth and started looking over the menu, which was one thing that hadn't changed. I lost myself in the menu, reading each item through the coffee rings and smeared pancake syrup.

"Coffee?" she asked shyly. She was young, maybe 20 or 22 years old, her long, black, wavy hair pulled back and fastened with one of those elastic bands with two clear, plastic, pink balls on them. Her shirt was buttoned up to her throat, but the two buttons over her chest were straining to stay fastened.

"Decaf," I replied.

"We just have regular coffee here." She brushed a strand of hair off her forehead and waited for my answer.

"Regular coffee's fine." As she turned to go get the pot, I glanced at her name tag. It was chipped at one corner and said *Celinda.* I watched her walk away. She moved like a graceful wild cat, with slow, purposeful strides. When she reached the end of the counter, she looked quickly back at me, and I pretended to be staring out the window, studying the grill of my dad's truck, or what was left of it.

She set the big thick cup and saucer in front of me and poured the coffee.

"Where are you from?" I asked her so she wouldn't leave.

She looked back at me with a moist pair of big, velvet brown eyes. "I'm from here. I've always been from here."

"No. I meant your nationality." She stared at me. "What country did your parents come from?"

"Italy. My parents came from Italy. I'm Italian. Do you want sugar?"

She kept rubbing the fingers of her right hand slowly back and forth along the edge of my table.

"Cream?" she asked.

"Yes. Cream. And sugar."

She slid the sugar bowl across the table and reached over to grab a spoon from the next booth. She picked up the creamer, lifted the lid and sniffed. "It's sour. I'll get you some fresh."

"That's okay. I don't really need any cream."

"I won't be gone long."

It was several minutes before she came back. There were other customers who needed waiting on.

"Want me to pour?" she said as she returned with the cream.

I nodded. With great concentration and with the tip of her tongue between her lips, she poured the thick cream into my cup. I noticed one of the buttons had worked its way out of its hole, and there was now a small gap in the front of her blouse.

"Have you decided what you'd like to eat?" she asked.

"How about two eggs over easy, hash browns, toast, and a steak, if you have it. And orange juice." She started to leave. "A big glass of orange juice."

"You must really be hungry."

"I didn't eat much yesterday," I said lamely. She nodded in understanding and then went to place my order.

I rubbed my moist palms on my jeans. I was thirty-five years old, and I was acting like I'd never seen a woman before.

The eggs were good. The steak wasn't "Morton's," but it was like eating your mom's cooking. As I ate, I watched Celinda wiping down tables and fetching hot plates of food. Although her skirt wasn't short, when she walked over to the booth, I could tell that she had great legs.

"Are you finished?"

"Yes. It was good."

I looked down at my empty plate and felt sad. I was done, and now had to leave.

She lowered her eyes, and I saw how thick her lashes were.

"Would you like your check?"

"Sure. I guess so."

She pushed the check across the table until it touched the tips of my fingers.

The next morning I stopped by Rosita's for breakfast. Celinda wasn't there, so I grabbed a cup of coffee at the counter. Two o'clock found me back at Rosita's for lunch. There was another girl waiting on tables, so I sat at the counter and ordered a BLT and a Coke. Rosita waved at me from the pass-thru and came out front.

"Hey, Antonio. How about a hug?" I leaned over the counter and squeezed her tight. I noticed her once-black hair had streaks of iron gray in it, but she wore it the same way — pulled straight back into a tight, braided bun at her neck. Big, cheap, Mexican silver earrings dangled from her ears, just like they always had. There were wrinkles now around her eyes when she smiled, and they cut deep into her brown, leathery face. Rosita had always been good to me. Once in awhile I'd get a free soda out of her when I was a kid.

"You come back for good?" she asked.

"Just a visit."

"You're goin' to get *muy gordo* eatin' at Rosita's three times a day. You know I use a lotta grease here."

"Well, hey, I love your food."

"It's not my food you love, it's the pretty waitresses I have." She put her hands on her round hips and laughed. "I know it wasn't old Rosita you come to see. She'll be here at four, Tony."

"*Gracias*, Rosita."

She grinned and shuffled back to the kitchen, her slippers slapping against the bottom of her feet. I paid my bill and headed outside. I glanced at my watch — 2:45 p.m. I walked down to the pharmacy and read the magazines on the rack. I bought a couple so the clerk wouldn't be mad at me for standing there over an hour. I walked outside, threw them in the trash can, and looked at my watch again — 4:05 p.m.

Celinda was filling the salt and pepper shakers when I walked in. I grabbed a menu from behind the register and headed for what I now considered to be my booth. She came right over.

"What do you want?"

"I'll have a cheeseburger and some fries."

"OK." She wrote it down on her little pad and passed it through to Rosita, who was smoking a cigarette. Rosita always had a cigarette dangling from the corner of her mouth when she cooked. She smoked the cheap Mexican kind that were probably made from banana leaves. I just knew a lot of the ashes were going to end up in my cheeseburger. There was only one other customer, and he looked like a lost trucker. I'd seen a rig parked up the street. Rosita dinged the pick-up bell, and Celinda picked up my order and brought it to the table.

She set the burger and fries down in front of me.

"You must have a great job to get off so early," she said, leaning up against the booth. She looked young and innocent in her black pleated skirt and her white cotton shirt; and, except for the cactus embroidered on the pocket, she reminded me of the Catholic girls I'd gone to school with.

"I'm just visiting. I grew up here. I'm a lobbyist in Washington, D.C., now," I said rather importantly.

"Oh," she replied, unimpressed. "You want something to drink?"

"Sure. A root beer float would be good."

She brought the float, and I noticed she'd removed the wrapper from the straw except at the very tip.

"Would you like to go to the movies?" I said. "I'm in town visiting my folks, and I don't know anybody here any more."

"Well..," she replied hesitantly.

Rosita dinged the pick-up bell, and she turned to go.

"Just to the movies," I said quickly.

"No, I can't..."

"I can come pick you up at your house. You can introduce me to your mother."

The bell dinged twice, harder this time.

"I've got to go," she said.

"My dad's the Tortilla King," I said desperately. There was a flicker of recognition.

I rushed in. "What about tonight?"

"Not tonight. Tomorrow."

"Celinda!" Rosita shouted, her head shoved through the pass-thru.

"I'm coming!"

"Where should I pick you up?"

"I'll meet you here. In front of the restaurant."

"Okay. Around 8 o'clock?"

"The movie always starts at 7:30," she said.

"Seven, then. I'll meet you here at seven. My name's Anthony. No — call me Tony. My friends call me Tony." I laughed.

Staring back at me, she extended her hand. "Celinda," she said as she solemnly grasped my hand. It was warm, almost hot, like it was on fire, but her face was cool, impassive, as she looked at me out of two deep, dark brown pools.

Stepping out of the cool restaurant into the heat, the sun felt warm across my shoulders. I flung myself into the cab of the truck and pounded the seat with my fists in happiness. Two dark brown eyes looked out at me from the rearview mirror. I squinted, and they squinted back at me. I ran my fingers through my black, curly hair, looking for signs of gray, but there weren't any. Grinning in the mirror at me was a set of white teeth my parents never had to have straightened. What a good-looking guy. I pulled my sunglasses from my pocket, slipped them on, turned the key in the ignition, and backed out of the parking space with a screech that I hoped Celinda heard. Cruising down the main street, I made a mental note to see if dad still had my old cowboy hat. Yahoo! I was home!

Mom lived down in the flat valley, at the opposite end of Sanibel from Dad. He'd given her the house I grew up in as part of their divorce settlement, but she lost it to her new husband when he sold it and high-tailed it to Vegas. I drove slowly by the old house on my way to see Mom, but it just wasn't the same when strangers lived behind the front door.

I turned onto Arroyo Street where she lived now. The houses were ranch-style and smaller. It wasn't much of a place.

Yellowed newspapers from the last two days were still lying where the paperboy had thrown them. There was a dead mouse on the front doormat, probably an offering from one of the neighborhood cats that

Mom fed. No animal, or human, ever went hungry when Mom was around. I picked the mouse up by its tail and flung it into the bushes, then knocked on the screen door. No one answered, so I went in. Doors in this neighborhood were rarely locked. Everything in the front room seemed smaller and shabbier, or maybe I was just taller and older. There was a layer of dust on everything. Each time I came, I hoped it would be different. How could she live like this? How could she not care?

I rubbed my finger over the dusty glass on the photograph taken of my father's parents soon after they were married. Mom had adored my dad's folks. They were the only real parents she'd ever had. Her dad had been a womanizer and left her mother when she was still a little girl. Her father ended up divorcing his second wife and married Mom's nanny. I'd met Nanny Ava. She was a piece of work. Mom hated her 'til the day old Nanny died. The only time she remembered spending time with her father was when he'd kidnapped her and her brother, my Uncle Tonio, and took them to Florida to live with him. She stayed for two years — or rather she stayed until her father got tired of having his kids around and sent them back home.

But Dad's parents, that was different. They adored Mom. I carried their photo over to the window to see it better. Two brown-eyed people stared out at me. My grandmother's long hair was swept up from her face, its massive waves secured with a comb on top of her head. I wiped the glass over my grandfather's face. He had an elegant, refined face, as befitted one of Mexico's wealthy landowners. Grandfather stood behind my grandmother, his hand resting gently on her shoulder. I admired his posture and the assured way he presented himself. Dad had told me that the photo had been taken before they lost all their land in the Revolution.

My parents' wedding picture was also sitting on the table. It had been taken in the Forties. The little dress Mom was wearing showed off her figure, the narrow waist and curving hips. On her feet were open-toed, high heels with a strap across the ankle. Dad was in his naval uniform, his hand around her waist. They looked so young and so happy. I glanced at the rest of the photos sitting in their tarnished metal frames. There were none of me over the age of fifteen. That's how old I was when my parents divorced.

I heard a television somewhere in the back of the house. They were sitting on the old sofa watching the movie "Fatso" with Dom DeLuise. It's always been her favorite movie. She'd seen it hundreds of times. I was surprised that her soft, wispy hair was no longer gray, but auburn like it used to be when she was younger. Al, her boarder, sat next to her. He was a tall, thin man with slightly stooping shoulders when he stood, which he rarely did. Some kind of "war" injury had left one leg with a bad limp, so he usually just sat around drinking beer. He had a can in his hand right now. A big, old tan cat lay in Mom's lap.

"Hey there."

"Tony?" Mom turned and looked at me. She smiled and stood, not too steadily.

"Al, it's my son Tony."

Al grunted, which is how he usually greeted me. He raised his beer can, but never turned around. Mom placed the cat gently on the floor and came over for her hug and kiss.

"Come on, Tony. We'll go in the kitchen."

"But this is your favorite movie, Mom."

"I know it by heart," she said. "Look," she pointed at the TV screen, "see — Anne Bancroft is going to start yelling at Dom." Mom repeated the speech verbatim as we walked down the hall to the kitchen. "'You're sorry? You eat 40 dollars worth of Chinese food and you're sorry? You scare the living shit out of everybody, and you're sorry? You ruin a Sunday night and you're sorry..?'"

I smiled. It was hard to be angry with her for the life she led when her sense of humor showed.

Al shouted after her. "Bring me another beer, would ya, Angie?"

I gritted my teeth and cringed with embarrassment for her. I'd been in the house five minutes, and already I wanted to leave.

"In a second, Al, in a second," Mom called back.

She hustled me into the kitchen and sat me down at the same table where I'd eaten my breakfast for years. I missed the house she'd lost, but at least the old furniture made it feel like home. It was all she had left.

"Do you want me to fix some pasta for you, Tony?" Cooking food for me is an act of love for Mom.

"No. I'll just have some of the coffee."

"It looks like you lost weight."

"Mom. I'm fine. I weigh the same as I did last time I was here."

"Okay, okay. You don't have to yell at me. I'm just worried about you." She was slurring her words. Mom stood there looking so worn I thought my heart would break in two. Where had the beautiful girl in the wedding picture gone?

"I'm sorry, Mom."

"It's okay. I know you don't mean it. I'll be right back." She took a beer out of the refrigerator for Al.

"For Christ's sake, let the man get his own beer."

"It's hard for him to get up and down with that bad leg of his."

"Mom..."

"I'll be right back."

I poured myself some coffee and carried my cup to the table. The coffee smelled of the cinnamon and Mexican chocolate she always grated into it. I ran my hand over the old table's white surface speckled with flakes of color, looking for the gouge where I had tried to pry out a gold chunk of plastic with a butcher knife. The hole was still there, and I rubbed my finger back and forth over it.

I stared gloomily into my coffee cup, then looked up into the eyes of the tan tabby, who was now sitting in one of the chairs.

"Hello there, Whiskers, old fella."

Whiskers bared his teeth and hissed.

There were dirty dishes piled in the sink. When I was growing up, there had never been a dirty dish in the kitchen. Two other cats wandered in and headed for the bowls of cat food. I hated the smell of cat food. Mom came back in and poured herself some coffee, then she went out the back door with the cup and headed over to her car. I watched her open the trunk, pull out a gallon jug of vodka, and pour a shot into her cup.

"Got to hide it from Al," she said as she sat down across from me, hoisting kitty into her lap.

"Why do you do this? Why do you live like this? With this bum."

"That's not nice, Tony."

I sat back, seething. Mom just didn't get it. That's one thing my mom has always been, nice. She's been too nice. Not a mean bone in her body. She lets everybody take advantage of her. I watched her stroke the cat's head.

"You remember Whiskers, don't you?"

Mom's favorite cat hissed at me again. Whiskers was a one-woman cat, and I had the scars to prove it. She sat there cooing and purring to the beast, and I consoled myself with the fact that at least she became friendlier when she drank. I was groping around for something to say and decided to pick neutral territory.

"All the neighborhood cats still hang around?"

"Oh, yes. They leave me presents on the doorstep — mice, lizards and an occasional live snake. Cats are always grateful for your love. They don't hurt you."

Was that remark aimed at me?

"Just last week Al and I took Missy to the vet. She'd had her ear chewed up pretty badly by the bully tom down the street." I looked over at Missy who sat nonchalantly licking her paw and wiping it across what was left of her right ear.

"When I die, Tony, if there are no cats in heaven, I don't wanna go. I'll go to cat heaven so I can be with my friends."

I nodded wearily, trying to be understanding. "Okay, Mom."

"Promise me, Tony, you'll never put me in one of those old people places. Shoot me first."

"What's all this? Sounds like you've been talking to Uncle Tonio again."

"He writes me. It costs too much to call."

"That's silly, Mom. I'll give you the money to call him."

"I don't want to call him," she said petulantly and stuck out her lower lip. She reminded me of a small child. "He's always talking about getting my 'affairs' in order. Everything will work out fine, I tell him. He gets on my nerves. Why do you care? You never come see me. All you care about is my money. You don't care about me." She wasn't talking sense now.

"I'm here now, Mom," I pointed out.

"That's just because you came to see your dad."

I looked at her sitting there in her funny old housedress. She had it buttoned wrong, and it took all my willpower not to reach over and button it up the right way.

"Mom, you've got a curler hanging in your hair still." She fumbled with it trying to get it out. I reached over and unrolled it for her. She kept trying to slap my hand away.

"Don't do that. I can do that. I don't need your help." She started to cry.

"Mom..."

"What's wrong?" It was Al standing in the doorway. He came over and knelt clumsily down beside her. Al started in on me. "What're you goin' and upsetin' her for?"

"I'm alright, Al. Me and Tony were just talking. You go on back to your TV." Al pulled another beer from the refrigerator and limped out of the room.

I reached for her hand and held it in mine.

"I'm sorry, Mom. I didn't mean to upset you."

"It's okay, Tony."

"Listen, I've gotta go."

"You're not stayin'? I fixed up the room for you."

"I can't," I said guiltily. "I'm just here today, and then heading to Mexico on business. I promised Dad I'd stop by and see him, too."

She dried her tears. "Okay. You give *her* a good kick in the butt from me. Why your dad ever married that witch, I'll never know."

"Okay, Mom."

She smiled and patted my hand.

"You're such a good son."

I met Celinda in front of Rosita's the next night. She wore a simple, blue cotton dress covered with small white polka dots. Her long hair was pulled up into a pony tail, and I liked watching it sway behind her as we walked to the theater. It was the same theater I had gone to as a kid. My buddies and I lived there on Saturdays. For three Pepsi bottle caps you could get in free, so we'd spend the week searching the ground around the stores in town for thrown-away caps. Times had changed at the old theater. There wasn't a first-run movie among the posters in the lobby. The movie that night was a very scratched print of *Old Yeller*, but it was the best movie I'd seen in years. Celinda cried and let me hold her hand.

After the movie, we walked the six blocks to Rosita's for a hot fudge sundae.

"What a sad movie," she sighed, sniffling.

"Yeah, I always hate it when an animal dies in the movie," I said. "I haven't been to a retrospective like this in a long time."

"A retrospective..," she repeated. She didn't know what I meant, so I helped her out.

"The theaters in Washington do it sometimes, too. They run old movies for a week."

"Oh, they play the old movies every week here."

"Every week? When do they play the new movies?"

"You can see the new movies in Albuquerque, but I don't go."

"Would you like to?"

"Yes. I would."

"I'll take you sometime."

Rosita had gone home, but Chubby was there, and he knew the routine. He fixed a double hot fudge sundae and brought it over to our booth with the two spoons.

"He forgot the cherries, Tony," she whispered to me.

Celinda went behind the counter and brought over the jar of cherries and the can of whipping cream.

"Give me the can," I said. "Stick out your tongue, and close your eyes." Celinda looked at me uncertainly. "I'm not going to hurt you." She closed her eyes, thrust her jaw forward, stuck out her tongue, and I squeezed out a little mound of whipped cream on the end of it. She pulled in her tongue and smiled as she tasted the cream.

"Hey! That ain't sanitary," Chubby yelled at us. He came over, took the can of cream away from us and wiped the top on his dirty apron. Chubby's a pain, I thought, and not real bright. "You know better than that, Celinda," he said, shaking a greasy finger at her.

She giggled and her eyes were sparkling, and every time she leaned forward, I got a glimpse of the most enticing cleavage.

"Celinda, let's go out to dinner. Some place really nice."

"But I'm not hungry, Tony."

"I don't mean tonight," I laughed. "Tomorrow night."

"Well...I'm not sure."

"I'll have you home by 10:30. I promise."

"I guess it would be okay then," she said, smiling coyly.

The three of them sat huddled around the kitchen table. The man was not old, but he moved as a very old man. His joints were stiff and swollen, and he fumbled with his hands when he tried to pick things up. The woman was not old either, but her face was lined and her eyes were tired. Her figure was still good, her hips curving out from a small, tiny waist. Looking at the woman, one could see the resemblance between her and the young woman sitting next to her. Celinda looked at her father and mother and shuddered inside. She never wanted to look as old and worn as they did. What fools they had been, working all their lives for pennies. She would show them.

"But who is this man?" her father asked.

"I told you. He is from Washington D.C., *Papá*," Celinda said. "He is in the government and makes lots of money. I am sure of it."

"But Celinda is promised to her cousin Carlos," the father protested.

The woman interrupted. "That was before your illness, Husband. Now we must think further than Nuevo Laredo and a small restaurant. Carlos is not a rich man. Celinda must do for all of us now. She must marry well. I clean houses all week and still we have nothing." She gestured at the shabby kitchen and its open window with no screen and a piece of fabric for a curtain.

"I do not know what to do," the father said. "Celinda, she is our only daughter."

"And our salvation..," the mother spat out.

"His father is the Tortilla King, *Papá*," Celinda added.

"Then he is a rich man," the man said sadly, thinking of his own misfortune. He rose clumsily. "It is up to you and Celinda to decide, Consuela." He walked slowly from the room. What was a man to do when all had been taken from him and he had to rely on women to take care of him, he thought.

Celinda looked at her mother.

"*La Vieja*," her mother whispered. "*La Vieja*."

Celinda nodded in agreement.

I borrowed my dad's Cadillac convertible. The look of surprise on Celinda's face when I drove up in front of Rosita's was priceless. I'd definitely impressed her. I jumped out, ran around and opened the door for her. She settled herself pertly in the seat and looked straight ahead. Tonight she was wearing a slinky, black dress that clung to her waist and hips. It had a scooped neckline that showed off her cleavage and shoulders, and a short, full skirt that nestled around her legs. She wore black shoes with spiked heels. Her hair was undone and hung in waves halfway down her back. I was accustomed to seeing women who wore fancy dresses and used plastic surgeons to look beautiful, or women who dressed in drab, ugly suits that made them look like men. Next to Celinda, they all faded into one woman, with an anemic, pinched face and too much makeup. Being with her was a refreshing change.

"I was thinking of Romano's," I said happily.

"Whatever you would like would also make me happy." She smiled at me. It was a dazzling smile that lit up her face and my heart.

It was warm and balmy. The wind felt like fingers running through my hair as we sped out of town and across the desert towards Romano's. Turning on the radio, the "south of the border" music my dad always listened to blared out of the speakers, so I changed the station. Her hand was fingering my cufflink.

"They were a gift from Nixon," I said casually.

"From Nixon, the President?"

"Yes."

"Is it gold?"

"Yes. Twenty-four carat. You can take it off if you want." She removed the cufflink and held it in the palm of her hand, pushing it over and over with her finger.

"You must be a very important man to receive a gift such as this from the President."

"Well, I don't know about that, but he was grateful." The cufflink didn't go back in as easily as it came out, so I pulled off the road. She slid over next to me, and I held the cuff together while she put it back in. Her head was bent close to my face, and I closed my eyes and breathed in her scent. Her warm, earthy, pungent smell wrapped itself around me, drawing me to her with its fragrance. It reminded me of fields of freshly turned earth when the soil is warm from the sun and crumbles sweet and musky between your fingers.

The radio announcer's voice broke in. "Here's a brand new one this week that's already jumped to Number Ten on the charts. 'Under Your Spell.'"

I reached over and turned up the volume.

Play CD Track 2
"Under Your Spell"

The fire in your eyes and the wetness on your lips,
It's the power of the night as we embrace in our first kiss.
Do I dare try to conquer your body's sacred ground?
Oh, the sweet nectar of love, love yet to be found.

And I can't control the passion that's burning
in my soul, 'cause when I hold you close to me
I'm under your spell.

You must be the Goddess of the Night.
Divine deity, what is guiding me to your light?
Is it love or devilry?
And as I breathe in your scent, I can no longer resist.
The chains of lust have bound me a slave to my nemesis.

And I can't control the passion that's burning
In my soul, 'cause when I hold you close to me
I'm under your spell.
Yea....Oh, Oh, Oh....Yea....Yea....

And I can't control the passion that's burning
in my soul, cause when I hold you close to me
I'm under your spell
I'm under your spell
I'm under your spell
Under your spell

"I love being here with you, Celinda," I whispered into her ear. Leaning over, I touched her lips gently with my mouth, then kissed her again, harder. She kissed me back. She put her head on my shoulder and held on to me. With one hand on the steering wheel and my other arm around her, I drove straight off into the desert.

When I turned off the car and the headlights, there wasn't a sound except for our breathing.

I laid her gently back against the seat and kissed her, my other hand running slowly up her leg. How far would she let me go? My hand slid past her knee and up her thigh. She was kissing me, murmuring my name. I pulled my hand from her leg and she moaned. I reached up her back and then unzipped her dress. She stiffened as I slid it to her waist. With one hand, I pinched her bra, and it collapsed into her lap.

"Tony, please," she whispered, "please don't," as I took my hand and placed it under her skirt on her thigh. I moved it up and felt a luxurious mound of hair and in the center she was moist and soft.

"Oh, Tony...."

I was inside her and we were both moaning. I could hardly stand to wait, and then I felt the ripple of movement inside her, and I pressed into her. Her cries rose and fell and then were lost in the stillness of the desert.

We lay together, breathing heavily.

"You're my angel. I'm under your spell," I sang.

She snuggled up next to me.

"Look at all those stars, Celinda. Back in Washington you can barely see a star for all the city lights, but out here you can see millions of them."

The Milky Way trailed out across the night sky like a woman's scarf, and I reached my hand up to see if I could touch it.

"What are you doing?" Celinda whispered.

"I'm touching the Milky Way," I said, playfully stretching my hand to the sky.

"You can't do that. It's too far away."

"Not for me." I closed my hand, grabbed a fist full of stars and threw them, letting them fall around her head. "See, I've covered you in stardust, Angel."

A smile broke slowly across her face, and her eyes sparkled.

"You try it," I said, reaching my hand upward again, swiping a path through the stars.

Celinda stretched her hand to the sky, her fingers spread wide. She grasped the air with a wave of her wrist, curling her hand into a fist. We held our closed hands in front of us, almost touching.

"Close your eyes, and make a wish, Celinda. When you open your hand, if the stars are gone, that means the angels have heard you, and your wish will be granted."

I watched her squeeze her eyes shut, then I closed mine. "I want money," I thought. "Lots of money. Money can buy me whatever I want. Money can make every star in my hand a diamond. No one will be able to take the jewels of this night away from me, ever."

I clenched my fist tight, squeezing it with all my strength. When I opened my eyes, Celinda was watching me. Together we uncurled our fingers and gazed into our empty palms.

"They've heard us, Angel," I said, brushing Celinda's hair back from her face with both my hands. Thick waves curled and twined possessively around my fingers. Shifting my weight, I traced the outline of her breasts in the moonlight with my fingertip.

I whispered in her ear, "Celinda, *Diosa de la Noche*, my Goddess of the Night, are you hungry? Do you want to go get something to eat?"

She wrapped her arms around my neck, and shook her head "no."

"What time is it?" she said sleepily, breaking the spell.

I pulled my arm out from under her and looked at my watch. "It's nearly ten."

"I need to go home. I have to get up early to go to school."

"Do you go to the junior college?"

"No. I go to Sanibel High, but it's my last year." She fluffed her skirts around her legs. "Can you zip me up?" she asked shyly, turning her back towards me and lifting her hair.

I fumbled with the zipper. "How old are you?"

"Seventeen."

Oh my God.... "Seventeen," I repeated, stunned. "Do you have a boyfriend?"

"I had a boyfriend once, and he wanted me to be with him like this and I wouldn't, so I had to give him his ring back. Do you want to be my boyfriend?" She pressed herself against me.

"Yeah, sure." My mind was racing. Seventeen. She was only seventeen. I'm in trouble now.

I turned the key in the ignition and pulled the lights on. The big old Caddy prowled across the desert back to the main road.

I dropped Celinda off at her house right on time. It was one of those stucco houses with wide porches and high-ceiling rooms. The porch light was on, and there was a light in one of the front upstairs windows. I guess her mother was waiting up for her. A ripple of guilt went through me as I looked at the lighted window. Celinda was exactly the same age as my son David. She waved at me from the porch as I drove off.

SLEEPING WITH AN ANGEL

Dad lives on Chapiquo Mountain, on a huge, flat ledge, five hundred feet below the crest. The house has no windows facing the mountains, but is a solid wall of glass on the side looking out over the valley. At night the whole valley is dark, except for the clustered lights of Sanibel and the headlights of cars snaking along the new interstate.

When I walked in the house, Dad was sitting in his big, old chair reading the newspaper. This chair is like his truck; he's had it forever. It's two-toned, like some old Chevy, and worn to the threads on the headrest and the arms. He won't get rid of it because he says it reminds him of who he is and where he came from.

"So I suppose I'm going to hear all that jazz music when I turn on the radio in my car tomorrow," he said without looking up.

I grinned. It was good to be with him again. I settled myself on the floor at his feet like I used to do when I was a kid.

"Dad, do you want me to come back to Sanibel?"

He lowered the paper and looked at me. "I miss you, Antonio, but Sanibel isn't the place for you. Washington is where you belong. You're involved in big, important things."

He was right. What would I do in a dumpy little place like Sanibel?

"But Mom..," And Celinda, I thought to myself.

"I know. She misses you and wants you here with her."

"She cries every time I leave."

"It's her drinking. When she drinks, she cries even more easily."

I don't really know why they separated, and it's not something I could ask Dad. Maybe it was the long hours he worked at the tortilla manufacturing plant. He wasn't home much, but he always came to watch me play baseball and football. He never missed a game. Dad had been a teacher, but Mom hadn't finished high school before she met and married him. She must have been about the same age as Celinda. One day, when I was about twelve, I remember my Aunt Lucia telling me how my mom wanted to surprise my dad by secretly attending classes to finally get her diploma. She wouldn't tell Dad where she was going in the evenings. He suspected she was having an affair and followed her to night school. He confronted her, demanding to know what was going on. Poor Mom was so shook up by his jealousy that she stopped going and never did get her diploma, my aunt said. Now that I think of it, maybe Dad's jealousy was partly the cause of their marriage breaking up.

"What are you thinking about, Antonio?"

"Just thinking how much I'm enjoying being home."

"When are you going to Mexico?"

"I leave in a week," I said, remembering the lie I'd told Mom.

"Good. So I have you for a little while longer. I'm very proud of you. It's a great honor to have been appointed by the President to this commission."

I had to admit, the Presidential appointment had come at a good time. This could be a very lucrative trip, especially since it would help me build my lobbying business. I was thinking about all the contacts I could make when Greta, Dad's wife, walked into the room. She was a redhead this time, with the usual inch of dark roots. She always wore tight tops and capri pants with backless high heels. Her eyes were trimmed with lashes coated with black mascara. I'd never seen the woman without lipstick in some bright shade of orange or red, and her skin had spent too much time in the Vegas sun. When Dad asked me if I thought he should marry her, I said "No way. She's a gold-digging bitch." She was just some bossy waitress in one of his restaurants, but I knew dad wasn't asking my opinion. He was telling me what he was going to do.

Greta walked up behind him, put her arms possessively around his neck and threw me a cold glance.

"You comin' upstairs, sweetheart?" she asked him.

He looked at me.

"You go on ahead, Dad."

"Good night, Antonio."

"Good night."

I got up, walked over, and sat down in his chair. It was still warm as I sank into the impression his body had made in it over the years. When we were kids, my brother Estefan, my sister Rosalie and I would sit in it when he wasn't home. No one ever caught us, but I often wondered if he knew. Leaning my head back, I closed my eyes and was eight years old again.

Every day I'd tell myself I shouldn't see her, but every night would find me in front of Rosita's, waiting. It was her youth, the firmness of her skin, her scent. It was everything about her that kept drawing me back. On her days off from the restaurant, I picked Celinda up after school. She never said too much, but she didn't have to. Just being with her was enough for me. One day while she was at school, I drove the two hundred miles to Albuquerque and picked out a gold chain bracelet. Celinda wore it every day, and it pleased me to know that she was wearing something from me next to her skin.

The two women sat with their heads together in the darkened room. One ancient in years and wisdom, *La Vieja*, the one who had the power to make dreams come true. The other, young with yearning and filled with dreams. They whispered to each other so quietly that their words could not even be heard in the corners of the tiny room. They met the way women have met for thousands of years, in quiet and in secret.

I was driving to Rosita's on an afternoon when Celinda was supposed to be in school, when I saw her coming out of a weather-beaten, clapboard building on one of Sanibel's side streets. An old woman stood behind the building's half-opened door. I could barely make out the woman in the shadows, but I could see that her face was creased with a fine web of wrinkles like some of the really old Mexican Indians I had seen as a boy.

"Celinda!" I shouted, waving from my truck.

The old woman quickly shut the door, and Celinda backed up against it. I pulled over and called out the window.

"How come you're not in school?" I said.

She came over to the truck. She was holding something in her hand.

"What's that?" I asked.

She held up a small vial, filled with something dark brown and thick. "My mother. She is ill. She likes the medicines of the old woman."

I was concerned. "Would you like me to drive her to the doctor?"

"No. No. She will be fine. She says the doctors are no good for her aches and pains, and she always feels better after taking the medicine of the old woman. Really. It is nothing."

It didn't seem like nothing. Celinda appeared very distraught.

"You're not ill, are you, Celinda?" My question seemed to calm her, and she regained her composure.

"No. It is my mother, Tony. I'm fine." She smiled sweetly at me. "I've got to go. My mother's waiting for me." She started walking up the street, and I drove along next to her.

"Do you want a lift?"

She shook her head. "No. You go on."

She turned, and I watched her hips shift back and forth beneath her skirt as she walked away from me.

That night, I borrowed the tortilla truck and drove Celinda out to Barlow on the old highway. Dixon's Bar is the only building left in Barlow. It's been a popular hangout for years, and people come from a hundred miles away just to "dance at Dixon's." Some of them tonight had probably just come from across the border. Celinda looked like a million dollars in her tight-fitting jeans and bright red shirt. When she walked into the room, heads turned, but she clung to me and let every one of those guys know she was mine. I didn't know then that her clothes were so tight, because she was too poor to buy new ones. She was literally growing out of them before my eyes. Her hair was pulled up in a bouncy ponytail, and I kept thinking how wonderful it was going to be later to take it down and let that mass of hair fall around her shoulders.

"You're my angel," I whispered to her as we danced slow and close. Her roving tongue moved over my ear, finishing with a playful bite on my ear lobe that sent a shiver through me. I moved my hands up and down her back, and through her shirt I could feel the strength in the curve of every muscle. My hands lingered over her buttocks, feeling their tight fullness, and slowly my palms moved out and over her hips as the music ended. We stood together on the dance floor, my hands resting lightly on her waist.

"Hey, Celinda." A stocky fellow with a shock of black hair ambled over, a beer bottle in his hand.

"Mickey." She turned to me. "Mickey used to work for my uncle," she explained. "This is Tony. He's a lobbyist from Washington, D.C."

"No shit." I don't think Mickey was impressed, but hell, what did he know. Mickey gave her the once-over from head to toe. "You look great, kid. How about a dance?"

"Is it okay, Tony?"

Well, it wasn't okay, but I could be big about it. "Sure. Fine. I'll be right here." I watched them for a few minutes, but watching people do the two-step made me dizzy, so I went to grab another beer. When I came back, there was a slow dance and the floor was crowded. I couldn't see Celinda or Mickey anywhere.

I circled the dance floor. No sign of them. I was starting to get irritated when I finally spotted them in the hall leading to the restrooms. Mickey had her up against the wall next to the pay phone. His hand was touching her shoulder, and they were deep in conversation. That did it.

I walked over and grabbed Celinda's arm. "She's leaving now, Mick." I didn't stop until I had her out in front of Dixon's.

"Just what the hell do you think you were doing?" I shouted, but I didn't give her any time to answer me. I pulled her across the street, yanked open the door, and slid across the seat dragging her behind me. I took off with the truck door still open and headed out of town as fast as I could. Celinda was crying and whimpering.

"What the hell was that?" I yelled.

"It was nothing," she cried.

"Yeah, right. Button your shirt up." I pushed my foot down on the accelerator.

"Tony, please," she begged, fumbling to button her top two buttons. "It was nothing. You don't understand. He's my cousin. He was asking me about my mother. She's been ill. He wanted to know what I was doing out there with you. He didn't know that I wasn't going steady any more. I haven't seen him for at least six months."

I refused to look at her. I kept my eyes glued to the road. She was quiet now, and when she spoke her voice was small and little.

"Tony, it's not what you think. I couldn't live knowing you thought that."

I turned to look at her, and I could see how pretty she was, and how frightened.

"Tony," she whispered, and then she crawled across the seat to me on her hands and knees. She laid her head down in my lap, and I stroked my hand through her hair.

"It's okay, Angel."

Celinda stood on the porch and gave me a little wave as I drove off. I looked in the rearview mirror before I turned the corner, and saw her slip off the porch and head down the street.

"What the hell?" I muttered under my breath. I made a U-turn. For a while I followed her in the car with the headlights off. After about eight blocks, I parked and followed her on foot. She'd taken her high heels off and was walking in bare feet now. If she was going to see that Mickey guy, I was going to be really pissed. Suddenly I realized where she was going. There are no streetlights in Mexico Town, only the lights from the houses to find your way. The streets had no names to the gringos, but the Mexicans had their own landmarks to guide each other through the dusty maze. I stood in the shadows on one of the dirt streets and watched Celinda enter an old adobe. Light spread across the porch as she opened the door, and I heard her greet someone in Spanish. "*Yo estoy aqui.*"

A woman replied, "*¿Cómo te fue?* How did it go?"

"Okay, *Mamá,*" I heard her say before she shut the door.

I stood there for a while, watching, before heading back to my car.

So my little Italian came from south of the border.

The next night when I drove Celinda home, I didn't take her to the stucco house with the big wide porch. I headed to Mexico Town. She'd been talking animatedly, but when I turned right instead of left, she became still, almost rigid.

"Where are you taking me?" she asked.

"I'm taking you home."

When I pulled up in front of the old adobe, she began to cry as if her heart would break.

"Why did you tell me you were Italian?" I said quietly.

"I didn't want you to know how poor we are," she sobbed. "I was afraid you wouldn't want me."

"Of course I want you. Whose house was it?" She looked at me, puzzled. "The stucco house."

She shrugged. "I don't know. They are usually gone most of the year. Our neighbor takes care of the house for those people."

We sat in silence, side by side. I could feel she was scared. She reminded me of a rabbit frozen in position, hoping you won't see them and shoot them.

"Celinda, I'm going to be leaving."

"Oh, I see. Because of what I have done?"

"No. It's business. I was appointed by the President to attend a commission on Mexican-U.S. relations in Puerto Vallarta."

"Puerto Vallarta," she said breathlessly. "I've heard it is a very beautiful place."

"It is. And I'd like you to see it. Will you come with me?"

She turned slowly towards me. I couldn't see her face in the dark. Now I was the one who was scared. Maybe she'd say no.

"Tony! You would want me to come with you?" she said excitedly.

I kissed her, and put my hand under her chin. "Yes. I would want you to come with me very much," I replied, mimicking her.

"But my *mamá* and *papá*, and school. I can't miss school."

"Don't worry. We'll fix it. Let's go talk to your parents right now."

"Right now?"

"Now."

The ceilings in the old adobe were low with smoke-darkened beams, and the wooden floor sagged beneath my weight. Celinda went into the kitchen, motioning for me to wait. I heard voices talking rapidly in Spanish behind the closed door. The room I was in was quite small. There was a shrine in the far wall, with votive candles flickering before an image of Our Lady. There was also one of those brightly-colored velvet paintings of a desert sunset above the old fireplace. A wood burning stove stood on the hearth. What was taking them so long?

"*Pero no es correcto por una muchacha ser esta cosa.* It is not right for a young girl to do this thing!" he said. "To go with a man."

"*Papá, por favor, no tan alto.* Not so loud. He'll hear you. *Mamá..,*" she pleaded.

"*Emos discutido todo estes antes,*" her mother replied. "We have discussed this all before. This is an opportunity, not just for Celinda, but for the family. *¿Que vamos a hacer?* What are we going to do? Wait for you to go back to work! *¿Y quando será eso?* When will that happen? *Mira a tus manos, son inutiles.* Look at your hands, they're useless," she hissed at him.

"*No es mi culpa,*" he whined. "It's not my fault."

"*¡Basta!* She goes! *Celinda, vaya con tu muchacho.* Go with your young man."

Celinda rose, anxiously casting a look at her father, relieved at what she saw in his face.

The door opened, and Celinda stood there with the light behind her, beckoning for me to come in. A lantern sat on the oilcloth-covered kitchen table; a bare bulb hung above the sink. There were no screens on the open windows, and flying night bugs battled each other for space in the light.

Her *papá* was a bull of a man, thick in the neck, with broad, muscular shoulders. His hands were rough with calluses, and his fingers curled over like he couldn't open them all the way. Her mother's face looked worn and older than her years, for she was probably near my age. Her hair was jet black with an inch-wide streak of white hair starting from her hairline on her forehead. I wondered what illness she suffered from, and if the medicine in the little vial was helping her. She wore a housedress, and I was relieved to see that she was not overweight like some older Mexican women, *las gorditas.* That meant Celinda would probably keep her figure, too.

"*Siéntese,*" her father said, gesturing with a small movement of his hand.

I pulled over a chair and sat at the table. Celinda and her mother stood quietly in the background.

"Celinda, she tell me you ask her to go to Mexico."

"Yes, sir." I explained my appointment by the President to the commission, and what an "educational" experience it would be for Celinda.

"Celinda is a good girl," her *papá* said.

"I know that. And I'll take good care of her, *Señor* Alvarez."

"You come from a good family, Antonio. Your father is a fine man, and well-respected in Sanibel. Celinda's *mamá* and I give our consent."

Celinda stood looking down at the floor and was very quiet until approval had been granted, then she gave me a shy smile.

Mamá and *Papá* were easier to convince than the high school. Celinda made up a story that an uncle had invited her to come with him to Mexico while he attended the commission. Celinda forged a note from her parents, while I called the principal, pretending to be her uncle. The school approved her absence, but her history teacher assigned Celinda a paper about Mexican-American relations and the outcome of the commission. All due on her return, of course. Celinda was furious.

"Tony," she wailed, "I can't write a long paper like that. I'll have to spend all my time in the library." She pouted.

"Don't worry. I'll write it for you on the plane trip home. I was an 'A' student all through college and I'm a law school graduate."

Two days later, we hit the road in Dad's big old Cadillac, with the top down, the radio blaring, and with Celinda and her mother, Consuela, in the back seat. We were heading to Albuquerque to outfit Celinda for our trip to Mexico. They chattered and laughed like two schoolgirls, their heads covered with scarves which did little to keep their hair in place. Long tendrils escaped and whipped against their faces and trailed out straight behind them. Whatever had ailed Consuela, the old woman's medicine certainly seemed to have done the trick. I watched them in the rearview mirror, their eyes hidden by sunglasses, their words carried off by the wind.

It was two disheveled, bright-eyed women that I dropped off for an afternoon of shopping. Leaving them with money to pay for the new clothes, I promised to be back at five to pick them up. I strolled up and down the streets, finally stopping in front of a swimsuit store. The mannequins were posed as if they were diving in an invisible sea. They hung suspended before me, swaying slightly, swimming above a display of bikinis, shells, mounds of sand, and cardboard seaweed. The store was cold when I went in, and a little bell rang as I shut the door. I looked through many racks of swimsuits before deciding on a tiny black bikini. So Celinda's mother wouldn't see it, I had the clerk wrap it up carefully and put it in a plain shopping bag.

They stood next to each other at the curb surrounded by packages. Consuela was beaming, but Celinda seemed cross and tired. Loading the trunk, I tried to peek, but Consuela playfully slapped my hand away.

"*Sorpresa*, Antonio, *sorpresa*," she clucked in Spanish.

I had a feeling I was going to love this surprise. Celinda slept the whole way home, and her mother talked in Spanish to me, but I couldn't understand a word of what she was saying.

I carried the packages into the adobe under Consuela's watchful eye.

"I'll pick you up tomorrow, Celinda, around eight."

She kissed me on the cheek, murmured her thanks, and bolted for the kitchen. I was beginning to feel uneasy.

The next morning when I pulled up, Celinda was standing on the front porch next to her suitcase. She was wearing the ugliest dress I had ever seen. It was floral, I think. There were big splotches of purple, green, red, and blue, and it had a ridiculous bow at the waist. We said our good-byes quickly, with Consuela smiling and waving until we drove out of sight.

Celinda rolled the window down. She placed her arms on the windowsill and stared down at the road racing by. I placed a package in her lap.

"What is it?" she said, finally looking at me.

"Open it."

She dangled the bikini from both her hands. "It's so tiny," she said, her eyes wide.

"You're going to look great in it. Do all the clothes your mother bought for you look like that?"

"Yes. I am sorry, Tony. All the money." She sighed.

"Cheer up. We'll dump them in a locker at the airport and pick them up when we come back. I'll buy you some new things on our trip." I grinned at her. She smiled back and slid over next to me. I put my arm around her and squeezed her tightly to me.

"*Damas y cabelleros, vamos a aterrizar en diez minutos. Favor de preparase para la llegada.*" The pilot repeated the announcement in English. "Ladees and gentlemin, we are goeeng to land in ten minoots. Pleeze to prepare for arrival."

Celinda was shaking my arm. I opened my eyes and took off my headset.

"Tony, Tony, we're getting ready to land," Celinda said.

I looked out the window. We were flying low over mountains, and I could see, alternately, clouds and flashes of sunlight illuminating the jungle vegetation below. It must have just rained, because the ground was dark and a small creek below us was overflowing its banks. We passed underneath the last of the clouds, and Puerto Vallarta lay ahead on the coast. A small brown river flowed through the center of the city, dumping a brown streak of rainwater washed from the mountains into the blue ocean.

"It's so beautiful, Tony. And big. I have never seen anything this big."

Thick, hot, steamy air met us as we stepped out of the airplane. I felt terrific in my bright tropical shirt and sunglasses, with the heat beating down on my head, and a good-looking woman on my arm. Celinda stayed close to me, her arm wrapped tightly around mine as we stepped into the limo.

I leaned back against the seat and watched the palm trees glide by.

"So, what do you think?"

"I think I like it very much," she said with a toss of her head. "Can I get some sunglasses?"

"Sure. Here, let me give you some money. Buy whatever you want."

Celinda took the money, carefully folded it, and tucked it into her little patent leather purse.

At the hotel, I put on my bathing trunks and headed for the pool to see who was there, leaving Celinda to unpack and get us settled. I was hoping to make some new contacts and didn't want to waste any time. Standing in the shade of a cabana, I spotted Phil Clybourn with two other men on the far side of the pool. He was the last person I expected to see. Phil headed up a multi-million dollar construction business in Dallas.

He was a big fellow with meaty jowls. He'd been a linebacker at Texas A&M, and still presented a massive bulk to anyone in his way. I'd had some dealings with him four years ago. Nothing big time, but you never knew where it would lead. I waved and called his name. He raised his massive bulk to a standing position and motioned me over. I pulled up a chaise lounge next to him, while he introduced me to the other men.

"Tony, this is Rod Springer. He owns KQRR out of Phoenix." A pudgy, bald man nodded his head and extended a hand coated with suntan lotion.

"A pleasure to meetch'a, Mister..?"

"Cassera. Tony Cassera." The other fellow was Martin Kitchner, a TV announcer from San Diego. He was a smooth one with a voice like silk, and craggy, hawkish good looks.

"So what's with the media guys?" I whispered to Phil.

"Nothing at all, Tony. Just shootin' the bull."

Whatever it was, he wasn't letting me in on this one.

I noticed Rod kept staring at Martin's full head of wavy gray hair. He was probably fascinated that someone twenty years older than he was still had that much hair. I ran my fingers through my own thick, black wavy hair.

"Hey, Martin. Is that all yours?" Rod finally asked.

"What?"

"Your hair. It's all yours?"

Martin gave a good hard tug on it. "All mine. My mom had a great head of hair."

"What about your dad?"

"Oh, he was bald. Everyone gets their hair from their mom." Martin gave Rod a playful pat on the head.

"My mom wasn't bald," Rod replied indignantly, rubbing the spot where Martin had touched the top of his head. "That's not a nice..."

Phil cut Rod off in mid-sentence. "Look at that!"

A bevy of beautiful Latin women in bikinis and high heels had just entered, transforming the pool area into a scene from a beauty pageant. Followed by cameramen, the young women struck poses and draped themselves on lounge chairs and diving boards.

"They're contestants in the Miss Puerto Vallarta Contest," Martin informed us.

Phil looked puzzled. "The Miss Puerto Vallarta Contest? You're kidding me. I never heard of it."

"No one has," Martin said dryly. "The Mexican officials dreamt it up and scheduled it at the same time as the commission." Very clever of them, I thought. All the high-level Mexican officials were undoubtedly attending this commission without their wives, but then, so were these guys.

"Look at that one." Phil gestured with his head. "She's gorgeous." We all turned to look. He was right. Celinda looked breathtaking in the scant black bikini I'd bought for her.

"She's coming towards us," Rod managed to squeak out.

I was really enjoying this. Celinda walked right up to us, and without saying a word, pulled a lounge chair up next to me. She proceeded to rub every inch of her body with suntan lotion in slow, circular motions. The men followed her every movement and never took their eyes off her. When she was finished with the ritual, she turned to me.

"Would you like me to rub some on your back, Tony?" I agreed, of course, and turned my back towards her. The look on the guys' faces filled me with great satisfaction.

"Celinda, would you like to meet some of my friends?" I was going to play this for all it was worth.

"Certainly, Tony."

"This is Celinda. She's from my home town of Sanibel, New Mexico," I said as I introduced each of them to her.

"It is very nice to meet Tony's friends," she said politely.

"We thought you were one of the contestants from the Miss Puerto Vallarta Contest," Martin said. "You could be, you know."

"Thank you for the compliment, but I am here with Tony."

Phil leaned forward eagerly, "What do you do, Celinda?"

"I am a student."

Phil pondered this for a moment. "Do you go to the University of New Mexico? I have a friend whose daughter goes there. You might know her. What are you studying?"

"History, but I don't go there."

"Where do you go?" Phil asked.

"I go to Sanibel High."

"You're in high school!" Rod sputtered. "You're studying what?" The way he said it, it was obvious that he thought she would be crazy to study anything.

"History," Celinda sighed.

"As a condition to coming down here," I informed them, "she has to write a paper on the commission meetings. It was the best deal I could negotiate for her." They all laughed at this. Celinda nodded graciously and settled back in her lounge chair. I lay back also and smiled to myself behind my sunglasses as I drifted off to sleep.

"*Señor Cassera. Teléfono, Señor Cassera.*" The steward handed me the phone, and I swung my legs over the side of the chaise.

"*Bueno*?"

"Hello, Cisco."

I recognized the voice immediately. It was Parker St. John, my oldest friend in Washington. He was a former ambassador to one of those countries that doesn't exist any more, but we still called him Ambassador. It was a nickname now. Tall and stately, he was the epitome of a diplomat. His name mentioned in the right places opened doors. Once the doors were opened, that's where I stepped in. We made a good team and some money together over the years.

"Ambassador. Where the hell are you? How did you find me?"

"I'm in Washington, and I've got only one word for you."

What had I done now? I'd been known to screw up on our deals once in a while, but I honestly couldn't think of anything. "What's that?"

"Cement."

"Cement?" That wasn't what I expected.

"It's beautiful. Russian cement."

"Do they use cement in Russia?"

"They build everything out of cement. When will you be back in Washington?"

"In about a week."

"Good. We'll go over it then. *Hasta la vista, amigo.*"

Russian cement? I couldn't put the deal together in my head for the life of me. Here I was in this beautiful tropical setting with a Latin beauty, and the last thing I wanted to think about was cement.

Sitting across the table from me at dinner that night, Celinda was bewitching. She wore a white, gauzy cotton dress we'd picked up for her in town earlier. The crocheted cotton lace hung off her shoulders and brushed her arms every time she moved her hands. She ate very precisely and made sure her fork and knife were exactly where they were supposed to be. Conversation was not her strong point, but I don't think the Mexican official next to her would have noticed if she was describing how to remove a brain tumor. You just had to look at her with the candlelight caressing her face to fall in love with her. The man on my right was *Señor* Juan Vega. He was starting up a computer business and was looking for someone to help sell and market computers in Mexico. I had some contacts for him in Washington and could probably put some contracts together for him. My future was looking bright and rosy. I felt on top of the world.

Following dinner, we all went out to the beach, where the Mexicans had erected a tent for after-dinner drinks. Torches blazed on bamboo poles, their flames reflecting off the black surface of the water. Celinda and I took off our shoes and walked hand in hand down the beach. When we looked back, the tent glowed with light and color, like a fairy castle. The water was warm on our feet even at night, and the wind surrounded us with the smell of a thousand thick and salty seas. We sat together on the beach at the edge of the surf, the water washing the sand from under our feet.

"I saw this movie once," I said. "It had Burt Lancaster in it and the actress was...I forget. It was set in Hawaii. *From Here to Eternity*. Have you ever seen it?"

"No, Tony. Tell me about it."

"It has this great scene. They'd been swimming, and they come out on the beach and make love in the surf as the waves wash over them."

I leaned back on my elbows and stared out at the water. Celinda stood, slid her dress off her shoulders, and let it fall to the sand. She knelt down next to me and unbuttoned my shirt.

"Show me, Tony," she whispered. And we made love on the beach with the waves flowing over and around us. I was floating, holding and being held in a deep warm, watery sea, suspended in a womb, feeling and not seeing.

During the mornings, while I attended meetings of the commission, Celinda headed for the pool or went shopping in town for presents for her family. One day she came back with one of those woven beach totes with "Puerto Vallarto" embroidered on it filled with thirty bottles of Tortuga Oil. She was sure that the turtle oil was responsible for the deep, honey-colored tan she was getting. Maybe she was right, but the mahogany richness of her skin was probably due more to our proximity to the equator. I told her so, but she wasn't convinced. She oiled herself religiously, and her natural musky scent became tinged with the salt of the sea. Every afternoon, after lunch and *siesta*, Celinda pestered me to take her out on the boat that the commission had chartered to take its members snorkeling. The day before we left, I gave in.

The water was blue, crystal clear, and warm like bath water. The intense heat and the Coco Locos made for a deadly combination, and all aboard had quite a buzz before we hit the first island and its coral reefs. The captain anchored the boat off the rocks, about fifty yards from the beach. Looking over the side, I could see all the way to the bottom, which must have been about fifteen feet.

I felt a heavy hand on my shoulder.

"*Señor Cassera*, let us talk some business, my friend. *¿Qué puedes hacer por mí?* What can you do for me?"

It was *Señor* Vega. He put his arm across my shoulders and started whispering like a conspirator. "Can you get American computer products into Mexico for me?"

"*Sí*. I can do it. Fax me your brochure, the types of products you need, and your company's financial report. If I like it, I can plug you into the biggest computer manufacturers in America."

"*¿Dices la verdad?*"

"I'm telling you the truth. I wouldn't lie to you, *Señor* Vega. You fax that report to me, then we'll talk."

"*Bueno*. It will be a pleasure doing business with you. I will have the report to you within one week." We shook hands, and he headed back to the bar. His English was perfect; no trace of an accent. He'd probably been educated at an American Ivy League school, like most wealthy Mexicans. I was embarrassed by my inadequate Spanish. After he walked off, I stood by the rail silently conjugating the verb "love" in Spanish. That, I hadn't forgotten from my high school Spanish class. "*Yo amo, tu amas, nosotras amanos, ellos aman*...they love."

Something rubbery touched my foot, and I jumped. It was Celinda in her goggles, slapping her flippers up and down the deck as she walked.

"Come on, Tony. Let's go in."

"You go on ahead. I'll be right behind you." I was not looking forward to this. Being in a boat on the water was one thing. Being in the water was an entirely different matter. I don't like going in any further than my waist. I was still hoping we'd be rowed to the beach, but it looked like everyone had to jump in the water from the boat. Celinda turned around before she jumped in and shouted to me.

"Don't forget to spit in your face mask."

Then she was gone. I put it off as long as I could, but she kept heckling me from the water. So, to shut her up, I jumped in. God, how I hate having my head under water. I popped back up and followed after Celinda, who was circling above one of the reefs. I was terrified of the dolphins. They'd swim amongst us, and I imagined they were sharks. Saturdays at the matinee when I was a kid, whenever the horror movies would be playing, my friends and I would sit with our legs pulled up off the floor. You never knew what might be lurking under the seats and come grab your legs. That's just the way I felt right now. I put on a bold front for Celinda, but I kept a keen eye peeled for sharks. I continually cautioned Celinda not to go out too far, and grabbed her leg one time as she floated by. She screamed with all her might and kicked me. By then I'd had enough.

I headed straight for the beach and was relieved when I felt my feet touch solid ground. A Mexican crew member waded out to greet me with a couple of Coco Locos. I took them both and sipped from one and then the other. On the beach, a raucous mariachi band was playing and singing in the shade of a huge palm umbrella. When the band took a break, a lone guitarist started singing. I drifted with each wave as it came in and curled around me. The sun's rays burned down hot and straight on my back, and the singer's voice carried out far across the water.

Play CD Track 3
"Under the Sun"

On this hot, balmy Mexico night
Walking on the waters edge, the moonlight was our guide.
And as the ocean wrapped around us, we made love in the sand.
I think I'm falling in love again, and it wasn't
What I planned.

I'd do anything for you
I'd do anything for you
I'd do anything for you
Under the Sun

Charmed by your kisses and the innocence of your style,
Oh, you put me at ease girl with the warmth of your smile.
And if I could have one wish, I'd wish this moment forever,
Cause I can't comprehend this world without your pleasure.
Oh, oh, oh, yeah.... Oh, oh, oh, yeah

I'd do anything for you
I'd do anything for you
I'd do anything for you
Under the sun
Under the sun
Under the sun

I stood rooted in the waist-high water with my toes curling into the sand, drinking one Coco Loco after another while I watched my angel float happily above the reefs.

Both Celinda and I felt sad when we boarded the plane for the flight home. Me, especially. I had a paper to do. Celinda slept while I wrote. All she had to do was write it over in her own handwriting when we got back.

The two of us sat in the old tortilla truck in front of her house. I was leaving for Albuquerque and my flight home to Washington D.C. Celinda's eyes were swollen from crying.

"Tony, don't leave."

"I have to. I'll come back. I promise. Here's my number in Washington. Rosita can show you how to call me collect from the restaurant phone."

"No. I know you'll forget me. You won't come back."

"Celinda, I'll come back. You have to finish high school. Two months, and you graduate. I'll come back then." I looked at my watch in exasperation. "I've got to go, Angel. I've got a long drive to Albuquerque, and I have to drop off the truck and pick up my brother, so he can drive the car back."

She nodded and started crying all over again. The door on my side doesn't open, so I had to reach across her and pull on the door handle. I slid over, nudging her, and she got out. I kissed her, climbed back in, and drove off. I felt like a jerk leaving her standing there crying, but that's the way it is sometimes. We had a great time, and that was it. Women always make everything into such a big deal.

She stood there, watching the old truck drive off. She didn't move even after it was no longer in sight, but she did stop crying, and a funny, tight smile played on her lips. She removed the gold bracelet he had given her and held it carefully in her hand as she walked the dusty streets to the house of the old woman.

SLEEPING WITH AN ANGEL

The car phone rang, and I answered it.

"*Cemento barato*," the thinly disguised voice on the other end said. Cheap cement. I laughed. "Hey, Cisco, you know anybody who needs cement?"

I played along. "You need to call Don 'Two Fingers' Rigatoni in New York. I can set you up." I heard Ambassador St. John's deep laugh.

"What's the deal?" I said. "Do you have some left over from your driveway, Ambassador?"

"Better than that. It's Russian cement. It's a sweet deal."

"I thought it was too cold to make cement in Russia," I teased.

"I have a client who owns a cement-making company in Russia," the Ambassador continued. "He wants to sell 4 million metric tons of Portland at $49.00 per metric ton. That's $2.00 under the world market price, so if we can find a buyer to pay current rates, we could make $8 million dollars as the broker. That's $4 million apiece, Tony."

I didn't know a damn thing about cement, but the money grabbed me. This was it. The big one. I could feel it in my bones. "That sounds like it's worth making a few phone calls. I'll call Armandi over at International Traders to see if he can help us, and I'll get back to you."

"Are you sure we want to deal with Armandi on this?"

"Trust me. I know he gives you the creeps, but he's our best bet. He's done deals like this before. We need his experience."

I could understand the Ambassador's hesitation. On first impression the trader looked harmless enough. Armandi was only four feet tall and moved his head like a bird, cocking it to one side and staring at you with one black, beady eye. He could have been Italian, he could have been Turkish, he could have been Greek, he could have been Arabic, or maybe even Argentinean. He could have been from Brooklyn. He spoke with an accent, but I never did know where he was from. One thing I did know for sure. He was no songbird. He was a vulture, who went where the pickings were good. I dealt with him because of who he knew, making sure I didn't slip and fall.

A couple days later, the Ambassador and I met with Armandi. He wanted us to cut him in at one-third and sign non-circumvent agreements, so none of us could go around the other and screw them out of the deal. That meant the Ambassador and I were down to $2.6 million apiece, but we said okay. We needed Armandi's contacts, and $2.6 million was not bad, we decided. Armandi had already located a buyer in Africa, some small country on the coast called Nigia. It was small and purple on the map; and it looked to me, with that much cement, Nigia could pave itself over and be a parking lot.

"So, Armandi," the Ambassador said, "who's the buyer? Tony needs to research his banking information."

"I can't tell you his name," Armandi replied innocently.

"Now wait a minute," I protested.

"Relax, Tony, the man who is acting for him will be in Washington in two weeks to meet with us."

Armandi was being evasive, and I didn't like it. But, I would have been the same way in his shoes.

At the door he turned his beady eye on me. "Not to worry, Tony. Just start thinking about how you're going to spend your millions."

The sound of water lapping against the hull of the boat, combined with the gentle rocking motion, caused me to sigh and reach for my drink. Without opening my eyes, I took a sip and held the cold glass on my stomach as I settled deeper into the hammock. I focused on the sounds of waves washing out from the shore and palm leaves swishing and brushing against each other. Below deck, I heard the faint beep of the fax. The phone rang. I groped for it, pushed some buttons, and heard the voice of my irritated secretary, Suzan, on the line.

"Mr. Cassera, I've been buzzing and buzzing you. I finally had to call you. There's a collect call for you on Line Two."

"I'll take it."

I lowered my feet from the desk and swung around in my chair. Looking out the window, I could see it was still raining in Washington.

"Hello."

"A collect call for Tony Cassera from Rosita's Diner," the voice said. "Will you accept the charges?"

"Yes, of course."

"Go ahead, ma'am," said the operator, and clicked off.

"Hi, Tony, it's Celinda."

My heart beat faster. "Celinda. How are you, Angel?"

"I miss you. Are you coming back?"

"Sure." From the corner of my eye, I saw Suzan gesturing that I had another call waiting. "I'm sorry, what was that you said?"

"I said I got a 'B' on the paper you wrote for me."

"A 'B'! That was an 'A' paper easy."

"Well, they gave me a 'B'," Celinda said. "That's a good grade for me, Tony."

My secretary was gesturing frantically at me.

"Listen. I've got to go. I'm in the middle of a big deal."

"Oh. Okay. You're still coming to my graduation, aren't you?"

"Listen. I've got to go. I'll call you back, Angel."

"Okay. Bye."

"Bye."

I was outraged. How could they have given her only a 'B'. I felt better, though, when I realized that her teacher probably knew she couldn't have written that paper. Yes, I'm sure that was it. I picked up the other call.

D-Day. The Plaza Club was a bastion of maleness. Women made rare excursions into the inner sanctum. Stepping from the noisy streets into the muffled quiet of its darkly paneled rooms spoke to me of luxury, wealth, and power that soon would be mine. Its overstuffed leather armchairs were occupied by men who looked like they hadn't moved in the last forty years. They still wore three-button suits and smoked pipes and cigars. Once upon a time, they had wielded the power in this town. Many still did, but quietly now, behind the scenes. It was the perfect place to impress the buyer's representative. The Ambassador had even arranged for a retired, one-star general to stop by our table while we were lunching.

The Ambassador, Armandi and myself were seated at the table, discussing our good fortune, when the maitre d' escorted the man we were meeting to the table. He looked like someone from the Mafia to me, but with better manners. Speaking with a slight French accent, he introduced himself as Phillipe Barent. Monsieur Barent had a thick, black moustache and drank three scotches to our one. His cigarettes were Algerian, and he smoked them one right after the other. The harsh smoke nauseated me, but the thought of my share kept me going.

"It is such a pleasure to meet you gentlemen at last," he said, exhaling a smoky haze. "Please have one of my cards." He withdrew a slim gold case from his inside coat pocket and handed us each a card. *Phillipe Barent.* Three cities were listed with phone and fax numbers: London, Paris, and Monte Carlo. I made a mental note to get myself a card case as I pulled my card from my wallet and handed it to him. Then he sat back in his chair and put the fingertips of his two hands together.

"My client is very excited about this deal," he said. "However, I have here a letter from him requesting some additional information about the cement." All of us looked cautiously at each other after reading the letter. Even though we had all signed non-circumvent agreements, everyone was still leery of each other.

"I would like to have the information on the seller now," Barent said, and he tapped his fingertips together.

The Ambassador handed Monsieur Barent the fax disclosing our source.

"Excellent. We are pleased." I guess by 'we,' he meant his client. To my disgust, he lit up another cigarette and ordered another scotch. This was going to be a hefty tab, and I was picking it up.

Armandi spoke next. "The cement is ready to ship from Russia once we get confirmation from you. Do you have any idea what we're looking at here?"

Before Barent could respond, a broad-shouldered gentleman approached our table. I'd forgotten about the general the Ambassador had lined up. Armandi glared at the intruder with his beady eye. I guess he'd forgotten to tell Armandi.

"Ambassador," the general said in a deep baritone voice.

Ambassador St. John stood, looking genuinely surprised. "General. It's good to see you. Gentleman, I'd like to introduce retired Brigadier General Schweiger. General Schweiger was in charge of Russian Affairs at the State Department." I glanced over at Barent. He looked suitably impressed.

"A pleasure to meet you, Monsieur Barent. It looks like you gentlemen are discussing business, so I won't linger. I have a meeting at the Pentagon within the hour." He addressed Monsieur Barent directly. "You're working with the best, sir. Good luck on your project." He shook hands all around. Exit the general, stage left.

Armandi started talking again. "Barent, what are we looking at here as far as a confirmation from the buyer?"

Monsieur Barent threw a steely glance at Armandi as he lit up yet another cigarette. The man definitely did not like being called by his surname. I kicked Armandi under the table as he started to open his mouth again. If Armandi blew this for us by a simple mistake.... I clenched and unclenched my fists under the table. We all sat quietly, as Monsieur Barent ordered another scotch.

Armandi was hunched over the table, tighter than a coiled spring. A woman passed behind him, and I was so startled when I saw her long black, wavy hair that I dropped my fork with a clatter on my plate. I followed her with my eyes as she made her way to a table. When she turned to be seated, I was both sad and relieved when I saw her face. Armandi and the Ambassador were staring at me. I directed my attention to Monsieur Barent, who was pulling another contract from his eelskin briefcase. I noted that his briefcase had some kind of fancy lock on it. Good, I thought. He's a careful man. We certainly didn't want the whole world knowing about this.

"To conclude the deal, I'll need this contract signed and filled in with the proper information." He handed it to the Ambassador, who passed it to me.

"...and we'll need fifty thousand dollars, up-front money...today."

The Ambassador, Armandi, and I looked each other. Armandi nodded his head, and we all three pulled out our checkbooks

I looked the contract over carefully and signed it before passing it to Armandi and the Ambassador, who also signed.

"Gentlemen." Monsieur Barent swayed slightly as he stood. "I have a plane to catch to London at four o'clock. Since it is now 3:00 p.m., I am afraid that I must leave." He put the contract and our checks in his briefcase and locked it. We escorted him out and deposited him in a cab with instructions to take him to Dulles Airport.

The three of us walked to the Ambassador's office, which was only a few blocks away. Those few blocks told the whole story of this city. Old, dilapidated brownstones were being demolished to make way for gleaming granite and marble ten-story office buildings, because no building can be higher than the nation's Capitol. What these new structures lacked in height, they made up for in power. Forgotten were the poor people whose homes were torn down and who were forced south of the Anacostia River, where the power belonged to the street gangs.

Armandi rubbed the palms of his hands together excitedly.

"That was great," he said. "The General was a nice touch, Ambassador, but for Christ's sake, tell me ahead of time."

"Sorry, Armandi, I thought I had," the Ambassador said apologetically, closing his office door.

"Thank God, he was so drunk, he didn't notice Tony throwing his silverware around. What was that about?"

I shrugged my shoulders. "It slipped. Just let it go, Armandi," I said irritably.

I was still fuming over the tab. "Five hundred dollars for lunch! Boy, can that guy drink. And what about the fifty grand up-front money? Why didn't you tell us about that, Armandi?"

"I didn't know. Honest."

"I thought you were so experienced," the Ambassador said.

"I am. Each deal is different."

"Relax, Tony," Armandi said from his perch on the arm of the couch. "The lunch and the up-front is a drop in the bucket compared to what you're going to get." Being lectured to didn't sit well with me, but I was excited. $2,600,000 dollars, and it was all mine. I'd invest it, get a good tax shelter going, and quit working. Armandi was right. What's a measly five hundred for lunch?

The Ambassador walked back into the front office. He had a handful of faxes in his hand and a troubled look on his face.

"These five faxes are about the cement deal. Some guys want a cut of our two dollar profit. This one's from some guy in New York saying he's representing the seller. I thought that was us!"

Armandi flew off the couch. "What guys? Another broker? Let me see those."

"I think we've got a little misunderstanding here. I'm going to call Russia," said the Ambassador. Armandi left for his office, and I raced over to mine. I'd given Suzan the afternoon off so the faxes from my machine littered the floor. I'd gotten the same stuff plus something else. I called the Ambassador immediately.

"Ambassador, it's Tony. Were you able to get through to Russia?"

"Not yet."

"Listen to this. I got the same faxes you did, but I also got one in Russian with an English translation." I read it out loud. "'We confirm the availability of four million metric tons of Portland cement at a price of forty-nine U.S. dollars per metric ton, with first delivery thirty days after receipt of Letter of Credit. One: Seller and Buyer execute the Kontract. Two: Buyer issue pre-advise Letter of Credit. Three: Seller issue performance bond at 1.5%. Four: Letter of Credit is activated. Shipment begins. We look forward to hearing from Zou.' I think they mean 'you'. So, we've got our confirmation from the seller, Ambassador," I said excitedly. Everything was going to be all right. I had a bad case of Potomac Fever and I was loving every minute. I was finally going to be rich!

"It sure looks like it. I've got another fax coming in, Tony. I'll call you right back."

My fax machine started up again. This one was another 'Kontract' with provisions in the event that the Buyer fails to perform, he will pay Seller 500,000 U.S. dollars.

My phone rang. It was the Ambassador. "Tony, I've got three more faxes from several brokers who want their share. They've got signed non-circumvent agreements with people I've never even heard of." Brokers were climbing out of the woodwork all over the world.

"Damn," I said. "It's over." I hit the ground hard. I could see my share barely covering the lunch tab, not to mention the up-front money I gave the guy.

"Hey, Cisco, not yet. I'll leave a message for Barent at his London office. We should hear back from him tomorrow. It's probably just a mix-up."

"Okay. I'll wait a couple of days," I said, hopefully.

Phillipe Barent called the next day. He didn't know who those other brokers were with the non-circumvent agreements, but he said our deal was going through after verification of the banking information. He'd contact us when everything was set. I let out a huge sigh of relief and spent the rest of the day prowling the docks at the Washington Marina, looking at all the 45-foot yachts.

Two weeks went by, with no calls and no faxes from Phillipe Barent. Armandi was pretty disgusted, but the Ambassador and I were doggedly hanging in there. I decided to call Monsieur Barent myself. I tried London first. "No, Monsieur is not here. He left for Monaco last week." I called Monaco. "No, Monsieur has departed for Paris." I tried Paris. "No, Monsieur had not arrived yet." I waited a couple days and tried Paris again. "Monsieur left for London this morning." I waited a day and called London. The line was disconnected, so I tried Monaco. "No, Monsieur is not due in Monaco for another two weeks. Yes, we have given him your messages."

I smelled a rat. I chased this guy around for thirty days. Then one day I received a fax from Phillipe Barent, but it was addressed to another broker, and it didn't bode well for our so-called deal. I called the Ambassador and Armandi and read them the fax on a conference call. "Please send quote for one million T-shirts at $1.00 apiece for African country."

There was silence on the line. The bastard was selling contracts for T-shirts now.

"I'm out," said Armandi. He hung up.

"Me, too," I said.

"Well, I guess I'm out, too," said the Ambassador. "I really thought this one was the one."

"That son-of-a-bitch," I said, "taking us like that. Fifty grand! Man, I'm so pissed off. We might just as well have thrown the money into a trash can! Christ!"

"Calm down, Tony. It's history now. At least we got a good lunch out of it. Right?"

"Yeah, right," I said, thinking of the credit card bill I had yet to pay.

"Say, Tony, I've got 150 containers of cigarettes. One container is 40 feet, 960 master cartons..." I could hear the Ambassador's calculator in the background. "...50 cartons in each master at $288 per master carton. Split with Armandi, that's almost three million dollars profit apiece."

"I bet they're from Algeria," I said, slamming down the phone.

Meeting at Cleveland's at the conclusion of a deal had become a tradition for us, win or lose. It was a bit of a joint, with dark red walls and lousy paintings that were always crooked. Last night's pretzels still littered the carpet under the tables. We'd spent a lot of hours here, hatching deals, watching them go under, or buying drinks for the house when one had gone through. The same guys hung out at the bar year after year, night after night, watching TV. There was a pool table in back, and I could never hear the clunk of a pool ball sinking without thinking fondly of Cleveland's.

Morty was seated on a barstool, his watery eyes on the football game. His face lit up when he saw me. "Drinks on the house tonight, Tony?"

"Not tonight, Morty. Seen the Ambassador?"

"Yeah. He's over in the corner. Some really squirrelly guy was with him for awhile. A dwarf, I think."

Armandi.

"How's the plumbing business?"

"Good. Real good. Lots'a tree roots to rooter out today."

"Keep up the good work, Morty. Washington needs you."

I made my way over to the corner. I could tell the Ambassador had been there for some time. Two empty martini glasses and two full ones sat in front of him. An ashtray held several half-smoked, smoldering cigarettes, and a lone green olive lay on the table, speared with brightly colored plastic swords.

"Hey, Ceeesco!"

"Ambassador. I thought you said 9:00 p.m.?"

"I changed my mind. Armandi just left. We were talking Algerian cigarettes. Are you in?"

"I'll let you know." I flopped down next to him in the booth and loosened my tie. "I'm getting too old for this, Ambassador. Maybe I should buy a business in Florida, or maybe in California. Someplace near the beach, where it's warm and sunny."

"That doesn't sound like you at all."

He was right. Deals usually never got me down. They just revved me up for the next one. I hoped I wasn't losing my edge, going soft.

"It's all just smoke and mirrors in Washington. You know that, Tony." He punched me in the arm. "You're the one who told me, remember?"

"I remember," I said, laughing.

"It's who puts on the best show, like in Hollywood. You gotta keep laughing, or you'll shoot yourself."

The Ambassador was right. The way I felt was stupid. So the deal didn't go through. So what? There would be others. All I needed was one hit, and I'd have it made. Look at Robert Vesco and the $200 million he walked away with. He lived on a yacht now in the Caribbean. Someday that was going to be me.

We sat next to each other in the booth and closed the place down. It was the middle of the night when I finally crawled into bed, my head fuzzy with drink and full of dreams of the "Big Deal."

A tendril of hair brushed across my face. The mattress gave beneath her weight, and I felt her thighs press into my sides, gripping them. She lay atop me, her smooth skin rubbing against mine, her heart beating rhythmically against my fiercely pounding one. Her breath was hot and close on my neck, like a desert wind. We moved as one, her tongue flicking over me, urging the dance to its completion. We whirled in the darkness, locked in a merciless tango. She would not stop nor let me go and rode me with her passion.

"Tony, Tony, Tony, you are mine, mine, mine... *eres mío, mío, mío...*"

The clock chiming in the next room silenced the dance. My eyes flew open, and I was alone in the dark, panting. The air in the room was thick and smothering, making me gasp for breath. I sat up, and out of the corner of my eye, I saw a luminous, transparent figure fade through the doorway. Someone was in the house!

I crept from the bed, flattened myself against the wall next to the door, and peered out. The moonlight coming in the window showed the hallway to be empty. I felt my way downstairs and stood at the base of the steps, listening. A lone car passed on the street, its headlights illuminating the living room, the light sliding from wall to wall. There was no one there.

I turned on the lights, checked every closet and the doors, to make sure they were still locked. I was alone in the house.

As I returned to bed, my limbs trembled, my heart pounded. I reached over and turned on the lamp next to the bed, and for a long time I lay awake, promising myself that I wouldn't drink so much.

I sat in my office staring out the window at a hazy, humid 95-degree day in June, with an ozone danger level of a hundred. Usually these days came in August and were the signal for the mass exodus from Washington of all the lawyers, politicians, and psychiatrists to their beach homes on the cool coast of Maine. I was felt restless, plagued with a yearning for something nameless. Walking down a street, I saw Celinda in every young woman with long, dark, wavy hair. There were some consulting jobs that were paying me well, but the excitement I'd felt during the cement deal just wasn't there. No adrenalin rush. I tapped my pen on the desk. It was almost 5:00 p.m., and a long, lonely night in front of me. For two and a half months the Ambassador and I had spun our wheels on the cement deal.

The fax machine beeped. The fax was from Martin Kitchner, the TV announcer I'd met in Puerto Vallarta. The paper emerged, slowly revealing a clipping from a Mexican newspaper. I couldn't decipher much of the article, but I recognized the man in the photograph. It was *Señor* Vega, the computer guy I'd met at the commission. He was in handcuffs, surrounded by policeman. I crumpled up the fax and threw it in the wastebasket. No deal going to happen there now. What a fool he was to get caught. I reached for the phone and dialed. A woman answered.

"*¿Bueno?*"

"*Hola, que tal, Rosita, es Tony. ¿Cómo está Sanibel?* How's everything going?"

"*Bien, muy bien,* Tony."

"*¿Está Celinda?*"

"*Sí está, pero está sirviendo a alguien.* Can you hang on? She's still with a customer."

"Sí, I can wait."

I heard Rosita calling to Celinda. Someone was singing in Spanish on the radio, and I could hear Chubby washing dishes and banging the pans around.

"Tony?"

"Hi, Angel."

"I graduated two weeks ago."

"Already?"

"You said you'd call me. You said you'd come."

"I was busy. I forgot."

"You promised."

"I know. I'm sorry."

"Did you make a lot of money on your deal?"

"The deal worked out great. What are you going to do now?"

"I am working more hours for Rosita. Some of the girls are getting jobs working for businesses over on the interstate. Maria is going to try and get me an interview for a job at Coleman's, answering phones."

"Who's Maria?"

"My best friend."

"You never mentioned her before."

"She is just my girlfriend."

"Good. That's good, answering the phones," I said absently.

"How is your deal?"

"Well, it didn't work out quite as we wanted it to."

"Oh. I am sorry for you, Tony."

"It's no big thing." What I said next surprised me, because I hadn't been thinking of it. "Listen, Celinda, I'm going to come home for awhile." I heard her breathe in deeply and hold her breath. "I'm thinking about coming next week."

"Oh, Tony."

"Does that make you happy?"

"Oh, yes, I am very happy."

And I heard the laughter and happiness in her voice even though she was not laughing.

"I'm not sure when I'll get a flight. I'll just show up and surprise you. Be good."

That night, Celinda pulled the box down from its hiding place behind the wooden beam in her room. The beam ran across the ceiling and close to the far wall, where she had dug a hole out of the soft adobe with a kitchen knife. She had been twelve when she first dug the hole, and no one had ever found it because it stayed in the shadow even during the day when the sun came in the room. But it was night now as she pulled down the box and opened it.

Inside was a stub of a candle in a glass, and a dirty, knotted handkerchief. The candle in the glass she lit, then carefully unfolded the handkerchief and lay it before the candle on the hard earth floor. The gold bracelet he'd given her glowed warmly in the folds of the handkerchief as she softly repeated the words the old woman had taught her. *"Madre Santa, Madre Sagrada, tú quien me has contestatado, bendice mi esfuerzo.* Holy Mother, Sacred Mother, you who have answered me, bless my endeavor. *Madre Santa, Madre Sagrada, tú que me amas, escucha mis palabras...* Holy Mother, Sacred Mother, you who love me, hear my words..."

Play CD Track 4
"*La Vieja*"
instrumental

The sun felt good on my face as I drove south from Albuquerque to Sanibel. The coldness I'd felt lurking deep inside me in Washington vanished in the warmth of the air. There were a few puffy white clouds, but they disappeared by the time I turned off the interstate and headed into Sanibel. The sky loomed huge and blue above the town as I descended into the valley.

I pulled up in front of Rosita's, turned off the engine, and sat there for a minute without moving. I walked up and stared through the plate glass window. Celinda was behind the counter, with her back to me. I watched and waited. She didn't see me for a while after she turned around, then she looked up after taking a customer's order, and I could tell by the expression on her face that she wasn't sure. The sun was at my back. She handed the order to Rosita, said something, and headed outside. Sanibel is a small town, so we didn't kiss or hug. We just looked at each other, and then she took my hand and pulled me inside.

My old booth was occupied, so I took the next one over. For the next two hours I ate and watched every move Celinda made. Rosita took a break and came over and kept me company. When 8 o'clock came, the next shift arrived and Celinda was free.

"Where are we going?" she asked as I drove out of town.

"Someplace where we can be alone."

"To the desert?"

"Wait and see," I said. "Why are you sitting way over there?"

Celinda slid over next to me, and I put my arm around her.

"I'm so glad you came back, Tony." She nuzzled her face against my neck, then rested her head on my shoulder.

Neither of us said a word as I drove along the old two-lane highway and took an old mining road up into one of the canyons. The road snaked back and forth, cutting deeper and higher into the canyon. The rocky walls and brush-like trees were bleached white in the passing sweep of the headlights. The road grew narrower and more rutted, until it finally ended in a space where the old mine shaft had its opening. I left the car lights on, so that we could see our way up a trail that cut though the side of the canyon.

"Where are you taking me?" Celinda demanded.

"Give me your hand. It's just a little bit further."

I pulled her up behind me on the top of a flat rock. Down below us was the valley and the shining lights of Sanibel.

"That's Sanibel?" Celinda whispered. "It's so tiny."

"And so far away. We're all by ourselves."

I pulled her gently towards me, and there in the dark, away from the eyes of Sanibel, I held her close and kissed her. She lay back against the side of the canyon, and I held her hands pinned there as my tongue found her mouth. Then her tongue was in my mouth. I released her hands, and she pulled her shirt out of her skirt, and I ran my hands over her back. Then her shirt was off, and I was cradling her breasts in my hands. She leaned into me and whispered into my ear, "Whatever you want, Tony. Whatever you want." And I lifted her up and she wrapped her legs around me, and we both tore into each other like wild animals howling to the moon and the stars.

We lay naked on the dusty ground, our legs entwined. I buried my face in her hair and breathed in deeply of her scent.

"Happy, Angel?" I said, covering her face with gentle kisses.

She sighed, stretching her body up against mine.

"Just a second." I stood and searched through the piles of tossed off clothes, looking for my jacket and the envelope in its pocket. I came back and lay down next to her. With the white envelope in my hand, I traced the outline of her body from her toes up over her calf and the curve of her hips, dragging it slowly between her breasts until it touched her chin.

"This is for you, Celinda."

"What is it?" She sat up and started to open the envelope. A breeze blew across us, tugging the envelope out of her hand.

I retrieved it. "It's too dark to read it. I'll tell you what it is. It's a plane ticket to Washington D.C. It's round trip, so if you decide you don't want to stay, you can come back to Sanibel. Will you come?"

"Yes, oh, yes, I'd like to come," she whispered, "but we'll have to ask my *papá's* permission."

"Don't worry, Angel. Let me take care of it. Come here." I pulled her on top of me and pushed *Papá* out of my thoughts. I'd deal with him later.

The breeze blew steadily, carrying with it the faint scent of a rose.

"So he has asked you to marry him?" the man said.

"Not exactly, *Papá*," Celinda said with some hesitation, "but he will."

"Then my answer is 'no.'" The man hit his fist on the kitchen table to emphasize his decision. "Good girls do not go off to live with some man like this."

"Now, Pablo," Consuela interjected soothingly. "Celinda, she is my daughter, too, and I think she should go. How many girls from our street get the opportunity to go to such a big city? To the capital of this country, where the President lives?"

"He has met the President, *Papá*. Even shook his hand, I am sure," Celinda interjected.

Her father shrugged his shoulders. "That means nothing to me. This President hasn't gotten me a job or my disability." He crossed his arms across his chest.

"You are a stubborn old goat, who starves rather than eat the food placed right under his nose," Consuela said, angrily. "Besides, once he has spent time with our daughter, he will be begging to marry her."

"It is just not the way it is done," the man insisted.

"Do we have a choice, Husband?"

"Please, *Papá*. Please listen to what he has to say," Celinda begged.

"I will talk to him, but I promise nothing."

The two women looked at each other, their expressions revealing nothing.

I sat by myself, practicing my Spanish in the front room of the old adobe, another chair facing me. I could hear them talking behind the closed door. I glanced at my watch, wondering what the hell was taking them so long. I watched the votive lights flickering on the altar. A flame flared up, startling me. I stood and glanced at the window to see if it was open. There was someone at the window, a face of a woman. I ran out to the porch, but there was no one there.

"Tony, where are you?"

"I'm here, on the porch."

"What are you doing out there?" Celinda asked.

Suddenly, my shoes felt too tight. Celinda's *papá*, leaning on an old wooden cane, stood behind her.

I walked back in the house. Her *papá* sat heavily in the chair opposite me and motioned for me to sit. He had a broad, Mayan face, like the ones I'd seen on the stone heads in the museum in Mexico City. All he needed was a headdress, a pyramid to stand on, and a sacrificial victim. I didn't feel as confident as I had last night with Celinda in the dark.

"*Señor* Alvarez." I swallowed. I couldn't think in Spanish fast enough, so I had to ask him in English. "I'd like your permission to take Celinda back to Washington with me. She could go to college, or work if she wanted to. I'd take good care of her, and if she wasn't happy and wanted to come home, she already has a return ticket."

He didn't say anything, but reached for the ticket he'd set on the table. I watched him struggle to pick it up with his stiff fingers. He held it carefully, the envelope smooth and white against his weathered, knotted hands.

"Celinda, she is my only daughter, and she is the youngest of our children."

"I will take very good care of her, *Señor.*"

"What are your plans for Celinda?"

"My plans?" I said uncertainly.

"Antonio, her *mamá* and I know what Celinda, she tells us is true. We know of your father. Everyone knows of your father. You come from good family and you are a very important man in Washington, and it is every parent's wish for their daughter that she marry a good man."

Marriage. So that's what he was getting at. Marriage was not uppermost in my mind when I thought of Celinda, but I would promise anything just to get the old guy to agree.

"I understand. You wish to know my intentions towards your daughter. Marrying her is my greatest desire, and this is a good way for us to see if we are compatible."

"How long would this take?" he asked.

"Two years," I said, hopefully, trying to buy myself time.

He stared back at me and said nothing.

"Or perhaps one year."

"One year is good. Do you promise one year then you marry my Celinda?"

"Sure. A year."

"Give me your hand on it," he said.

We shook hands.

"I want you take good care my daughter, and be good to her. *Mamá* and I give permission."

"*Gracias,*" I said, the sweat forming on my brow.

Papá stood solemnly, pulling himself up on his cane, and then he smiled at me. One of his front teeth was gold. When he realized I was looking at his tooth, he rubbed it with his thumb and said "*Buena suerta,*" — "for good luck" — and at that moment, I felt very lucky.

He rested his hand on my shoulder. "And now we eat, Antonio." He escorted me into the tiny kitchen where Consuela and Celinda were finishing the meal. Celinda passed by me with a plate of enchiladas, smiled, and lightly stroked my hand. We all squeezed in around the table. Her mother brought plate after plate of food: tamales, tacos, enchiladas, barbecued ribs, steak and tortillas, of course. Tortilla King wrappers were lying all over the kitchen counter. We toasted the future with Coronas, clinking our bottles over and over again.

Two weeks later Celinda Alvarez was at National airport in her too small pink suit and her too high, high heels, and she was all mine.

We drove up in front of my Georgetown row house. It dated from the 1850's and was on a cobblestone street. Most people had to park in the street, but I was lucky to have a small cemented space in front that doubled as a driveway. Fortunately, the Washington, D.C. police thought it was a driveway, too, so I escaped the usual parking tickets. Furnishing it had been the fulfillment of a dream for me. I covered the hardwood floors with oriental rugs from estate sales where I would haggle over the prices just like in Mexico. My pride and joy was the master bedroom set. The bedstead was massive, with carved wooden scrollwork, and sat high off the floor. There were matching bureaus, dressers and mirrors. It was opulently rococo, and sleeping in it made me feel like a king. I couldn't wait for Celinda to see my home and to love it.

While I went through my mail, Celinda went exploring. I heard her open the French doors leading off the kitchen which opened out into a tiny garden. I wondered if she liked to plant things and watch them grow. She shut the doors and came quietly back into the library.

"Is it always so hot here?" she asked.

"It's hot in New Mexico," I said.

"But here, it's hard to breathe."

"You'll get used to it soon."

She started looking at the pictures on the walls. She studied each one in the same deliberate way that she spoke. There were photos of me with Nixon and Ford, framed letters from them both, and the desktop was covered with political mementos: an ashtray with the Presidential seal, inscribed pen and pencil sets, and numerous glass paperweights with government agency seals in them. The object that fascinated her the most was the photograph of me standing next to the 150-pound sailfish that I had caught off the Florida Keys. She took the photograph from the wall and brought it over to me.

"Why did you have your picture taken with a fish? Did the President give you the fish?

"No. I caught it deep sea fishing off the Keys."

"Did it taste good? It is a strange-looking fish."

"Well, I didn't eat it." She seemed surprised. "I had it mounted. It's downstairs in the basement." I could tell by her face that she wasn't sure what I meant. "It's hanging on the wall." She shrugged her shoulders and hung the photograph back up.

"Can I go upstairs?"

"Of course you can. You don't have to ask. It's your home now."

I heard her walk up the stairs and soon the floors above me started creaking. I'd been reading for about ten minutes when I realized I hadn't heard a sound for some time. I went upstairs and looked in the rooms. I couldn't find her anywhere.

"Celinda?"

"In here, Tony." Her voice sounded like it was coming from the master bedroom. I went back in, but still didn't see her.

"Celinda. Where are you?"

"I'm here." I whirled around as she stepped out of the closet.

"It's so big, Tony."

I was really proud of my closet. I'd taken the small front bedroom and changed it into a dressing room, lined with wardrobes, drawers for shirts and ties, and special shelves for my shoes. A friend had referred the carpenter to me. This guy should have been making furniture. He was one talented woodworker. I'd been talking to him about paneling the den downstairs and making it into a gentleman's library.

"Come on." I took her hand and pulled her back into the closet. "Let's make some room for your things." Her one suitcase was lying open on the floor. She seemed lost, so I took charge and pulled out a hanger. "Hand me your dresses, and we'll hang them up here."

"No, just show me where, and I'll hang them up, Tony."

I made space for her in one of the wardrobes and cleared out several drawers. I guess women like to put their own things away. When I went in the closet later, I saw five dresses hanging in the wardrobe, each one more hideous than the next. I recognized them. They were the dresses we'd hidden in the locker at the airport on our way to Puerto Vallarta.

We ate in the dining room by candlelight that night. She'd showered and put on one of her floral dresses. It was the green and brown one with orange spiral things printed all over it. Candlelight helped that dress. You couldn't see it very well. Celinda, however, was radiant.

"Do you like the house?" I asked her.

"I love it, Tony. It's perfect."

"We'll get you some new clothes."

Celinda looked down at her dress.

"I guess I am very ugly," she said.

"Not you, Celinda. You are always beautiful to me, and tomorrow you will have clothes as beautiful as you are."

New clothes transformed her. She smiled and laughed more. She even walked differently. I would leave her money in the morning, and in the evening I'd come home to a fashion show. We'd end up on the living room floor, and she wouldn't be wearing a thing.

Our life settled into a routine, with me heading out to work, and Celinda reading fashion magazines and trying to copy the newest looks. One night I came home, and found her walking around waving her hands in the air. I knew from my phone bills that she was calling home a lot. I figured she'd been talking to her mother, who was talking to the old woman, who probably told her if Celinda walked that way on the full moon, life would be great. They were a superstitious bunch.

"Tony, look." She walked up to me and spread out the fingers on both of her hands. Her nails. She'd had her nails done. Actually, it looked like she had new nails. They were an inch long and bright red. She looked so pleased.

"They're sure long."

"Yes. They put this porcelain on them and build them up. They are so hard. Look." She whacked her nails on the table. I was impressed.

"I liked your nails the way they were before. You could hurt me with those."

She wiggled her fingers in front of my face.

"Stop it, Celinda," I said. I was irritated now. "I really don't like those things."

"Men," she hissed. "What do you know about such things. Why can't you say anything nice?"

"Aw, Celinda, calm down. They're beautiful." I tried to hug her, but she pushed me away.

"Stop it. You're lying to me." She ran upstairs and slammed the door. I'd never seen that side of her before. I got to know it intimately. She'd love me with all her heart or she'd want to cut my balls off. And it was usually over nothing.

The next few days were pretty bleak, until I left her some money in the morning for new clothes. We had a fashion show that night, and things went better after that until...

I came home early one afternoon to surprise Celinda and spend the afternoon making love. I closed the front door softly and peeked into the downstairs rooms. I was disappointed when I didn't find her right away. I called upstairs. "Celinda?"

"Tony. You're home early. I was just changing."

"Don't bother, Angel. I'm going to take all your clothes off, anyway." I ran up the stairs two steps at a time, pounced on her in the bedroom and pulled her T-shirt over her head. I stood staring at her, her shirt in my hands.

"You cut your hair."

"Do you like it?" she said, posing seductively.

"You cut your fucking hair! Are you crazy, or what?"

I threw the shirt violently to the floor.

"What's the matter, Tony? See, it's like in the magazine." She pointed to a model with shoulder length hair.

"Fuck the magazine," I said, grabbing it from her and ripping it up.

"I want to look like all the women we see when we go to the receptions," she shouted at me. "I look stupid with long hair. No one else wears long hair."

"I love your hair long," I yelled back. "I love you because you don't look like all the other bitches in this town."

"But we're not married," she screamed at me.

"Okay, but we're thinking about it," I said lamely.

"We are?" She put down the lamp she was going to throw at me.

"Yeah, sort of, we are."

"Oh, Tony." She put the lamp down and came over to me. I picked her up and threw her on the bed and leapt on her. She was laughing and giggling as I pulled off her underpants, but soon she was moaning and begging me not to stop. But I did. Her eyes flew open.

"Tony, what are you doing?" she gasped.

"Promise me you'll never cut your hair again."

"Let me go. You're holding my wrists too tight."

"Promise me."

She was getting ready to knee me, but hesitated.

"Promise me."

She started to laugh. "I promise," she said. "I promise."

I took her to the White House, the Smithsonian, the Kennedy Center, all the top restaurants, and to Capitol Hill to have lunch with some congressmen. We drove by Watergate, and I explained Nixon's undoing by the burglary. She listened, but I don't think she understood much, or cared about what I was trying to teach her about Washington.

That became evident when I found her stash of stolen ashtrays in the basement. One from every place I'd ever taken her. When confronted, she said they were presents for her family.

I was always invited to receptions on the Hill to mingle with business leaders, congressional staff and others trying to peddle their influence. Ambassador St. John would sometimes be there, and we'd chuckle over our cement deal, but not without a little yearning for what might have been. He seemed down lately, especially after his cigarette deal had gone up in smoke. Plus, I had Celinda now, and he and I weren't seeing as much of each other. I took Celinda with me to the receptions. I was proud of the impact her presence made when she entered a room. She was always gracious as the men flocked around her, but I could tell she was bored. She'd had to promise me not to steal anything as a condition to coming.

At one reception, she pulled me aside. "Tony, I really like coming to all these places with you. I love Washington and you, but when these people ask me what I do, I have nothing to say. I do not do anything."

"You're with me."

"I know and I love that, but I'd like to do something during the day, while you're gone."

"You want to work?"

"Yes. I would like to have a job."

"Of course you can get a job, if you want. What do you think you'd like to do?"

She thought very carefully. "Well, I took typing and computers in high school. There are always a lot of lawyers here. Do you think I could work for a law firm as a secretary?"

"That's possible," I lied, knowing she wouldn't have a snowball's chance in hell with her skills. "I have a friend who has a big law firm here in D.C. I'll give him a call tomorrow."

"Thank you, Tony. You're wonderful. I'll work hard, and maybe someday I can help you in your business."

"Maybe someday. We'll see."

My business. I was walking on the edge in my business. For Celinda, everything was either black or white. She did not understand the gray areas that most of us in Washington D.C. worked in. This was a real gray area right now. Sitting across the lunch table from me was Leon Kobetski. He'd called me on a referral from someone in Illinois, wanting to go over some business, and implied he might need my services. The poor guy didn't know I'd already worked for him several months ago as a subcontractor through a lobbyist friend of mine, Ted Townsend. Ted and I worked together when he had contracts that needed someone who knew the ropes in government contracts.

"You know, Tony, I never hired a lobbyist before Ted. I had no idea how expensive you guys are. It's been six months now, and I'm not seein' a whole lot of progress out of him. That's why I called you."

What was he talking about? There was a federal investigation going on, and until it had been concluded, Ted's hands were tied. That's why I submitted my final invoice months ago, and I bet that son-of-a-bitch was still billing Kobetski for my services. I hedged.

"Leon, I wish I could help you out, but I can't take you on as a client right now. I'm just too busy. I'm sure Ted's doing the best he can. Lobbying takes time, and getting everything lined up is tricky. I doubt it will be much longer."

"I hope you're right, Tony. I hope you're right. I need that government contract. You don't know how much I need it."

"I'm sorry, Leon."

"Maybe next time. Want another drink?"

I glanced at my watch. "Wish I could, but I've got to get over to the Hill," I lied.

"I understand," Leon said.

At the door of the restaurant, I turned and looked back at Kobetski sitting by himself, drinking. Here I had been working for this guy to the tune of five thousand dollars a month, and he didn't even know it. I didn't even know it.

I called Ted from my car.

"Hey, Tony. Long time since I heard from you."

I turned onto Pennsylvania Avenue. "I haven't heard from you in a while either, Ted."

"Been busy. You know how it is. We should get a game of golf in soon."

The light turned red. "Ted, I had lunch with Kobetski today, at Old Ebbit's Grill."

There was a long silence. The light turned green, and I turned right into one of those traffic circles.

"Leon Kobetski's in town? I thought he was still in Peoria. He wasn't due here until next week."

Damn, I'd missed my turn onto K Street.

"Ted, you've been billing the sucker for my services the past five months, haven't you? I'm going to have a talk with Leon about you."

"Tony, please don't. I'll get you your money, the whole twenty-five thousand you would have earned. Just don't say anything."

"You got a fancy lady on the side, Ted? Or you back into cocaine again."

"No. It's nothing like that."

"You're working a good scam this time."

I shot onto K street.

"Twenty-five thousand dollars is a lot of money, Tony."

"You're damn right it is, and it's mine." And I could use it. Celinda and I had piled up some hefty bills.

I pressed him. "Okay, Ted. When do I get it?"

"Friday."

"If I don't have it by 2:00 p.m. Friday, I'm calling Kobetski."

"You'll have it, I promise." He hung up.

I headed up Wisconsin Avenue, knowing a promise in Washington didn't amount to beans. Ten to one, by Friday, Ted would have skipped town, and in six months poor Leon Kobetski would be bankrupt, and Tony Cassera would be kissing twenty-five thousand dollars good-bye.

Celinda was sitting on the floor next to the bed, her arm wedged between the mattress and box spring.

"What are you doing?" I asked irritably. This had not been a good day, and it didn't look like it was going to get any better.

"Tony." She wouldn't look me in the eye.

I reached in under the mattress and felt around.

"Tony, no." She looked so upset that I pulled my hand out.

"Show me what you put there." Reluctantly she reached in and pulled something out.

"Let me see it."

In my open hand she placed this thing. I'm not sure what it was. It looked like a piece of bone that had been dipped in tar with a feather tied to it.

"Christ! What the hell is that?"

She took it out of my hand. "It's for good luck, Tony. So that for us everything is good. For your business and our loving each other."

"And you put it under the mattress?"

"Yes. You're supposed to. We go to the old woman. She makes them for us when we marry. Well, we are not married, but it is the same."

"Throw it out. We don't need it. I'm not sleeping with that thing under me."

"Tony, please. It won't hurt anything." She seemed frightened at the thought of throwing it away. "It's like throwing my love for you away."

I reconsidered. "You can keep it, but not under the bed. Find some place else for it. I don't ever want to see it again."

This town was driving me crazy. After the thing with Ted (he'd skipped town) and the cement deal falling through, and with Celinda acting weirder every day, I was starting to lose my taste for Washington. It was a sure thing that we'd have a new Administration before the year was out, and I wasn't looking forward to the scramble. Maybe I was just getting frustrated with my bad luck. I sent Celinda to New Mexico to see her folks. Something compelled me to call the Ambassador, and we decided to get together at Cleveland's.

The Ambassador was sitting at our usual table, waiting for me.

"Is that a Bombay Gin martini, Ambassador?"

"You bet, Tony. I invited Congressman Betts to stop by tonight."

"That old fart."

"You're in a lousy mood."

"Sorry, Ambassador. Bad day."

"I heard him talking at lunch about a friend of his who's looking for a business partner. It's in Santa Fe. This might be just what you're looking for."

"What kind of business is it?" I said, half-heartedly.

"A radio station."

"A radio station?"

"That's right, Tony, a radio station."

"Congressman Betts," I said, standing.

"Sit down. No need to stand on formality here." Congressman Betts laughed at his pun.

"Do you mind?"

I looked at the huge cigar he was rolling between his fingers, and became instantly nauseous.

"Go ahead. It won't bother us," I said. "So tell me about this radio station."

The Congressman puffed on his cigar a few times before wedging it in the corner of his mouth. His huge, fleshy lips glistened as he spoke. "KSFE is owned by a friend of mine, Red Granger. He's looking for a partner, and this could be a golden opportunity. It's a good long-term investment, and you can sell it to a big corporation for a lot more money than you paid for it, Tony. It's happening every day. That's what Red's aiming to do."

"How come you're not leaping on this one, Congressman?"

"I'd like to, Tony, but I just don't have the capital available right now."

"How much?"

"He's asking for fifty grand."

"Fifty's a lot."

"Sure it is, but think of the influence you'll have."

"Influence?"

"Radio stations reach a lot of people. Gives you some leverage here in town."

"I'll think it over, Congressman. Thanks for the tip."

I drove the Ambassador home and headed for Georgetown. All the way I mulled over the idea of the radio station, and the fifteen thousand dollars the Ambassador and I had each recently lost. Armandi had come out fine. He wrote a bad check to Barent. I wasn't ready to lose any more money, but if Congressman Betts was involved, it had to be legit.

When I arrived home, I poured myself a drink and headed upstairs. The house was so quiet without Celinda. I flicked on the light and stared at the center of the bed wishing she weren't two thousand miles away. I ached just thinking about her. I took my drink and walked into the closet. I opened her wardrobe and ran my hands down one of her dresses. She loved silk. I reached for my favorite, the white cotton dress I bought for her in Puerto Vallarta. It had been cheap, only a hundred and fifty pesos. I put it back, turned off the light and went to bed.

Her skin was hot to the touch and damp as my body quivered and rose beneath her. I grabbed her hair and pulled her head back. She was moaning and her skin was pale, like she was bathed in moonlight. She wrenched free from my hands and arched her back, her hair now totally covering her face. She lowered her face to mine, and I felt and tasted the salty sweetness and wetness of her lips and tongue in my mouth. And then I was inside her and she lay on top of me and she kept moving faster and faster. Celinda, Celinda, Celinda...

"Tony?"

"Celinda. It's 4 a.m. Why are you calling me this early? Is anything wrong?"

"No, no, everything is fine. I just miss you."

"I miss you, too."

"*Mamá* and I would like to go to Nuevo Laredo to see some of my cousins and my aunt."

"Into Mexico?"

"Yes. Do you mind if I go?"

"No, that's fine. Actually, I was going to call you. I'm flying out there on Tuesday. I heard about a possible business venture in Santa Fe."

"What is it?"

"A partnership in a radio station."

"Does it seem a good thing?"

"I don't know yet."

"Are you coming to Sanibel?"

"Yes. I'm going to go by and see Mom after I leave Santa Fe. When will you and your mother be back?"

"Thursday. I'll come by your mom's house as soon as we get home."

"Okay. Have a good visit, Angel."

Red Granger met me at the Albuquerque airport and drove me to Santa Fe. He was one of the partners in KSFE. He was a good ole boy, with lean, mean cowboy good looks, a big old Stetson, and chewing tobacco wadded up in his cheek. He dressed in worn blue jeans, a blazer and snakeskin cowboy boots. He was flashier than I expected, and the thought crossed my mind that Greta, my dad's wife, and he would get along just great. We met the other partner, T.J. King, for lunch. T.J. was a drinker and a tease, always out for a good time, but when it came to talking numbers and money, he laid it out line by line. They were an impressive pair. Red had gone to law school, and T.J. had taken over his father's lumber business at the ripe old age of twenty-one, when his dad had been killed in a plane crash. They were a nice change from men in three-piece suits, and the deal seemed like a good one. I would be the 51% majority shareholder of the radio station. Being Hispanic, I qualified as a minority, so my partners would receive tax deduction benefits which the FCC allowed for minority participation. All I had to do was invest $50,000. They would run the business in Santa Fe, and with my connections, I could bring in Washington insiders to build up the talk show format. It would be right up my alley, and I'd have something in the works when the Administration changed. My spirits were lifting as I saw a way out of Washington open up before me.

After the meeting, Red was flying down to Mexico in his plane, so he offered to drop me off at the landing strip outside Sanibel.

When flying in a small plane, it seems like you're moving so slowly that you could fall from the sky. When the nuns in school would talk about heaven, I'd stare at the sky hoping to catch a glimpse of an angel flying from cloud to cloud. Heaven seemed so far away when I was eight years old, but I knew then right where it was, in the sky above me. Now I've flown among the clouds myself, but heaven still seems far away.

The sun was getting lower in the sky, and the shadows were lengthening as we came in to land. I saw the top of my dad's Cadillac, parked off to the side of the landing strip, as we touched down. Red taxied right up to the car and let me out without even turning his engines off. He wanted to reach Juarez before night fell.

Dad and I hugged. He looked the same, maybe a little thinner.

He started up the car. "I told your mom I'd drive you to her place. You know she never was a good driver, and she doesn't see so well anymore."

There isn't really a road into the airport at Sanibel. You drive about ten miles west of town out the old blacktop road. When you see the windsock on the right, you just head off across the desert, driving straight towards it. There'd been a building there once, but it collapsed twenty years ago. It was a pile of boards and home to the lizards now. I smiled as we drove by, remembering when we used to get cold sodas there.

"How's Mom?"

"Pretty much the same. She still has that boarder. Don't know why she puts up with him. How can you stand wearing those things?"

"What things?" I looked down at my jacket.

My dad tapped his finger next to his right eye.

"My sunglasses?" He nodded. "Everyone wears them."

"You trying to be a big movie star? No one in Sanibel wears sunglasses except you."

He was right. I'd never noticed. I liked the way I looked in them. He'd never understand my spending $550 on a pair of glasses that I could only wear on a sunny day, so I decided to focus on the health aspect.

"They filter out the ultraviolet rays, Dad. You know, the bad rays from the sun."

"If you say so, Tony, but I never saw a bad ray come from the sun."

Mom dried her eyes on a dish towel. She always cries when I come home, because she thinks she will never see me again. She still wants me to come home to Sanibel to live.

"Is Celinda here? I'm looking forward to meeting her."

"She and her mother went over to Nuevo Laredo to see some cousins, Mom. Consuela is going to drop her off here tonight."

"Nuevo Laredo?" She seemed thoughtful, then shook her head as if she was shaking the thought out of her mind.

"What's wrong, Mom?"

"I've heard things about what goes on down there. You be careful, Tony." She looked really worried.

"There's nothing to worry about. They're just going to visit her family, that's all."

Mom changed the subject. "I got the front bedroom all ready for you two. You don't have to go to your father's at all."

"I promised, Mom." I felt guilty. "But, thanks. We'll stay tonight."

She poured us some coffee, then tottered off to the bottle of vodka in the trunk of the car.

"I've got something for you, Tony," she said when she came back in. She rummaged in one of the cabinets and pulled out an empty green wine bottle in the shape of a fish.

"Do you remember this bottle?" She set it down with a thump in front of me. I looked at her blankly.

She prodded my memory. "Your grandmother's funeral in New York. 1974. We drank the wine together, you and me." Well, I remembered the funeral, but not the wine. "Yes, I remember," I lied.

"I want my ashes placed in this bottle, Tony. You take this bottle with you and keep it until it's time." She was serious, and she seemed to have sobered up suddenly.

"Sure, Mom, if that's what you want." I looked helplessly at the cheap glass bottle. And then I knew exactly what to say. "I'll put your ashes in it, and put it on my fireplace mantle so I can see you every day." She smiled a little smile. I knew that would make her feel good, because I knew she was unhappy that she couldn't see me every day.

"Mom, there's a chance I may go into partnership with two fellows who have a radio station in Santa Fe. If I do, I'll be able to come down and see you a lot."

"Oh, I'd like that. Wouldn't we like that, Whiskers?" She rubbed the cat between the ears. "Why don't you come live here with me and drive to Santa Fe?"

Here we go again. We go through this every time I come home.

"You know I can't do that. I'm going to have to be in Santa Fe, and I'm going to try to keep my lobbying practice in Washington D.C., but you'll see me more often. I promise, Mom."

"Well, we'll see, won't we, Whiskers. I'm tired. I think I'll go to bed. I'm glad you're here, Tony, even if it's only for tonight. Tell Celinda I was sorry I couldn't wait up for her."

"You'll meet her in the morning." I kissed her on the cheek. She felt so soft and she still had the soap-like smell I remembered as a kid, only now it was tinged with vodka and bourbon. "Good-night, Mom."

I watched her get up and make her way unsteadily out the door. I knew she'd probably have another drink to help her go to sleep, and I was relieved that she would be in bed before Celinda came home.

I went out on the front porch. Night is so dark in Sanibel. I could hear the crickets and the distant sound of the television. I don't know why my mom put up with Al. He only got up from the couch to go to the bathroom and get another beer. I guess she was lonely and he was company. I went inside and got a couple of Al's beers from the refrigerator, came back out and sat on the top step. The beer felt cool going down. What was I going to do about Mom and Al? She was drinking more since he moved in, and it disgusted me. At least if I bought into that partnership in the radio station, I'd be closer, but every time I saw her, she drove me away with her drinking. My guts were all twisted inside with rage and sorrow for what my mom had become. Why did my dad go and leave her by herself?

I put the beer down on the porch. I couldn't drink any more. A fluttery gust of wind blew the leaves on the bushes, rustling them against each other. It blew against my cheek and brought with it the sweet smell of roses on a warm, summer's day. I closed my eyes and remembered a day in the backyard of our old house. My mom was there, holding the garden hose so I could run through its spray. My sister Rosalie and my brother Estefan were there, too, and we were laughing and running under the falling water drops. And there was a woman with blonde hair standing there, laughing.

A car turned onto the street and pulled up in front of the house, and I opened my eyes. I could hear her saying good-bye to her mother in Spanish, and then she started up the walk. She couldn't see me sitting in the dark on the steps, but I could see the faint outline of her figure and recognize her languid walk in the dark. I whispered her name.

"Celinda, *Mi Diosa de la noche*, my Goddess of the Night."

She gasped, and I reached over and ran my hand slowly up her leg past her knee and up under her skirt. She stood very still in front of me. I moved my hand ever so slowly up her thigh, marveling at the smoothness of her skin and how firm and hard her muscles were. She ran her fingers through my hair while I drew light little circles with my fingertips on the soft inside flesh of her thigh. She shifted slightly and widened her stance. As she stood there, I inched my fingers further up her thigh. She wasn't wearing anything. Her body undulated and contracted around my finger. She gripped my shoulders and moaned in pleasure. I stood up behind her, and right there on the front porch I made love to her. I wanted to love her again and again. I couldn't get enough of her. A loose floorboard creaked when the warm, perfumed air blew across the porch. Celinda sensed me tense.

"What is it, Tony?"

I turned her towards me and kissed her. "It's nothing. I just thought I heard something."

"It's getting windy, Tony. Let's go inside."

I glanced over my shoulder at the street. I couldn't see anyone, but I felt like we were being watched. I followed Celinda inside, closed the door and locked it.

Four months and $50,000 later, I was a senior "brown" partner in a radio station. My white, non-minority partners were ecstatic. I was looking forward to making a lot of money. The Administration had changed, so the new focus for me was much needed. I'd spend a few months in D.C., arranging appearances for the talk show, then a month in Santa Fe. Celinda was always upset when I left her behind, but I'd always bring her back something special to make up for it.

It was a Friday afternoon when everything started to unravel. Suzan poked her head in and signaled that I had an urgent call waiting.

"Tony, it's T.J."

"Hey, T.J., what's the weather in Santa Fe? It's..."

He cut me off. "We've got a problem. Red resigned."

"Resigned?"

"I think you better come out here. I've been going over the books with the accountant. Your fifty thousand dollars is gone."

"Gone?" T.J. had my total attention now. "Where the hell did it go?"

"My bet is, south of the border, with Red."

"That son-of-a-bitch! What the hell were you doing, T.J.? You're supposed to be managing this."

"I know. I know, but we've been running so lean that I've been having to cover sales. I'm not here as much as I'd like. What are we going to do?"

He was getting on my nerves. "I'm coming out there today. I'll get the first flight I can." I hung up. Damn. I had Suzan book me a flight, and I headed home.

I slammed the front door and took the stairs two steps at a time. I could hear voices talking in Spanish in one of the upstairs rooms. A man and a woman. They were in the master bedroom. I flung open the door, not knowing who or what to expect. Celinda was standing in front of the ironing board with the iron in her hand watching television. That's where the voices were coming from. I walked over and looked at the picture. It was some Spanish soap she watched every day. I would get a blow-by-blow of each episode. That dark-haired guy must be Rodrigo, the one who's sold his soul to the Cartel to pay for his younger brother's operation. I wasn't sure who the woman was. Maybe his mother. She was yelling at him. I flicked it off.

"What's the matter with you? Don't turn that off." Celinda grabbed the control and clicked it on again.

I turned on my heel and went into the closet, grabbed my suitcase, hauled it out to the bedroom, threw it on the bed, and started packing. Celinda looked frightened now.

"Tony. What are you doing? You're not leaving me, are you?"

I threw some shirts in the suitcase. "I have to go to Santa Fe. There's been a screw-up." She followed me into the closet. I couldn't decide which ties to take, so I took them all from the drawer. From the television in the other room a woman's voice pleaded. "*Rodrigo, no hagas esto. Nosotros conseguiremos el dinero de alguna forma.* Don't do this thing, Rodrigo. We'll get the money somehow."

I threw the ties in the suitcase. "He took the money, Celinda. My money. My investment."

"Who? What money?"

"Red. I got a call from T.J. Red resigned and took my investment with him."

Celinda stood there staring at me, one of my shirts in her hand.

The television was the only sound in the room. "*Mama, tú no entiendes,*" Rodrigo said. "You don't understand. Raul has to have the operation. *Raul tiene que tener la operación. Sin ella él morirá.* Without it he'll die. *No llores, Mamá.*" The actress on the TV started to wail, and I couldn't take it any more.

"Turn that damn thing off, Celinda."

She pointed the control at the screen and the picture faded.

"He took my money," she said, not believing. She seemed stunned. "That wasn't supposed to happen."

I exploded. What the hell was she talking about? "Your money? Since when was it your money? Tell me that." I was yelling at the top of my voice.

"Well, it's my money, too," she screamed. "We're together, Tony." She grabbed the iron and threw it at me. I ducked, but it left a huge dent in the wall behind me. She ran into the bathroom and locked the door behind her. I heard her running water in the bathtub. Damn her. I picked up the hot iron. There was a scorch mark burned into my oriental rug. It smelled like burning wool, or burning camel hair, or whatever the hell those rugs are made out of. I sat on the edge of the bed, waiting for the water to stop. As soon as it did, I got up and tapped on the door.

"Celinda," I said quietly. She didn't respond. "I'm sorry." I heard her unlock the door. I waited a few seconds before I opened it. I was prepared to duck. Her clothes were strewn all over the floor and she was submerged in bubbles. I picked her clothes up, put them in the hamper, and sat down on the floor next to the tub. "I'm just really upset."

"It's okay," she said, but she was still pouting. "What are you going to do?"

"I'm going to Santa Fe tonight. Suzan booked me a six o'clock flight into Albuquerque."

She shifted ever so slightly, and I could see the outline of a breast underneath the bubbles. "I want to go with you, Tony."

I was going to say no, but she was right. I didn't want to leave her here all by herself. "All right," I said. "I'll call Suzan and have her get you a ticket."

When I came back, she was soaping her leg with one of those sea sponges. I watched the soapy water run down her leg into the tub.

She sat in the tub beating the water with her fists. What the hell was going on? *La Vieja* had promised her that they would be rich and that he would marry her. Something was going wrong. This wasn't supposed to happen like this. She would force the old one to give her exactly what she wanted.

It was worse than I'd thought. T.J. went over the paperwork for me and discovered that Red had cooked the financial statements, so that I'd invest in the company. Others were involved, so I fired everyone but T.J. Essentially I was running it now. Yesterday, I'd been a partner. Today, I was the sole owner of a radio station. My mind was working overtime. This could be the opportunity I'd been looking for. I could bring in Congressmen and federal officials as guest speakers on the programs, then sell shares of stock and watch the money roll in. But, I had very little in savings. I took a second mortgage out on the Georgetown house, and Celinda and I moved to Santa Fe. I brought Celinda into the business as office manager. With her there, I felt confident that I could travel and bring in business. She blossomed under the responsibility, but we were both running at a frantic pace. I put the $25,000 from the second mortgage into the station, but it was gone in two weeks after I'd paid off creditors. Every time I turned around, someone was holding out their hand. I couldn't sleep nights for worrying about where I was going to get the money to ease our cash flow problems. The Ambassador came through for me with a solution, a private loan. What would I do without that guy? By the end of the week, I'd applied for a $200,000 loan from a private placement financial company because no bank would touch this. It was a chance in a million that we'd get it, but I had to try.

I was on pins and needles, pulling daisy petals in my mind. "They will give me the loan. They won't give me the loan." Celinda suggested I go along with her on her planned trip to Nuevo Laredo to keep me busy, so I agreed. It was the usual round of family visiting, with so many cousins that it was impossible to keep them all straight. They all looked alike to me. Tamales at every house. I thought I'd gain twenty pounds by the end of the weekend. When Celinda suggested dinner at her cousin Carlos' restaurant, I baulked, but she was so insistent that I finally gave in.

La Paloma Ensuciada was a small restaurant with not a chair or table that matched. The old, zinc-topped bar was lined with customers, some standing, some perched on rickety stools. The adobe walls had big cracks running from floor to ceiling. The cooling system was three ceiling fans, the edges of their blades covered with gray dust. Mongrel dogs lay under a couple of tables, their tongues lying on the tile floor. Flies hummed above everyone's heads as the diners ate, laughed, and drank tequila. I didn't think there were this many people in Nuevo Laredo who'd want to come to this place.

"You're not eating, Tony."

I looked down at my plate, watching a fly crawl around its edge. "Just not hungry, I guess. I'm eating tequila today." I took another swig. I was sitting with my back to the front door, so that I faced the interior stairway. Something strange was going on here.

"Celinda, what's upstairs?"

"What do you mean?" She seemed tense, but her eyes were bright, almost feverish.

"Well, we've been here an hour and a half, and I keep seeing men go upstairs, but they don't come back down. Is your cousin running a 'house' upstairs?"

"Don't joke about it. Be careful what you say." She turned and looked at the stairway just as a young man headed upstairs. Other heads turned to watch him.

"Celinda, what is this place?"

She was not telling me something. We were definitely not here to eat. That had never been her intention.

She leaned towards me across the table. "Upstairs there is an old woman, *La Vieja*, we call her. She is the most powerful. My cousin said he could get us in to see her. We need to get this loan. She can help us."

"So that's why you wanted to come to Nuevo Laredo. Mumbo jumbo. We're leaving." I signaled the guy for the check.

"Ssh, Tony. Not so loud. Please. It can't hurt. Carlos arranged this for me."

"Behind my back."

"I did it for us."

Carlos came over to the table. I tried to imagine this skinny, nervous man married to Celinda. She'd told me they'd been "promised" to each other. His wispy black hair was plastered to his forehead with sweat. He was wiry, but muscular, and probably stronger than he looked. He had a lean, angular face, and small black eyes that glittered and darted around the room. He'd done the best financially of anybody in the family because of this restaurant.

"*Hay algo malo, Celinda?*"

"Tony won't go see the old woman. Tell him, Carlos."

Carlos dragged a chair over and hunched himself over the table and began speaking in a low tone.

"I have seen things. Things the old woman can do. Celinda has seen things, too. We know her power is real. I will tell you something I have seen with these two eyes." Carlos shook two fingers in front of his face. "I saw a man go in her room and a few minutes later, he came out a woman." Carlos held his hands in front of him like he was cupping a breast in each one.

Oh, brother. Working in Washington you live in the world of bullshit, but this was the craziest thing I'd ever heard.

"*Veo que no crees, Antonio, pero es cierto.* I see you do not believe, Antonio, but it is true. I saw him change before my very eyes, *con Dios como mi testigo*, as God is my witness." Carlos crossed himself. "I sat on a bench facing the doorway. The door was draped with a curtain, but I could see through it. I know you are thinking it was too dark to see, but I will tell you. The man he undressed and stood before the old woman. She took his thing in her hand and rubbed something on it while she chanted in the old language. It bent," Carlos curled his finger to show me how it drooped, "and then I could no longer see it. Then she puts both her hands on his chest and rubs her hands in circles, like this." Carlos rubbed his hands on his chest demonstrating the old woman's technique.

All I could think of was that I must be nuts to be sitting here, listening to this. "This is crazy. Celinda and I are leaving," I said. But Carlos clamped his hand down on my arm and held me there.

"I have not finished telling you of this. The man he came out from behind the curtain and put on a dress that the old woman had given to him, and I could see that he had no thing and he had breasts. *Es la verdad.* It is the truth." He sat back in his chair, satisfied.

Yeah, right. "Why were you going to see her?" I asked Carlos. He lowered his voice further. "My sister was shaming my family. *La Vieja* gave me something to put in her drink. Now my sister is married and has children and only one man. *Celinda te dirá que así es.* Celinda will tell you that this is so."

"It is true, Tony. After Carlos went to see the old woman, his sister changed."

Carlos was becoming impatient. "If you want to see her, you will need to go up now. I asked her as a special favor for Celinda."

"Please, Tony," Celinda said. "We came all this way."

"Okay. Okay. You win." Both Celinda and Carlos seemed relieved.

"You will see it is the truth that I speak, Antonio," Carlos said.

"I hope not," I muttered under my breath.

We followed Carlos upstairs, and he ushered us into a darkened room. Once we were seated, I had time to look around. There were others like us, sitting quietly in the rows of wooden chairs. Music played. I recognized it. It was Bach, from the Orchestral Suite No. 3 in D Major. The room had been whitewashed, and a single cross hung on the one wall. The only light came from tiers of burning candles. There must have been a hundred flickering flames. I wanted to leave.

"Celinda," I began.

"Sshh. Be quiet."

I could tell I wasn't going to go anywhere real soon. She was determined. I decided to get back at her by looking incredibly bored even though I was terrified. It was then that I noticed the smell. The room smelled like the incense they burned at Mass when I was growing up in Sanibel.

"If she touches me, I'm going to deck her," I whispered to Celinda.

"Nobody but me touches you," she whispered back.

The door opened, and everyone in the room jumped at the sound. A small man with a crippled leg came out and spoke to a woman in the row in front of us. The woman stood and followed the man into the other room. You could sense everyone relax. For me, it was like sitting in the waiting room of my doctor's office when I was a kid.

"I've got an idea," I whispered. "Why don't you go talk to the old woman, and I'll wait here for you."

"Tony, you have to come, or it won't work."

"What won't work?" Celinda didn't answer me. She was too busy rummaging through her purse.

"Tony, we're going to have to give her an offering," she whispered.

"Like what?"

"Hold this for me." Celinda emptied half the contents of her purse into my hands. "She'll take anything — money, food, something of value that we have, so that she can bless us." I decided on money at that point. It seemed easy. She evidently found what she was looking for. She pulled out her wallet.

"I have money, Celinda," I whispered.

"I know. I was looking for this." She pulled out a picture of the two of us taken in Puerto Vallarta.

"You're just going to give her a picture of us?"

"Not just this. She'll need this, but we have to give her an offering, too. What shall we give her?"

"Money," I said. "Here." She held out her purse, and I dumped everything in my hands back into it. I pulled out a twenty- dollar bill and handed it to Celinda. That seemed to satisfy her. She held the money and the photo tightly in her hands and watched the door, waiting for it to open. Two more times the man limped out and led someone into the room. Each time the door closed, my whole body relaxed. The next time he came out, he walked up to Celinda and whispered in her ear. When she rose, I started to stand, too, but Celinda motioned me back.

"I go first, and then he will come for you," she whispered.

I started to protest, but they were gone. The others in the room stared at me, then turned back to each other, whispering. After about five minutes, the room became quiet again.

She saw the old woman, as she had seen her many times before, standing motionless in front of the unpainted wooden table, covered with mounds of melted wax, with bits of blackened wicks embedded in them. *La Vieja* gave no sign of recognition nor looked at her as she approached and kissed each withered cheek. She stood, waiting for a sign from the old one.

The old woman spoke no words, but raising a hand to her head, she tugged at a long, yellow-gray strand of hair. The girl took from her pocket, where she had kept it hidden, a square of paper which she carefully unfolded. Approaching the table, she lay it in a stone bowl filled with ashes. The lock of dark hair lay curled on the sheet of paper.

Still the old woman did not look at her or speak, and she was afraid that she had done something wrong and not brought the right thing. The outside door blew open rattling the lock and spewing dust into the room, causing the candles to flicker, a chair to fall over, and the lock of hair to rise and flutter on its bed of ashes. She saw fear in the old woman's eyes as she cringed in the light before the crippled man could shut and bolt the door. She saw that he was frightened, too.

"*¿Lo tienes?*" the old woman asked, extending her hand.

"*Sí, y a él también, Mamá Vieja.* Yes, I have it. And him, too, Old Mother."

She handed the photograph and the twenty-dollar bill to *La Vieja.*

The old woman burned the hair and tore him out of the photo and burned the half in the stone bowl lying on the altar.

Everyone in the waiting room stopped talking when they heard a loud bang as of something falling to the floor. I was staring anxiously at the door when the man opened it and beckoned for me to come. I hoped this wasn't going to hurt.

I stood in front of the old woman thinking she must be a thousand years old. There was some kind of altar behind her, with a black, wooden cross above it and two large candles burning on the wax-covered table. An acrid smell filled the room. It wasn't incense, like in the other room. It reminded me of the time my sister Rosalie had tried to straighten her hair with an iron and singed it so badly that Mom had to trim six inches off.

"*Celinda, ella me dice que nosotros podemos ajudarte con tus negocios,*" the old woman said.

I looked at Celinda, who translated.

"She is asking if we are here to be successful in business."

I nodded. I couldn't believe this creature in front of me was actually able to speak. She could have passed for a mummy in the Egyptian exhibit at some museum with her dry, hoarse voice.

"*Tú tienes mucho exito en tus negocios, pero hay gente celosa que te quieren arruinar tu negocio.*"

Celinda translated. "She says there are people who are jealous and do not want our business to succeed."

"Who? What people? *¿Quienes*? I want names," I said.

The old woman replied, "*Debes hacer lo que yo te diga.*" The sternness in her voice alarmed me. "*No te preocupes. Celinda te ayudará. Yo ayudaré. Venceremos a los que destruirían. Tomará un año, para tendrás mucho dinero. El dinero te empezará a llegar en cuatro días.*"

I looked at Celinda.

"She says we must do what she tells us, and the people will have no power over us. She says we will have much money in a year, but the money will start to come in four days time."

"The loan. It must be the loan," I said excitedly. "Celinda, this is great." Now I was glad we had come. If I could just get this loan, everything would be okay.

The old woman had us turn and face north, east, south and west, and at each direction, she sprinkled us liberally with holy water. Then she placed two large candles in our hands, telling us to burn them every night, all night long, until they were gone.

"*Cuando se terminado las velas, entierra lo que quede lejos de tu casa y negocio,*" the old woman rasped.

"What did she say, Celinda?"

"She was just telling me what to do when the candles were gone. It's not important."

Celinda bent down and kissed the woman's hand which looked more like a claw to me. "*Gracias, Vieja,*" she said. The old woman extended her hand to me. I shook it. The hand in mine was light, the skin dry like parchment.

"*Gracias,*" I mumbled.

Celinda and I followed the limping man out of the room. I turned and looked back, but the old woman was gone.

The bright sun blinded me after having sat in the darkened rooms for so long. "I hope this works," I said, squinting into the sun.

"It will work," Celinda said. "She is a very powerful *Vieja.*"

When we arrived back at the cousin's house where we were staying, Celinda went straight to our room and lit the candles. I was exhausted and suffering from a terrible headache, so I crawled into bed. I awoke several times during the night, and Celinda was still sitting in front of the candles, watching them burn. When I awoke to the sun pouring in the window, Celinda was asleep, sitting in front of the burning candles. When I stretched, she awoke, carefully blew out the candles, crawled into bed next to me and fell asleep.

On Wednesday, I got a call at the radio station saying that we'd gotten the loan. For once in my life, I didn't have a smart-ass remark to make.

Celinda and I found a Spanish, hacienda-style house up in the hills outside Santa Fe. Some poor jerk had gotten himself in financial trouble, and we got it for a song. It had tile floors that feel cool on your feet no matter how hot it is outside. It also had a swimming pool that was supposed to be self-cleaning, but that summer I found out that there is no such thing. I filled the shelves in the linen closet with the bottles of Tortuga Oil that Celinda had bought in Puerto Vallarta, but I never had much time to get a tan. I still had my lobbying business, and spent a lot of time traveling between Santa Fe and Washington, D.C. That left Celinda with the task of furnishing the house. I'd give her cash at the beginning of the week, and when I flew back into town on Sunday, the money would be gone. She'd pick me up at the airport, and tell me what she'd gotten for the house. Then I'd get upset about how much she'd spent for a lamp, and we'd argue half the way home. Midway to Santa Fe we'd pull off the road and make love, so by the time we'd pull into the driveway, I'd forgotten about the money. Then the whole process repeated itself the next week. But I had to admit, I loved the Indian rugs on the floors, the old wooden refectory tables and the Mexican pottery.

Money problems hounded me all the time. The equipment was old and was constantly in need of repair. I changed the format from country to oldies, in hopes of attracting a wider range of advertisers and listeners. Celinda kept tabs on everything at the station while I was gone, and she seemed to work well with Brad, the new office manager I'd hired. When I was in town, Celinda and I would end the day sitting out by the pool, watching the sun set. That's where we were one evening when the phone rang. Celinda got up to get it, and my eyes followed her into the house. She still looked great in a bikini. She reappeared a moment later.

"It's for you, Tony."

"Is it Brad?" I sighed.

"I do not know who it is. I do not recognize the voice. He asked for Mr. Cassera."

Oh, oh. "Okay, I'm coming."

I took a deep breath before I picked up the receiver. I just didn't want any bad news. I'd already had a rough day. "Hello?"

"Hi, Dad. It's David."

"David!" It was my son. I hadn't talked to him much over the last two years. I'd invited him to come visit me in Washington a few times, but we could never get it worked out. I hadn't seen him in eight years. His voice was so deep.

"I called Grandpa in Sanibel for your number. I'm calling you from Atlanta."

"Atlanta? What are you doing in Atlanta?"

"I'm only here for a few days. I'm touring with a rock band this summer. I'm gettin' paid."

"No kidding. That's great."

"Yeah. We're gonna be in Albuquerque, at the Regency Hotel, on the twenty-third."

"I wouldn't miss it for the world. Celinda and I will be there."

"Who's Celinda?"

"She's the woman I live with. You'll like her."

Silence.

"How's your mother?"

"She's fine. Listen, Dad, I gotta go. I'll see you on the twenty-third?"

"I'll be there."

Celinda came into the living room, munching a celery stick. "Who was that?"

"My son."

"You never told me you had a son. How old is he?"

"Eighteen."

"I'm eighteen," she said.

"I haven't seen him for eight years," I explained. "He lives with his mom and her husband in Colorado."

"How come you never told me about him?"

"I was going to. I just never did." If I don't tell anyone about him, I don't have to feel guilty about having left him. "He's going to be in Albuquerque in two weeks, with a band. He's asked us to come see him."

"He knows about me?"

"He plays guitar and sings."

"Really." Celinda sounded a little cool, but I was too excited to notice.

The rest of the week was hell. With word out that I'd gotten the loan, the phone started ringing with more people I'd never heard of, wanting the money that was owed them. I hired an outside accountant to come in and audit the station's books, and I spent the next two weeks with him, trying to unravel the finances of the last three years. T.J. spent the week skulking in corners. I thought he felt bad about my going to an outside accountant, and I kept apologizing to him. By the end of the first week with the accountant, however, I was ready to strangle T.J. Instead, I fired him for total and complete incompetence. The books were a mess, and Red and T.J. had been in it together. T.J. had been siphoning money to Red in Juarez. In the middle of all this, Celinda decided to run off to Nuevo Laredo again, though why she'd want to spend so much time with those relatives of hers was beyond me. Mom kept calling wanting to know why I didn't come see her. What kept me going was the thought that I'd be seeing my son. I just had to hang in there for a few more days.

The sun was a glorious orange sphere as it sank behind the mountains and turned the desert a dusky purple with its departure. Damn if I wasn't turning into a poet, or I'd had too much to drink. I used to come home and sit by the pool with a beer. Now I was sitting with an ice bucket and a bottle of Johnny Walker Red. With Celinda in Mexico, it was the only way I could relax. The sun was little more than a faint glow above the mountains when the phone started ringing. I decided not to answer it. It was probably Brad from the station, and I'd had enough bad news for one week. The hours went by, and I just sat there in the dark, listening to the night. Something was howling in the distance. The front door slammed, and I heard the heels of Celinda's shoes on the tile floor as she headed down the hall to the bedroom. It was a minute or two before her footsteps came back towards me. There was a click, and light flooded across the patio. She paused at the open door. The back of the chaise was towards her, and I could sense she wasn't sure if I was there.

"Tony?"

"I'm here."

She came over and knelt down by the chaise. "What are you doing, sitting out here in the dark?"

"Missing you."

"Move over," she said. I turned on my side, and she squeezed in next to me. I ran my hands over the familiar curves of her body.

"I'm glad you're back."

"I missed you, too. Stop, Tony." She removed my hand from where I had placed it. That made me angry, and I crushed her to me.

"Stop it, Tony. Stop. I have to talk to you."

"But I don't want to talk."

"You're drunk."

"So what if I am? Come here."

"It's getting late, and we have to go."

"Go where?"

"The candles are all gone. We have to bury the candle wax tonight in the desert. Then the men who want to ruin you will stay away from us forever."

"Oh, Christ, Celinda. Can't it wait? You just got home."

She disentangled herself and stood up. "No. We have to do it tonight."

"Why tonight?"

"The moon is right."

"The moon?"

"You would not understand. We have to go now, or it will be too late." She sensed I wasn't moving, so she bent down and whispered in my ear all the wonderful things she was going to do to me out on the desert.

We left the car about a mile off the road and walked the rest of the way. Celinda wandered from one spot to another, with me weaving along behind, carrying the shovel and the blanket. She had one of those paper lunch bags in which I guessed were the "remains. After about twenty minutes she finally decided on the right spot, though it beats me what made it any better than our backyard. I put my back into shoveling, as I wanted my reward.

"That looks deep enough to me," I said.

Celinda shined the flashlight down into the hole. "A little bit more, Tony." Jeez. Okay. I rattled my shovel in the hole and that seemed to satisfy her.

"Okay. Let's dump it in," I said impatiently.

"It's not time." She shined the flashlight on her watch. Five minutes to midnight. We sat side by side, waiting for both hands on the watch to hit twelve. As soon as they did, she placed the paper bag in the hole and I covered it up.

"Aren't we supposed to say something?" I said.

"She didn't tell me." Celinda sounded worried.

"Well, maybe we should do something then," I hinted. "You know, to celebrate."

I spread the blanket on top of the newly dug "grave. I don't know what it is about making love outdoors under the sky, but it feels right. It probably harks back to our animal beginnings. Afterwards, as we lay there together, I felt my confidence coming back. I felt stronger, more powerful, like a warrior prepared to go into battle to fight whatever threatened us.

On Monday, I called Ambassador St. John.

"Hey, Ambassador."

"Cisco."

"I need your help. I've got to find an investor fast."

"I thought you got your loan." He sounded tired.

"I did, but as soon as word hit the streets, the vultures descended."

"I understand. I've got another idea. I just might be able to hook you up with an investor."

"Who?"

"Let me make a few calls first. You'll be at the station the next few days?"

"Yeah. We're switching to oldies this week, and Ronald Stone, a former Senator from New Mexico, is flying out for the talk show. We should get lots of listeners calling in, with questions about how the government works—or, as we know, how it should work. Anyway, I've got to wine and dine him, and I'm pulling money out of thin air at this point."

"Sit tight. I'll see what I can do."

"Thanks, Ambassador. Got a big deal in the works?"

"You could call it that. Florence and I are separating."

"Oh, man. I'm sorry." I could almost hear him shrug over the phone.

"She was having an affair right under my nose with some State Department nerd, a low-grade GS'r, maybe a 12 grade. Besides, Lynn is back."

"Oh, no." Poor St. John. His wife had a multiple personality disorder. He adored Florence, but when Lynn showed up, life was hell on wheels.

"I don't want to talk about it. I'll see what I can do for you, Tony. Call you in a couple of days."

"Thanks, Ambassador."

"*De nada*, Cisco."

I hung up and felt like a heel for burdening my friend with my problems.

The Ambassador, though, was as good as his word. He had someone lined up for me in Washington by the end of the week.

Hugh Hightower had made his money in commodities and was looking for a place to park $150,000. Since he loved the Southwest, KSFE in Santa Fe seemed like a match made in heaven. Hightower needed a favor from me, though. He had a friend who wanted a $1,500,000 government contract. That was no problem for me, as my specialty was finding government contracts. I started work on locating a contract, and signed over a third of the radio station to secure the loan Hightower had wired to me. I owed the Ambassador big time. "I owe you two," is how we'd put it in Washington. By the time David's band hit Albuquerque, I was sitting pretty. I had given myself my $50,000 initial investment back. The new format was working well, and the response to Ron Steinberg's appearance on the talk show had been good, over fifty call-ins. We still had lots of rough edges, but Celinda, Brad and I were breathing easier.

You'd think I was going to my first dance with a girl. That's how nervous I felt, getting ready to drive to Albuquerque to hear David perform. I was running late, and the faster I hurried, the longer it took. I was midway through my shower when the water turned cold. My electric shaver stopped working, and I had to use Celinda's shaving lotion and her razor. I had pieces of toilet paper stuck on my face where I'd cut myself, and I couldn't find the gold cufflinks that Nixon had given me. I stood in the center of the bedroom and howled like a wounded animal. This wasn't fair. God knew I had to be perfect to meet my son.

"Celinda, where are my cufflinks?" I yelled.

"They're in the box on top of the dresser."

"No. Not those. My gold ones. The ones Nixon gave me."

"But you haven't worn those in a long time."

"I want to wear them tonight."

"I don't know where they are. Listen, Tony, we're going to be late if you don't hurry."

"They've got to be here somewhere."

"They're not here."

"What do you mean?"

"You can't find them so they must not be here."

"That's not what you meant. What have you done with them?"

"I didn't do anything."

"Celinda, where the hell are my cufflinks?"

"You buried them."

"I buried them? You're kidding. They weren't in that paper bag?"

One look at her face told me the answer.

"She said I needed something you valued."

"That was a stupid thing to do," I shouted, but I didn't have time to argue. I grabbed any old pair of cufflinks and right before I reached the doorway, I turned and shook a finger at her. "You're never going to Nuevo Laredo and see that old hag again." I left the room.

"I am not stupid," she shouted after me.

Damn bitch. I reached the car and stood breathing deeply. She'd ruined everything. I fought to regain my sense of balance and recapture some of the joy I felt at seeing my son, but all I could do was stand there and pound my fists on the top of the car.

She sat in the front seat and cried halfway to Albuquerque.

"You look like hell," I said.

That snapped her out of it. She pulled down the visor and looked in the mirror. She had big black circles around her eyes and smudgy black streaks running down her face. I gave her my handkerchief, and she rubbed off all her make-up. She hauled out her make-up case and started repairs.

"Tony, you're driving too fast. Slow down."

"Thanks to you, Celinda, we're going to be late, so just be quiet and fix your face."

A sign on an easel said "Soul Circus" was performing in the cocktail lounge. We were seated at a small table off towards the right. I was mad that we weren't dead center, but there wasn't much I could do about it. A twenty waved at the maitre d' didn't do any good. He just shrugged his shoulders. The place was packed, and it seemed like a good crowd. I was scared they wouldn't like my son. I was scared he wouldn't like me. The lights dimmed, and we heard drums, and then music, as the stage rotated into view. A spotlight pierced the darkness and illuminated the lead singer. He had the same thick, curly hair, only his was brown and mine was black; but the face, it was my face. When he started to sing, I beamed at Celinda and blinked tears from my eyes.

That was my son up there in front of all these people, their eyes focused just on him as he began to sing.

Play CD Track 5
"Prayer for my Angel"

Each day when the sun meets the sky
Reflections of you run through my mind
And when we met that cold winter night
I felt the winds of change within me breathing in new life

When you found me I was steppin on the edge of darkness
Disallusioned by lies of loves past
But, in time my dream has come to show me
With every breath I'm closer to you

So, each day I say a prayer for my angel
My heart beats faster at the thought of holding you
Each night I say a prayers for my angel
Close my eyes and run to my dreams,
Run to my dreams to you

When I look into the deepness in your eyes
The secret of this visino is finally realized
Through the fire the eagle is soaring
And he knows his destination cannot be compromised

With reckless abandon I was searching for some meaning
Twisted perception of things not clearly seen
But, you held the key that opened heaven's door
With every step I'm closer to you

His voice trailed away, and as soon as he lowered his mike, everyone started to applaud. They loved him! They loved my son!

"Wasn't he great?" I said to Celinda.

She smiled. "He's a good-looking boy," was all she said.

At intermission, I sent a message to David to come out to our table. I watched the curtain, and pretty soon he stepped out. I saw him scanning the crowd. Which one of these men was his father, I'm sure he was wondering. I stood and waved to him.

"Sit down, Tony, you look like a fool, standing up like that."

"He's seen me. He's coming over," I said excitedly.

I hugged him to me and looked into eyes that never knew me. I didn't know what to say, so I introduced him to Celinda. She extended her hand and smiled.

David sat down, and I noticed everyone in the room was staring at us. I was with a celebrity, and I liked the feeling.

"How about a drink? A Coke?"

"No thanks. I'm drinking water backstage."

"You're great. I mean it. I had no idea you could sing like that!"

He ran his fingers through his thick hair, and I noticed how long and slim his fingers were. Not like my hands at all. He had Julie's straight, narrow nose, but his jaw was square like mine.

"You've got a good voice," I said.

"Maybe I got it from you or Grandpa."

"I didn't know you could sing, Tony," Celinda said. She turned to David. "He's never sung for me. Sometimes he sings in the shower, but that probably doesn't count."

David looked embarrassed. "Listen. I gotta go change. Thanks for coming."

"David, why don't you come out to Santa Fe while you're here. We've got a pool at the house." I was desperate. I didn't want him to leave yet. I needed for him to have a good time to make up for all the years I wasn't there. David hesitated and looked at Celinda.

"We'd love to have you come visit, David," Celinda said politely.

"I'm free after noon tomorrow, but I have to be back to the hotel by seven on Saturday."

"That's not a problem. We'll have to leave soon, because I have to be at the station at 6:00 a.m. tomorrow morning, but I'll come pick you up at noon."

"Okay, Dad." And then he was gone.

He was sitting out front, waiting for me, when I drove up in the convertible. I had to admit he was a good-looking kid, but then I'd been good-looking myself. I looked in the rearview mirror. As he walked towards the car, I noticed he was taller than I was.

"Cool car," he said, as he settled back and leaned his arm on the windowsill. He was wearing silver sunglasses that made him look like he was from outer space. They must be the "in" thing. I smiled to myself as I remembered my dad's comment about my own sunglasses.

"You got your ear pierced."

"It didn't hurt much."

"How's your mother?"

"She's okay. Did you know I have a brother now?"

"No way. How old is he?"

"His name's Eric, and he's ten. He's a great kid, but sometimes he can be a real pain."

We headed out north of Albuquerque, and the country opened up into desert with distant mountains.

"You can turn on the radio if you want."

"No, that's okay."

"When we get closer to Santa Fe, we'll be able to pull in my station. What have you decided about school?"

"I'm thinking about the Guitar Institute in Atlanta. I got a scholarship to the Cincinnati Conservatory School of Music, but I didn't take it."

"You turned down a scholarship? Are you crazy?"

"You're starting to sound like Mom."

"It's up to you, but an education is a good thing to have. Grandpa used to say it's one thing no one can take away from you."

"I'm not interested in going to school right now," he said defensively. I backed off.

"Are you and Celinda going to get married?" he asked.

"She wants to, but I don't know yet. Maybe when the business settles down a bit."

"She's pretty young."

"What are you saying? That I'm too old for her?"

"I didn't say that. She's just, young. She looks like she's just a little bit older than me."

"Actually, she's the same age as you."

"Jesus, Dad."

"You don't approve?"

"It's weird is all, but she's a looker." I glanced over and he was grinning at me. I grinned back.

At the dinner table, Celinda and David sized each other up. The food was great, though. The chilies were hot, and the blue corn tamales were the best I'd ever had. Celinda started the conversational ball rolling.

"Your performance the other night was really good, David. Have you been playing together for a while?"

"Only two months," David replied. "We just clicked the very first time we jammed together. That doesn't happen often."

"I had no idea David was so talented," I said.

My son beamed at me and blushed. I was happy that we were all together, and that they were getting along so well. I looked over at Celinda and smiled at her.

"Dinner is fantastic, Celinda. The best tamales you've ever made."

"Dad's right, Celinda, you're a terrific cook."

"I do more than just cook."

"I'm sure you do," David said, glancing at me uncertainly.

Celinda smiled sweetly at him. "Your dad says you're dropping out of school."

"I'm not dropping out. I'm not interested in going right now. My music's more important."

"I didn't say that, Celinda. I said David was taking some time before deciding where he wants to go to school. He's really a talented musician and singer. He even turned down a scholarship at the Conservatory in Cincinnati."

"That doesn't seem too smart."

"It was real smart," David said. "That school's too conservative for me. Where do you go to school, Celinda?"

"I graduated. I'm helping your father build a business. He needs me."

"I bet he does," David spit back at her. I felt like I was watching a tennis match.

"What do you care about your dad? He didn't even tell me he had a son."

David threw me a sharp glance.

"You live some place in Colorado, but I'm here. He's with me. He left you."

"Celinda..," I began.

"Maybe if you don't shut up, he'll leave you too," David snapped at her.

"If abortion were legal, David, you'd have never been born." Celinda threw the words in his face and ran from the room. I heard the front door shut and the car start up. She backed out of the driveway with a screech and was gone. I looked over at David. His face was white.

"That's some real classy lady you got there, Dad."

"Don't start. I'm sorry, David. She should have never said that. It's not true."

"Maybe she was right. I want to go back to the hotel."

"It's late. You can stay here, in the ..."

"I don't want to stay here."

"David..."

"I don't want to stay here."

"Okay, I'll drive you back."

It was the longest, darkest ride of my life. I couldn't get him to talk to me and finally stopped trying. I pulled up in front of the hotel. He got out, shut the door and leaned on the windowsill.

"Thanks, Dad. Bye."

"David..."

He didn't turn around. I watched him walk away and disappear into the hotel. At that moment, I felt as if I'd been shot. My life was draining out of me, and there was nothing I could do about it except feel it slowly slip away.

I decided that the best thing for me to do would be to spend more time in Washington, rebuilding my lobbying business while Celinda and Brad kept the station going. I'd be back in the network again, and could make money to pay off the loan. I'd fallen behind on the payments, and I hadn't pulled a paycheck once from the station. Celinda drove me to the airport in Albuquerque. We hadn't spoken since David's visit. We pulled up at Departures, and I got my bag out of the trunk and had it checked through at the curb. I walked over to the driver's side and pulled out my wallet.

"Here's some money to tide you over 'til I get back."

"I'm sorry, Tony," she said quietly. "I'll make it up to you."

"Take care of the station for me."

She nodded.

After he was gone, she pressed her forehead against the steering wheel, and hoped and prayed she hadn't blown it. She knew the other one was in the car with her, and she did not like it. The sweet smell of roses nauseated her. She got out, walked around to the passenger side, yanked open the door, and screamed at her to "get out and leave me alone." Everyone was watching, but she didn't care. When she got back in the car, she was the only one there.

The billowing clouds passed below and around me. I wanted to reach out and hold a piece of them in my hand, to step out and walk on them. Would they hold me? Would I fall to earth? My grandfather refused to set foot in an airplane. He was of the "if God had meant me to fly, he'd have given me wings" school of thought. He said flying cut your threads, the threads that attach you to people, places, objects; and when you land, you have to spin your threads again to ground you and hold you to the earth. Outside my window, the sun shone brilliantly on the clouds. It never rained in heaven, I guess. David's visit hung around me like a black, smothering fog. It weighed me down, saddening me, and fed on the guilt I felt for not having been there for him. I could feel myself slipping into despair, and I couldn't let that happen. I adjusted my mental armor, steeling myself against the thoughts, pushing them down into a distant part of my mind.

We descended through the clouds, and they turned wispy and gray and pressed against my window, and then I was lost between heaven and earth. Something was wrong. I was sure of it. It was taking too long. I should be seeing the ground by now. Still we made our descent, and the clouds pressed against the window, trying to get in. My heart was beginning to pound, and then the grayness broke and the ground was so close. It was rushing up to meet me. There was a jolt as the wheels hit the runway. I was back.

Hugh Hightower and I were getting together for dinner at the Willard Hotel that night. He said he had someone he wanted me to meet. Actually, it would be the first time Hugh and I had met. All of our business had been conducted by fax and phone. I called the Ambassador, but his secretary told me he was out of town for the week, so I made a few business phone calls and prowled around the house. The garden out back looked scraggly, and I'd have to have Suzan get a new maid service. It appeared to me that they were vacuuming only in the center of the room and dusting where they felt like it. The master bedroom was particularly bad. I got a dust cloth and wiped every carved scroll on my bed and dresser.

As I dusted, I had a queasy feeling just below my heart. I sat on the edge of the bed and hoped I wasn't having a heart attack. I'd felt like this once when I was on vacation with my parents, when I was ten years old. We'd rented a cabin in Yellowstone National Park, and it happened one night when I was getting ready to go to bed. "Homesick," my mom had said. "You're just homesick." Seeing all my things again had made me homesick, and I realized for the first time how much I'd missed my house in Georgetown. The clock downstairs chimed six, and I stood up with a start. I had to be at the Willard by seven.

I arrived at the dining room at about 7:15 p.m. As I was being led to the table, I spotted Congressman Betts at one of the tables by the window. He was working on something for me. He motioned me over.

"Tony, I've got that letter of introduction for you to the Department of Defense. That big electronics procurement is coming out. Don't know how you got wind of it before me. Call my office in the morning." That was good news. The $1,5000,000 contract for Hightower's friend looked like it was going through. "Congratulations, boy. I hear you're the sole owner of a radio station. You're goin' to make a fortune of that one. Don't know how you ever got Red to sell out to you like that."

"Sell out? You've talked to Red?"

"A couple of days ago. He called me. Good luck to you."

"Thanks, Congressman. Appreciate it. Give me a call if you need anything."

Congressman Betts winked back at me. "Will do, Tony, will do." I smiled expansively and shook his hand, but inside I was cursing a blue streak for him getting me into this radio station mess.

I looked at my watch. I'd kept my investor waiting twenty minutes now, but Mr. Hightower didn't look the least bit perturbed that I was late, and when I saw his companion, I understood why. She was one gorgeous blonde. Hugh stood and shook my hand. He was a big man with broad shoulders, a steak and potatoes sort of guy. He had thick, red hair, the reddest hair I'd ever seen in my life, but not one freckle on his face.

"Tony, I'd like you to meet my associate, Laura Ruston."

I looked into Laura Ruston's green eyes, and they smiled back at me.

She extended her hand, and I noted that she wasn't wearing a wedding ring.

"Laura manages some of my other investments for me."

I bet she does, I thought.

"I'd like her to be your contact on the radio station."

My lucky day, though I didn't think Celinda would be pleased. I'd just have to make sure these two never met.

"That's fine with me," I replied. "How long have you been working with Mr. Hightower?"

He didn't give her a chance to answer. "Laura and I have been working together about three years, and it's been a good business relationship. She keeps my investments in line for me." He grinned at her. "She's one sharp, little lady."

"I have an MBA from Wharton, Mr. Cassera, so I'm quite qualified."

"I never thought you weren't, Miss Ruston." I smiled back at her, and I felt her catch my admiration of her body.

"Where are you from, Miss Ruston?"

"Laura. Call me Laura. I'm from Alabama. You noticed my southern drawl, didn't you?" Her eyes sparkled at me over her glass of champagne.

I felt my face get hot. I reached for my drink to hide my confusion. The meal was superb. I told them both how successful the new format had been and who I had lined up for the talk show. Actually, the station was in a slump like the rest of the economy, but I didn't want to bring that up. We were waiting for our dessert and coffee, when Laura looked at her watch.

"It's ten o'clock, Mr. Hightower."

"Damn." Hugh threw down his napkin. "I've got to run. Another appointment. You two stay. I want Laura to go out to Santa Fe and become familiar with your operation. Why don't you both set up something and then get back to me?"

I saw him stop and talk to Congressman Betts on his way out.

"Mr. Hightower knows the Congressman?"

"They go way back, Tony." Laura's eyes were smiling at me again. She put her champagne glass down. "It's his wife."

"What?"

"She wants him home by ten-thirty, every night." So that was it. He was more than Mr. Hightower to her.

"That bothers you."

"No. It's just hard to do business sometimes. Let's have a nightcap and plan my visit to Santa Fe." I leaned back in my chair, but she stood up. The waiter came over with our desserts. "Tony, do you still want your dessert?"

"No. Sorry." The waiter's face didn't change expression.

We went upstairs to her room. There was a bottle of chilled champagne sitting on the bar. We opened it and started discussing her business trip to Santa Fe.

The phone rang about midnight, but I didn't stop what I was doing.

"I have to answer it," she said breathlessly. I eased up and she lifted the receiver. I toyed with her, giving little thrusts. She yawned to hide her gasps as she spoke into the receiver.

"No. I'm just tired. Yes. It's all set. In about two weeks. Me, too. Good night."

I looked at her lying beneath me, her blonde hair spread across the pillow. I ran my hands up her belly and over her breasts and then pinned her shoulders to the bed.

"He's rich and he takes good care of me, but he's lousy in bed." She smiled as she said it. I held her shoulders, and she began to move her hips slowly. I stayed where I was and watched her convulse and tremble beneath me. The explosion traveled through her whole body, and it filled me with wonder at the intensity of the passion. I wasn't in love with this woman, I thought to myself as I drifted off to sleep, but to give her such pleasure filled me with love for her.

I woke in the middle of the night, moaning and writhing. I kept my eyes closed and immersed myself in her movements, moving my body in rhythm to hers. This lady knew what she was doing. I opened my eyes. Laura was asleep next to me, but my body was reaching its climax. There was a weight on my chest, a heavy weight as if the palms of someone's hands were pushing down on my heart. Then I noticed the smell, the earthy, musky smell. It was starting to hurt. My thighs were cramping. I flung myself out of bed and stood shaking in the middle of the floor.

I looked over at the bed. Laura hadn't moved. She was still sound asleep. I made my way to the bathroom and flipped on the light. I leaned over the sink, gasping for breath. I turned the faucets on full blast and put my head under the spout. Raising my head, I was startled by what I saw. My face was gray and my eyes were bulging in terror.

I started talking to myself. "You're okay. It was just a bad dream. You're fine." My heart pounded in my ears. I kept talking to myself. "I am calm. Everything is fine. You'll be fine." I sat on the edge of the bed and held my throbbing head in my hands. I felt the mattress shift as Laura turned over and placed her hand on my bare back.

"Tony, are you all right?"

"I'm fine. Just a bad dream."

She sat up and leaned against my back. "Your hair's soaking wet. Let me get you a towel." She wrapped the sheet around her and came back with a towel.

"I took a shower," I mumbled. She didn't say a word, but slowly rubbed the towel on my head. The motion of her hand moving on my head calmed me, and I leaned up against her as she carefully dried my hair.

"There." She lay the towel down and rubbed her hands over my shoulders. "That's better." The sheet was slipping off of her, and she pressed my head to her breasts and held me. I pulled her down into my lap, and let her hug me tightly. She slipped into the bed, pulling me after her, and I fell asleep in her arms. For two days we didn't leave the hotel room.

I called Celinda from Dulles airport before I took off, but couldn't reach her, so I rented a car in Albuquerque and drove the forty hot miles to Santa Fe with a barely functioning air conditioner. A dip in the cool, clear water of our pool was going to be my reward when I reached the house. It was with a great sense of relief that I pulled into the driveway. I couldn't wait to jump in the pool. I yanked my bag out of the trunk and headed for the front door.

My key wouldn't work in the lock. I tried all the keys, then I started pounding on the door in frustration .

"Celinda," I shouted. "Celinda. Open the door."

I pounded again, rueing the day someone had put these heavy mission doors in. I left my suitcase and walked around to the back. I tried the French doors leading to the pool. Locked and bolted. The house alarm over by the kitchen was armed. I looked again. There wasn't a stick of furniture in the living room. I walked around the entire house, trying every door and window. There was no furniture in any of the rooms. The phone rang, but no one answered.

I went back to the front door. My suitcase was gone. Celinda was inside! I tried my keys in the door again. They still didn't work. I ran around back and pounded on the doors. I peered in, and that's when I saw her. Celinda stood at the far end of the living room, smiling. I turned around angrily and stalked over to the edge of the pool. The water lay there sparkling and winking at me in the sunlight.

"Why the hell are you doing this to me?" I yelled.

When the door didn't open, I glanced over my shoulder.

She wasn't there any more.

I inserted my pass key in the door to the radio station, and punched in my code. Nothing happened. What the fuck was going on?

I found the nearest phone both and called the station, relieved when Cindy, the receptionist, answered.

"Oh, Mr. Cassera. This is just terrible. I really liked working here." She sniffed.

"Cindy, what's going on?"

"Celinda told me about the loan being in default. It seemed T.J. was honest, to me. I had no idea about him being that kind of person. Celinda said the IRS is going to lean on you. If I'd known T.J. was bad, I would have told you, Mr. Cassera."

"Cindy, what are you talking about?" I'd fired T.J. several weeks before.

"Honest. If I'd known, Mr. Cassera..."

I interrupted her. "Cindy, where's Brad?"

"I don't know."

"Cindy. Open the door for me."

"I can't. The attorney says I can't."

"What attorney?"

"He told me if I let you in, I wouldn't get my walking money, and I need that for my kids."

I calmed her down. "Okay. Okay, Cindy. You don't have to let me in, just tell me the attorney's name."

She hesitated, "I'm not sure if..."

"It's okay, Cindy. You'll get your money." I was losing my patience. "Cindy..."

"His name is Ramirez. Reynaldo Ramirez, but I don't know his phone number, so don't ask me."

"Thanks, Cindy. You're a good kid."

"Good luck, Mr. Cassera. I hope everything works out for you."

I hung up. The IRS was putting a lien on me? There must be some mistake. I stood in the booth, looking through the glass walls at what was left of my life.

I drove out of town and checked into a motel. It wasn't much of a place. The bed sagged in the middle, and the grout was falling out of the tile in the bathroom, but I told myself it was only temporary. I found a phone book and a Gideon Bible in the bottom dresser drawer. Opening the Bible randomly, I closed my eyes and placed my finger on the page. A woman I dated once swore that she got answers to her problems that way, or advice if she needed it.

I moved my finger and read: "He began making an east wind burst forth in the heavens and making a south wind blow by his own strength." Psalms 78, Verse 26. The phone book definitely had more to offer at this moment.

"Mr. Ramirez, this is Tony Cassera."

A voice with a thick, Spanish accent replied. "*Si, Señor Cassera*?" He didn't seem to know who I was.

"I own the radio station KSFE here in town, and I want to know what the hell you think you're doing telling my staff not to let me in."

"*Señorita* Alvarez has retained me to protect her interest in the radio station. She called me when she received a notice from the IRS placing a lien against the radio station. The officers also received a lien individually, including my client. *Señorita* Alvarez told me she tried to reach you in Washington for two days, but couldn't, so she retained me. Apparently, even your secretary did not know where you had gone on your business trip with a Laura Ruston."

I decided to ignore the insinuation I heard in his voice. "Where'd she get the money to retain you?" As soon as I asked the question, I knew the answer, our joint account.

"That I do not know, *Señor Cassera*," he said smugly.

I bet this guy charged her plenty, too.

"What's this about an IRS lien on the station?"

"Evidently, you have not spoken to *Señorita* Alvarez yet." Evidently. "Payroll taxes were not paid for the last four years. The unpaid taxes, plus penalties and interest amount to..."

I could hear papers shuffling.

"...325,428 dollars and 16 cents."

"What! But that's before I bought the radio station." I was stunned. No wonder Red had left town.

"It does not matter, *Señor Cassera*. The IRS goes after whoever has signature power over the company. That's you and *Señorita* Alvarez. She has hired me to get herself out of this IRS problem. I've contacted them and requested that she be removed from the lien. We haven't heard back from them yet, but it's doubtful they'll let her off. My client feels, however, that you are solely responsible."

"I can't believe this is happening."

"Yes, well, my client has also informed me that you took $50,000 out of the station for your personal use, instead of paying the taxes."

"That's not true. T.J., our accountant, said they had been paid."

"Well, *Señor Cassera*, the IRS says they haven't, and you are responsible now."

"Now wait a minute, Mr. Ramirez. I had the books audited and..."

"*Señor Cassera*, I would advise you to seek your own legal counsel. I really cannot speak with you about this matter any further. I also must tell you that I filed a restraining order against you at my client's request. I would advise you not to see her, or you will risk going to jail."

"A restraining order!"

"Yes. *Señorita* Alvarez fears that you may harm her, so we think this is best for all concerned."

"Harm her? What about my safety? She's the one who's..."

"I must repeat, *Señor*. I advise you to seek your own legal counsel. Once you have retained your attorney, as a courtesy I'll fax him all papers pertaining to the case."

"My attorney is Hal Buckman."

"I'll see that he gets a copy of everything. *Buenas dias, Señor Cassera.*"

He hung up. The bastard hung up on *me*! I decided to count to ten in Spanish before I ripped the phone out of the wall. By the time I reached six, I had calmed down. It was just as well. I had another call to make. Hal Buckman had taken care of some small legal matters for me before, regarding the station. I called, filled him in, and made an appointment to see him. I swung by the bank on my way to his office and discovered I'd been right about Celinda. Our joint business account had only a hundred dollars left in it. My personal account was untouched, but there was a hold on it.

Hal Buckman's office was in old Santa Fe. He looked like a grizzled rancher rather than the high-powered lawyer he was. He was pretty well known in those parts. We shook hands, and I noticed how leathery and rough they felt in mine. Buckman wore western shirts and boots, and those funny string ties my dad sometimes wore. His bolo had one big chunk of turquoise set in silver, and his shirt was adorned with silver and turquoise collar points. He used a silver cigarette holder to smoke his cigarettes.

"Hal, I've got a problem."

Buckman nodded wisely. Didn't everyone have a problem who came to see him?

"I'm locked out of my house and the radio station. Celinda has a restraining order against me; and Celinda's lawyer, Ramirez, said there's an IRS lien against us."

"Calm down, Tony. Sit down and stop jumpin' all over the room. I got the papers from Ramirez right here. I've looked them over, and here's what I think. We can file a motion to contest the restrainin' order, but in all probability, the court won't sustain it. So, I think you should just stay away from Celinda and save your pesos."

He leaned back in his chair and cracked his knuckles. He looked at me with piercing gray eyes beneath incredibly bushy, gray eyebrows. "Who," he asked, "is Laura Ruston?"

I swallowed before answering. "She's a business associate of Hugh Hightower, the investor who loaned me $150,000. Why?"

"Seems Miss Celinda thinks you're havin' an affair with this Ruston gal, and she's tellin' Ramirez all about it."

"She's crazy. It's strictly business. Laura Ruston works for Hugh Hightower." Buckman's eyebrows wiggled like two furry caterpillars when I said that.

"Okay, Tony, that's good enough for me, but promise me you'll stay away from Celinda and Miz Ruston 'til all this cools down."

"But what about the furniture she took?"

"I'll look into it. The IRS, though, can take ev'rythin you own."

"Without even notifying me? Come on, Hal, I doubt that. I didn't receive any notice from them."

"By law, Tony, when you owe overdue taxes, they can take you for whatever you own."

"But I wasn't responsible, Red and T.J. were."

"Listen here, Tony, you're the owner. You're responsible. Celinda, too."

"You're scaring me, Hal."

"I don't mean to scare you none. I jus' want you to be real clear on what the situation is. Has your accountant mentioned filing Chapter 11 Bankruptcy?"

"Bankruptcy!"

I started pacing back and forth in front of his desk.

"I'm jus' bringin' it up as an option. Chapter 11 would protect your company assets while you reorganize the station. If we file Chapter 11, the IRS will probably back off, givin' you time to work out a payment plan with 'em."

"I've never filed for bankruptcy," I said. What would my dad think? I could never tell him.

"We're talkin' reorganization, Tony, not total liquidation. I know one company that spent five years reorganizin' and came out at the end profitable. Lots'a businesses doin' it these days, with the economy bein' what it is."

"Well, I don't know about..."

"We should seriously consider it, Tony. Let me review your financials an' then I can recommend better."

"I've got copies in my Washington office. I can have my secretary send them on to you."

"Why don' you head back to Washington, and let me handle things at this end? I think I can get you outta this, but it will take some time to sort through it. I'll need $15,000 to get me started, though. Can you handle it?"

I had to handle it. "Sure, no problem. I'll have to send the money from my account in Washington. There's a hold on my account here."

"Sure thing. I understand. I'll get started today. I'm goin' to call a friend o' mine at the IRS, and see if we can get this lien released offa you."

"How long will that take?"

"Coupla weeks at the most. You jus' get back to Washington, and send me your financials."

"Okay," I sighed. I'll leave this afternoon. I'll be able to wire you the money and Fed Ex the financials to you tomorrow."

Buckman stood. "Sounds good. Let's shake on it."

We shook hands, and I felt a little better. "Have a good trip," he waved at me as I left. "And don' worry none."

When I got back to my motel room, I booked an afternoon flight out of Albuquerque, and I called Suzan at my office in Washington.

"Thank God you called, Mr. Cassera. I've been trying to reach you at home all morning. Mr. Hightower called. He's pretty angry. Something about misappropriation of funds. He said his attorney will be contacting you. A Laura Ruston called. She sounds frantic to get in touch with you. Actually, she called first. And, oh, yes, the new maid service called and said they can't get in to clean. You must have left me the wrong key. Can you send the right one to me?"

"No. Suzan, I've changed my plans. I'm coming back to Washington today."

"What's going on?" I could tell by her voice that she was worried.

"Listen, Suzan, call the Ambassador and ask him if he could pick me up at National Airport. Hang on a second." I had to find the paper with my flight information. "Flight 2022. United. Arriving 3:15 pm. Thanks, Suzan. Sit tight. I'll explain later."

The car rental guy stared at me. I'd left a few hours ago in my perfectly pressed suit, starched shirt, and buffed shoes. Now I stood before him with no tie (I'd forgotten it at the motel) my shirt crumpled and dirty, my hair plastered to my head with sweat, my shoes covered with dust and a less than composed look on my face.

"The air conditioning is not working," I said.

The Ambassador was standing by his car, arguing with airport security, when I walked out of National Airport into a hot, muggy August afternoon. My flight had been a half hour late, and I'm sure the Ambassador had parked himself there and was not moving until I showed up.

The Ambassador looked over and saw me.

"Here he is, Officer." The Ambassador called loudly to me. "Mr. Cassera, I was getting worried. The Congressman is holding the start of the meeting until your arrival. We've got to hurry."

The security officer looked uncertainly at my disheveled appearance. He glanced at the license plate on the Ambassador's car. I knew he was checking to see if they were diplomatic plates. I knew they weren't. The Ambassador gallantly opened the car door for me, before scurrying around to his side and getting in. He glanced in the rearview mirror. The security officer stood behind the car glaring at us.

"I could probably stall him a little longer, while you go to baggage claim and get the rest of your luggage, Tony."

I stared straight ahead of me. "I don't have any more luggage. This is it."

We turned and looked at each other, and our eyes exchanged a hundred stories. The security officer gestured for us to get moving.

"Where do you want to go?" he asked.

"The house in Georgetown, I guess."

Looking at the keys in my hand, I wasn't surprised that none of them worked in the lock. The Ambassador stood on the porch, a puzzled expression on his face. When I said I was going to break a window to get in, he just nodded his head. We entered the house through the side vestibule window. The only things left inside were the nail holes in the wall and the phones sitting on the floors. My desk, my books — everything was gone. Without my political mementos and photos, it was like I'd never existed. We walked upstairs. I was hoping against hope that my bedroom set was there, but the master bedroom was empty. I looked into the bathroom and remembered the bath Celinda and I had taken together right before we moved to Santa Fe. There wasn't even a bottle of aspirin left in the medicine chest. She hadn't left a coat hanger in the closet, but I could still smell her faintly where her clothes had been hanging. Even the big sailfish that had been hanging on the wall in the basement was gone, and she hadn't even liked that fish.

"That fuckin' bitch. If she thinks she can steal everything from me, she's wrong."

"Tony, what's happened?"

"Everything's just gone wrong, Ambassador."

I sat on the kitchen counter, in front of the wall phone, and picked up the receiver. I was almost surprised to hear a dial tone. Had she left the phones on purpose, or was it an oversight? The Ambassador sat on the counter next to me, and I thought to myself what a sight we must make, two men in business suits sitting in the an empty kitchen. She'd even taken the stove and the refrigerator. I dialed the radio station in Santa Fe. Cindy answered. I spoke in my thickest, oiliest, Spanish-accented English.

"This is *Señor* Ramirez calling for *Señorita* Alvarez."

"Oh, yes, Mr. Ramirez," Cindy said importantly. "I'll get her for you," What a little turncoat she was.

"*Hola, Señor Ramirez,*" Celinda said.

"Where's my fuckin' furniture!?" I said.

She hesitated before answering. "Where are you?"

"I'm in the Georgetown house." I spoke the next words slowly and carefully. "Where is my furniture?"

"I did it for us, Tony, so the IRS couldn't get our furniture."

"'Our' furniture? It was never 'your' furniture. Where is it?"

"I put it in storage."

"Where in storage?"

"Someplace safe."

"Celinda, you tell me where you put it. Now."

"I earned it," she shouted at me through the phone. "You took my youth."

What the hell was she talking about? She was eighteen years old!

"I want my furniture back," I shouted.

"You owe it to me," she shrieked back. "They leaned on me because of you. I know about her. I know about the blonde. The furniture is mine. You got fifty thousand dollars out of the company. I didn't get anything for all my work."

"Celinda, what are you talking about? You know I put that money back into the station."

"You can talk to my lawyer. I am not talking to you anymore. You lied to me."

"You can consider this a divorce," I screamed back at her. And then I did what I'd been wanting to do for days, I ripped the phone from the wall and threw it across the room.

It was the Ambassador who broke the silence. "Let's go to Cleveland's and talk this through."

We crawled back out through the window. My next door neighbor, Mrs. DeWitt, was on her front porch watching us.

"It's you, Mr. Cassera," she said. "I was thinking I should call the police."

"It's okay, Mrs. DeWitt. I forgot my keys."

She looked over my shoulder at the window frame I'd destroyed, then narrowed her eyes as she looked back at me. "I thought you had moved out a couple of days ago."

"Do you remember the name of the moving company who came?"

She stared at me as if I were crazy. "How do you expect me to remember, if you don't?" Mrs. DeWitt threw an alarmed look at the Ambassador, then went into her house. I heard her bolt her front door.

"Let's get out of here, Ambassador, before she does call the police."

We left and went to Cleveland's , licking our wounds.

"What should I do about the house, Ambassador? I could lease some furniture and..."

"Cisco, I'd let it go. You're going to lose it anyway. From what you tell me, there's no equity left in it. The bank or the IRS is going to get it."

I knew he was right, but I didn't want to hear it.

"You can come and stay with me. I'm living in this mansion in Washington, DC, renting one of the bedrooms. There are eight bedrooms in this place, and there's a couple that are vacant. I'm sure you could work out something out with the woman who owns the house."

"Florence has your house, then?" I said.

The Ambassador nodded. "Actually, Lynn has it. You know, Tony, Florence and I had the best time all over Europe. It was wonderful, and I still love the woman I married. But I knew I was in trouble the day Lynn told me that Florence was dead. Now she's Lynn all the time, and she's one mean bitch."

"I know what you mean," I said gloomily.

"So, what do you say, Cisco? To the mansion?"

"Okay, Ambassador. To the mansion."

The driveway curved up the slope between a row of trees before opening in front of a massive Tudor facade. I wondered why someone had to rent out the rooms. I stood in the entrance hall and gazed upwards. A wide stairway curled up against the wall ending at an arched second floor landing. Clutching a plastic grocery bag in my hand (we'd stopped at the Safeway for some necessities), I followed the Ambassador as he led the way up the stairs. The upstairs hallway was paneled in a dark wood. There were a few paintings on the walls, and nails where paintings used to hang. I stared at the lone nail next to the door where I would be sleeping tonight. I sighed audibly.

"Come on now, Tony. It will get better. We're in this together, you and I."

"I know, Ambassador."

The Ambassador opened the door and adjusted the dimmer switch. The room grew slowly in brightness, to reveal an elegantly appointed room with walls the color of a robin's egg. A crystal chandelier hung from the center of a plaster medallion in the ceiling. The bed was huge, wide and high off the floor. Ambassador St. John bid me good-night and left for his room two doors down the hall. He said we would meet with Madam, his name for the woman who owned the house, in the morning.

I waited until I heard his door close, then walked slowly around the room, enjoying the way my feet sank into the thick carpet. The bathroom was huge, with two dressing rooms off of it. This must be the master bedroom suite, I decided, and wondered how much she would charge me for it. Sitting on the edge of the bed, I set the plastic grocery bag next to me. How could my life have changed so much in twenty-four hours? I was living my worst nightmare and my greatest fear. Here I was, practically destitute and almost homeless. Bankruptcy. How would I ever come back from this?

The most important thing was for me not to panic. I knew plenty of people in town. If anyone could get back on their feet, it was Tony Cassera. Celinda wasn't going to get the best of me. I looked down at the white plastic bag. It, and the clothes on my back were just about all I had in the world...and my education. My dad said they can never take that away from you. Audibly sighing, I dumped the contents of the plastic bag on the bed. I'd forgotten to buy a toothbrush.

She followed Carlos and Enrique, as they struggled to carry the huge fish between the tables and chairs without breaking off its long, sharp, pointed nose. They were taking so long, and the cardboard box she carryied in her arms was getting heavy. Those in the restaurant stood and stared as the big fish passed by them. None of them had seen such a fish in Nuevo Laredo before. The two men lifted the fish to the bar, and she set her box down next to it. She lifted the cardboard flaps and started taking out the framed photographs and setting them on the bar.

"¡Ah! El Presidente," Carlos said, pointing to President Nixon and holding up the photograph for all to see. *"Captureste un pez grande."*

"Sí," she said. "I caught a big fish."

Rachel

I saw her before she saw me. She was reclining on a chaise in the solarium, talking on the phone. The sunlight fell across her head and shoulders, highlighting a blazing copper mass of wavy hair. Her cheeks were rouged to match, little circles of coral defining a pair of magnificent cheekbones. The Ambassador called her Madam behind her back, but her real name, he said, was Ellen Parker Jamison. Daddy had been in oil and his "little darlin" had married into the Washington political scene, where life was one party and one deal after the other. The husband was gone now, but Ambassador St. John told me she was still pretty well connected. He'd met some high-powered people at her parties. There had been a daughter, but Madam never talked about her. That's all the Ambassador could tell me, other than the fact that she needed help paying the mortgage on this place. I guessed she must be at least 65, but she was still extremely attractive. I watched a slipper dangle from the end of her foot, bouncing gently in a counterpoint to her thick, flowing drawl, that was smooth and rich like a glass of Southern Comfort. She shifted the phone to her other ear.

"Now, Congressman, I am counting on you coming. We can make millions on this, hon. General Malcolm Rogers will be attending, and you know he's a careful investor. There's tons of potential here. You will? I am *sooo* pleased, Congressman. About 8 o'clock? Do bring Elizabeth. Haven't seen her in simply ages. See you Friday." She replaced the receiver and sat back with a satisfied smile on her lips. Then she noticed me.

"Hello? Do I know you?"

"Well, actually, no. I'm a friend of Ambassador St. John."

She squinted to see me. "Come closer. I have misplaced my glasses somewhere. Who did you say you knew?"

"Ambassador St. John."

"He's one of my guests, you know. What's your name, hon?"

"Cassera. Tony Cassera."

"Please sit down, Mr. Cassera."

She graciously indicated a wicker chair next to her. "Tell me, Mr. Cassera, what do you do?" She leaned towards me, her bright blue eyes peering intently into mine.

"I'm a lobbyist."

"A lobbyist. That's absolutely perfect." She laid a hand on my arm. The fingernails were long, oval, and red. "Well, I've got people for you to meet. I've been in this town for over forty years, hon, and I know everyone."

Madam leaned back in her chaise, but kept her hand resting languidly on my arm. "Do you live here in Washington?"

"I've just moved back to town from Santa Fe. I was in business out there for a while."

She patted my arm in sympathy. "How dreadful for you, hon. Never could understand what people see in that place, all those cow skulls, and that ghastly turquoise jewelry, and all that lumpy pottery. And dust. That awful, dreary dust everywhere. But anyone can see from looking at you, Mr. Cassera, that you belong here in Washington. You need to be in a powerful place." She paused for a moment. "Are you married, Mr. Cassera?"

"No."

She held her breath, waiting for me to continue, but that was as much as I felt like saying. Thwarted, Madam let out a long sigh. "I know how lonely it can be, darlin'. Richard died some years ago, now. Since then, I've been wined and dined all over the world, but no one has captured my heart."

Her hands fluttered about her head like butterflies, and I could imagine the long line of rich and powerful men who had been attracted by the heady scent from this exotic flower. She watched me carefully from half-closed lids, waiting to see if her allure was working.

"Where are you living?" she half-yawned and half-drawled.

"Well..."

She sat up abruptly.

"I know. Why don't you stay here with me? I have so much room I don't know what to do with it all. I could introduce you to some of my friends, and women. A handsome man like you needs to meet just the right woman."

I beamed at her, and her eyes sparkled. If I played up to her, she might give me a break on the rent.

"Please excuse me," I said, "but I stayed here last night." I rushed on. "You weren't home. The Ambassador was hoping to introduce us this morning..."

She clapped her hands, and her gold bracelets jangled. "Then it's already settled. Are you in the Blue Room? You are, aren't you? That's the one I would have picked for you."

"How much would you like for the room?"

Madam rose to her feet and pulled me up with her, putting her arm through mine. "We can discuss that later. First, let me give you the tour. Do you play tennis? I have a court and a pool, both of which you are free to use." She whisked me off down the hall, stopping only to comment on the thermostat. "Don't ever touch it. It's set automatically, so there's no need to ever adjust it." I assured her that I never would. She led me through the living room, dining room, butler's pantry, kitchen, morning room, library, garden room and out to the pool, and then we circled the tennis courts, twice, her arm still resting in mine.

We stopped by the edge of the pool. I noticed leaves clinging to its side walls. There was a waterbed sitting next to the pool, and a dirty tennis ball floating in the middle of the water.

"Richard never would listen to me," she said, eyeing the floating tennis ball. "I told him not to put the courts so close to the pool. Friday I'm having a cocktail party. I shall expect you to be there, Mr.

Cassera. I do hope you shall enjoy living here. We're one big family, you know. I have an appointment, so I've got to run. Let me know what you think you can afford, and we'll work something out. I hope she didn't take you for everything, hon." She gave my arm a confidential squeeze, a dazzling smile, and left me standing speechless next to the pool.

What a windfall. I had nothing, but I was living in a mansion. With Madam's connections, I could get some clients and deals going, and the money would start flowing in.

From the library window, I saw Ambassador St. John drive up. I headed to the front hall to meet him. His face looked haggard, but the worry left his eyes when he saw me.

"Cisco, so what do you think? Should we talk to Madam?"

"It's all set. I talked to her this morning."

"We're *compadres* now, then. Excellent. Come with me to the kitchen. Meeting with my lawyer always stimulates my appetite."

There was already someone in the kitchen — a tall, good-looking Ivy Leaguer, with Kennedy hair that sprang up thickly from his forehead.

"Peter, let me introduce you to Tony Cassera. Peter Fannon, a lawyer at Stearns, Waverly, Parson and Holtz — soon to be Stearns, Waverly, Parson, Holtz, and Fannon, he hopes. Tony's a lobbyist, newly returned from the great Southwest."

"So, you're going to be a partner. Congratulations," I said enviously, shaking his hand. Everyone in Washington knew of the firm.

"The Ambassador is rushing my promotion a bit," Peter replied in a thick Boston accent, "but hopefully by the end of the year." He grinned, a set of huge teeth filling his mouth.

Then he said, "You'll excuse me. Company." He loaded two plates onto a tray and headed for the door. "Welcome to St. Elizabeth's, Tony," he called over his shoulder.

"Why did he say that?"

"Peter's Yankee humor." The Ambassador nodded towards the

door through which Peter had just departed.

"Separated from his wife. Says he's here for some solitude, and to think things through."

"But you think different," I said.

"I know different. He sneaks women in through the side, garden room door. My room's right above the door, and that door's getting a lot of use late at night. Had breakfast yet?" He pulled a carton of eggs from the refrigerator and started cracking them into a bowl.

"No thanks. I'm still digesting my encounter with Madam."

The Ambassador chuckled. "She's a character, but she seems to know the right people. It was through her that I found the consulting job I'm doing now."

"Why's there a waterbed by the pool?"

"Rumor has it she used to tumble with the gardeners out there, and a few government officials, too. But that was before the Reverend."

"The Reverend?"

"You'll meet him."

"Ambassador, you just put the eggs back in the freezer."

He looked perplexed. "I did?" He opened the freezer, took the carton out and put it on the lower shelves. "Would you like some orange juice?"

"You poured me some already."

"Yes, so I did." He stood in the center of the kitchen looking lost, like he couldn't remember what he was doing. He opened several drawers, looking for a whisk. I watched, knowing better than to ask. He would tell me when he was ready.

He beat the eggs in the bowl for a full two minutes without saying a word.

"I think they're ready," I said finally.

"I'm losing everything, Tony." He stared into the bowl at the foaming eggs, then turned to look at me with the resigned eyes of a dog about to be put to sleep. "She's the one who's crazy. She's the one who's sleeping with some low-life government guy, and I'm paying through the nose."

"I know." We looked at each other. "Oh, hell, Ambassador, we'll get out of this mess somehow."

"I don't know, Cisco. I'm getting too old for this." He poured the eggs into the skillet and gently scrambled them. "Florence was beautiful. When I had that post in Europe, she was a treasure. With the kids, she was great, a little moody sometimes, but now...." He sighed.

I couldn't think of anything to say to make him feel better, so I tried a question. "Are you going to Madam's cocktail party on Friday?"

"Yes. She's got quite a guest list. She's working on putting some investors together for an international art deal. If I were you, I'd go and work the crowd. Lots of politicos and diplomats coming."

"...and General Malcolm Rogers."

"Really?"

"I overheard her talking on the phone."

"She's got more pull than I thought. He's hard to get. Sure you don't want some eggs?"

The Ambassador looked at me thoughtfully over his half-eaten breakfast, then reached into his coat pocket, and pulled out a plastic baggy which he placed in front of me. Inside there was a brown mass. He tapped his forefinger on it.

"This could be it, Cisco."

I lifted up the bag and peered at it. "Looks like shit to me."

"It is, in a way." The Ambassador took the bag from me, opened it and poured the contents into his hand. "A friend of mine in the State Department, his son gave this to me. Luis works as a horticulturalist for the U.S. Agency for International Development, in the Dominican Republic. He's the one who developed this. It's an artificial soil replacement and fertilizer made from coconuts."

"Coconuts?"

"This fiber is extracted from the husks of coconuts. When I was Director of Asian Affairs, we were looking for agricultural products like this one, to help build the economies of the different countries, to give them an export product. Tony, it retains six times its weight and significantly enhances plant growth. Luis, the son, is working on a process that sterilizes the fiber, so it doesn't carry any soil parasites or diseases. That means it will pass USDA inspection for importation into this country." The Ambassador sat back with a triumphant look on his face.

"So..?"

"So, we round up the funding, get a trial project going, and we're in business. Think about this. Coconuts grow on tropical islands, Cisco. We could retire to an island somewhere and run our business from there. What do you think?"

"I think cement."

"No. This is nothing like that. That was bogus. This is legit. Luis is faxing me the University study. My friend's son is not a businessman. He needs us."

"I do know where we might be able to get some funding through the World Bank and some other international agencies," I said, "but I want to read this report and anything else you've got about it."

"Then you'll consider it?"

"I'll consider reading the report.

I drove up to the mansion on Friday night, after leasing a car, and was amazed at the number of Mercedes, Cadillacs, BMW's and limousines parked out front. Madam had teamed up with some guy in the art world to set up an International Art Exchange, similar to the stock market. Through this Exchange, investors, artists, and gallery owners could invest in works of art from their home, via computer. There was to be a presentation and lots to eat and drink. It would be the perfect setting for me to make contacts and meet potential clients. Getting back into lobbying would help me get back on my feet financially while I was waiting for Hal Buckman to resolve my tax problem. People had always been willing to pay for my knowledge of government contracting and contacts. I thought back to how it all began. How the summer after graduating from law school in San Antonio, I worked on a local congressional campaign. How, after winning the election, I was offered a position in Washington on the congressional staff. How I gave up my dream to practice law with a small firm. What if I had become a lawyer? Where would I be now? Probably stuck in an office somewhere, preparing for another boring case. Washington really was the best place for me. This is where I belonged. Big things and big money were happening here, and I was going to be part of them. I was sure of that.

It was with great anticipation that I walked up the steps to the front door in my new suit that I'd bought with a credit card, and a designer tie I'd borrowed from the Ambassador. Madam was there, greeting each guest personally. She looked radiant in a green sequined sheath that skimmed the floor. The emeralds and diamonds in her necklace sparkled in the light and screamed "money". As soon as I walked through the door, she grabbed my arm and pulled me next to her.

"Tony, I was so afraid you wouldn't make it. What a beautiful tie. Versace?"

I nodded.

"I can always tell, hon."

Her voice was spreading honey on everyone as they walked in. "Congressman Curtis, this is Tony Cassera. He's a lobbyist here in Washington. I think you two should talk."

I shook hands with the Congressman, and made plans to meet later. He moved on, and then I was exchanging pleasantries with a gallery owner. Yes, of course, I looked forward to talking to him later. I spotted the Ambassador by the bar, hovering over a woman in a bright red dress. I envied him, as he was where I wanted to be. After about six more introductions, I made my escape to the bar.

"Tony, over here. I've got someone for you to meet." The Ambassador circled his martini glass over his head.

"Is that a Bombay Gin martini, Ambassador?"

"The very same. Tony, this is Countess von Kemmler. Countess, Mr. Tony Cassera."

"Mister Cassera." She spoke with a slight Austrian accent and extended her hand with a very large diamond on it. She was a petite woman, with dark auburn hair, a wickedly alluring smile and impeccable manners. Her red lace dress dipped low across her breasts and clung to her every curve. This was my first brush with an aristocrat, and it was a pleasant experience.

"Are you an investor in paintings, Mister Cassera?" she inquired.

"A few minor works, Countess. Nothing at the level of your investments, I'm certain." I thought of the black velvet painting of a desert sunset that Celinda had insisted on putting up in my house in Georgetown, and my few estate bargains that Celinda now had in "safekeeping."

"Will you gentlemen excuse me? There's someone I need to talk to."

Both the Ambassador and I bowed slightly from the waist as she left. Our eyes followed her red dress until she disappeared into the crowd. The back of the dress curved low, revealing beautiful back muscles, and I noticed she had a tiny beauty mark on her left shoulder blade.

"A few minor works?" the Ambassador crowed. I punched him playfully in the ribs.

"Watch that, Cisco, you're making me spill a first-class Bombay Gin martini."

"Gotta get to work, Ambassador. See you later."

I headed for Congressman Curtis and circled, waiting for a lull in the conversation. It wasn't long in coming.

"Congressman, Tony Cassera. I'm a lobbyist here in Washington."

"Who do you lobby for, son?"

"I mainly represent government contractors seeking business with agencies." In other words, I represent anyone who has enough money to pay me to lobby for them. "What committees are you on, Congressman?"

"I was a Representative from Wyoming before leaving Congress two years ago, and served on the Agriculture Committee for one term."

Damn. I can't use him for anything. He's out of power. Most of my clients in the past had been defense contractors. I decided to see if I could salvage something from the conversation.

"Do you know Congressman Wynett from Georgia?" I asked him. "He's a friend of mine. We've worked on some international deals together." Actually, I'd only met the man twice in Armandi's office, during the cement deal, but that made us practically best friends in Washington.

"I've met Congressman Wynett. But right now, I'm working with Brooks & Sturgess on an international sugar sale. We should have lunch some time next week." He handed me his card. Bingo.

"I'll call you the middle of next week, Congressman." He nodded and headed off towards the bar. I stood there for a moment, sipping my drink, trying to look unobtrusive as I planned my next move. A woman laughed behind me.

"Oh, Mister Petrucci, we made ten million dollars each, off of our investments," the woman said. My ears perked up.

"Countess, you're extraordinary," her companion said. "I passed on that one, myself." I turned, and there was the "Countess of the Red Dress," surrounded by four wealthy-looking businessmen.

She raised her eyebrows in recognition. "Mister Cassera, won't you join us?" The four men turned to look at me, and I could tell they would just as soon I didn't, so I went right over.

"Come, Countess. Would you like a glass of champagne?" I sailed away with her on my arm.

"What do you do here in Washington, Mister Cassera?" That was the typical Washington conversation opener. You are what you do in this town.

"I'm a lobbyist, Countess. Defense contracts mainly, but I've worked some international deals." I handed her a glass of champagne and took one for myself.

"Perhaps we could work together," she said. "Let me introduce you to one of my clients."

Her client was Lyle Westerley, from Nassau, an imposing, distinguished man with a full head of white hair and an amazing tan. I wondered if he used Tortuga Oil. Westerley owned a casino in the Bahamas, and wanted to expand into Maryland. We discussed his getting an operator's license, and he invited me to Nassau to see his operation. I was really excited. This party had been incredible for me so far, and it wasn't over yet.

"Everyone. Everyone please." Madam's voice boomed into the far corners of the house. "Please adjourn to the living room."

Westerley escorted the Countess out, and the rest of us dutifully filed into the living room. I noticed that the buffet had been plundered. Only a few, sad-looking hors-d'oeuvres were left on Madam's magnificent silver platters.

A slide projector was set up, and some artsy guy in tweed and a bow tie was passing out materials in a folder. I wondered if this was what a Tupperware party was like. Celinda went to one, and came back with all these tubs with lids you had to burp. She showed me how to do it. The Ambassador sat next to me, in one of the chairs that had been neatly arranged in a semi-circle around the living room.

"Did you meet General Malcolm Rogers?" he asked.

"No. Have you?" I whispered back.

"No. He's probably out of uniform."

The guy in tweed was thanking Madam for hosting the event in her lovely home.

"Who's the black man standing next to Madam, Ambassador?"

"That's the Reverend. He's some kind of holy roller. Madam doesn't make a move without him." I looked the guy over. He wore glasses with black rims that made his eyes look as if he were staring through a pair of magnifying glasses. His hair was a wet, shiny black, and slicked straight back from his forehead, which he was constantly wiping with a snowy white handkerchief. I eyed the biceps bulging from under his suit coat, and would have bet money that I was looking at a former prizefighter if his nose hadn't been so perfect.

"In your folders, you'll notice we've prepared a prospectus," Tweed Man began. "Investment opportunity of a lifetime. We are seeking one million dollars from investors...projected sales of fifty million dollars..."

Forty-five minutes later it was over, and I'd hardly heard a word. Everyone mingled, talking in small groups. What I overheard indicated a favorable response to the presentation. I scanned the groups, wondering who I should introduce myself to next. I spotted a likely person and headed over. He was wearing an expensive suit with a decidedly European cut.

"Tony Cassera. I'm a lobbyist here in Washington."

He looked at me and smiled. "I'm Ambassador Uneke from Nigeria. What did you think of the presentation, Mr. Cassera? Are you going to invest?"

I thought for a moment, then said, "Well, actually, I'm considering it. It has a great deal of potential." I paused diplomatically before changing the subject. "Ambassador Uneke, I know a Congressman who's looking for some connections in Africa, to sell sugar. Does your country have any need for this commodity?"

"Well, yes, perhaps we should talk further. Why don't you come by my office in the next couple of weeks, and bring the Congressman." We exchanged business cards, and he left for the evening. There were very few people still around, and the Ambassador was nowhere in sight nor was the countess. Madam was still holding court in the living room, so I slipped upstairs.

As I turned on the light in my room, I noticed a small raised lump in the bed. I looked around to see if Celinda was in the room. Carefully, I approached the bed and pulled back the cover.

It was a coconut. Underneath it was a university report: "A New Technology for Coconuts: CocoBono."

I crawled into bed and fell asleep reading about "the enormous potential of coconuts for building an agricultural soil base in soil deficient areas of the world such as deserts, arid plains, and islands." Islands. Beautiful, lush, tropical islands.

The Ambassador lay in wait for me in the kitchen the next morning. I poured myself a cup of coffee while he read out loud.

"Listen to this part, Tony. Adding just twenty percent CocoBono to peat/perlite doubled the number of leaves, while the width of the foliage increased by fifty percent, and the plants grew twenty-five percent taller." The Ambassador shoved the graphs across the kitchen table to me. "The report is signed by some professor from Polytechnic University, College of Horticulture."

I drank my coffee. My silence didn't stop the Ambassador.

"But wait 'til you hear this. I just received this fax this morning. It's a letter from the USDA's Plant Inspection service saying that the coconut fiber is free of pests or contaminants, and is acceptable packing material for imported plants. There's also a letter from Luis, saying that there's some area called Samana in the Dominican Republic that produces about eighty million coconuts per year. That's a lot of coconut fiber, Tony."

"Are there any other places in the world, besides the Dominican Republic, that produce a lot of coconuts?" I asked.

"Well, there's the Philippines."

"I don't know much about that place. Would it be a nice place to live?"

"Tony, you've got contacts at the Agriculture Department. Let's verify these letters."

"I'm not..."

"All you have to do is verify the letters. You're not committed to anything."

"Okay, okay, Ambassador. I'll make some calls."

I picked up our coffee cups and took them over to the sink to rinse them.

Madam's voice reached the kitchen a full ten seconds before she did. "Who touched the thermostat?" She planted herself in the doorway and repeated her question. "Who touched the thermostat?" Her red hair stuck straight up from her head. She wore a bathrobe and shabby slippers, with ostrich feathers on them.

"I drew that line on the thermostat for a reason, and it's not supposed to go beyond that. You both know that. People are so inconsiderate!" Madam twirled around and stalked out. A few minutes later we heard her raised voice coming from the morning room.

I looked at the Ambassador. He shrugged his shoulders.

"Women are crazy," I said.

"The evidence does seem to be weighted in their favor," he replied.

Over the next week I managed to meet the others who were sharing the mansion.

"Big" Ed was a real estate developer who "had a big land deal" in the works in the Washington area. The television ran in his room twenty-four hours a day — a thin, glowing blue line showing under his door late at night. He said he had a "big house in Jersey," but was living here temporarily, to save commuting time. He also had a "big car." Everything about "Big" Ed was big, including himself. He must have weighed close to three hundred pounds, but he was no slouch. His suits were custom-made for him, and he always looked the dapper gentleman, with nails manicured, shoes buffed, every wavy brown lock on his head in place. His after-shave lingered long after his departure from a room.

Markham B. Colter II, it was whispered around the mansion, was on probation for some felony white-collar crime, but no one really knew what. Markham came and went at odd hours, sneaking in and out of his lower level room. My theory was that he was allergic to "Big" Ed's after-shave. I bumped into him in the front hall one night at midnight. He invited me down for a drink and seemed a friendly enough guy, but too scholarly for me. He wasn't very old, thirty-five at the most, with a tall, wiry build and a head of prematurely gray hair which he wore too long. He had an irritating habit of scrunching his eyes nervously every thirty seconds while he was talking. Sitting downstairs with him, sipping a drink, was nerve wracking, and the room didn't help. The lower level was eerie, with its exotic oriental furnishings and draped divans. Markham explained that Madam and her husband had dragged the stuff back from their trips to India and the Orient. All the statues had at least six pairs of arms, which I found disconcerting. He launched into an impressive explanation of Buddhism and Hinduism which left me nodding over my drink. There was even a meditation room, empty except for a buddha sitting on a shelf, a silk pillow on the floor, and a couple cardboard boxes filled with the odds and ends of life, waiting to move on. Staring at the boxes made me feel inexplicably uncomfortable and anxious, so it was with a great sense of relief that I made my way upstairs and left "Buddha" Markham to his incense and chants.

"Kennedy-hair" Peter worked for the prestigious law firm that wanted to make him a partner, so he said. He and his wife had separated, so he could have the solitude to think things through and, conveniently, date as many women as possible.

Dr. Delbert Rosenthal had lived in the mansion the longest. He supposedly had a problem with alcohol, but I rarely saw him take a drink. The Ambassador said he'd been a dentist, but "Big" Ed swore he'd been a psychiatrist in Beverly Hills, because a friend of his had gone to him for two years. Delbert had a kindly face, dominated by a red, bulbous nose, the only outward sign of his imbibing. I could see people wanting to tell their troubles to a man with such a pleasant countenance. He was soft-spoken, obviously well-educated, with three passions in life — reading the New York Times, which he did religiously every morning in the kitchen, eating Wonder Bread and Velveeta cheese sandwiches, and listening for hours to opera.

And then there was Madam, the erratic, charming, common denominator in all our lives. One afternoon, Madam approached me and the Ambassador, carrying two empty bottles.

"Someone's been drinking my liquor," she said in cold, even tones. "I found this bottle in the trash, and this one behind the couch in the living room. Do you two know anything about this?"

The Ambassador and I glanced at each other. We were both thinking Dr. Delbert, but there was no way we'd turn him in.

"Maybe they were left over from one of your parties?" I suggested.

"No they weren't. I recognize these. They're from my private liquor cabinet in the library. You're protecting someone, aren't you? Thou shalt not steal," she thundered, and she shook the two bottles at us. She hurled them into the trash can, and I winced at the sound of breaking glass. Madam was full of surprises, I soon discovered.

I was lying in bed trying to read, after trying to call Laura Ruston, who was never home. She hadn't returned any of my calls. I was broke now, so she'd probably hooked up with Hightower again, I thought, feeling sorry for myself. The door flew open, and Madam swept into the room. She was a master of the grand entrance.

"Most people knock," I said, without looking up from my book.

"I don't knock on doors in my house. Besides, hon, I have great news for you. Look."

Madam thrust a card in front of my nose. It was an engraved invitation to the Debutante Ball at The Mayflower Hotel in Washington, D.C.

"You do have a tuxedo, hon, don't you?"

Without waiting for my answer, she opened my closet and looked pitifully at my meager wardrobe. "I guess you'll have to rent one. I'll tell you where to go. Trust me. Sid has the latest cuts, and for me, he's cheap. You'll go as my guest. The most eligible and wealthy young women on the East Coast will be coming out, and we must be sure you are there."

Madam came back over to the bed and studied my face.

"Why do you have all those coconuts in the bottom of your closet?"

"I collect them," I said as seriously as I could.

The Ambassador had been leaving coconuts in my car, under my pillow, and this morning there was one floating in my toilet.

"I must ask you to get rid of them. They bring in all sorts of nasty insects. Your hair's too long. I'll make an appointment for you with my stylist." She sailed out of the room and down the hall.

I heard the Ambassador's door open, and he came into my room.

"The coconuts have got to go, Ambassador."

"I heard."

"Who the hell does she think she is?" I was furious. How dare she come into my room and go through my things. The Ambassador went over and shut the door.

"Not so loud, Cisco," he said.

"I don't care if she hears."

"What's this?" he said, picking up the card Madam had left behind.

"An invitation to the Debutante Ball," I said irritably.

"Really? You lead a charmed life. These are hard to come by. I suggest you bite the bullet and suffer through the evening."

"You're probably right." I brightened considerably, thinking about all the beautiful women I was going to sweep off their feet. Madam really wasn't such a bad person after all.

The Ambassador handed me a sheaf of papers and sat down on the bed.

"I came in to show you these reports. CocoBono is a real product.

It's legitimate. Everything's checked out, and it does all they claim. All we need now is a host country and some capital. Are you in?"

"I'm in." I wanted to make some money fast, and get back on my feet again. "I'll start calling around tomorrow to the agencies, and see if I can drum up some funding."

"I'll check out islands with lots of coconuts, as a possible base for our operation."

"Sounds good to me."

"I tell you, Cisco, this is going to be it."

"I sure hope you're right, Ambassador."

My phone rang, and the Ambassador left, closing the door behind him.

"Tony? Is that you?"

"Laura. I've been trying to reach you for the past two weeks."

"I know. Things have been nuts since Hugh got a phone call from a woman named Celinda. She said the IRS had put a lien on the radio station and that the accounts were frozen. Tony, what's going on?"

"You know more than I do. Evidently, there were back taxes owed when I bought the station, and before I could even deal with the situation, the IRS slapped a lien on everything and everyone. Celinda is the office manager, and she panicked and called Hightower."

"Hugh's livid. He doesn't even want to talk to you. Celinda told him you misappropriated some of the funds he put into the company. Is that true?"

"That's an out-and-out lie," I said angrily. "I've got a lawyer working on it, Laura. Hang on a second."

I watched the door to my room open slightly and a hand rolled a coconut into the room. The door closed.

"Listen, Laura, can we get together?"

"Tony, I think it would be better if we didn't see each other until things quiet down. You understand how it is."

I understood.

"Okay, Laura. Call me when you can."

She hung up. I knew she wouldn't call.

They sat together side by side in the dark, before a hundred flickering candles. Celinda held the gnarled claw of the old woman, and it seemed to her that she held the root of a tree or a bone of some animal, not a human hand. Her eyes were closed and looking deep into the darkness of her eyelids, she saw him asleep and reached out and touched his face.

She was startled when his eyes flew open, and he stared with the fixed stare of the dead. She watched, unmoving, as *La Vieja* flew at him, her hair splayed out behind her, the long nails on each of her fingers arced like talons. He tried to cry out, but no sound came from his open lips. Celinda watched in horrified fascination, but just as *La Vieja* was to claim him, there was a rustling sound and she felt the brush of feathers against her face. The old one grabbed her by the arm and pulled her out of the light that filled the room. When she saw the one who made the light, Celinda was furious.

When she opened her eyes, she was alone in the dark, and there was a pain in her arm where the old one had grabbed her, and she could feel the cut and the warmth of her own blood.

She was angry with the old woman. *La Vieja* had promised her everything, but all she'd gotten was some stupid old furniture. She shrugged her shoulders. Her *mama* would like the furniture. She had never had much. None of them had had much. She was not sure what was going wrong, except that it had gotten harder and harder to get to him. *La Vieja* was becoming afraid. She could see it, and she could smell the fear on her, but she wouldn't let the old one stop now. If she hadn't got the money from him because of that interfering white witch, then she was going to go for something bigger.

If she couldn't have him, no one would.

That night, I had a dream. It started with flickering lights — thousands of flickering lights. A big black bird was attacking me, and I tried to protect myself, but I couldn't move my arms. Celinda was there. I saw her face and felt her hand caressing my forehead. The bird kept flying at me, its beak open, as if it wanted to tear at my face and my heart. Every time it came close, a small white bird would dart at its head, trying to peck its eyes out. Then the white bird became larger than the black bird and chased it away.

When I woke in the morning, a shattered coconut lay on the floor in the middle of the room, its milk seeping slowly into the carpet. I knew Madam would not be happy about that.

One hundred virginal girls dressed in white descended the staircase, an escort in military uniform beside each one. They were officially presented to the audience, and then it was over. The debutantes had come out. I mingled with them, sipping champagne, but none of them interested me. They were too young. Celinda had cured me of the young ones. I found their mothers much more interesting. They were dressed to impress, wearing their best jewels. I quizzed Madam about some of them.

"No, hon, not that one," she said. "She's divinely happy with her husband. See the woman in blue. That's Babs Connally. She cheats on her husband all the time."

I eyed the strikingly beautiful Babs.

"Tell me more about the one who cheats."

Madam lowered her voice. "She's careful, though. Her husband is fabulously wealthy and adores her. If its money, you should look to her daughter, Bria."

I followed Madam's glance. Bria evidently took after her dad. She had none of her mother's beauty. Her pale red hair was braided around her head, and it looked like she had no eyebrows. But, after all, her wealth outshone all her faults, so I strained to find some quality that would overcome her average looks. I gave Madam a wry smile and chased down another glass of champagne.

"Perhaps an older woman is what you need, hon," Madam purred in my ear. I looked at her in alarm, and my look was her answer.

She straightened, fussing with her hair and dress to hide her disappointment. I'd just been propositioned by a woman old enough to be my mother. I'd been old enough to be Celinda's father, but that was different. Or was it? What had I been thinking when I went after Celinda? What was I doing here? How had I got myself into this mess?

The questions whirled through my mind the next morning, as I drove downtown to my office. My lawyer, Hal Buckman, was going to call me. I'd had to let Suzan go, and I wasn't sure how much longer I'd be able to keep the space. I was hanging on to it out of shear stubbornness...and pride.

While I sat in my office waiting for Hal's call, I decided to try Congressman Betts' office again. I'd been calling for over a week, trying to get past his receptionist. Once again, I was put on hold. Someone picked up.

"Darryl, it's Congressman Betts. How you doing, my boy?"

"Congressman, this is Tony Cassera. I've got a..."

"Tony, hang on a second." The Congressman put me on hold. His secretary came on the line and asked if I could call back another time.

"Sure. No problem," I said.

They'd gotten to the Congressman, too. No one would return my phone calls. The Ambassador had hinted that rumors were flying all over Washington about how I was bankrupt, maybe even a convicted felon. I'm sure my lobbying buddies were fueling the rumors in hopes of taking away my clients. That's the way its played in Washington. Anything goes to get what you want. That's the rule in this town, and no one knew the rule better than me.

The phone rang. It was Hal.

"Ya know, Tony, I've been married four times. The last one was a sweetheart who treated me like gold, but she had an ornery streak that caused me a lot of problems. I ended up having to start over from scratch."

I didn't like the way this conversation was starting out.

"What has Celinda done?"

"Well, Tony, she hasn't done anything except overreact. She's upset because the tax man cometh, and she doesn't know what to do except protect her own behind."

"What about mine? I haven't given her any reason to screw me."

"Women don't need no reasons. I jus' got off the phone with Brad. She's high-tailed it out, and left the keys to the station with him."

That figured. No money, no broad. "When did she bail out?"

"Yesterday. I don't think she'll cause ya any more problems. She's got signature power over the accounts in the station, same as you. That makes her liable, same as you."

"Hal, offer the IRS thirty thousand dollars to take the lien off. I'll get the money somehow."

"I've already worked out a payment plan with the IRS for two thousand dollars a month. If you agree to it, they'll remove the lien from you and Celinda. But, you'll have to give up the radio station, Tony. They want it to liquidate the back taxes."

"Damn it, Hal. Is that the best you can do?"

"Hold on a second. You've got yourself in a hell of a tight spot here, buster. I looked over the financials you gave me, and you got no equity. Chapter 11 is out. You give 'em what's left of the station, and that'll pay half the taxes owed to 'em. I can cut a deal to get you and Celinda off personally."

"What about my furniture?"

"As I see it, you got two choices. Give it to Celinda, or the IRS. You're lucky to be gettin' off the way you are."

"She can have the things in Santa Fe, but I'm not giving up my Washington things. I'll sue her for it, if I have to."

"Send me five grand, and we'll make things hot for her."

"You're starting to sound like a Washington lawyer, Hal."

"Hey, Tony, I'm your friend. I'm jus' tryin' to help ya."

"I know. And thanks, Hal."

I hung up, and went downstairs to make arrangements to sub-let my office space. Then I headed to the bank, to wire the money to Hal. There wasn't much left in my account.

Usually I loved the drive home up Rock Creek Parkway, savoring every twist and turn, but today it was different. I looked at the rock-filled creek and the trees arching overhead, but didn't really see them. Trying to peer into my future, I couldn't see that either. Why was this happening to me? What did I do wrong? I didn't deserve this. I turned the radio up to drown out my thoughts, but the song echoed my feelings of frustration.

Play CD Track 6
"Depths of Despair"

My life is flashing past my eyes.
It's hard to see through the tears,
It's hard to realize.
But my friends tried to warn me,
Tell me you're the devil in disguise.

Betrayed by my so-called lover,
How could I know that you were undercover,
That your heart wasn't even in the game,
How I'm I supposed to ease the pain?

You don't care!
What's going on here?
And life ain't fair
In the depths of despair.
I should have seen it coming.
I should have known all along
And now my head is reeling.
How could my heart be so wrong?

You don't care.
What's going on here?

And life ain't fair
In the depths of despair.

I shared my secret thoughts
All my dreams with you.
I gave you everything,
and you played me for the fool.
You think your cunning ways
Are gonna get you free.
We'll, I've got news for you,
That ain't, ain't gonna be, woe, yeah.

You don't care.
What's going on here?
And life ain't fair
In the depths of despair.
Woe, yeah.
In the depths of despair.
Woe, yeah.

It was late afternoon when I finally turned into the drive leading to the mansion. The sun was low in the sky, casting long shadows. I pulled up next to a car I'd never seen out back before. Connecticut plates. There was a sticker on the back bumper, *Expect A Miracle.* I sighed.

So My Lady of Fatima is driving a Toyota Tercel now.

Mornings at the mansion were quiet. The Ambassador was out of town for two weeks. As irritating as it was to stumble over coconuts every time I turned around, I found that the last few days I was missing their hairy little heads. Madam never emerged from her room before noon lately. By sheer luck, I'd signed a contract to provide lobbying for an energy company while the coconut deal simmered. I tormented myself by roaming the house meditating on my past mistakes, and thinking "if only I had..." The leaves were starting to change and the nights were chilly. Madam was extremely protective of her thermostat, and I was seriously wondering if we'd have heat this winter. The breakfast room off the kitchen had a fireplace, and I took to building a fire every morning. Someone once told me about a theory they had, that major upheavals and disasters seem to occur most when the seasons change. The forces in the earth are seething, the energy levels are fluctuating, and we all feel it — maybe not consciously, but we feel it. I was feeling it.

This particular October morning was especially cold, damp and gray. The sun would break through only occasionally, turning the drab leaves a warm, coppery gold. I made myself a scotch and soda and sat in front of the roaring blaze. Its warmth comforted me, for the coldness I felt went deep inside. For the first time in my life, failure gripped my shoulder. I'd seen other people's lives disintegrate countless times, but it was never going to happen to me. I was too smart for that. I'd known men who'd taken their own lives rather than live with defeat. I'd been on the south lawn of the White House when Nixon boarded the Presidential helicopter for the last time, waving his victory sign in the face of personal and political disaster. But it always happened to someone else. I never thought it would happen to me. When I drove through Washington at night and saw the homeless people curled up on grates to stay warm, I was scared out of my wits. My heart pounded in my ears, as I prayed to God that it would never be me lying there. I knew most of them were crazy, but there were days when I thought the stress would push me over the edge. I'd lay awake at night tossing and turning for hours, worrying, frightened about the future.

"It's a lovely fire," she said.

"What?" I said, startled.

"The fire," she said, "it's lovely."

She walked over and knelt before the fire, holding her hands to the flames. She looked vaguely familiar, like I'd seen her before. Her hair was blonde, and when she turned towards me I noticed it curved under her chin like a half moon or a bird wing, framing an exquisitely beautiful face with delicate features. Her eyes were sea green, with a soft, unfocused gaze about them. Across her nose was the tiniest bridge of freckles.

"It's cold downstairs, even wearing a thick sweater," I said.

"I just came from upstairs, and it's cold up there, too," she said.

"This whole house is pretty cold most of the time," I said, apologetically, like it was my fault, which it wasn't.

"It's warm here."

"Yes. It is warm here." I couldn't believe that I couldn't think of anything more interesting to say than that.

She settled herself on the rug in front of the fire. "I just moved in yesterday."

"Are you from Connecticut?"

She seemed surprised. "Why, yes, I am. It must be my accent."

"Actually, I noticed the license plates on your car."

"My car? Oh, yes, of course, my car."

"Which room do you have?"

"I'm next to Mrs. Jamison. It's a nice room, all paneled in wood, but cold."

"I'm at the other end of the hall. Mine's cold, too. Madam has a thing about the thermostat. If you want to stay on her good side, don't touch it."

"Madam?"

"Mrs. Jamison. That's what we call her behind her back."

"Thanks for the warning about the thermostat. I'll talk to her about it. Well, I've got to finish unpacking." She stood to go. "I'm Rachel."

"Tony." I held onto my drink with both hands.

"Tony," she repeated, and I liked the way she said it. "It's nice to meet you, Tony."

I spent the afternoon in business meetings, but my mind kept returning to the pretty woman now living at the other end of the hall from me. As I was leaving the office, I received a handwritten fax from the Ambassador. It had only one word scrawled across the page, *Tapa'u,* and a drawing of a coconut.

As soon as I got home that night, I borrowed the huge Rand McNally Atlas from Madam's library. At the top of the stairs, I paused and glanced down the hall. I could see the blue glow emanating from under "Big" Ed's door. Rachel's door was ajar, and light spilled out across the hallway. In my head, I told myself to go to my room; but my heart said just stop by and say "hello." Head and heart. Heart and head. I stood rooted to the floor at the top of the stairs while the voices flew back and forth.

"She probably won't like me," my head said.

"It won't hurt to just see how she's doing," said my heart.

"Women are nothing but trouble. Go to your room and shut the door," said my head.

"Maybe she's lonely. She'd probably appreciate my company," my heart replied.

"You're broke. Women like men with money," my head fought back.

"I'll only stay for a couple of minutes. What harm can that do?" my heart said hopefully.

"Forget it. Why open yourself up to getting hurt again?" said my head.

"She seems nice, though," my heart said.

"What's with all this 'nice' talk? You just want to get her into bed," my head said.

I knocked on her door.

"Rachel, it's Tony."

"Tony, hi. Come on in." She'd piled her hair on top of her head, and she was busy putting books away on a bookshelf. Stacks of books were everywhere, including the room's only chair. She moved things to one end of the bed and patted the mattress for me to sit.

"I'm glad you came by. No one's been around all day."

My heart spoke to my head. "*See, I told you so.*"

"It looks like you like to read," I began.

"They're mostly reference books for my job."

"What do you do?"

"I've just completed my one year internship at a drug and alcohol abuse center in Connecticut. I lived there and worked with the counseling staff as part of my training to be a psychologist. I've accepted a position with the Westwood Psychiatric Institute, here in Washington, as a staff psychologist." She pointed to the atlas I had set on the bed. "It looks like you like to read, too."

"It's just an atlas. Ever heard of this place?" I showed her the fax the Ambassador had sent me.

"No. Let's see if we can find it." She sat on the bed next to me, her leg up against the length of my thigh, and started going through the index. I watched her profile and the way a lock of her hair had fallen down next to her ear. She wore no make-up I noticed.

"Here it is. Page 216." Page 216 was primarily blue Pacific Ocean with a few brownish, greenish dots on it. Rachel seemed disappointed. "There's nothing there."

"Oh, yes, there is. Coconuts."

"Oh, are you the one who has a coconut collection?" I could tell by the way she looked at me that she was trying to figure out what childhood aberration would surface in an adult as coconut collecting. She'd obviously been talking to someone in the house.

"The coconuts are a joke between a friend and me. Do you have a magnifying glass?"

"Yes, I do. I'll see if I can find it." I watched her as she bent over a box and rummaged through it. I liked the way her jeans fit. "Here it is." She stood and turned quickly, and I pretended to be studying the map.

"You should look more into a woman's heart," she said as she handed me the magnifier.

I blushed, knowing she'd caught me staring at her.

I held the magnifier over the page and focused all my attention on the map. The island of Tapa'u was located between Fiji and Samoa. It appeared that the Ambassador had found our host country in the middle of the South Pacific, on a little hunk of rock.

"Have you ever been married?" I asked casually, as I peered through the magnifying glass at the open atlas.

"I was once, a long time ago. I have two children, a boy and a girl. They're off on their own now."

I looked at her. "You don't look that old." She blushed, and I could have kicked myself.

"I'm older than I look," she said. "What about you?"

I told her a little about me, though not much, because I didn't want her to know about Celinda, or my business failure. I wanted this woman to like me, so I talked in generalities — about graduating from law school, my work in Washington, being captain of the football team in high school — all the good stuff.

"So you've never been married, or had any children?" she said.

"No," I lied. "Listen, would it be okay if I borrowed your magnifying glass?"

"Sure, go ahead."

I hurriedly said good-night before she asked me any more questions, and left her to her unpacking.

Rachel stared at the door after he left, then went over and shut it. He certainly liked to talk about himself. She sighed. Everyone here seemed about as deep as a rain puddle; or, rather, they'd only let you go into their puddle a little ways and then splash water in your face, so you wouldn't find out their secrets. She'd bet money that Tony had been married, and she was pretty sure he was financially floundering, if not floundering in other ways, too. Rachel knew why she was where she was; and she knew, too, that Tony had no idea why he was where he was.

As I lugged the atlas down the hall, the dialogue began again.

"I think she liked you," my heart said brightly.

"Wait 'til she finds out the truth," my head said, knowingly. I crawled into bed with the atlas.

I stared through the magnifying glass at the little brown speck in an ocean of azure blue. The waves were lapping at the sides of my yacht as I lay anchored in the bay at Tapa'u. On the sandy shore were the lush groves of coconut trees responsible for my success. My phone and fax were within arm's reach, as the creaking and rocking of my boat on the waves lulled me into the best sleep I'd had in weeks.

Madam emerged from her cocoon two days later. When I drove up to the mansion, I knew something big was afoot. The Reverend's big old black Cadillac was parked out front. A florist was delivering huge bouquets of flowers, and as I entered the front door, Madam supervised their placement with the authority of a movie director. She was followed by a pimply-faced delivery boy and kept making him shift the bouquets two inches this way, then two inches that way.

"No, no, no, hon, not there." The boy shifted the bouquet back to where it was when I entered the front hall. "Yes, that's perfect, hon." She threw the delivery boy a dazzling smile that made him feel like the world's best flower arranger. A huge tip from the Reverend surprised me, and the young man floated on air out to his delivery van.

"Tony, you are coming to my party tonight?" Madam said, as she fluffed the flowers and pulled off a perfectly healthy leaf.

"I didn't know..."

"Nonsense, hon, you have a standing invitation. Reverend Mike, tell Tony how wonderful it's going to be. The Countess is coming," she added, before the Reverend could answer. "I know she has some business she wants to discuss with you."

"You should come." Reverend Mike spoke with great conviction in a deep, theatrical voice. Listening to him was like riding a roller coaster. Up at the beginning of the sentence, down in the middle, then finishing on the up with an "Amen" tacked on at the end. I'd like to hear him order breakfast in a restaurant. "The banquet is being prepared by Latins from my congregation who have a catering business. The most beautiful women from South America will be here tonight."

"They're contestants in a beauty pageant," Madam interjected, "and the reception will introduce them to the diplomatic community here in Washington." She looked at me knowingly. Contacts were money in

Washington, and I'd like to add a few new ones to my list.

Damn, I'd almost forgotten, I'd invited Rachel out for the evening. The thought of Latin women after Celinda made me feel a little uneasy, but I really wanted to see the Countess again. I told them I'd consider it, and escaped upstairs during the confusion created by the arrival of the rental chairs.

I stood in front of Rachel's door and looked at my watch. I knocked right on time.

"Come on in, Tony. I'm almost ready."

She looked stunning, in a glowing, soft peach sweater and skirt. The sweater was a lacy one and exactly matched the pleated skirt. In her hands were the two ends of a necklace. Looking over her shoulder, I saw that the bed was covered with all the outfits she'd been trying on. The smile disappeared from her face when she looked at my expression.

"It's no good? The skirt's too long. It's not in style?"

"What?"

"What I'm wearing. It's no good?"

"Oh, no. I'm just used to seeing you in blue jeans with your hair all up. You look beautiful."

She relaxed visibly. "It was the look on your face."

I reassured her. "You look gorgeous. Maybe I should go change?" I turned, as if to leave.

"No. You look handsome, very handsome."

I puffed out my chest a little bit at that, and she smiled. I could see how pretty and straight her teeth were, except for one on the side that poked out a little bit, but it was that tooth which made her smile so appealing.

"Do you want some help?" I said. She looked around behind her at the clothes piled on the bed. "With your necklace."

"Please."

I took the necklace from her hands. It was an unusual design in gold and pearls with a pink, faceted crystal pendant.

"What kind of stone is that?" I asked, pointing to the pendant.

"I'm not sure. Some kind of pink crystal. It's quite old, and has been in my family for a long time."

I lowered the necklace over her head, and she raised her hair so that I could clasp it for her. The nape of her neck had a little "V" of golden, downy hairs on it. Her perfume was sweet and delicate, like the scent of a pale pink rose in full bloom.

She lowered her hair and fluffed it. "What about this coat?"

"It's perfect. That coat is perfect."

"You're teasing me now," she said, laughing.

I'd almost forgotten. I reached into my pocket and pulled out her magnifier. "Here. Thanks for letting me borrow it."

When she took it from me, her hand brushed against mine, sending a tingle through my whole body. I helped her on with her coat and rested my hands lightly on her shoulders.

"Rachel, would you mind if we stopped in briefly at the party? There's someone I need to talk to. It's business."

"We won't stay long though, will we?"

I assured her we wouldn't.

The party was in full swing as we made our way down the staircase. Guests were pouring in the front door, and Madam, with Reverend Mike in tow, flitted from one group to the next. It was not hard to spot Countess von Kemmler in her vibrant, coral dress and diamonds. Rachel and I made our way through the party of admirers surrounding her.

"Mister Cassera, how good to see you again." She extended a graceful hand, more for me to kiss than to shake. I bowed low over it, my lips brushing the back of her hand. She slipped me her card. "Please call me at your earliest convenience, Mister Cassera." I assured her I would, bowed again and turned to introduce Rachel, but she wasn't there.

I found her standing by herself against the wall by the staircase. "What are you doing over here? I wanted to introduce you to the Countess."

"That woman's a countess?"

"Of course she's a countess. What's the matter?" I said, irritably. "Do you want to meet her, or not?"

"No. That's okay. Can we go now?"

"Sure."

We made our way to the front entrance. Rachel and I arrived at the front door at the same time as one of the beauty contestants and, for a brief moment, I regretted having to miss the party. Miss Ecuador had been poured into the tightest, lowest-cut dress I had ever seen, and literally had to wiggle in tiny steps to walk at all. I sensed Rachel hesitate so I put my hand lightly around her waist to let her know she had my full attention. Women can be so jealous sometimes.

"Do you like to dance?" I asked her.

"I love to dance, but it seems like I haven't danced in a hundred years."

"We'll go dancing then."

I took her to a small local nightclub that I'd just discovered. It was dark, with the lights catching on the mirrored facets on the walls and light fixtures. It was louder than I had remembered, so I found a nice table tucked away in a corner. I ordered a scotch on the rocks, and Rachel ordered water. When I asked her again if she'd like a drink, she demurred.

"I don't ever drink," she said, firmly.

"Is it because..?" I started, then stopped.

"My father drank," she said.

I thought of my mom, and felt a hollow sadness creep inside me. I pushed the feeling down and smothered it with a sentence.

"Is that why you want to work with alcoholics?"

"It probably has something to do with it. I like helping people."

"I bet you're a good therapist."

"I really hope so. I do the best I can. Tell me about the countess."

"The way you say it, it sounds as if you don't think she is a countess."

"I didn't say that. Just tell me about her."

"The Countess von Kemmler and her partner, Lyle Westerley, own a casino in the Bahamas. They're thinking of opening a casino in Maryland, and want to me to lobby for them to get the license approved by the Governor."

"What does it mean when you say 'lobby?'"

I launched into an explanation. "A lobbyist works with elected officials to help them understand an issue that you're advocating, so a particular provision can be written into a piece of legislation. Some people call it influencing legislation, or reaching into the pork barrel. Lobbyists call themselves 'communication facilitators.' My dad calls it '*chicharrones*,' fried pork rinds. I call it 'contacts and contracts.' You see, it all boils down to who you know in this town."

Rachel stared blankly at me. "Can you really make a living doing this 'lobbying'?" she asked. "It sounds so intangible, Tony. How can someone know if you're doing it?"

"Well...sure you can. For example, I just signed a contract with an energy company called Alternative Energies, Incorporated, to lobby for them. They're a small company, and they want to go after government contracts. Most of the contracts right now go to the big Fortune 500 corporations, and most of the regulations favor the big guys, so Stan Owens at Alternative Energies has hired me to go in and get the regulations amended to allow a greater share of the contracts to go to small companies, specifically his company."

"But how can one person do that?"

"Through their contacts. It's who you know and how you work it. While in the White House, I had a special assignment of tracking legislation dealing with Federal government reorganizations. That's when I started really getting to know people in Washington. The Government Operations Committees and Subcommittees of the House and Senate were monitored frequently, so I spent a lot of time on the Hill, presenting Administration-sponsored bills, or changes to Congressional versions of bills before Congress. One piece of legislation I worked on involved a complete overhaul of the nation's energy programs, and I served as a special consultant to implement the provisions contained in the legislation. After leaving the government, corporations started approaching me to lobby for them, to help them get through the maze of the bureaucracy to get contracts. That's what I do."

"It certainly sounds complicated, Tony, and impressive. I wouldn't know where to begin if someone asked me to do that."

She sounded so sincere and genuine when she spoke to me, something I'd never felt about anyone else. I looked into her eyes in the candlelight, marveling at the pale green clarity of them. It was bullshit. Everything I'd said to her was bullshit, and I felt guilty doing it to her. I'd been talking the talk so long, I'd started to believe it myself. I felt something inside me start to crumble, but I couldn't let that happen. If I did, who would I be? Believing my own bullshit was my protection, my armor.

"Let's dance."

I took her by the hand and led her to the dance floor. She wasn't a good dancer, but it didn't really matter if she could dance well or not. Being with her gave me such a feeling of peace, whereas dancing with Celinda was always like doing the rhumba with an active volcano. When the slow dances came, she'd curl up into me and let me hold her in a close, protective embrace. I loved holding her close. It had never felt this good before.

Our evening ended abruptly, when some Fred Astaire wanna-be landed with all his weight on my foot while I was teaching Rachel one of the new dances. I was in so much pain that she offered to drive us home. If I'd known what a poor driver she was, I would have never agreed. She confessed to just having learned how to drive.

There were very few cars in front of the mansion when we pulled up, and it wasn't even midnight. The guests seemed to have departed rather early, which was unusual for one of Madam's parties. I limped across the marble floor and up the stairs, with Rachel by my side. We'd made it halfway up, when I heard Madam's raised voice coming down the hallway.

"Faster, Rachel." She shouldered more of my weight as we hurried up the stairs. Out of breath, we slid behind the arches on the landing, as Madam entered the front hall, Reverend Mike right behind her.

"I'll never trust those Latins again," Madam said. "They've got a lot of nerve, embarrassing me, making promises, and then breaking them. They ruined my party."

The Reverend's deep voice attempted to soothe her. "Ellen, that was never their intention. You're thinking uncharitable and un-Christian thoughts again."

"Reverend, I am a God-fearing, Christian woman, and you know it. Courtesy and good manners have nothing to do with religion. I don't know if I'll donate to your building fund, after all."

Madam started up the stairs. I hobbled as fast as I could to my room, leaning on Rachel. Madam was almost to the landing, and Reverend Mike was still with her. He wasn't about to lose a donation for his Church. His Cadillac needed a new set of tires.

"Ellen, you're blowing this out of proportion. I'm sure there's an explanation. The food was excellent, like I told you it would be."

"It was an hour late, Reverend! Those goddamn caterers!"

"Ellen, you're swearing."

They reached the landing just as Rachel and I entered my room and closed the door. I was out of breath, and my foot throbbed. I hoped my toe wasn't broken.

"That was close. What are you doing, Rachel?"

"Trying to find the lock."

"None of the doors have locks in this house. Sssh."

They were in the hall now. Reverend Mike pleaded with her. "Ellen, calm down. We'll get the investors."

"Stuff it, Reverend." With that, we heard Madam slam the door to her room and lock it. So Madam had a lock on *her* door. It was quiet for a minute, then we heard the Reverend's heavy footsteps descending the stairs.

I hopped over to the bed and turned on the light. Rachel massaged my foot for a few minutes.

"That feels great. Thanks. Sorry to ruin the evening for you."

"You didn't ruin it. Actually, it was fun. Is she always like that?"

"Madam can be very nice, but she has her days. Lately, it seems like she's been having more of them."

"I've got to go, Tony. I want to get up early and call the director at the clinic about the start date for my job."

"Do you have to go?" I hinted.

"Yes. You'll be fine." She gave me a gentle kiss on the cheek, so pure and innocent that I felt like a heel for thinking what I'd been thinking.

I walked down the stairs to the kitchen with barely a limp. Peter was eating at the table.

"So, Peter, what happened last night at the party?"

Peter ran his hands through his thick hair and started to laugh. "The Latins who were bringing the food were supposed to be at the mansion at eight o'clock, and they showed up at nine."

"Oh, no. Madam..?"

"Threw an enormous temper tantrum, screaming and yelling to the high heavens. You should have seen it. There was a traffic jam in front of the mansion, as everyone tried to leave at once. Beauty contestants were crying." He sighed contentedly. "The food was fantastic. These people were professional caterers, you know. I've filled the refrigerator with it. Help yourself."

I smiled to myself. Madam just didn't know that when you tell Latins, even caterers, that a party starts at a certain time, they always show up late. She should have asked me. I could have told her that.

After work the next day, I came home and put in a call to the Countess, but her secretary said she was out and wouldn't be back until late. My curiosity about what she had in mind would have to wait. I turned my thoughts to Rachel, her inviting smile, and her pale, sea green eyes. There was something different about her. She was unlike any woman I'd ever known, and it left me feeling uncertain. Her door was slightly open, so I knocked softly. There was silence, and then her muffled reply.

"Yes?"

"It's Tony."

Another hesitation. "Come in."

Rachel was sitting on the floor with her legs crossed Indian style. It was obvious by her eyes that she'd been crying.

"Rachel, what's wrong?"

"I d-don't have a job," she sobbed. "I don't know what I'm going to do. I don't have very much m-money." She was very agitated and kept twisting a Kleenex in her hands, shredding it.

"What happened to the position you'd accepted at the Institute?"

"It's g-gone. They're downsizing, whatever that means, and there's n-nothing for me. I c-came all this way..."

"You'll find something else. There are lots of jobs in Washington," I said. "You'll be fine. I'll check on you later."

She nodded at me. I was halfway down the hall to my room when the voices started.

"You can't leave her sitting there, crying all by herself," my heart said.

"I don't want to get involved," my head said.

"You just want to fuck her," my heart sneered.

"I'm not so sure," my head said.

"What?" my heart answered, surprised.

"She doesn't know anyone in this town," my head reminded me.

"I've got my own problems," my heart said.

"You can't just walk away from her," my head pleaded.

I walked back and stared at the door. What was this woman doing to me? I always minded my own business and didn't get involved. Other people's problems were their problems. I knocked on Rachel's door and went in. She was still sitting on the floor, surrounded by little mounds of shredded Kleenex. I sat down next to her.

"Rachel, maybe you could work at the company I lobby for. It wouldn't be anything great, probably secretarial, but at least it would be something until you found another position."

"Oh, T-Tony, thank you. That would be w-wonderful." She'd stopped crying, but she had the hiccups now.

I patted her knee awkwardly. "Don't thank me yet."

"T-Thank y-you." She hiccupped and laughed.

"Don't worry. We've got to cheer you up. Let's go dancing."

She sighed and hiccupped again. "I'd l-like that. But...your f-foot."

"It's good as new. See?" I stood up and did a little shuffle. "I don't know what you did, but it worked." My foot wasn't sore at all. She smiled up at me as I did my little jig, and I felt like I was ten years old again and walking on top of a brick wall at school to impress Maria Sanchez, the prettiest girl in my class.

The dance floor wasn't crowded, which was fortunate, because Rachel used up a lot of space when she danced. Her arms were everywhere, and she was always two or three beats behind the music. She swooped up and down as if she were waltzing, but she was smiling, and it made me feel good to see her happy. That was a another new feeling for me. Usually I feel happy if I'm happy, not if someone else is. Such a glow radiated from her face that I felt a little tug at my heart.

When we returned to the mansion, the Reverend's Cadillac sat ominously out front. I parked around back and headed for the garden room.

"Where are we going?" Rachel whispered loudly.

"I'm showing you the secret entrance. Madam doesn't know we come in and out this way to avoid her."

"Why do you call her Madam?"

"I'm not sure. We just do. Not to her face, though." I couldn't tell Rachel that a Madam was a woman who ran a brothel. I opened the door. The garden room was in total darkness, but we could smell wet earth in the cold, moist air that blew into our faces. There was a layer of palms two deep around the perimeter, and the path through them required ducking to miss the palm fronds. I took Rachel's hand and pulled her in behind me. I crouched low. She did the same. We wended our way between the two rows of trees and came out close to the door into the back hall.

"Hey, watch it," someone called out. I was startled. Rachel gasped and gripped my hand more tightly.

"Peter, is that you?"

"Tony?"

"Yeah, it's me. Sorry."

Gently, I pulled Rachel past two dark forms. One was Kennedy-hair Peter, and the other was wearing a very nice perfume. Rachel and I scurried up the stairs. At the end of the hall, Madam's door was closed, but we could see a crack of light underneath. The two of us stood in shadow on the landing, listening, waiting for any signs of movement. A good two minutes passed before we felt confident enough to take off our shoes and creep cautiously towards Rachel's room.

A door slammed somewhere downstairs, and we both jumped, staring in terror at Madam's door. I decided I wasn't going to wait to see if it opened. I put the palm of my hand on the small of Rachel's back and propelled her to her door as fast as I could. Seconds later we were safe in her room, smothering our laughter with our hands. I helped her off with her coat, and she went over and turned on the small lamp next to her bed. Since Rachel's room was right next to Madams', we spoke as quietly as possible.

"I really had fun, Tony. Thank you."

"Me, too." And I really meant it for the first time in a long time. Being with her *was* fun.

"You want a hug?" she asked.

Without thinking, I nodded my head. I closed my eyes, and I felt her arms going around me. I rested my cheek against her hair and put my arms around her. I could smell her and feel her heart beating and my heart beating, and I would have sworn they started beating together. I felt safe for the first time in a very long time.

"You're loved," Rachel whispered.

I opened my eyes with a start. Her words confused me, and I felt my heart close up like a fist. I took a deep breath and let the air out of my lungs as I ran my hand lightly across her cheek. She turned her face and kissed my fingers.

"I should go," I whispered in her ear. "Madam."

I felt her nod. I kissed her on the forehead, telling her I'd check about a job for her tomorrow. I opened the door quietly and peered out. The hall was deserted. I let myself out, and as I eased the door closed, I heard a tiny hiccup.

When I entered the kitchen the next morning, Rachel was already there getting herself some coffee. Dr. Delbert was there, too, eating breakfast, a Velveeta cheese omelette. Rachel and I looked at each other without expression or emotion, as if we barely knew each other.

"Hey, Tony, what've you been up to? Haven't seen you in a while." Delbert turned the pages of the newspaper, flattening them against the table with his palm.

"I've started lobbying for an energy company. What about you?" I looked over his head at Rachel, who gave me a secretive smile.

"The usual. A little of this. A little of that. I've got a conference in New York the end of the week." I didn't believe him. Ten to one, the end of the week would find him sitting here reading the morning paper.

"Really. Well, if I don't see you before then, have a great trip." I went over to the refrigerator and pulled out an apple to eat on the way. I stepped close enough to Rachel to smell her sweet fragrance. "I'll see you two later," I said as I left the kitchen.

There was frost on the ground as I headed across the lawn to the driveway. Winter was coming, and I was no closer to having my financial affairs resolved than I had been a month ago. Every time I thought about Celinda or said her name out loud, my stomach grew nauseous. My finances were still a shambles, and my credit card balances were getting higher and higher. Fortunately, I'd gotten the lobbying job, and I consoled myself with the fact that I had the Countess and the coconuts on the back burners.

As soon as I arrived at work, I talked to Stan Owens, the owner of the energy company I was lobbying for, about a position for Rachel. He said he just might have something. His secretary was going on maternity leave next week, and he would need someone to answer the phones.

On the way home, I stopped at a florist and picked up a bunch of white daisies with cheery yellow centers. I ran up the front steps to the mansion, but came to an abrupt halt when I saw Madam standing dead center in the front hall, hands on her hips. I hid the daisies behind my back, managing to slip them under my suit coat and shove them into the waistband of my slacks. With both hands free, I felt ready to do battle with the dragon lady.

"Someone's been in my room," she said, pacing back and forth across the front hall.

"Really?" I tried to sound interested. None of us wanted to go within twenty yards of her room.

"None of you care about how I feel. You just want my money."

Oh, brother. She was turning neurotic on me. "That's not true," I said soothingly.

"It's gone. Maggie's gone."

"Who?"

"Maggie. My daughter. Her picture. It's always on my dresser. It's not there. I don't know what she'll think when she sees it's gone. Somebody stole it from me."

"Now Mrs. Jamison, I don't think anyone would..."

"I've got to find it," she said absentmindedly. She stopped pacing and walked over to look at her mail, which was always left for her on the front hall table. I waited, but she seemed to have forgotten I was there, so I headed for the stairs.

I reached the landing and turned right as if I were heading for my room. Once past the archway, I flattened myself against the far wall to keep Madam from seeing me from the front hall and headed towards Rachel's room. I knocked softly and entered. Rachel sat in a chair by the window, reading, a cup of coffee on the windowsill. Outside, the late afternoon sun slanted in, creating a faint halo of light around her. I pulled the crushed daisies from under my suit coat and handed them to her.

"Hello, gorgeous."

"Oh, they're beautiful. I adore daisies. Thank you." She rose and went into the adjoining bathroom to fill a glass with water. I sat on the edge of the bed and talked to her, while she snipped their stems and placed each one carefully in the glass.

"I got you a job."

She whirled around. "Oh, Tony, thank you."

"It's not much, just answering phones, and Stan said he could only pay ten dollars an hour."

"But, Tony, that's okay. At least I'll be working." She took a deep breath. "When do I start?"

"Next Monday."

"Thank you for remembering to ask for me," she said shyly.

"We'll have to celebrate."

Her eyes sparkled like sunlight on an ocean wave as she came over and hugged me.

"I'll take you someplace special," I whispered.

"Why are you whispering?"

I cautioned her to be quiet. Someone was walking down the hall, heading this way. The footsteps paused outside the door. I held my breath and didn't move. The footsteps resumed, and we heard Madam's door open and shut.

"She scares me, Rachel. I'm not sure she's mentally all there."

"She's harmless, Tony, just a little kooky."

"I resent having to sneak around in a house I'm paying money to live in."

"Things are hard for her right now. I hear her sometimes, on the phone..."

"Let's not talk about her," I whispered. "Do you want me to come visit tonight?"

Rachel smiled shyly. "Of course I do."

Rachel couldn't believe he'd actually asked about the job for her. She knew it was the first time in a long time he'd thought about someone besides himself, and she was terribly pleased for him.

I was relieved when I closed the door to my room behind me. There was a coconut resting in the middle of the bed, its two brown "eyes" staring at me. The Ambassador was back! I went out and knocked on his door, but there was no answer. Peeking in, I saw his suitcase sitting on the floor next to the bed. It looked like he'd run in and out. My phone was ringing when I went back to my room.

"Mister Cassera?"

"Yes."

"I have the Countess on the line for you."

I heard a click, and then the Countess' voice with its slight accent. "Mister Cassera? This is the Countess von Kemmler."

"You can call me Tony, Countess."

"Tony. Would Tuesday afternoon around 4 p.m. at the Prime Rib suit you?"

"Tuesday at four o'clock is fine, Countess. I'll be there."

"I look forward to seeing you again. Good-bye, Mister Cassera."

Things were definitely looking up. They had to. I was living way beyond my means. Waking up in the middle of the night in a cold sweat was getting on my nerves.

I waited until around ten o'clock before heading to Rachel's room, but as I started down the hall, Peter came out of his room. I walked downstairs with him, pretending to be on my way to the kitchen. He left the mansion, and I bolted upstairs again. This was ridiculous, I said to myself. It reminded me of Julie, my high school sweetheart, and me sneaking away to make out in the peach orchard. I didn't want to take the chance of rousing Madam with a knock, so I turned the doorknob on Rachel's door and let myself in.

She was sitting on her bed, an afghan wrapped around her, reading. The only light on was next to the bed. She reached over and turned it off. I lay down on the bed next to her, burying my face in her silky hair. Neither of us made a sound. Her fingers stroked my hair, and with every gesture I felt my body relax and melt into her. Her touch was magic, stroking me, removing every doubt, every fear, restoring and healing me with every caress. We were lying there quietly when we heard Madam's voice.

"You lied to me."

I tensed. It seemed like she was in the room with us. Rachel pointed silently in the direction of the wall she shared in common with Madam. The words were muffled, but we could hear what was being said.

"I trusted you," Madam went on. "Please give it back. You promised me millions." She was pleading hysterically. "I need it back. Please give it back." She was sobbing now with every word. The reply from the person on the other end turned her hysterics into rage. "He'll be sorry," she shouted. "I'll get that bastard. He can't hide from me. My friends will take care of him."

There was a crash as though she threw something against the wall, and we heard whatever it was shatter into pieces. Her door opened and slammed shut. Two minutes later the front door slammed, and we heard her car drive off.

"What the hell is going on?" I said, anxiously.

"I don't know. I can hear her every word, and there's something terribly wrong, but she's gone now. Go to sleep."

The day dawned bright and clear, with a touch of crisp coolness to the air. The autumn leaves were at their peak. As I shaved, I tried to decide where I would take Rachel for the day, to celebrate her new job. She'd hardly seen anything of Washington, so I was overwhelmed with options. I had decided on a walk on the Mall, and renting canoes on the Potomac River, when someone knocked on the door.

"Hey, Cisco."

"Come on in, Ambassador. How'd your trip to New York go?"

"Very well. We signed a big contract."

"That's great."

"Look at this." The Ambassador handed me the front section of the *Washington Post*.

"Ambassador, this paper is three weeks old."

"I know. Look at the caption under the picture."

General and Mrs. Malcolm Rogers are greeted by the President and First Lady at a Tribute Dinner in the General's honor.

"So?"

"That was the night Madam supposedly had the General coming here."

"You're right! You think Madam never had him lined up at all? She was just dangling his name as bait?"

"I'm not sure. I just thought you'd find it interesting, but never mind about that. I've got some great news about coconuts. I met the personal trainer for King Haal'a pua Kami, Monarch of the island of Tapa'u."

"How'd you happen to 'just run into' this personal trainer guy?"

"Believe it or not, I met him in a donut shop. There was some big Polynesian conference in New York. This guy was standing there wearing some kind of skirt and a grass rug, so I asked him if he'd ever heard of Tapa'u. I couldn't get an audience with the king, but I did find out that one of his daughters, Princess Sava, is going to be in Washington in two weeks. I've lined up an audience with her so, that we can present CocoBono."

"Ambassador, I am amazed."

The Ambassador bowed with a courtly flourish.

"What's new with you, Cisco?"

"Well, I've got a meeting with the Countess next Tuesday afternoon about lobbying for the Casino."

"No, I don't mean that. I mean a woman."

"A woman?"

"You look different. I attribute it to a new 'amour' perhaps. A twinkle in the eye and a bounce to the step, sir, do not go unnoticed to my trained eye."

I stared at my feet in response.

"So, I'm right. I question no more, my friend. Your secret remains safe with me." With that, he sauntered off downstairs.

It was a day "fit for the Gods" as my grandfather used to say. Rachel and I headed down Rock Creek Parkway into Washington. She was delighted to see this beautiful creek slicing through such a dense urban area. You could forget the millions of people surrounding you as you made your way down into the city. We walked on the Mall from the Lincoln Memorial to the Capital. I bought her one of those huge pretzels and a Coke. I couldn't believe she'd never had a Coke before. She explained she didn't drink soft drinks very often. In the afternoon, we went to Fletcher's Boathouse on the C & O Canal. I rented a canoe, and we spent hours paddling and floating on the Potomac. We pretended we were sailing around the Caribbean Islands, or floating down the canals of Venice, or along the magnificent Seine. When we were tired of paddling we'd rest and drift, bobbing gently.

"Are you happy, Rachel?"

"Oh, yes," she sighed, "I'm really enjoying this."

"Julie enjoyed it, too," I said, thinking back to another afternoon a long time ago.

"Who's Julie?"

"Julie was my wife. She came to visit me once in Washington." The words were out of my mouth and said, when I realized I'd been caught in my own lie.

"I thought you told me you'd never been married?"

"Once, to my high school sweetheart, but that was a long time ago. It didn't last long, so I just don't count it as being married."

"What happened?"

"We were too young, barely out of high school."

"And you never married again?"

"No. There was someone, but we never married." The specter of Celinda loomed before me and a gray cloud blotted out the sun. "It looks like a storm is coming. Let's head in. I'll take you to dinner at one of my favorite places in Georgetown."

Rachel stared at the sky, puzzled. "There aren't any dark clouds."

I looked up, and she was right. It was blue sky and white, fleecy clouds as far as the eye could see.

"Race you to shore," I said to distract her. I started paddling and she had no choice but to paddle, too. By the time we reached the dock, we were out of breath and laughing, and she'd forgotten what we were talking about.

I looked at her sitting across the table from me at The Guards, marveling at her simple beauty and gentle manner. Being with her, everything seemed brighter. I relaxed and didn't worry like I did most of the time. What was she doing with me? She was good for me, but could I really be good for her?

"I got a call from the Countess," I said. "I'm going to meet with her early next week. By this time Tuesday, I'll probably have a lobbying contract and a trip to the Bahamas lined up, to look over the casino operation there."

Rachel's eyes grew wide. "I've never met anyone like you before. You know so many important people. I met Stevie Wonder once, after a concert — a friend took me backstage. But mostly I know ordinary people. My patients have been ordinary people with extraordinary problems. Of course, I do know Madam, and she's an extraordinary person with extraordinary problems."

"What do you mean? You said she was just a kook."

"No, there's more to her than that. Did you know she had a daughter who died very young, only nine years old?"

"Madam did mention a daughter the other day -- Maggie. But she was talking about her coming to visit. Did she have several daughters?"

"No, she only had one child, and she was beautiful. I've seen her."

"You've seen her photograph? Madam said she'd lost her photograph. She was really upset."

"No. I saw *her*, the child."

I lowered my voice so the other diners wouldn't hear. "But you just said she's dead."

"I know that. Delbert's seen her, too."

"Well, that figures," I said, disgusted.

"He was sober, Tony."

"Are you telling me you saw a ghost?" I spoke a little too loudly. The man at the next table turned and glanced over at us. I warned Rachel with my eyes that someone was listening. "Your sherbet's melting."

"I'll tell you later, on the way home."

It gave me an eerie feeling hearing her tell the story. The hair on my arms stood straight up. There were no street lights on this part of the Parkway, so I couldn't see her face, only her voice coming from the darkness on the passenger's side of the car.

"It happened a week ago. I went down to the kitchen to get some orange juice. It was about three in the morning. Delbert was there, sitting at the counter, eating a sandwich he'd made. I poured my juice and sat down across from him. We were chatting about not much in particular, when I saw the strangest look on his face. He was staring past me, so I turned in time to see this little girl with long blonde hair, wearing Mary Jane shoes, walk by us. She never looked our way, but kept her eyes straight ahead. She walked through the doorway into the dark breakfast room."

"Maybe someone had a child visiting, and she was sleepwalking."

"Her shoes didn't make a sound on the kitchen floor."

"What did Dr. Delbert think?"

"He said she was a 'ghost child.' He also said she wasn't the only one in the house."

"There's another ghost?"

"That's what he says."

She was spooking me, behaving this way.

"If you believe in ghosts, I bet you believe in angels. I suppose you believe in that past lives stuff, too," I said.

"I don't discount anything," Rachel replied quietly.

She was making me uneasy. When people die, they're dead. They can't go walking around. They don't have any bodies, and yet I remembered as a child celebrating the *Día de los Muertos,* the Day of the Dead, in a small Mexican town where my relatives lived. We all walked by candlelight to the local cemetery, where the spirits of the dead were returning to visit living friends and relatives. I remember eating a skull made of candy and laying food on the grave of the old grandfathers.

"Did I scare you, Tony?"

"Naw, not me. It just seems a little hard to believe." She scooted over next to me and laid her head on my shoulder. I rubbed my cheek against her hair. "What perfume do you wear? It smells so good."

She snuggled closer. "I don't wear perfume. I'm allergic to it."

"Then how is it you smell so good?"

"I really don't know."

"Damn."

"What is it?" Rachel said, sitting up.

I gestured irritably towards the car in front of us. "That guy must be going twenty miles an hour, and the guy in the right lane isn't going much faster. They've got us all blocked in here." I put on my left turn signal, waited a moment, then cut in front of the car in the right lane.

"You had your left turn signal on, Tony!"

"I know. You can't let them know what you're going to do. You keep them confused, then you can beat them out. If you put on your right turn signal and change lanes to the right, the guy will speed up and not let you in."

"You could get hit that way," Rachel said.

"I know what I'm doing. This is Washington, and that's the way it plays here."

"It sounds dangerous."

"It's just a game with different rules here."

"The rules are the same everywhere, Tony."

"What do you know about the Washington rules?" I said.

"I'm not talking about the Washington rules, as you call them. I'm talking about life's rules."

"You don't mean that 'what goes around comes around' shit?"

"You're so stubborn," she said, with the first indication of a temper that I'd seen.

When we arrived at the mansion, Rachel went in the front door, and I came in through the side garden door, so Madam wouldn't suspect we were seeing each other. I met Madam coming down the front staircase as I was going up. What rotten luck, I thought angrily. I was still irritated by Rachel's comments. Just like a woman to try and tell you what's right.

"You've been out all day? Rachel was out all day, too," Madam hinted.

"Was she? I have some calls to make."

Madam narrowed her eyes at me. "My prayer meeting is tonight. I think you should come."

"Tonight doesn't look good for me. Business, you know. Proposals to write. Oh, by the way, I'm seeing the Countess on Tuesday." Rachel's words earlier prompted me to add, "Thank you for recommending me."

Madam softened a bit. "I knew you would be the person to help her. I'll look for you tonight." She swept past me, and I almost made it to the landing when I heard her voice again.

"Mr. Cassera, you are leaving dirty coffee cups in the sink. You know the house rules."

"I'm sorry. It won't happen again."

"There was mold floating in the old coffee. That tells me you are leaving your cups in your room. There's no telling what kind of filthy creatures it's attracting."

"I promise. It won't happen again."

The look she gave me told me she didn't believe me.

My door was slightly ajar when I heard a gentle scratching sound. I opened the door and she slipped quietly in.

"Are we still friends?" she asked.

"Sure. Come on in."

"Madam's talking so loudly on the phone, I can't sleep."

There was a knock, and we both tensed. Rachel ran to the bed and hid underneath it.

"Who is it?" I called out.

"It's me, Cisco. Can I come in?"

"Could we talk later, Ambassador? I'm kind of in the middle of something."

"No *problema, compadre*. I'll talk to you in the morning."

"Thanks. See you *manaña*." I heard him walk down the hall and close the door to his room.

"He's gone." I walked over to the bed and looked under it.

"I'm up here." Rachel peered out from under the covers, not six inches from my face.

"How'd you do that?"

She laughed and pulled the covers over her head. I dove under the covers and grabbed her ankle as she headed out the other side and pulled her back in. She shrieked, and I had to kiss her to keep her quiet. She was startled, then smiled at me with her eyes.

I heard her voice like it was inside my head, and it was saying, "I love you, Tony."

Why do women have to go and ruin everything by talking about "love?" I'd had enough of "love" and all the pain and heartache that goes with it.

But I smiled at her, and tapped my finger on her nose. "Go to sleep, sweetheart. You start your job tomorrow." She smiled back at me and fell asleep in my arms.

From downstairs, voices were raised in the opening hymn of the prayer meeting. I thought about the Catholic Church, Our Lady of Mercy, where I attended mass as a boy in Sanibel. I thought about the nuns at school, and felt the waves of guilt and fear I used to feel at catechism. Was I a good man? I wasn't sure. Was I good enough for Rachel? I didn't think so. Besides, how could I take care of her if I couldn't even take care of myself?

A long, sung 'Amen' floated up the stairs, and I said a silent prayer for the first time in a long time. *Dear God, please help me find the money to get out of the mess I'm in. I'm going under fast.*

Rachel was gone when I woke up the next morning. The room wasn't cold like it usually is in the morning. Had Rachel got Madam to turn on the heat? I took a shower, and headed off to the office for a meeting with Stan, and a lobbying lunch at the Capitol. Rachel was already sitting at the receptionist's desk when I walked in. She gave me a sly wink that was merely a dip of her eyelid.

"Good morning, Mr. Cassera. Mr. Owens is waiting for you in the conference room." The phone rang. "Good morning, Alternative Energies. How can I direct your call?"

Stan and I had a brief strategy meeting, and then I went to my office. There was a message on the desk from the Countess von Kemmler. She'd had to postpone our meeting for a week. That was disappointing, because after filling out the bankruptcy, personal assets and liabilities forms for the IRS, I'd discovered that I was in deeper trouble than I thought financially. My liabilities exceeded my assets by five to one. I needed a quick financial fix, and now the countess had put me off for another week.

My phone rang. It was Rachel.

"It's a Hal Buckman from Santa Fe on Line One. Do you want to take it?"

"Yes. Put him through."

There was a click, then I heard Hal's drawl on the other end. "Hiya, Tony. Buckman here."

"Hi, Hal. Did you get the forms I sent you?"

"Sure did. And I gotta tell you, it don' look good, kid."

My heart sank into the pit of my stomach. "You'd better tell me."

"I sure feel bad, givin' it to you with both barrels, but you'd best file for corporate bankruptcy."

"There's no other way?"

"Nope, 'fraid not. You got yourself a pig in a poke, Tony. Wisht I could do better for you, but we're up against the wall here. Should I go ahead and file for you?"

What would Rachel think of me?

"Tony, are you there?"

"Yeah, Hal, I'm here," I sighed. "Okay, go ahead and do what you've got to do."

"I'm real sorry, Tony."

"I know, Hal, and thanks for trying." He hung up, and I sat there for a long time just staring into space, trying to figure out what I had done wrong. It just wasn't fair. I went to the men's room and was violently sick. When I returned to my office, the intercom was buzzing. It was Rachel again.

"It's your friend the Ambassador, Tony."

"Tell him I'm in a meeting, and take a message for me."

"Are you okay?"

"Yeah, I'm fine. I'm just tied up right now."

She called back in a couple of minutes.

"He says your audience with Princess Sava is set for the 24th of November, 3:00 p.m., at her suite in the Mayflower Hotel. That's good news, isn't it?"

"Yes, it's good news. Actually, it's great news. Thanks, Rachel."

I sat there for a while, daydreaming about running my coconut business from a yacht in Mala Bay in the Kingdom of Tapa'u. That cheered me up immensely and distracted me from my problems, though the rest of the week I walked around in a daze, trying to adjust to the twist my life had taken. I'd known filing bankruptcy was a possibility, but I never seriously thought it would come to that. What the hell was I going to do?

Having Rachel in the office made it easier to bear my financial disaster. Stan was real taken with her efficiency, and everyone always seemed in a better mood when she was around. I loved it when she'd call me on the intercom and tell me in her soft voice that I had a call waiting. What she was really telling me was that she couldn't wait to see me tonight. Every evening there would be this scratch on my door, and Rachel would come in and crawl quietly into bed next to me.

After only a few days on the job, Stan was already considering offering Rachel a full-time position. She'd taught herself how to use the computer and was typing letters for everyone. How she learned everything so quickly was unbelievable. One night, Rachel told me how Stan had said she could use the conference room after hours to start a group therapy session. She assured me it would only be on Tuesday and Thursday nights that she'd be coming to my room late. I was pleased for her when I saw how much it meant to her, but I was envious, too. Her life seemed to be falling into place with such ease, and I was still floundering. Of course, the kind of deals I do take time to develop, I kept telling myself.

With great anticipation, I left the office early the following Tuesday to meet the countess at The Prime Rib. I was wearing a new suit and tie that I'd charged. I barely had enough money to pay the shoeshine boy, because my wallet was filled with plastic. There was no way I was going to touch my bank account. I needed that money for my lawyer. I hadn't been to The Prime Rib since I moved to Santa Fe, and it brought back a lot of memories when I saw the black walls, hung with black and white artwork. The people provided the color here; the restaurant, the backdrop. I noticed many familiar faces that afternoon, congressmen and people I'd lobbied for over my years in Washington. Even some people from my days on the White House staff. The maitre d' seated me, and I ordered a drink.

The countess was a fashionable fifteen minutes late, and I rose for her as she approached the table. She was wearing a stylish European suit in a brilliant tangerine orange. As one of the few women in the restaurant, she created quite a sensation, because most women in Washington wear black, gray or brown box-cut suits. Besides, she was gorgeous. Doing what I thought was a good imitation of a European bow, I bent over to kiss her hand. Glancing sideways, I noticed everyone was still staring at us. I pulled out the huge leather wing chair for her and seated myself opposite. She had my full and undivided attention. I was calculating in my head how much I would charge for lobbying for her and Lyle Westerley. We ordered lunch, and exchanged pleasantries over our Caesar salads. It wasn't until our main course arrived that she got down to business, but not before gazing in astonishment at the inch-thick piece of prime rib that was larger than the plate.

"Mister Cassera..."

"Tony, Countess."

"Tony. I am so grateful to Ellen Parker Jamison for recommending you."

"I won't disappoint you and Mr. Westerley. It will be difficult getting the operator's permit, but I think with my contacts, getting to the governor's office can be accomplished."

"Excuse me, Mister Cassera — Tony, I mean. I believe there has been some mistake. Didn't Ellen tell you?"

I lowered my fork. "Tell me?"

"Oh dear. I can see she did not. I'm moving."

I still didn't get it. "You're moving to the Bahamas?"

"What are you talking about, Mister Cassera?"

"I thought you and Lyle Westerley wanted me to do some lobbying for you for the casino he wants to build in Maryland."

"Casino?"

"The other night at Ellen Jamison's party, you and Lyle mentioned..."

"Oh, that casino. No, no, he's changed his mind. He wants to buy one of those little islands, I think in the Caribbean, and build it there. I need help moving. Ellen thought you'd be willing to help me. I don't have a car, you see." She gestured helplessly.

"Oh yes, of course, helping you move. I remember now," I lied.

The countess looked relieved. "Oh, thank you. I've been so worried, and then when it seemed you did not know what I was talking about, well, I...."

"I'll be happy to help you move," I said cheerfully, but I was secretly making plans to strangle Madam when I got home. "When do you want to do it?"

"I thought now, after we've finished eating. It won't take long."

I looked down at my half-eaten meal and realized who was paying for lunch. Me. I thought I was going to be sick when I had to pull out my credit card.

We picked up my car from the valet, and I asked the Countess to tip him, explaining I only had a hundred-dollar bill in my wallet. We drove the few blocks to her building. All the way up to the eleventh floor in the elevator, I was cursing my luck. She had a few packed cardboard boxes, two armloads of clothes on hangers, and four suitcases. She carried her overnight case. I handed her my suit coat, tie and cufflinks, and lugged everything down to the lobby. The doorman held the door for me while I loaded the stuff into my car. The countess came out last with her case, tipped the doorman, put on her sunglasses and stood next to the car door, waiting for me to open it. Once she was comfortable, she began directing me through the streets of Washington.

We ended up in front of a rundown building in the northwest part of town, by the National Cathedral. There was no elevator, so I carried everything up two flights of stairs. It was a hole of a place. I stood in the center of the living room with her stuff not sure what to do next.

"Where's your bedroom, Countess?"

"You can leave it here in the living room, Tony. My friend has the bedroom." So the countess was going to be bedding down on the couch. "It is so expensive staying in hotels, and I won't be going back to my house in Salzburg for another two months."

I pretended to believe the lie. "That must be rough. Listen, I've got to be going."

"You won't stay? Even for just a little while?"

I ignored the invitation. "Gotta run. Dinner with friends. You know."

"Ah, yes, I know. Perhaps..."

"So long, Countess, and good luck." I fled out the door and ran down the stairs to my car.

When I pulled up to the mansion, it was the time of day called the gloaming, the time between twilight and dusk when nothing seems to have substance, and all is merely shadows of the day past. I parked and turned off the ignition. How could I have been such a fool? I stared down at my hands. They were strong, broad hands, and I thought about all the footballs they'd carried across the goal line in high school.

Victory and success were so simple and sweet, then.

"Tony?" Rachel tapped hard on the car window. "What are you doing sitting out here? I've been waiting for you to come home."

"Just thinking."

She tried the door, but it was locked, so she ran around the car, opened the passenger door, and got in.

"What happened?" she said.

I looked down at my disheveled clothing. "I stopped to help a guy change a flat tire on the Parkway." I couldn't tell her the truth. It was too embarrassing.

"You're such a wonderful man." I cringed when she said that. "So, tell me all about it. How was your meeting with the countess?"

"It was fine. It went well. There's still some things to be ironed out, though."

"Oh, I see. Too soon for the contract yet, I guess. Well, don't worry, I'm sure it will all work out. Tony, you've got to come with me. Right now."

"What's wrong?"

She didn't answer. Instead, she pulled me out of the car and around the back of the mansion. The door to the lower room was open, and she dragged me in. In the fading light, the room looked more grotesque than usual. The sofas seemed bigger and more ominous, the pillows more garish and sinister as they lounged seductively in the corners of the sofas. The dancing statues from India with all the arms looked like they'd grown at least six inches in height. The room was cold, too, colder than outside. I was definitely not in the mood for this.

"Rachel..."

"Do you see anything?" she whispered fiercely in my ear.

"I see one hell of an ugly room."

"No. I mean, do you see *anyone*?"

"Aw, Rachel...."

She nudged me in the ribs. I looked. The light was failing, but, no, there was no one there.

"I saw someone, Tony. Something. I saw him walking. There." She pointed to the space between the far couch and the window.

"I don't see anyone," I said, but the hair was rising on the back of my neck. As a matter of fact, the back of my neck felt prickly, like someone was breathing on it.

We moved cautiously forward until we stood behind the closest sofa. There was a swift movement behind us, and the whole room was suddenly awash in a riotous blaze of bordello reds and golds. Rachel screamed, and I clutched her to me as we whirled to face the unknown.

Dr. Delbert stood in the doorway, with his hand on the light switch.

"What are you two doing?" He took one look at our faces. "So you saw him."

With that, he turned and headed up the stairs to the kitchen. He was never happier than when he was making a sandwich, but this hardly seemed the time. I followed him to the refrigerator.

"Wait a minute." I said. "Saw who?" I looked over at Rachel. Her eyes were clear and bright as she waited in breathless anticipation of his answer.

"The Congressman," Delbert said. He slapped two huge pieces of Velveeta cheese on his slice of Wonder Bread. "Madam told me about it. It was at one of her cocktail parties for some bigwig from Ohio. There was quite a scandal. Rachel, could you pass me that jar of pickles at the end of the counter? Thanks. Apparently, the Congressman's mistress invited herself to the party, as well. The guy's wife was there, see, but she was unaware of the existence of this other woman. In a fit of rage, the mistress spikes the wife's drink with poison, but it gets mixed up when the waiter turns and gives it to the Congressman. Sounds kinda like an Agatha Christie mystery, doesn't it? Anyway, the Congressman, see, keels over with a thud next to the bar. Dead. And the mistress runs out of the house screaming."

I suddenly remembered reading about it. "I remember when it happened. It was on the front page of the *Washington Star* a couple years ago."

Delbert nodded his head solemnly, his mouth full.

I was impressed. "And to think it happened right here."

Rachel gave a shiver.

"Hey, I thought you liked ghosts," I said to her.

"She told you about the little girl?" Delbert said.

I nodded.

"It was the damnedest thing I ever saw," he said.

"I'm staying out of that room downstairs," I swore. "How can Buddha Markham live down there?"

Delbert said, "He's so spaced out all the time, I'm sure he doesn't notice anything."

"The Congressman needs someone to tell him that it's okay to leave now," Rachel said.

"Rachel, what are you talking about?"

"Oh, nothing." She changed the course of the conversation. "Have you seen the Congressman, Delbert?"

"I saw something once. Madam says she sees him all the time. She's very thankful he has the good sense not to show up and ruin another one of her parties."

"Well, he's got more sense than I have," I muttered.

Rachel said, "I'm going to run downstairs. I'll be right back."

"Rachel, you're not going to go down and talk to the Congressman?" I said snidely.

"Oh, give it a rest," she snapped.

"Someone has a temper," remarked Dr. Delbert.

All this talk about ghosts was making me uncomfortable. Once someone dies they just don't keep reappearing. Rachel said that there are more worlds than we're aware of; but me, the only world I believe in is the one I can touch and smell and see. Give me a good solid oak table, a firm handshake —something concrete. I had to admit that even my faith in God was weakening, if not altogether gone. I muttered silent prayers to God, but things just seemed to be going from bad to worse for me. He wasn't listening to me or sending me any help, so praying seemed to be pointless. One thing I was certain about. Peter was right about calling this place "St. Elizabeth's," after the mental hospital in D.C.

"Peter's moving out," Rachel said to me later that night as she lay next to me.

"Did he and his wife patch things up?"

"No. He's having too good a time on his own. It's Madam. He says he's fed up with her temper tantrums and prying. She actually stood over me in the kitchen to make sure I did my breakfast dishes this morning."

"She's something else, but this house is so great to live in."

Rachel rolled over, propping her head on her hand. "It's not normal behavior, Tony."

"You're the therapist, not me. I like living here." Living in this house made me feel important. It was all I had left. I could pretend I was successful when I came home every night and was surrounded by all these expensive things.

Rachel was quiet for a moment. "What happened with the Countess today?"

"Everything's okay. It's just going to take some time for the Countess and her partner to get everything in place for me."

"You're disappointed."

"No. I'm actually too busy to start lobbying for them right now. Besides, the Ambassador and I have our presentation for Princess Sava. Deals like this take time, Rachel — sometimes months — to fall into place."

"I see. I guess it's like working with a patient. Results take time. Breakthroughs are small, but each one builds on the next."

"Yeah, that's exactly how it is." I was grateful for her understanding and for her not forcing the issue with me like any other woman I'd ever known would have done.

She fussed with my hair, mussing it up, then putting it back in place. My mom used to do the exact same thing when I was little. "Tony, I've been talking about doing Thanksgiving dinner here at the house for everyone. Do you want to come?" she asked shyly.

"Of course." A home-cooked meal rather than happy hour dinners was very appealing.

I reached over and turned out the light. "Come here," I whispered. She curled up into me, and I held her until she fell asleep. My desire for her was so strong, but I didn't want to jeopardize the one good thing in my life.

Two o'clock the following day found the Ambassador and me in his car heading for our audience with Princess Sava at the Mayflower Hotel. I had three bound copies of our CocoBono proposal in my briefcase. They were just a bunch of papers, but my dreams were wedged between every sheet. We had plotted out our presentation. He would start, set the diplomatic tone, and then I'd come in and present the financials and operational logistics. He had a pretty good closing speech prepared. I felt confident, but nervous.

"Are you supposed to bow, Ambassador, when you meet a Polynesian Princess?"

"Yes. You put your feet together, bend from the waist, and put your hands together like this." The Ambassador took both his hands off the steering wheel and put his palms together. The car started to drift into the other lane, and the guy next to us laid on his horn.

"Jeez, Ambassador, be careful!"

"Calm down. We're fine. Grab that package on the back seat."

I undid my seatbelt and leaned over the seat to grab the package. Inside was an ornate, inlaid, wooden box and a T-shirt.

"Open the box, Cisco."

I lifted the lid, and saw that the box was filled with shredded coconut husk. "What's this for?"

"It's a present for the Princess. We can't just hand her CocoBono in a plastic sandwich bag."

"Good thinking, Ambassador. What about the T-shirt?" I'd unfolded it. It said "Hard Rock Cafe, Washington DC."

"That's for the Princess, too. Her secretary said she likes American T-shirts. I hope it fits. I got an extra large, you know, thinking Polynesian ladies have got big..."

"Keep your hands on the steering wheel. You're going to get us killed before we get there."

"Relax, Cisco. What's with you?"

"I just really need this to work out, that's all."

The Princess kept us waiting forty-five minutes in the hotel lobby. For such a prestigious hotel as The Mayflower, the lobby was rather small; but what it lacked in scale, it made up for in grandeur. Every square inch was made out of marble whose smooth surface reflected the polished brass fittings. Each time the elevator doors opened, I'd sit up a little straighter, but the person would walk right by us. The Ambassador had the wooden box balanced on his knees, and I had the briefcase and the T-shirt. I was worried that maybe we should have gift-wrapped the shirt.

The elevator bell dinged again, and a man stepped out. This had to be the secretary. He wore a bright blue polo shirt and a black cotton skirt wrapped around him that went down almost to his ankles. Around his waist was what looked like a grass mat secured with a black cord. He had well-worn flip-flops on his feet, and was carrying a clipboard. The Ambassador and I stood, and the secretary spotted us. The fancy wooden box gave us away, I guess. We were obviously on a diplomatic mission.

"I am Mr. Van'uloa. Her Highness will see you now."

The Ambassador and I followed him into the elevator. The secretary pushed the button for the 8th floor and planted himself dead center in front of the elevator doors, staring straight ahead. I stole a sideways glance at him and noticed his polo shirt said "Jake's Bar and Grill" on the pocket. He was wearing a Rolex watch, and his clipboard had *The New York Times* crossword puzzle on it. It was half done.

Outside the door to the Princess' suite, he asked us to wait. A few minutes later, he opened the door and escorted us in, but not before telling us not to look up until the Princess had spoken to us first. I walked in, obediently staring at the heels of the Ambassador's shoes in front of me. In a very grand voice, the secretary announced us.

"Ambassador Parker St. John and Mr. Anthony Cassera, from the United States of America, desire an audience with Her Most Gracious Princess, Sava Tupu Palua'panga, of the Kingdom of Tapa'u."

"Sit," she said.

I raised my eyes, took one look at the Princess and knew we were in trouble. The T-shirt was never going to fit. She must have weighed 400 pounds. They'd dragged the couch out into the center of the room for her to sit on. Her face was as round as the full moon, and her blue-black hair rippled in waves across her shoulders. The Princess had the most beautiful hair I had ever seen. Around her neck and across her chest was a woven mantle of grasses, shells, and palm fronds. Her dress was really a huge, pale pink sack that fell to the floor. From under its hem, her pudgy bare feet stuck out.

Mr. Van'uloa brought chairs over for us. Once we were seated, she graciously offered us some food. I don't care for McDonald's, but felt it would be rude to refuse so I munched on some french fries.

The Ambassador began. "Your Highness, we have brought gifts for you." He handed the wooden box to Mr. Van'uloa, who then gave it to the Princess. She opened it and grunted. Sensing her disappointment, the Ambassador rushed in with an explanation of its contents.

"It's CocoBono, Your Highness."

She poked at the husks with her finger. "It is coconuts," she stated matter-of-factly.

"We have another present for you." The Ambassador paused. "Mr. Cassera, the Princess' gift?"

I had missed my cue. "Your Highness, please accept this small gift in thanks for granting us this audience." I handed the T-shirt to Mr. Van'uloa who then walked it over to the Princess. The Ambassador and I watched in ominous silence as she unfolded the T-shirt.

We were rewarded with a huge smile. "It is Hard Rock Cafe. This I do not have. Many thank you's for this gift."

"Your Highness," said the Ambassador, "we are pleased that you like our gifts." Evidently, the size was not going to be a problem. I sighed inwardly with relief. The Ambassador continued. "Your Highness, have you had a chance to review our letter concerning the CocoBono project?"

"I have read, but tell me more."

"We believe that our product, which is made from coconut husks, has great potential for export to soil-deficient areas of the world such as deserts, islands, and arid plains. It could be a low-cost alternative for more expensive soil conditioners. For example, CocoBono would provide a water-conserving, inexpensive mulch to improve soil quality and food production. As a packing medium, it would revolutionize the plant import business. It has already been approved by the USDA as a packing media for imported, rooted plants, so the horticulture and florist industries would greatly benefit. Mr. Cassera will tell you how we envision the Kingdom of Tapa'u as part of the project."

I stood and performed the royal bow before speaking. The surprised look on the Princess' face told me that the Ambassador had pulled a good one on me by showing me how to bow to a Polynesian Princess.

"Your Highness, in order to demonstrate its potential, we propose a small start-up project on Tapa'u. Coconut husks would be collected from farmers, helping them with what we understand is an agricultural waste problem on your island. Turning the husks into CocoBono would stimulate the agricultural development in Tapa'u, as well as create a product for export to the United States and other countries. The project will employ local Tapa'uans. What we are proposing is a joint venture to set up an operating company in Tapa'u, and we would like to ask you to be a partner in this project." I finished and sat down.

The Princess sat for a couple of minutes in silence, which evidently was her royal prerogative. "Yes, this sounds interesting," she eventually replied.

I jumped in again. "We will need a letter from the government of Tapa'u agreeing in principle to our proposal. With this letter, we will be able to approach agencies like The World Bank and the International Trade Program at the State Department for funding for a pilot program." I reached into my briefcase and brought out the bound proposals, which I handed to Mr. Van'uloa. "Here are copies of our proposal, Your Highness."

The Ambassador picked up from me. "Also, Your Highness, we will need to know the volume of coconut husks, the best method of collecting them, and we will need some land with a building for our operations."

Once again, she waited several minutes before replying. "That will be no problem. This sounds like a good project. I return to Tapa'u in two months, after my trip to Europe, and you will hear from me then."

That was it. The audience was over. The Ambassador never even had a chance to give his closing speech. Mr. Van'uloa escorted us to the elevator and bid us good-bye on behalf of the Princess. We were ecstatic. The meeting had gone better than either of us had ever expected. Standing at the curb in front of the hotel, waiting for the valet to bring our car, the two of us kept patting each other on the back and shaking each other's hand. I couldn't wait to get home and share my success with Rachel.

"What was all that about, telling me I had to bow to a Polynesian Princess?" I said.

"You did it great!" the Ambassador crowed.

"That could have jeopardized everything for us, Ambassador!"

"But it didn't, did it? She loved it."

I gave him an angry punch in the arm, but inside I was really happy.

I surprised Rachel at the kitchen sink. I came up behind her and put my arms around her waist. "The Princess loved it, Rachel. When she gets back to her island in two months, we're going to discuss a building for our operations on the island of Tapa'u." I looked down into the sink. "What the hell is that?"

"It's a turkey. For Thanksgiving."

"It's huge."

"Twenty pounds." She turned to face me and gave me a hug. "So, the meeting was a success. I'm so happy for you, Tony. What was she like, the Princess?"

"She was huge, like that turkey. I bet she weighed four hundred pounds."

"No, you're teasing me."

"Honest. Ask the Ambassador."

"Ask me what?" said the Ambassador as he walked into the kitchen.

"Tony said the Princess weighed four hundred pounds. Was he telling the truth? You wouldn't lie to me, would you, Ambassador?"

"I swear upon this bag of Pepperidge Farm dressing that he speaks the truth. That's the biggest turkey I've ever seen, Rachel."

Rachel beamed. "He's a beauty isn't he?"

"Is it going to fit in the oven?" The Ambassador's question raised a worried look on Rachel's face.

"Well, I didn't think..."

"Of course it's going to fit," I said. "Are we having cranberry sauce, too?"

"Yes, Tony, we're having cranberry sauce, and dressing, and giblet gravy and..."

"...pumpkin pie," the Ambassador threw in. "I saw the cans of pumpkin in the pantry." The Ambassador opened the refrigerator. "It appears we're having a Fed Ex box, too. What's this doing in here?"

"I forgot about that," I said. "I was in such a hurry this morning that I put the whole box in the refrigerator. That's my contribution to Thanksgiving. I had my dad send me some of his tamales. You know, a little cultural diversity at the Thanksgiving table. We always had tamales at home on the holidays."

Rachel was thrilled. "Tony, that's a wonderful idea."

Thanksgiving Day, Rachel and I woke up early and headed downstairs to begin the dinner preparations. I built a fire in the breakfast room, while Rachel scrambled some eggs and made coffee. A leisurely breakfast in front of a roaring fire gave me a feeling of contentment that I'd seldom felt before. I lingered over my cup of coffee, watching the sunlight filter through the window. I could hear Rachel doing the dishes in the kitchen, and I felt at that moment like a rich man. That struck me as a funny thought. Possessions and money in the bank were the only things that had ever made me feel that way before. I wondered where my son David was today, and if he was happy and surrounded by family. Should I call? I thought not. I was too embarrassed from the last time we were together. I didn't think he wanted to hear from me ever again. Someday I'd make it up to him. I'd make everything up to him. It was Rachel's voice calling from the kitchen that woke me up from my mournful reverie.

"Tony, what are you doing? We need to get started."

"I'm coming. I just need to put another log on the fire."

Delbert was perched at the kitchen counter with a huge bowl in front of him. Rachel had started him on the dressing, and he was busily tossing bread crumbs with celery. If he didn't stop nibbling, we'd have nothing left for the turkey. Rachel came over and stopped his hand halfway to his mouth.

"Delbert, you forgot to cut up the onions."

"You're right. So I did. Sorry Rachel." He picked up the knife and the onion and began chopping away. "So, who's coming, Rachel?"

"I invited everyone in the house."

"Everyone?" I said.

"Yes. I invited Madam, but she said she had plans."

Dr. Delbert's silent sigh of relief matched my own.

"I'm hoping she'll change her mind."

"Rachel!" I said.

"It's Thanksgiving," she snapped back at me.

Fortunately, "Buddha" Markham from downstairs came into the kitchen carrying a can and a bottle of wine. He was taller and thinner than I remembered.

"Hi, everybody. I brought some oysters for the stuffing, and some wine." Buddha shoved the can of oysters and wine bottle into Rachel's hands. He stood back awkwardly, then leaned against the counter trying to look relaxed. This guy was definitely a bundle of nerves, his eyes squinting in an out-of-control facial tic. It was obviously some serious crime he'd committed.

"Thank you, Markham," Rachel said. "We can have the wine

with dinner." Two bright pink spots appeared on Buddha's cheeks. I was jealous of the attention she was paying to him. Rachel put the wine in the refrigerator and passed the can of oysters to Delbert.

"Oysters in turkey dressing?" he said unhappily. Rachel knew it would put an end to his snacking. Dr. Delbert detested oysters.

The Ambassador appeared next, carrying two coconuts and a pineapple. "Happy Turkey Day!" he said as he plopped the armload onto the counter. "I will be creating a delectable Tapa'uan dish for our feast — pineapple chunks with grated coconut, floating in coconut milk laced with..." and he pulled a bottle from his coat pocket, "rum."

"That sounds good," said the Doctor, eyeing the bottle of rum.

"Has anyone a hammer?" asked the Ambassador. Buddha stood up and started rummaging through the kitchen silverware drawer. I couldn't believe he found a hammer in there.

"Good work, man. Will you be my assistant at the sacrifice to the great coconut god?

Buddha looked pleased to be asked, and he and the Ambassador headed outdoors to whack the coconuts with the hammer. Rachel handed them a bowl on their way out.

"For the milk," she said.

The Ambassador looked over at me and said, "She's a brilliant woman, Cisco." He left, followed by the Buddha, cradling the coconuts in his arms.

"That guy has the weirdest sense of humor," Dr. Delbert said.

"He has a great sense of humor," I said, defensively.

"Whatever."

Rachel pulled out a stack of plates and silverware and handed them to the doctor. "Delbert, you can stop with the dressing now. Why don't you set the table for me?"

"I'll help you with that," a young woman said, entering the kitchen. "Hi, Rachel."

"Hi, Colleen. Colleen just moved in a couple of days ago. She's attending school at American University," Rachel explained as she introduced us.

The girl didn't look more than twenty years old. She had a mop of thick, wavy red hair, pale white skin, and wide, brown eyes. I wondered why she wasn't at her parents' house for the holiday.

Colleen and Delbert went down the hall to the dining room to set the table. As soon as they were gone, Rachel turned to me.

"Quick, Tony, start toasting that loaf of bread in the refrigerator."

"Every slice?"

"Yes. Look at this mess." We both looked down into the bowl with the dressing. The doctor had turned it to mush.

I laughed. "There's nothing like Thanksgiving with your family," I said as I gave her a little kiss on the cheek. I was surprised when she brushed my kiss away.

"Hiya, kids. Ready for the parade?"

Oh, God, it was Big Ed and his big 26-inch TV. "Thanksgiving is just not Thanksgiving without the Macy's parade," he said. "Hey, give me a hand with this."

Rachel looked irritated. "Ed, there's really no room in the kitchen. Tony can help you set it up in the breakfast room."

"Okay, Mom. C'mon, Tony, put some muscle into this." I felt like leaving him there until he sank through the floor from the weight of the thing, but it was Thanksgiving and I was in a good mood. I helped Big Ed set up the TV in the breakfast room, then went back to my bread toasting. We could hear Buddha Markham and the Ambassador chatting outside as they chipped away at the coconuts.

"This is great, Rachel. Thanks for doing this."

"You're welcome. The turkey's ready to be stuffed. I'll go ahead and start cutting up the bread. What a soggy mess this dressing is. I hope we can save it."

Delbert came back in and set the dishes and silverware back on the kitchen counter.

Rachel threw him a funny look. "What's the matter?"

"Madam says we use the good china and silver for Thanksgiving dinner."

"She's here?" I said, anxiously.

"Yep. She and Colleen are hauling out the fine linens and polishing the silver."

I was filled with dread. "Is she..?"

"Yep," replied Dr. Delbert. "Guess who's coming for dinner."

"Oh, no."

"Well, after all, you two, it is her house," Rachel said. "I think it's wonderful that she's joining us." She spoke calmly, but I noticed she started chopping up the toast with a fury.

"Rachel, your therapist side is showing," I told her.

Big Ed called out from the breakfast room. "Hey you guys gotta come see this. It's Roy Rogers and Dale Evans on a float. They're so old. You know, Roy actually stuffed Trigger and put him in his museum. I wouldn't be surprised if they stuffed these two. C'mon in here."

Rachel glared at Delbert and me. "Why don't you two go watch television. I'll call you if I need your help."

The doctor and I obediently left the kitchen.

Outside I heard the Ambassador and Buddha singing some song from the musical *South Pacific.*

Now, nothing is more irritating to me than the Macy's parade, with all those bands, but I decided to stick with it out of a sense of Thanksgiving camaraderie. I had been lulled into a stupor when I heard Rachel call me. She needed help lifting the bird.

We hoisted the pan, and headed for the oven.

"Oh, Tony," she wailed. "It's too big."

No matter what we did, we couldn't wedge it in. The sides were fine. It was the top of the bird that was the problem.

"We can use the lower oven, Rachel."

"No, it doesn't work."

"Okay. We'll slice an inch off the top of the turkey."

"Everything's ruined," she said, throwing the dishtowel into the breakfast room. She sat on the kitchen stool and started sobbing. That wasn't like Rachel.

I put the bird down, went over, and hugged her. "We can still cook it. No one will mind." I grabbed the roll of paper towels for her tears.

"It's not the t-turkey," she sobbed. "It's my k-kids. This is the f-first Th-thanksgiving we've been apart."

"Let's go call them."

"I already did. It's just that I m-miss them t-today." She buried her face against me and cried.

"That must be so hard," I said. I held her close and stroked her hair.

The turkey looked beautiful sitting in the center of the table. It was flat on top, but a nice golden brown, and it smelled heavenly. Madam had outdone herself. The tablecloth was snowy white, and the table glittered in the candlelight from two silver candelabras. We each had three crystal goblets, and the correct number of forks. Individual salt cellars like I'd seen at Embassy dinners were at each setting. The Ambassador's Tapa'uan dish nestled in a silver serving bowl. We'd all gone back upstairs and gotten dressed up for the occasion. Madam would have it no other way. She was radiant at the head of the table, her red hair elegantly coifed. But it was Rachel who glowed. She always glowed when she wore white like she did today. She looked absolutely beautiful.

"I will say grace now," Madam announced. We all looked at each other before bowing our heads. Since Madam didn't say anything, I assumed it must be a silent grace. I was eyeing the rolls when she began.

"Heavenly Father. We are most grateful to you for all the blessings you have bestowed on us this year. Please, may you find us all worthy of your generous gifts. We, who are humble sinners, beg forgiveness for any wrongs we may have done. We beseech you to watch over those of our families who cannot be with us today and to take care of our loved ones who sit with you in heaven. May this coming year see the banishment of hunger in our world, so that no child may die of starvation. We ask this in the name of Our Lord, Jesus Christ. Amen. Ambassador St. John, will you carve please?"

"With pleasure," said the Ambassador, graciously acknowledging the compliment paid to him by Madam.

He picked up the carving knife and fork, and deftly portioned out the turkey. Somehow I didn't feel quite as hungry. Images of starving children came to my mind after Madam's grace. I looked around the table at my Thanksgiving "family" and wondered what tricks of fate had washed us ashore here. We were a highly educated group of people who had somehow lost something, were at a crossroads in our lives, or were changing careers or directions. Some were coming from broken relationships, some from shattered dreams. For all of us the mansion was a temporary haven, a place to pick up the pieces and begin putting our lives back together. We all had ended up here for the same reason. We just took different roads getting here. I watched Colleen eating her meal. She looked so young, too young to be here with the rest of us. How could she have lost so much already? Madam was rambling on, entertaining us, as the perfect hostess should. Rachel watched her from the other end of the table, a bemused smile on her face. Madam's hands fluttered and swooped, keeping company with every word she uttered.

"I remember a Thanksgiving in Marrakech. My husband wanted turkey, but pigeon was the best that I could do. Our chef, however, prepared it exquisitely. He was Moroccan, a gifted cook, but quite short for a man. I often wondered if malnutrition as a child played a part in his lack of stature. Ambassador, I understand you are the creator of this Polynesian dish. It looks most interesting." Madam helped herself to a spoonful.

"Yes, Ellen," said the Ambassador. "It is a recipe passed down to me from the king of the island of Tapa'u in the South Pacific. Markham and I labored carefully in its preparation."

Madam raised the spoon to her mouth. "Markham, too? I had no idea you were still interested in international foods."

Buddha Markham looked extremely uncomfortable. I was curious why Madam mentioning international food should cause him to squirm in his chair.

The spoon reached Madam's mouth, and we waited for her reaction.

"Delicious," she pronounced. "There's quite a bit of rum in it, I believe?"

The Ambassador cleared his throat. "Yes. Rum is one of the main ingredients in the island's cuisine."

"I think I've had something like this at a bar," Madam said thoughtfully. "Isn't it usually served in a glass, Ambassador?"

"You're right," Big Ed interjected. "They put those little paper umbrellas sticking out over the edge."

We all laughed and got into seriously eating dinner. Later, we all referred to it as "the Last Supper," for it was the beginning of the end of our little family. It all started with a chance remark from Colleen during the pumpkin pie.

"Where's the little girl?"

"What little girl?" Big Ed said between forkfuls of pie. "There's no little girl here."

I glanced over at Rachel. She was looking at Madam. I followed her gaze.

Madam had gone alarmingly pale. Both hands were at her throat. "Maggie's here?" she said to Colleen, who had stopped eating.

"Well," Colleen said hesitantly, "I thought I saw a little blonde-haired girl in the upstairs hall. I assumed she was visiting someone. What's wrong?"

None of us bothered to answer her. All eyes were on Madam who was becoming fretful.

"I can't leave her. She won't be able to find me," Madam whined. She stood up, and her chair crashed onto the floor. She began pacing like she did that time in the front hall when she lost Maggie's photograph. The Ambassador and I went to her side.

"Ellen, let's go in the library." The Ambassador put her arm around his and walked her across the hall. The transformation in her appearance was alarming. In the space of a few minutes she had shrunken in on herself. We helped her into the wing chair, and I found myself hoping she wouldn't die on us.

The Ambassador took charge. "Get her a brandy, Tony. Stay with her. I think I should call a doctor."

Madam would have none of that. "No. No. Call Reverend Mike. His number's by the phone, in the black book."

I got her to drink some brandy. She grabbed my arm and pulled me down next to her. Her voice was getting louder and more hysterical.

"You're the only one I can tell. You helped the countess. It's the house...it's..."

I got her to take a little more brandy, and the Ambassador came over and started talking to her in quiet, soothing tones.

"Reverend Mike is on his way over. He said he'd be here in thirty minutes."

"I always feel stronger when he's with me. He carries the Lord with him."

The Ambassador kept talking to her quietly and pouring her brandy.

I found everyone else in the kitchen, gathered around Colleen, who was quite distraught and looked like she'd been crying. Rachel was talking to her. "Colleen, it's not your fault. She gets upset easily. This will blow over in a couple of days, and she'll forget all about it. Why don't you help Delbert put the china and silver away. You know where it goes. Tony and I will wash the dishes, and Ed and Markham can dry."

"Okay," Colleen sniffed. "But who's the little girl?"

"She's the daughter of a friend of mine," Big Ed lied.

Soon everyone was involved in their tasks. I admired the way Rachel took charge of the situation. Delbert took the china and silver to Colleen in the dining room as soon as they were dry. Rachel and I stood side by side at the sink, doing the dishes.

"How is she, Tony?"

"The Ambassador got her calmed down. He called Reverend Mike for her. He's on his way over."

"What's going on?"

"I'm not sure."

She nodded silently. We were almost done with the dishes when the Ambassador appeared in the kitchen.

"Reverend Mike's with her in the library. You two need any help?"

"No, we're fine," I said.

"In that case, I'm going to bed. I'm ready to call it a day. I'll leave the first draft of our follow-up letter to the Princess on your desk upstairs, Cisco. We can go over it tomorrow. Thank you, my dear Miss Rachel, for such a lovely Thanksgiving dinner."

"Good-night, Ambassador," I called after him.

"He's really a good friend of yours, isn't he, Tony? Have you two known each other a long time?"

I had to stop and think for a minute before answering. "About ten years. We met at the White House mess."

"You mean, during Watergate?"

I laughed. "No. The White House mess is the cafeteria in the Old Executive Office Building. It's run by the Navy. That's why they call it a 'mess.' It's a military term for where everyone eats."

"Oh, I see."

"For three years he was posted in Europe. We hooked up again once he got back to the States. Listen, how about if I build up the fire in the breakfast room?"

"That sounds nice. I'll make coffee."

I had a blaze going by the time Rachel brought in the mugs of coffee. We turned off all the lights and sat in the dark, watching the flames. The house was quiet, the only sound the crackling of the logs. I put my arm around Rachel, and she laid her head on my shoulder.

"Some Thanksgiving, wasn't it?" I said.

"You can say that again."

"It was perfect, except for one small thing."

Rachel sat up. "What?"

"You forgot to put my dad's tamales out."

"Oh, Tony, I'm sorry. Will he ever forgive me?"

I laughed and kissed her nose. "Don't worry. I'll never tell him."

There were a lot of things I was never going to tell my dad. He'd never understand my financial troubles. Everything had always gone well for him.

We had survived Thanksgiving. Rachel typed up the letter to the Princess for me and mailed it. It would be the first of February before anything happened, so I put it on the back burner of my mind and threw myself into lobbying. Madam regained her equilibrium, and there were no more Maggie sightings. Colleen moved out, and someone named Fred moved in. He lasted two weeks, then he was gone, too. I guess we'd all gotten so used to Madam's large eccentricities, the little ones didn't bother us anymore.

Rachel's practice was growing; she'd started her first group session. She'd broken the leg off of one of Stan's conference tables, moving it to accommodate her group. Stan made such a big deal out of the incident that Rachel made arrangements to rent space from the Westwood Psychiatric Institute starting the first of the year. With Christmas coming, a lot of her patients were getting depressed, so Rachel and I weren't able to spend as much time together, which irritated me, even though I was pleased with her success. Stan Owens and I were starting to butt heads over how little money he was paying me for as much lobbying as he wanted me to do.

My restlessness and frustration came out on Rachel one Saturday night. I wanted to go out dancing; she wanted to stay home and relax. I kept pestering her, and she kept calmly repeating what she needed. Sometimes dating a therapist can be a real pain.

"Tony, I'm tired. I just want to sit here in front of the fire and become a vegetable."

"You never want to do anything, anymore. Wednesday night, you didn't even come to my room. I always sleep better when you're there."

Rachel stood, and her green eyes became more brilliant in color as she stared levelly into my eyes. "Maybe you should start thinking about someone else besides yourself," she yelled at me.

And then she said the most amazing thing. It wasn't what she said, but how she said it, so matter-of-factly, without a trace of the previous anger. "We're not even doing anything, but you're no different than the rest. All men really want to do is fuck. Then what? What happens after that? Men want the conquest, but then what happens after that? Is that all there is? Is that all there will ever be for you?"

She didn't wait for an answer. She turned and left.

I sat there feeling like I'd been punched, not physically, but emotionally. What the hell was she talking about? Who got her a job? I thought about what she'd said, though. It's true. When men meet someone they're attracted to, they don't think "I'm going to find out all about this woman, get into her head, delve deep into her innermost thoughts to get to know her better." All men think about is sex, and how good a woman would be in bed. That's the first step to developing a relationship with a man.

I was no different. When I first met Rachel, all I could think about was having sex with her. I didn't want a relationship, just pure sex for fun and no commitment. That was what was on my mind. It was exciting meeting a new woman I was attracted to and fulfilling my need to conquer her. The act always gave me such a power surge. I craved it. I needed it. She should know that. I wasn't pushing her or making demands. Well, if she wanted to go to sleep, fine. I was going out.

Saturdays were always hot at the club. The music was loud, and I stood nursing my scotch, watching the dancing. The women were all dressed up, many in short skirts and low-cut tops. There was a woman on the dance floor who kept looking over her partner's shoulder at me. Her body undulated to the music, and my eyes were riveted to watching her skirt stretch tightly over her thighs. When the dance ended, she dumped her partner and came over and stood next to me, her back against the wall. She was a knockout. Her curly, auburn hair fell to her shoulders.

"Do you dance?" she said in a deep, husky voice.

I and leaned my hand on the wall above her head. "Yeah, I dance. Do you drink?"

She ran her finger around the rim of my glass. "Yeah, I drink. I'll have whatever you're having. My name's Jessie."

"Hey, Eddie, the lady needs a scotch on the rocks." Eddie saluted me from behind the bar and made up the drink for me. "Jessie — that's a funny name for a girl."

"My parents had a strange sense of humor," she said wryly. She smiled, and her teeth were white and straight, and I liked the way her lips curved.

We drank and danced and I held her close. I liked the way she moved her body with mine. Her breasts were firm and pointed as they pressed against my chest, and I wanted to see what she looked like with no clothes on. After the dance ended, she led me by the hand to the entrance. I walked her to her car and leaned on the windowsill.

"I'll follow you home," was all I said.

She smiled and nodded.

I watched the taillights of her car as they wove in and out through the traffic ahead of me.

"What the hell are you doing?" my heart said.

"I'm following the lady home, so I can screw her! What do you think I'm doing?" my head said.

"So you screw her, so what's that going to do?" my heart replied.

"It'll make me feel better," my head sneered back.

"Really?" my heart whispered.

"Well, not really," my head sighed.

"So what do you really want?" my heart asked.

"I want to be home in bed, lying next to Rachel."

"So, what the hell are you doing?" my heart asked.

I slowed the car, pulled over to the left lane, and made a U-turn.

Rachel was asleep in my bed when I got home. I stripped my clothes off, took a shower, then crawled quietly under the covers. She didn't wake up, and I lay there thinking about what she'd said earlier, about what men want. I reached over and held a lock of her hair in my hand and let the strands fall back into place one by one.

What did I want? My furniture back. Money. Love. I sighed. I knew what I wanted, but was it what I needed?

The room was dark, but I could make out Rachel's silhouette where she lay sleeping next to me. Her back was towards me, and I could hear her slow breathing. I kissed her shoulder. It was intoxicating, her scent, her body lying next to mine. I wanted to pull her nightgown over her head and let it drop on the floor. When she turned towards me, stretching her body against mine, I ran my fingers lightly over the curve of her hips. Wrapping my arms around her, I pulled her closer, feeling her leg slip between my thighs. I could wait for her. I could wait for as long as it took. I wasn't going to lose this. This woman with the delicate face who was so strong, yet so gentle, capable of great anger, yet so patient. She was a mystery to me, and I was awed and fascinated.

I woke Rachel in the morning with a kiss on the cheek.

"Hi," she said sleepily. "When did you get home?"

"Late. You didn't even wake up. Feeling rested?"

She stretched and yawned. "Yes. Did you have fun?"

"It was okay. I should have stayed home with you."

"Well, I could have told you that."

"You're pretty sure of yourself," I said.

"Yep, I am," she replied playfully. Then she said, "I'm thinking of driving up to Connecticut for Christmas. Do you want to come?"

"Is your family there?"

"Well, they were. My dad died a long time ago. When my mom died, she left the house to me. My kid's are going to be with their dad in Las Vegas."

"What does your ex-husband do in Vegas?"

"Umm, he's an architect. That's what he does. He builds and designs those awful casinos. Anyway, we have the house for Christmas if we want it. Do we want it?"

"What happened between you two?"

"We just drifted apart. It started when he got the job offer in Las Vegas. The money was good, and everything that went with it was exactly what he'd always wanted — beautiful women, fancy cars, the night life. It was different when we first met. He was going to be an innovator, another Frank Lloyd Wright, but there was no money in that. Harry was always lured by a facade, and he finally found one that paid off." She shrugged. "That was a long time ago now. Do you want to come to Connecticut with me?"

"Yes, I'd like that."

"We'll have a white Christmas," Rachel murmured happily as she fell back to sleep.

I'd never seen so much snow. The house was about eight miles outside of Old Mystic on a country road. Rachel called it a "saltbox." It sat back from the road on a hill, and there was a huge boulder among the trees down below the front of the house. I pointed it out to Rachel. She stopped the car.

"That's Old Man Mountain. That's what we used to call it when we were kids. It was left behind by the glacier, my father said."

"It must be twenty feet high." I craned my neck to look at it. "You should see the mountains out above Sanibel. There's an old canyon..."

I stopped. I didn't want to start thinking about Celinda. "I'm going to take a picture of it." I pulled my instamatic out of my pocket.

"Take a picture?"

"With my camera. I hope they turn out. I'm really unlucky when it comes to these gadgets. Come on, Rachel, stand in front of Old Man Mountain."

"Tony, I take a terrible picture."

"Please."

Reluctantly, she got out and stood in front of the ancient rock so I could get my shot. We climbed back in the car and headed up to the house. The snow was piled up in front of the barn doors. Rachel got a snow shovel from the house, and I dug the doors out so I could pull the car in, while she took the groceries into the house. I soon smelled wood burning, and looked up to see smoke coming from the chimney. Rachel came back out and watched me finish up.

"I thought there'd be more snow," she said.

"More snow? There's lots of snow. There must be a foot on the ground."

"That's not very much, Tony."

"It seems like a lot when you're shoveling it."

"Stop complaining. Come on in and have some coffee."

"I'll be right there."

I drove the car into the barn and parked it. I pulled the wooden door closed. I felt like I'd just shut out all my problems and left them in that musty, dark barn. For the next four days, I vowed to myself that I wasn't going to think about the creditors who had started to hound me.

From the side porch, I could see down behind the house where the land sloped to a little creek. Near the creek, were mounds of snow. They looked like a half-melted snowman family.

"Rachel, what are those things?"

She stuck her head out the mud room door. "They're tombstones. That's the family cemetery."

"You have your own cemetery?"

"Doesn't everyone?" she teased. "My family has lived on this hill for generations — over two hundred years, we think. My mother and father are buried there. The poinsettias I brought are to put out on their graves."

I shivered. "I don't like cemeteries, and I sure wouldn't want one in my backyard."

"Are you afraid of dying, Tony?"

"I'm a little worried about it, aren't you?"

"Not particularly. Most people think of it as a big deal, like it's the end of everything, but it's not. It's just a change."

"A big change, if you ask me. If someone dies, you never, ever see them again. That sounds like forever and final to me."

"That's because you have to physically 'see' everything."

"What else is there? This is it," I said, pointing at the ground and the trees. "What else is there to see?"

"It's not so much *seeing* something or someone. It's *knowing* they're there."

I was confused. I had no idea what she was talking about.

Rachel laughed. "Don't look so serious." She pointed to the creek that wound by the cemetery. "That's Gooseman Creek. Wild blackberries grow in the cemetery in the summer. They're delicious."

"That's awful. You might be eating your Uncle John."

"I don't have an Uncle John," Rachel said mischievously.

There was a huge stone fireplace in the old house, and pine floors that sloped in all different directions. They were shiny and worn in different places, particularly on the door sills. There was a threadbare runner on the stairs, and the doors had black metal latches that you lifted. No doorknobs. The furniture had edges and corners rounded from use and deep nicks scarring the wood. On the shelves were rows of books. None of them had been published within the last sixty years except for copies of *National Geographic*, but even they dated from the Fifties.

"Everything here is really old," I commented as I pulled out yet another book and checked its publication date. 1868.

"There's no TV either. Look at this." Rachel pulled out a Monopoly game in a worn, tattered box and handed it to me. "This was our favorite game when we were growing up. We'd play it as a family on the long winter nights. This whole cabinet is filled with photo albums. See, they have the black pages and the corners for holding the pictures in. There are even some tintypes in here somewhere."

"You're lucky to have all this, Rachel."

"I think you're right."

"My grandfather lost all his land, his house, everything he owned, in the Mexican Revolution. He fled with his family to New Mexico, leaving his gold with his best friend for safekeeping. He never saw his friend or his gold again." I'd lost everything I owned to Celinda. At that moment I felt my grandfather's rage, his sorrow, and his disappointment, and they became mine.

Rachel put another log on the fire. "That must have been very hard for him. He was a proud man, I have a feeling."

Sitting there in front of the flickering flames, I told myself that I'd have a nice house again some day.

"I thought you had a house out in Santa Fe?" Rachel said.

"How'd you know that?" I said, startled. "You're spooky, sometimes."

"Know what? You just said you wanted to have a nice house again, and I thought you'd told me you had a house in Santa Fe."

"Did I say that out loud? I lost it."

"What do you mean?"

"I don't like to talk about it much."

There was something in her look that made me feel I could tell her anything and not be judged, so I told her the truth. I told her about the bankruptcy, and losing my houses, and I told her about Celinda, and about how I was trying to get my furniture back. I talked and talked, and by the time I'd finished, the logs in the fireplace were burning embers.

"It's only furniture, Tony. There are other things you can lose that are more important."

My son, David, came into my mind. To hide how upset I felt, I started rebuilding the fire.

"I had beautiful furniture, Rachel. I wish you could have seen it, and now Celinda has it." Sitting back on my heels, I watched the fire take hold.

She shrugged. "I've lost things, too."

"But you still have your kids." I jabbed at the logs with a poker.

"I could lose everything else, but I wasn't going to lose my kids," Rachel said firmly.

I looked down at my hands, and watched the firelight play across them. I wasn't sure if I could get the words out. They seemed stuck in my throat.

"I lost my son on purpose."

"How old is your son? Where is he?"

"He's nineteen now." The words tumbled out. "We were too young, Julie and I. We had to get married. We were eighteen years old, and she and David lived with my folks while I went to college. I didn't know how to be a father. Julie finally left and took David." I stared into the fire. "I didn't even fight for him, Rachel. Julie remarried years ago. David told me he even has a little brother now."

"Why didn't you tell me you had a son?"

"I didn't want anyone to know what I'd done, especially you, Rachel.

He doesn't even want to see me, I'm sure. He came to visit us, Celinda and I, in Santa Fe. Celinda said something to him. She should have never said it."

"Where is he this Christmas?"

"I don't know, probably with his mother in Colorado." I was waiting for Rachel to start chewing me out for being such a lousy person, but she didn't.

"It's hard to know why we make the decisions we do," she said. "Looking back, it's always easy to see what we should have done. I've cried a lot over some of my mistakes, but when it's all said and done, we have to live with them and accept what we've done and forgive ourselves. I don't think you've done that yet about David."

"Have I become one of your patients, Rachel?"

"No, but I hope you've become one of my friends."

I blinked my eyes fast to keep the tears away.

"It sure is smoky in here," I said.

"Yes, it is a little bit. I'll open the kitchen window a crack."

With Rachel out of the room, I wiped my eyes. I heard her open the window in the kitchen.

"Tony, come in here."

I walked into the dark kitchen. She was peering out the window. I stood next to her and looked out. Standing by the creek near the cemetery were two dark forms.

"Aren't they beautiful?" Rachel whispered.

"What are they?"

"Deer. Two deer."

The deer raised their heads and looked up. I expected them to run, figuring that the wind had carried Rachel's voice to them, but they didn't. They stood very still, then started slowly walking up the hill towards the house and Rachel's voice.

"Come on." She beckoned to them. "Come and see me."

"Rachel, they're coming this way!"

"I know," she whispered excitedly.

The deer stopped within twenty feet of the window. They stared straight at us with unblinking eyes, and we gazed back. At that moment I felt time stop, leaving us suspended in the space between two seconds. Then one of the deer broke the spell by dropping its head. It turned back down the hill, and the other followed. They crossed the creek, and the two dark shapes melted into the black shadows of the woods.

I touched the rumpled covers where Rachel had lain next to me last night. I was alone in bed. I looked out the bedroom window, thinking about the two deer we'd seen. The morning sun shone brilliantly on the white snow, so dazzling in its brightness that I had to squint. I saw Rachel down at the cemetery, moving among the graves. There were bright red poinsettias in front of two of the headstones. I dressed and hurried down to join her.

"Hello there," I called as I headed down the slope.

"You're up already?"

"What are you doing?"

"Setting out the flowers I brought with us."

I walked up to the first tombstone. *Miriam Whitaker Gabriella 1925-1989.* That must be Rachel's mother. The next one was probably her father. *Michael Ruben Gabriella 1915-1959.* I looked up, and there was Rachel perched on a tombstone, holding a pot of white poinsettias.

"Rachel, you shouldn't sit on top of a stone."

"She won't mind. The flowers are for her."

Rachel hopped down and put the flowers in front of the headstone. I looked over her shoulder as she knelt in the snow. *Rachel Isabella Gabriella 1832-1874.*

"Rachel, that's your name," I said uneasily.

"I was named after her. She was my father's great-great grandmother."

"Oh, I see. Some of these stones are really old." I peered at a worn stone face where I could barely make out the year, *1779.*

"What's really amazing is that they're all family, every one of them." Her arm swept out in a gesture indicating all the stones.

"Look at this little lamb," I said, brushing a mound of snow off the top of the stone lamb's head.

"There are actually two lambs. They're my favorites."

I watched as she unburied the second lamb hiding in the snow. She brushed the snow off as if it were a real lamb, gently and carefully.

"Hello, my little babies," she said. She read the names on the stones out loud, "'Daniel Elijah Gabriella, Aged 3 mos and 7 dayes, 1849. Rebecca Mary Gabriella, 1850-1854, Taken too soon.'"

Rachel looked around. "Most of the others you can't read, and under the snow are some markers that have been broken off." She reached down and cleared the snow from around the two little lambs before standing.

"Are you ready to go cut our Christmas tree, Tony?"

"You mean we're not going to go to a lot and buy it?"

Rachel rolled her eyes. "Wait here. I'll get the saw."

We crossed the creek, following the trail of footprints left by the deer from last night. The tracks veered off to the left about a hundred yards from the creek. Rachel struck out to the right, with me following. It was obvious that she knew exactly where she was going. Jeez, it was cold. My coat wasn't made for this weather. The trees were close together here, with not too many pines. We came out into a clearing of fresh snow, and Rachel hooted in delight.

"It's perfect," she cried out.

She threw herself in the snow and started moving her arms and legs.

"Rachel, what the hell are you doing?" Why anyone would deliberately throw themselves into the freezing snow seemed crazy to me.

"I'm making a snow angel. I haven't done this in years."

She sat up, then carefully tiptoed away. "See, her wings you make with your arms, and your legs make her robe. I guess growing up in New Mexico you didn't make a lot of snow angels?"

"That's true. Are we almost there? I'm freezing."

She pouted. "You're no fun."

"Sorry, but I'm cold." I jumped up and down to keep myself warm.

Off we went through the woods again, hunting for the elusive perfect tree.

"Tell me more about your son, Tony."

"He's a musician. He sings and plays the guitar. I saw him perform in Albuquerque. He was terrific."

"Does he write songs, too?"

"I think he has written some of the ones he performs."

"Are you a musician?"

"No. I don't know where he gets it from. Julie isn't musically inclined either. I used to write poetry sometimes, just for myself. What about that tree?"

"It's flat on one side."

I was certain I was in the advanced stages of frostbite by the time Rachel made her choice, but I had to admit it was a pretty little tree. We carried it home and set it up in an old bucket in a corner of the living room. Rachel disappeared upstairs and came down with two old cardboard boxes full of ornaments and lights. The strings of lights were the big bulbs, in all different colors with flecks of paint chipped off.

"Maybe we should get some of those little Italian lights," I suggested.

"These are perfect. There's nothing wrong with them."

I began to string them on the tree. When I was done, I sat back with a mug of hot chocolate and watched Rachel put on the ornaments. There was a story that went along with each one. She'd unwrap it carefully from its tissue paper and tell me its history while she looked for the perfect spot for it.

"See this black and white cat with the red collar." She dangled the ornament in front of me. "We had a cat just like this named Hannah, who wore a red collar that Mom put a bell on, so the birds could hear her coming."

Rachel hung the ornament, then stood back critically to observe the effect. It was a pleasant afternoon for me, watching Rachel decorate the tree. I took a few more pictures with my camera — of Rachel by the tree, Rachel building a fire, Rachel sipping hot chocolate. She indulged me, because she really hated having her picture taken. By the end of the afternoon, the tree was done, and the sky was beginning to darken. I went out for some more firewood and noticed gray clouds rolling in.

"I think we're going to get more snow, Rachel."

"Oh, good." Her eyes sparkled. "I love it when it snows on Christmas Eve. In the morning when you look out, there's a whole fresh blanket of snow over everything."

"I think we're in the middle of a down comforter," I said the next morning as I stared glumly out the window.

"Or a snow globe," Rachel added brightly.

I couldn't see the creek. I couldn't even see ten feet from the house. We were caught in a Christmas blizzard.

"Merry Christmas, Tony," Rachel said. She handed me a tiny, wrapped box. I opened it, and inside was a clear stone about an inch and a half long. I held it up to the light and was amazed at how deeply you could look into it.

"It's a quartz crystal. It was given to me by my father, to protect me. I want you to have it now."

I was very touched. It was obviously something she had really treasured. "Thank you, Rachel." I slipped it into my pocket. "I'm going to keep it with me always."

I handed her a little box. "This is for you." Inside was a necklace, with a gold heart locket with a tiny diamond in the center.

"Oh, Tony, it's beautiful."

"It's just a little something. I wish I could have gotten you more." I thought about all the fancy jewelry I'd bought for Celinda.

"I love it. I want to wear it. Help me put it on." She lifted her hair. I fastened the clasp, then bent down and kissed the back of her neck.

"Merry Christmas, Rachel."

It snowed all day, so we spent the time in front of the fireplace, playing cards, talking, and listening to Christmas music on an old radio from the Forties. Being snowbound was not half-bad, I decided. Around noon, Rachel went into the kitchen to fix Christmas dinner. I could hear her banging cabinet doors and talking to herself.

"What are we having, Rachel?"

She came to the kitchen door. "Roast beef and Yorkshire pudding and..." she pulled a plate from behind her back and carried it over to me, "...tamales."

"You didn't."

"I sure did."

I pulled her down onto my lap and nuzzled her neck. "Thanks."

"You're welcome. I'm glad you're pleased, because that's all we're having. I must have left a bag of groceries back at the mansion. I didn't notice when I put everything away after we arrived."

"It sounds like a perfect Christmas dinner to me," I said.

"I think I can make a little salad to go with it. I hope the snow eases up tonight. I'll have to go into town to get us some groceries tomorrow."

"Do you need some help?" I asked. I think she was remembering Thanksgiving when she said she could handle it by herself. As she headed back into the kitchen, I threw another log onto the fire and watched the flames leap around it. That's when I made my decision.

"Rachel," I called out. "Can I use your phone? I think I'll call David."

"Sure, go ahead," she called back to me.

I sat in the chair and put the phone in my lap.

Julie answered. "Hello?"

"Merry Christmas, Julie. It's Tony. Is David there?"

"Yes," she said coolly, "but he's busy. Now's not a good time."

"Can't I just talk to him for a second?"

"I told you. He can't come to the phone right now."

"Tell him I called."

"I will," she said, but I doubted it.

Rachel came in carrying a tray with our salads. "Did you reach him?" she asked.

"No, nobody was home."

"Let's eat. Maybe you can try again later."

"No. That's okay. I'll call another time."

The house was strangely quiet. I looked at the clock, its numbers glowing through the darkness. It was midnight. For hours the snow had blown hard against the walls, but now the wind had stopped and the moon had come out. I walked over to the window and looked out at the newly fallen snow. The tops of the tombstones were barely visible. Rachel's poinsettias had been totally buried. I made my way downstairs to the living room. I turned on the desk lamp, lit a fire, and pulled one of the old wing chairs in front of it. My eye was caught by the crystal Rachel had given me. It was sitting where I'd put it on the desk, winking in the firelight. I walked over to the desk, sat down. The scrap of paper with David's number on it stared back at me. I crumpled it up and threw it in the wastebasket.

I decided to write Rachel a poem. It was many years since I'd written anything other than a business proposal, but after a few false starts, I lost myself in the words, writing, "Am I sleeping with an Angel?" I finished the poem and slid the paper in my pocket. I started to write again, and the words flowed from my pen...

"My nights are filled with dreams of her. I've been searching for half my life. I know that she'll be coming soon."

Play CD Track 7
"She'll Be Coming Soon"

My nights are filled with dreams of her.
I've got a heart that's longing for a smile
And sweet caress,
And I've been searching for half my life.
Oh Lord, what's a man to do?

SLEEPING WITH AN ANGEL

I know that she'll be coming soon.
All my fears will be forgotten, my heart
will be singing a different tune.
I know that she'll be coming soon.
All those years of anxiously waiting
will be over soon.

Hopin' and prayin', on star lit nights,
For the woman I love, I'd send ten thousand
ships to fight.
She's all I've ever wanted, and it's hurtin' me inside
That a gift of so much love could be denied.

I know that she'll be coming soon.
All my fears will be forgotten, my heart will be
singing a different tune.
I know that she'll be coming soon.
All those years of anxiously waiting
will be over soon.

I can see you clearly as a moonlit night.
And just to touch your hand would make it
all worth while.
My fair maiden, won't you come fulfill my soul
From this deep slumber? Oh, come make me whole.

I know that she'll be coming soon.
All my fears will be forgotten, my heart
will be singing a different tune.
I know that she'll be coming soon.
All those years of anxiously waiting
will be over soon.

My fair maiden, won't you come fulfill my soul
From this deep slumber, Oh, come make me whole.

I was interrupted by a voice whispering, "Tony...I love you."

I whirled around in my chair.

"Rachel?" I peered toward the stairs, but no one replied. I turned back to the desk and wrote and rewrote long into the night.

Everyone had come up from Nuevo Laredo to celebrate Christmas. She watched her mother in a new red dress and black patent leather shoes accepting compliments on the new furniture. And the curtains in the kitchen, they were real lace? All the women, one by one, reached out and touched the flimsy material. "Light as a feather," they said. Even her papá was smiling and laughing and drinking beer. She looked at the clock and counted the hours until tomorrow. Oh, no, Carlos was coming to see her. If he asked her one more time to marry him, she was going to scream.

"Tony. Wake up, Tony."

I lifted my head from the desk.

"How long have you been down here?"

"Rachel. What time is it?"

"It's nearly eight. It's stopped snowing, and I need to go to town for groceries. What were you doing?" She glanced curiously at the papers on the desk.

"I was just writing some stuff."

I folded the papers and put them in my pocket.

Drifts had blown up against everything, so we spent the morning digging our way to the barn. Rachel flagged down a truck that was clearing the main road, and the driver plowed the road to the house for us for fifteen dollars. When he was finished, she backed the car out of the barn.

"You stay here, Rachel. I'll drive into town."

"I can do it, Tony."

"I know you can, but I'd feel better if you weren't on the roads."

"Tony..."

I opened the car door and pulled her gently out. Reluctantly, she let go of the steering wheel.

"I'll go with you, Tony."

"Rachel, I'll be fine. Have you got the list of what you need?"

She pulled it from her coat pocket and handed it to me. I sat in the driver's seat and rolled down the window. "Don't look so worried. I'll be back before you know it."

"Drive carefully. There may be ice under the snow."

I rolled up the window and waved to her reassuringly. I turned the car around so I wouldn't have to back all the way down the long, curving driveway. Pulling on the headlights, I started slowly down the hill. I looked in the rearview mirror one last time before rounding the corner of the house, and Rachel was still standing there, watching.

I'd barely gone thirty yards when I felt the car start to slide out to the left. I guided the wheels carefully in the direction of the skid and the car righted itself. The steering wheel jerked sharply to the right. I must have hit a pothole in the road. I pulled on the steering wheel, but something was tugging it away from me. I pulled with all my might, but the wheel wouldn't budge. The car slipped off the plowed road and slid sideways down the hill. Whatever was holding the wheel suddenly released its grip, and the car flipped as it gained momentum. I was hanging by my seatbelt, and I wasn't sure if I was upside down or if the car was still on its side. The snow surged against the windows, and I heard and felt the glass shatter. There was a tremendous jolt as the car hit something hard, and the snow poured in. My face was full of snow and cold air rushed past my head. My heart was pounding out of control, then stopped.

A blinding light burst around me. It was hot, so hot. I ran as fast as I could, my shoes kicking up clouds of dust every time my feet hit the ground. I left the road and cut behind the cactus, so that I would beat the men on horseback to the house. Faster and faster my feet carried me, pounding the ground. I heard the horses and the voices of the men urging the animals on.

I could see him now, my grandfather, standing in front of the hacienda. I ran and ran, crying his name, "*Abuelo*!" He knelt down and opened his arms to me. My grandmother came out onto the porch, her long skirt swaying and sweeping across the wooden boards.

"Antonio," my grandfather said, gently smiling at me.

"*Los hombres, los revolutionarios*," I cried as I flung myself into his arms.

"*No tengas miedo, pegueño*," my grandfather said. "Don't be scared, little one." But his words did not calm my fear of these men.

And then they were there, in front of us with their guns, and my grandfather stood to face them. I buried my face against his clothing, feeling the scratchiness of the cloth against my closed eyelids.

From out of the darkness came the bobbing flames of candles carried by unseen hands. A white, sugar-spun skull heaved up, and my grandfather spoke to me, and it brought tears to my eyes to hear his voice again.

"Antonio, what are you doing? So much you have forgotten that I taught you. Things I learned from my father and that he learned from his father. What it is to be a man of honor in this world. You are the reason your ancestors ever existed. For who we have been, you are now."

I reached my hand out, fumbling for his hand, wanting him to take my small hand in his big, rough one, but he shook my hand away from his. I pressed my face closer against him.

"What of my great grandson, your son, what have you passed on to him?" he said. "He is of us, and you have forsaken him. You must go back."

"No, grandfather," I pleaded. "How will I know what to do?"

"*Cada paso determina tu camino. Toma el primer paso, Antonio.* Each step determines your path. Take the first step, Antonio."

The leather thong gave way under my fingers, and the armor slipped off my chest. I rose, swaying, the bodies stretching out on all sides of me, reeking of death. She was there, the woman in white, still kneeling amongst the dead, cradling the dying in her arms. I called to her. "Zeptha."

She turned and looked at me, then smiled.

Rachel stood watching the car make its way slowly down the plowed drive. She watched intently, willing the car safely to the main road. A strangled gasp escaped her throat as she saw the car fishtail to the left. Then a huge blow to her back sent her sprawling face down in the snow. She struggled to get up, but something was holding her down, pushing her face further into the snow. She summoned all her strength and slipped beneath the powerful grasp. When she was standing, she could barely see, the snow was blowing so hard, whirling and eddying with gale force. She knew that they were there, the old one and the greedy one who would have a man's soul. The wind whipped against her face like the blades of a hundred tiny knives. Her hands were around her head, fighting off the pricking blows. If she could only find it, and hold on to it. The wind began to shriek, louder and louder, and she wanted to cover her ears, but she knew that would be a fatal mistake.

Celinda watched in awe as *La Vieja* flew in a fury at the woman standing in the snow. The woman's arms and hands were around her head, trying to protect herself, and the girl trembled with fear and excitement. The girl clung to the old one, held to her by the sheer force of the old one's power. *La Vieja* shrieked an unearthly scream and lunged for the woman, but the woman was stronger than she looked and fought back with a great power. Then the girl felt the thrashing and flailing of the old one, and for the first time, she began to be afraid for what she had tried to do. *La Vieja* squirmed and writhed in the grasp of the beautiful woman. Celinda held on and felt the final tremor when it shuddered through *La Vieja.* All her hopes, her dreams, she was losing them all. Then there was nothing holding them, and they were falling, falling through darkness. When everything became still, she was aware of the hard floor against her cheek. She opened her eyes. The old one lay, unmoving, in a crumpled heap on the floor, and she knew, then, that he was lost to her forever.

Rachel stood limply in the silence, gasping, gazing numbly around her at the snow-plastered walls of the house and barn, then down at the circular patch of bare ground where no snow remained. Tony!

She ran around the corner of the house and saw the tire tracks heading off through the snow of the front yard. The car lay on its side against the boulder. The entire front end was smashed in; the windows were shattered.

She raced down the hill towards the car, slipping and sliding on the drive which was a solid sheet of ice under the snow.

"Tony!" she screamed. "Tony, answer me!"

She reached the car and looked in. It was empty. Something must have gone wrong. He should be fine. They couldn't have won. She pulled off her gloves and frantically started digging under the car. Her hand touched something, and she dug harder. It was a boot. Frightened, she dug carefully around it. The boot came free and slid into her hand. She peered into the hole she'd cleared, but couldn't see anything. She stood up and looked around, trying to figure out how she was going to get him out from under the car when the car settled and shifted deeper into the snow with a muffled, crunching sound. Rachel stood and looked around to see if anyone was watching, then bent down to lift the car. She stopped, listening. It came, faintly at first, and then louder. A cough, then another. She slid down the hill, below the glacier boulder. Tony was standing on one foot, leaning against the rock, wiping snow off his face. His other foot was bare.

"Tony." Her knees went weak with relief. "How? How did you get here?"

"I'm not sure," he said.

I had no idea how I'd gotten out of the car and below the boulder, and after I saw the car and the shape it was in, I would have thought it was impossible.

"Are you okay?"

"I think so. I can move everything, but my foot's cold."

"You scared the hell out of me, Tony." Rachel knelt in front of me and rubbed my foot in her hands before putting the boot on.

When she stood up, I pulled her towards me and hugged and kissed her, tears streaming down my face.

"Rachel..."

"I'm so glad you're all right, Tony." We stood there in the snow hugging each other.

"You folks okay?"

It was the snow plow driver. We hadn't heard him approach up in his noisy plow. "I heard the crash from near a quarter mile away." He whistled when he looked at the Toyota. "Looky there. Looks like you'll have to write her off. You okay, ma'am? I can drive you into town to see a doctor. Your ears look like they're pretty bad."

I hadn't noticed that there was a thin trickle of blood coming from each of Rachel's ears.

"Rachel, what's wrong? Have you been hurt?" I asked anxiously.

"No, it's just the cold. It happens sometimes. Perhaps you should go see a doctor to make sure you're all right, Tony. And we could use some groceries and a rental car." She brushed the snow off my clothes, smiling at me.

On the way home the roads were clear, with huge banks of dirty snow lining the sides. Why New Jersey was called "The Garden State" had always been a mystery to me. It was always downright ugly whenever I drove through it. It's true that I'd never left the interstate, but there never looked like much of a reason to.

I glanced over at Rachel, curled up asleep, her pillow jammed against the car window. What a wonderful time I'd had with her. I was so thankful that we were both safe. I found myself thinking of my grandfather, and all he'd lost, and how he went on to a new life in a new country. I understood the courage of this man. I understood things I had never understood as a child.

"Would you like me to drive?" Rachel asked in a sleepy voice.

"I thought you were asleep."

"I was, but I'm awake now." She stretched, pressing her hands against the roof of the car.

"No, I'm fine. I was planning on stopping soon to get a cup of coffee."

"This car rides pretty nicely for a rental. Maybe I should get one like this."

"I'm sorry I wrecked your car, Rachel."

"It's just a car. I'll get another."

"That's it?"

"What do you mean?"

"Rachel, I wrecked your car!"

"I know. I was there. It was just a car, Tony."

"I'd be so upset if that had happened to my car."

"That's because you get attached to things so much."

"I'll go with you to help you get a new one."

Rachel sighed in exasperation. "Will you please stop worrying about it?"

"Okay, okay. I'm stopping right now."

"Good."

I turned on the radio, flicking through the stations, trying to find something good.

"Do you have to keep doing that?" Rachel sounded like she was getting more irritated.

"I can't just listen to anything."

She gave me a look, and buried her head in her pillow.

I left it on the last station I'd flipped to, and I adjusted the sound so it wouldn't disturb her.

Play CD Track 8
"I Wanna Know"

In the face of grace, I've turned and run away.
My heart knows the truth,
and somehow I'll find a way back to you.
I felt the passion of it all,
So why do I see myself backed against the wall?

Restless and confused, bound by nothing new,
Know it's only in my mind, oh, what am I to do?
Living inside, you see, there's more than meets the eye,
Fighting for my soul 'til the day I die.

Shades of gray internalized, troubled by this life of mine,
I wanna know...
I change like the wind.
Will I ever find myself again?

Sometimes, inside my head, I hear whispers in the dark
Tryin' to make their way straight between the heart.
In the right, I see the freedom of it all,
But somehow I lose the feel, and I stumble and I fall.

I wanna know
Shades of gray internalized, troubled by this life of mine.
I wanna know
Will the colors of my heart set me free?

I wanna know
Shades of gray internalized, troubled by this life of mine.
I wanna know
I change like the wind,
Will I ever find myself again?

I wanna know
Shades of gray internalized, troubled by this life of mine.
I wanna know
Will the colors of my heart set me free?
I wanna know...will the colors of my heart set me free?
I wanna know...
I change like the wind.
Will I ever find myself again?

The song ended, and I turned the radio off. "That's how I feel," I said to Rachel, but there was no response from her. She was asleep again, but I kept talking to her anyway. "I can't imagine what it would be like without you in my life, or where I'd be right now, but I know it wouldn't be as half a good a place."

The light was fading behind the gray skies, so I turned on the headlights. The road lay flat and straight in front of me, and I knew I had a chance if I stayed to the right of the white line.

The first few days back at the mansion, I wandered from room to room, trying to get my bearings. Something had changed, but I wasn't sure what. I was still jittery from the accident, of course, but what I decided it came down to, was that the house was the same, but I had changed. The Ambassador had noticeably changed, however. He was nursing a rather nasty black eye given to him by his ex-wife on Christmas Day. She'd thrown an ashtray at him, and he had to have twelve stitches. Nothing ever dampened his spirits though, and we were genuinely happy to see each other again. I'd received a Christmas card from

Hal Buckman out in Santa Fe. It was a lone Indian on a horse staring up at a single, bright star. I found some symbolism in that one for me. Big Ed had moved out and taken his 26-inch TV with him. Madam was nowhere to be seen. The Ambassador said he'd thought she'd spent Christmas with some friends from her church. Buddha Markham was gone, too. He'd finally been nailed on some fruit and vegetable scam in Mexico. My answering machine had a Christmas message from my dad. He and his wife Greta had gone to Texas to be with her family. He sounded like he had a bad cold. What an end to one of the worst years of my life...

New Year's Eve found me seriously depressed about my future. I kept sending money to Hal, but results were eluding me. A long talk with Stan Owens, Jr. after the first of the year, regarding my salary, or, rather, what I considered the lack thereof, would definitely be necessary. New Year's Eve itself was quiet. It was the first time I hadn't gone out partying all night. Rachel, the Ambassador, and I played cards until a quarter to twelve, when the Ambassador excused himself and went to bed. It never crossed my mind until much later that he left so Rachel and I could be alone at midnight. Rachel picked the cards up and started shuffling.

"Gin rummy?" she said.

I looked at my watch. "Sure. We still have a few minutes to go. I hope this will be a good year." I wasn't sad to see this one end.

"It will be."

"You sound so sure."

"I am. You start. I dealt."

"Do people ever get as irritated as I do about your always being right?"

"It irritates you?"

I arranged the cards in my hand.

Rachel laid down the last of her cards. "Gin."

"See what I mean! I still have a hand full of cards. Either you're cheating, or you've got God on your side!"

"Do you hear that?"

"What?

"It's the clock in the hall. Happy New Year, Tony."

"Happy New Year." I leaned across the table and kissed her, and I felt like I was floating in a sea of roses.

"Nice," she murmured, and I wasn't sure if it was a statement or a question.

It wasn't three days into the new year, when Madam surfaced and reared her ugly head.

"Are you two sleeping together?"

Rachel and I had been doing our breakfast dishes and laughing over a joke, when we heard Madam repeat the question.

"I said, 'Are you two sleeping together?'" She stood defiantly in the doorway. Next to her was one of her friends from church. Rachel took one look and turned back to doing the dishes.

"It's none of your business," she said. "Whatever our relationship is, it's between us. You have no business and no right to pry into our personal lives."

"As long as you are in my house, you need to play by my rules."

Her church friend chimed in. "Besides, it's a sin."

I took one look at the friend and decided it wasn't a sin, but an impossibility, for her.

"Sleeping together is not going to be tolerated here," Madam said firmly. She stamped her foot to emphasize the word "here" and threw back her head haughtily.

I was furious. "You have no right to..."

I didn't get a chance to finish my sentence. Rachel interrupted me by laying her hand on my arm. "Tony, I have to get ready for work, or I'll be late," she said quietly. She left the kitchen, walking past Madam and her friend as if they didn't exist.

Losing one-half of her audience didn't stop Madam. "You two have been warned. I won't have this going on in my house." With that, she turned abruptly and left, with her friend in tow.

"You're lucky to still have us!" I shouted after her.

I went upstairs and knocked on Rachel's door, but there was no answer. I tried the door, but it wouldn't open, because she had something jammed up against it. I heard the shower running, so I decided I'd talk to her later. I went to my room and got ready for work. I decided that today was the day Stan and I were going to have our little talk about my salary.

The phones were ringing constantly when I arrived at Alternative Energies, so Rachel and I could do nothing more than exchange a quick glance. My talk with Stan, Jr. didn't last very long. He accused me of diverting business to other companies with my outside lobbying, which wasn't true; and I accused him of not living up to his promises of higher pay, which was true.

I said, "I quit."

He said, "You're fired."

I was gathering my stuff in my office, when the intercom buzzed. It was Rachel.

"Tony, Hal Buckman's on Line Three. Do you want to take it?"

What lousy timing the guy had, but I had the feeling no time would be a good time to talk to Hal. "I'll talk to him. Rachel, I quit."

"I know. I think everyone in the building knows."

"We were that loud?"

"Tony, the phone's ringing. I'll see you later."

I pushed Line Three. "Hello, Hal."

"Hiya, Tony. How's it goin' in the nation's capital?"

"Could be better, Hal. What's up?"

"Cougar's been sighted, prowlin' 'roun the foothills here."

"No kidding." I sighed. When he started with the local news, I knew he was easing into the bad news slowly.

"I got some developments for ya. Some good and some not so good."

"Start with the good, Hal."

"The Chapter Seven liquidation of the radio station is almost finalized, and I've worked out a deal with Ramirez and Celinda on your furniture. She wants everthin'..."

I interrupted. "That's the deal?"

"Hold on! She wants everythin', excep' she'll give ya back your antiques from the Washington townhouse. You can have a mover take 'em to your folks in Sanibel."

"Hal, the antiques were less than a fourth of what I owned. That's not good news. Besides, why move everything to Sanibel?"

"All your furniture's right here in Santa Fe." Hal hurried on before I had time to comment on her lugging my furniture half-way across the country. "It'll save ya money, Tony."

"Jeez, that woman never saved me money. What's the rest?"

"This is the bad part. A Mr. Hugh Hightower has sent a letter to the bankruptcy judge, allegin' that you misappropriated company funds. Now, Tony, this is serious. We're talkin' indictment here, if'n we don't handle this right. What's the true dealin' on this?"

"I never misappropriated a dime, Hal. This is coming from Celinda. Laura Ruston, who works with Hugh Hightower, told me that Celinda called and told Hightower I took fifty thousand dollars of his investment. What I did is take the fifty thousand dollars I loaned the company up front, and I paid the station's bills. We were behind on rent payments and equipment leases. It's all legal and proper, Hal."

"I see. My read on this is that Hightower wants the radio station. If he can prove fraud, that kicks out your bankruptcy protection. I'm a gonna talk to this Hightower guy, an' see what he's got up his sleeve. Hate to say this, Tony, but I'm gonna need another five grand."

I heaved a big sigh. "Okay, Hal. I'll get it to you this week."

"I'm goin' to prepare a letter to the court protestin' Hightower's letter. We don't need another wrinkle in this case, so I'm goin' to ask you straight out. There any skeletons danglin' in any closets that I need to know about?"

"No, Hal."

"Good. I was hopin' you'd say that. Your financials should support our case, so I'll keep my eyeballs peeled for the fifty thousand loan payment. Your accountant would've made a notation on somethin' like that."

"Keep me posted, Hal."

I hung up the phone and felt like the walls were closing in on me. I had to get out of here. I put the rest of my stuff in a cardboard box, lugged it out to the car, and threw it in the trunk. I headed for Rock Creek Parkway, pulled off the road, and sat staring at the creek for a couple of hours until I got cold. For the first time in my life, I understood why someone would shoot himself.

Her mother was furious. Consuela was screaming and crying at the same time, while her father just sat there, looking at the floor. She could tell that he was going to be no help. Celinda spoke quietly to her mother, hoping her voice would calm her.

"Mamá, I told the lawyer I would let Tony have the bedroom furniture."

"No. No. No," her mother wailed. "All my life I have wanted such a bed as this, and such a dresser, and now I have them."

"Consuela, please," her father pleaded.

"Shush," Consuela hissed. "I have a beautiful bed, and no man for it." She threw herself defiantly into the center of the bed. "I will tie myself to the bed."

"Mamá," Celinda said wearily. "All right, you can keep the bedroom set. I will pretend I didn't understand, and give him something else back."

"Give him the couch. It is ugly," her mother said, smiling triumphantly.

It was dark when I awoke from my nap. I wondered where Rachel was, then realized it was her group therapy night. I opened my door and looked down the hall. I saw a crack of light coming from under Madam's door, so I decided to confront her about her accusations. I knocked and didn't even wait for her answer. She was seated at her dressing table, putting on her makeup.

"Mrs. Jamison, you and I need to talk."

"Now? I'm busy, can't you see that?"

"It's important. Otherwise, I wouldn't be disturbing you right now."

She turned towards me impatiently, and my anxiety level went up a few notches. I didn't want to get myself kicked out of the house. I'd lost my job. I sure as hell didn't want to lose the roof over my head, but I just couldn't let this morning's incident go by. I was going to have to be real careful how I said this. I began very calmly.

"I found your insinuations this morning about Rachel and myself very upsetting, especially since they aren't true. I'm puzzled as to why you would want to hurt us, when we've done everything we can to get along with you and do things the way you want."

She looked down at all her jars of makeup on the table and burst into tears.

I was astonished, and I acted like any man confronted by a woman's tears. I stood there looking helpless.

"I am so very sorry, Tony," she sobbed. "It's not you and Rachel. I shouldn't take it out on you two. It's just that I'm so scared. I don't know what I'm going to do."

"Aw, Mrs. Jamison, don't cry, please." I pulled a chair over and sat down next to her. She looked so frail and vulnerable sitting on her upholstered bench. I was becoming unglued at the sight of her misery, which could have equaled my own.

Tears rolled down her face as she talked. "I took the money, the equity I have in the house, and I gave it to these friends of Reverend Mike's. It's been so hard since Richard died. Once he was gone, no one would have anything to do with me. So I gave the money to these men to invest. They said I would make millions, but now they own the house, and I pay them rent from what you and everyone else pays me, and the heating bills are so high. Tell Rachel I'm sorry. Half the time, I don't know what I'm saying anymore. I never thought I'd be in such a mess. I don't want to give up my house. Maggie died here."

Madam reached over and picked up a framed photograph of a little girl with long blonde hair, wearing Mary Jane shoes. She'd evidently found the missing photograph. "She's used to my being here.

We thought it was only a cold..."

Madam broke into wracking sobs. I fought not to break down and sob with her.

"I'm sure Maggie understands, Mrs. Jamison." It was Rachel. We hadn't heard her come in. She came over and put her hand on Madam's shoulder, and Mrs. Jamison leaned against her and wept.

"I'm so sorry, Rachel, for what I said to you and Tony."

"We know that. Maggie loves you. I'm sure of it, and wherever you go, she'll be there with you," Rachel said reassuringly. "I promise you."

"You promise me?"

"Yes, I do."

Madam let out a long sigh. She reached for a Kleenex and started dabbing at her face. "My makeup is such a mess." She smiled at herself in the mirror.

Rachel nudged me. "Come on, Tony. Mrs. Jamison needs to get ready."

Madam peered closely into the mirror. "My eyes are so red. I'm expecting some senators and congressional aides this evening. You know..."

We left her gazing in the mirror and attaching her fake eyelashes. Rachel and I were at the door when she called shyly after us.

"Rachel, do you really believe that Maggie still loves me?"

"Yes, I do," said Rachel. She smiled at me with her eyes as we softly closed the door.

I tossed and turned on the hard, cold metal, cold even through all my layers of clothing. The steam was rising around me, and even it couldn't keep me from trembling with cold. I clutched at the grate with my fingers, pulling myself...

I sat bolt upright in bed. It was night, and I was in a cold sweat. It had been a terrifying nightmare, with me as a homeless person, sleeping on the streets at night. I was relieved to look over and find Rachel next to me, sound asleep. The dream had felt all too real. It couldn't be very late, because I could still hear the voices of Madam's guests and music playing. I decided I was hungry, and opened the door to head into the hallway. Standing near the door of Big Ed's old room stood a child — a beautiful little girl with long blonde hair. Her dress was the palest of pinks, with a round, white collar. She turned her head, looking back over her shoulder towards the other end of the hall, as if she were making a gesture. Then she started walking slowly towards me, with a soft, sweet smile on her face — not sad, not happy, but content. At the landing, she turned towards the stairway and disappeared. I slowly closed the door and crawled back into bed, no longer anxious or hungry, and fell into a deep, peaceful sleep.

"Tony, the phone's for you"

"Rachel, what time is it?"

"It's eight in the morning, and you have a phone call."

Rachel handed me the phone and crawled back into bed.

"Dad?" the voice on the other end said.

"David! Where are you? How are you? Are you all right?"

"I'm fine, Dad. I'm out in L.A., doing a recording session."

"A recording session? That's great! Tell me about it."

"I recorded two songs in Colorado. The local radio station played them. Then a guy at the station hooked me up with this studio out in Los Angeles, and here I am. I'm doing a demo to see if I can get an agent. Mom and my step-dad are financing it, and they're cutting me a deal."

"I'm impressed, David, and very proud of you."

"I know this is kind of off the wall, but I'd really like to have you come out to L.A. to watch me record."

"I'd love to come, David. Listen, I'm sorry about what Celinda said. She was wrong. She's out of my life."

"I know. Rachel sounds like a great lady."

"Rachel?"

"I gotta go. They're waiting for me. Call me with your arrival time. Bye."

I hung up the phone, speechless and not just a little confused. "Rachel, what do you know about this?"

She waved a scrap of paper in front of my nose, with David's Colorado phone number on it. It was the paper I'd thrown away when I was at the house in Connecticut at Christmas.

"You called him?"

"I did. We've been talking for weeks, and I already have the tickets for us to go."

"Oh, Rachel..."

I barely made our flight for Los Angeles. Rachel was meeting me at Dulles, as she was heading out straight from work. I got it into my head that I had to pick up the pictures of our Connecticut trip, that I'd dropped off to have developed, so we could look at them on the plane. Rachel was standing by the gate, worriedly looking up and down the concourse. When she saw me, she waved me on.

"Hurry, Tony, they're going to close the door."

I sprinted for the gate, and we dashed on board just as the stewardess sealed the door shut behind us. Rachel led the way to our seats. I was barely settled by the time the plane took off.

"What happened?" she asked.

"I wanted to pick up the photos from our Connecticut trip, so I could show David."

"But you nearly missed the plane."

"I know."

"So, how did they turn out?"

"I haven't looked at them yet." I pulled the envelope from my suit coat pocket, and was disappointed to find that every frame was so overexposed you couldn't see anything.

Rachel laughed. "It looks like there was a lot of snow."

"Rachel, don't tease. I don't know what I did. I had some great shots of you. I always screw them up somehow," I said dejectedly.

"I told you I took terrible pictures," she said with mock seriousness.

"It's not you. It's me. It's mechanical things. I've never been able to use a camera. I think I can see your face in this one."

I angled the overhead light down onto the photo. I could barely make out Rachel's face, but it looked like the one I took of her sitting on the bed in the upstairs bedroom. "Remember the one I took of you on Christmas morning? I think this is it."

Rachel squinted at the photo in my hand. "Those do look like my eyebrows, Tony. I look like a ghost."

That reminded me about last night. "I saw her, Rachel."

"Saw who?"

"Maggie. Madam's daughter. She's very beautiful."

"Yes, she is."

"Not scary at all. But, I don't understand how it's possible."

"Some things can't be explained, Tony."

"I know you're always telling me that, but I feel better if I know exactly how everything works."

Rachel smiled at me. "So what are you going to do with the photographs?"

"I'm going to keep them anyway." I put them back in the envelope and tucked them into my pocket. "I like them."

Rachel yawned. "I'm going to get some sleep. Is David meeting us at the airport?"

"Yes, he's going to pick us up and drive us to the hotel. The recording session is tomorrow at 10 a.m."

Rachel went to sleep. I pulled out the photos I had taken of her and tried to figure out what I'd done wrong.

Rachel pretended to be asleep, and through half-closed eyes she watched Tony look at each photograph in turn. He'd been so upset when they hadn't turned out. No doubt he was going to want to take her picture again, and she dreaded the thought. But she comforted herself with the fact that he'd seen Maggie and not been frightened. He'd begun to accept things he would have rigidly denied in the past. Opening up was the hardest part, but it paved the way for a new person to emerge.

David was waiting for us when we disembarked, but he wasn't alone. She was petite and dark, and stood only as high as his shoulder.

"Hi, Dad. This is Sara."

I wasn't prepared for this, my son with a girlfriend. I always think of him in my mind as eight years old since, that's how old he was when Julie and I split up. Sara looked like a very nice girl.

I introduced Rachel to David. He gave me a secret sign that he thought she was okay.

"Dad, Grandma called and asked me to have you give her a call as soon as you landed."

"Is anything wrong?"

"She didn't say."

"I'll call her now."

I found a fairly quiet pay phone and dialed.

"It's Tony, Mom."

"Oh, I'm so glad you called. Your flight was okay?"

"Yeah, Mom, it was fine. Is anything wrong?"

"It's your father. He's in the hospital."

My heart skipped a beat. "Why?"

"He went in today for observation. He's been complaining of chest pains and trouble breathing, so the doctor thought he should go in for some tests. She didn't even call me, that wife of his. I found out through your brother. Estefan always calls me after he visits your father."

"You haven't seen him?"

"No. That woman he married doesn't want me to go near the hospital, but Estefan said he'd call me every day. I just wanted you to know."

"Thanks, Mom. What hospital is he at?"

"He's at Twin Oaks, out by the new highway."

"Do you think I should come?"

"No. Not now. He should be out in a couple of days. They'll probably tell him to stop eating all that spicy food," she said, laughing.

"Thanks for letting me know. I'll call you tomorrow."

I hung up and stared at the phone. I was scared. I didn't remember my dad ever being sick. I couldn't imagine my life without my father in it. He must be almost eighty years old, but I couldn't believe that either. It seemed like only yesterday he was coming to watch me play football.

Rachel, David, and Sara were still in the waiting area. Rachel could tell something was wrong.

"Is everything okay, Tony?"

"Dad's in the hospital."

David looked alarmed now. "Grandpa?"

"It's probably nothing," I reassured them. "He's having some tests. Mom just wanted to let me know. Let's go get dinner. Know any good places, David?"

"What about sushi, Dad?"

"Sushi," I replied thoughtfully.

"What's sushi?" said Rachel.

Sushi is definitely pretty interesting stuff. It wasn't bad, but then, I'll eat anything. I prefer my fish grilled over mesquite, but hey, when in L.A....

After dinner, we dropped Rachel off at the hotel, and David and I drove Sara home. On the way back, we took the Pacific Coast Highway, and as we headed past the cliffs in Santa Monica, I decided I wanted to walk along the beach.

"Right now, Dad?" David exclaimed.

"Yeah, why not?" I was so happy to have my son back in my life. What a gift Rachel had given me.

"But it's almost midnight."

"It's a beautiful night."

"Okay." David turned off the road and parked. We took off our shoes and headed for the water's edge. It was unseasonably warm and balmy for a January night in California. The clouds covered a moon trying to peek out. The smell of the ocean was invigorating as we walked along in the rippling surf, our footprints sinking into the wet sand, then disappearing under the next wave.

"This is great," I said, sitting down on the sand.

David dropped down next to me. "You know, it is nice. I hadn't realized what I'd been missing. Rachel seems like a really nice person."

"So why is she with me, you're wondering?"

"Naw. I'm just glad you found her."

"I think maybe she found me, and I'm glad she did, too. Tell me about Sara."

"I think I love her, Dad," David said, bashfully, " but I'm not sure. How do you know when you're in love?"

"I'm not sure I'm the one to ask," I said, ruefully. "I think I got love and sex all mixed up, like they were one and the same thing. And they're not. I think it's loving someone for who they are, and not for what they can give you, or how they make you look good when they're next to you."

"Did you love my mom?"

"Yes, I did. I loved her very much, and I only wish I knew then what I know now. But one thing's for sure, I love you. I was so happy the day you were born. I'll never forget the first time I saw you, and when I held you, I was so proud. You were, and are, my son."

"I wasn't sure. You were never there."

"That was stupid on my part. I was just plain stupid and very young, but I'm here now, and I'm planning to stay."

David grinned at me.

"So, it sounds serious between you and Sara," I hinted.

"Not yet. What about you and Rachel?"

I shrugged my shoulders. "I don't know."

"This is weird, talking 'girlfriends' with your dad."

"It is, isn't it?" I said, laughing. "David, I've written something. It's for Rachel. It started out as a poem, but I think it might make a good song. Would you mind looking it over? Maybe you could do something with it for me. If you need to change any of the words, it's okay."

David took the papers from me and glanced at the words. "Sure, Dad, I'll play around with it."

"Thanks. Well, I guess we'd better get going," I said, standing. "Early day tomorrow."

She loved the sushi last night, but this morning her stomach felt very queasy. She asked them to stop at the pharmacy on the way to the recording studio. Tony brought her out something called Alka-Seltzer, along with a bottle of water. Fortunately, it seemed to be working. David told her that the recording studio was owned by a friend of his from his days of touring. They were recording a new song, which he was planning to submit to an agent in hopes of getting an audition. Rachel had never seen anything like it before. All those levers and lights. She didn't quite understand how it worked.

"It's your first time in a recording studio?" David asked her.

Rachel nodded. "It all seems very complicated."

"Not really, once you get the hang of it. It's fun."

"You really love music, don't you?"

"More than anything. You known my dad a long time?"

"Not too long."

"He really likes you, you know," David said, awkwardly.

"I like him, too, David."

"He seems different."

"Different?"

"I don't know what it is. He's just nicer, and he looks happier. Is that because of you?"

Rachel laughed. "I can't take credit for that."

"I'm not so sure."

"He's very proud of you, and your music."

"I sometimes wonder. He was irritated when I didn't take the music scholarship."

"He was just being a father."

"A father?"

"Yes. A father. Fathers worry sometimes."

"You're nice. I'm glad he met you. I guess they're ready for me."

She watched him walk over to the producer. She noticed that he held his body and moved the same way as his dad.

Rachel and David seemed to be getting along very well. I wondered what they were laughing and talking about, and felt a little jealous being excluded. Right before David was to start, Rachel got us all together in a circle. We stood quietly holding hands for a minute, then Rachel lowered her head and spoke. "Heavenly Father, bless the music that fills this place, and hear the words his music makes."

We dropped hands and left David alone in the studio, but I felt I'd never been closer to my son and his dreams. When he put on his earphones and began to sing, he was singing for both of us.

Play CD Track 9
"Dear Rachel"

I hear you calling my name,
Whispering words of love again,
And just the sound of your voice fans the flames.
Graceful, lovely, like some angelic Princess,
When I'm with you I lose my defenses,
And if I said, "I didn't love you", I'd be a liar.

Dear Rachel, I just want to say
That I love you, and this love is here to stay.
Let's hold each other forever in the night
And let the sun wake us with her light.

While we sit by the fireside
Telling stories about each others lives,
How can I contain this love I'm concealing?
Am I willing to take a chance,
Express my feelings about our romance
To finally shed some light on just how I'm feeling.

Dear Rachel, I just want to say
That I love you, and this love is here to stay.
Let's hold each other forever in the night
And let the sun wake us with her light.

Dear Rachel, I just want to say
That I love you, and this love is here to stay.
Let's hold each other forever in the night
And let the sun wake us with her light.

And let the sun wake us with her light.
And let the sun...
And let the sun...
And let the sun...

I looked over at Rachel. She was leaning forward, staring intently at David while he sang. I watched her for a long time, and she must have felt my eyes on her, for she turned and smiled knowingly at me.

I had no idea how much went into a recording session, so it was about midafternoon before I realized I hadn't talked to my mom. I called her, but there was no answer, which made me feel uneasy. The call came about an hour later, just as David was wrapping up. It was Mom, and she'd been crying.

"Tony, you'd better come home."

The tone of her voice scared me. "What do you mean? I thought it was nothing," I said.

"Oh, Tony, you've got to come," she wailed. "Something's wrong. He had a bad spell this morning. I don't know what to do."

"Okay, Mom. I'm on my way. I'm leaving right now." I could hear her crying. "Mom, did you hear me?"

"Yes. Get here as fast as you can, Tony."

It was night, and the corridor was endless. I turned at the doorway of the airplane to wave goodbye to David. His face was white, drained of all color, his eyes two small, dark circles. He was scared, too. Rachel's hand lay firmly on my arm. She talked to me as if I'd been injured and needed reassurance that I would be okay.

"Tony, our seats are on the right, 17A and B." I felt her hand on my arm, stopping me. "They're here, Tony."

I sat down and fastened my seatbelt. Through the window I could see the ground crew loading the baggage. It had started to rain, and the water ran in rivulets down the glass. It was late at night; only a few passengers had their overhead lights on. I stared straight ahead at the seat in front of me, and found myself wondering about the person who chooses fabric for airplane seats. Then I realized Rachel was speaking to me.

"Are you all right, Tony?"

"He's never been sick, you know. Allergies once in awhile, but never really sick." I turned to face her. "I'm sorry. What did you just ask me?"

"I asked if you're all right."

"I'm okay. It's the idea of my dad being in a hospital."

"Do you want something to drink?" she asked.

"Coffee would be good. Not decaf. Real coffee."

The flight attendant brought my coffee. I wrapped my hands around the hot cup, and it comforted me. Rachel had her bring me a pillow, too. Then Rachel pulled one of those airline magazines out of the pocket in front of her and started reading.

I stared out the window, but there was nothing to see but my own reflection staring back at me, so I pulled the shade down. I slowly sipped my coffee and drummed my fingers on the pull-down tray in front of me. The plane was not moving fast enough, and I imagined myself rocketing through the skies and to my dad's room in a matter of seconds. I thought about the last time I'd heard his voice, the message on my answering machine wishing me a Merry Christmas. Why hadn't I paid more attention? I thought it was just a bad cold. I played the message over and over again in my head, as a way to hold on to him.

I turned to Rachel for comfort, but I noticed she was very absorbed in what she was reading. I glanced at the article's title. *"Living in Paradise"* it said, and underneath the heading was a color photo of an island in the South Pacific, complete with palm trees and a curving sandy beach. I pointed to the picture.

"Where is that?" I said excitedly.

Rachel read the caption out loud, "'Mala Bay on the island of Tapa'u. This beautiful island is paradise for the inhabitants of this tiny kingdom in the South Pacific. No one has to work in the Kingdom of Tapa'u. Postage stamps and Tapa'uan passports, $35,000 for a family of four, are the major sources of revenue. Life on this tiny island is...'"

I interrupted her. "Let me see that."

She handed me the magazine. "What's the matter?"

I held up the magazine, pointing to the photograph. "It's the island where the Ambassador and I are trying to get our CocoBono project started." I stared at the photograph. "It's beautiful!"

"They don't work, Tony."

I looked at Rachel uncertainly. "What?"

"They sell passports, Tony, for thousands of dollars. They don't have to work."

I had no idea what she was getting at. "Can I read this when you're done?"

"You can have it now," she said.

I read the article from front to back, twice. When I closed the magazine, I felt like the floor had opened up beneath me, and I was falling through thousands of feet of darkness to earth. There was going to be no yacht floating on Mala Bay. Princess Sava was never going to call. They didn't need us, or our project. I could see the Ambassador and I in wrap-around skirts, tossing coconut husks into a truck, while the natives sat around watching color TV.

"Lots of money isn't going to fix it," Rachel said to me.

"Fix what?"

"What you think is wrong," was all she said.

I slumped back in my seat, feeling discouragement and utter despair. The numbness, the hollowness, the pain, a black wall looming in front of me was all I could see. I plugged in the headset and closed my eyes.

Play CD Track 10
"Search my heart, Search my soul"

This valley is deep, and I can't seem to find my connection.
Somewhere down the line, I misplaced my direction.
I saw a wise man, he was sitting at the station.
And I said, "Hey man, can you help me find my destination?"

And he said...
Search your heart, well, search your soul,
Don't you know you're more than skin and bones?
You're at the crossroad, in need of some religion,
Don't you know, deep down, he's given you the vision?
Yeah

But, it's hard, so hard, when you've been living in a fool's paradise.
Well, deception, lies, they've cut me down to size,
And I can hardly recognize myself anymore.

Search my heart, well, search my soul,
Don't you know I'm more than skin and bones?
I'm at the crossroads, in need of your redemption,
Oh, my Lord, my God, please give me inner vision.

Well, search my heart and search my soul,
Don't you know I'm more than skin and bones?
I'm at the crossroads, in need of your redemption,
Oh, my Lord, my God, please give me inner vision.

Well, search my heart and search my soul,
Don't you know I'm more than skin and bones?
I'm at the crossroads, in need of your redemption,
Oh, my Lord, my God, please give me inner vision.

I'm in need of your religion.
I need some redemption.

I slipped the headset off and stared down at it in my hands. The song was playing faintly when I pulled the plug out of the jack.

I slammed the door on the rental car trunk and went around to the other side to let Rachel in. She laid her hand over mine as I put it on the door handle.

"It's late. We could stay in Albuquerque tonight and get a fresh start in the morning."

"My mom's waiting."

Rachel nodded wearily and got in. I relaxed a bit once we got away from the harsh city lights and into the darkness of the desert. There were very few cars traveling on the highway; the only other light was the crescent moon hanging off to our west, above the mountain range. Rachel fell asleep, and I soon followed.

I woke up with a start when the car came to a lurching stop. A few rocks and a scraggly cactus were lit by the headlights. I had no idea where the road was. I got out of the car and looked around. The moon was behind us now. Our front wheels were in a ditch and the bumper was up against a rock. Rachel got out of the car, looked around, then looked at me across the top of the car.

"Where are we?"

I could tell by the sound of her voice that she was exasperated with me. I leaned both hands against the top of the car and looked at the ground.

"I know. We should have stayed in Albuquerque. I fell asleep at the wheel."

"Where's the road?"

"I don't know," I shouted. "Why is it everything always goes wrong? Everything always works out for you. Your practice is booming. My dad's a success. He's made lots of money. Everything worked out for him." I was pacing like a madman in the light from the headlights. "It's not fair. I deserve better than this for all I've done and how hard I've worked. But, no, what do I end up with? A big fat zero."

I came up short and glared at Rachel who was still standing by the car door.

"But you don't want to be successful," she yelled at me.

Her words were like a bomb going off in my head. "You're crazy!" I shouted at the top of my voice. "Do you think I like living like this, going from deal to deal, scrambling for money?"

"Look what you're choosing, Tony. Cement in Russia, coconuts in Tapawonga..."

"Tapa'u!" I screamed. "Tapa'u!"

"It doesn't matter what it's called," she shouted back at me. "You're chasing rainbows. Of course you're going to fail. You can't catch a rainbow."

Her words echoed across the desert. "You can't catch a rainbow. You can't catch a rainbow." The wind carried the words to the mountains, and the mountains sent them back to me with a force that nearly knocked me off my feet. I slumped sobbing to the rock. I felt Rachel's arm go across my shoulders as she sat down next to me.

"My dad never cried," I sobbed.

"You're not your dad," Rachel said gently.

"What if I don't get a chance to talk to him again?" I wept.

"You'll talk to him."

"How can you know that?"

"I just know."

Sanibel was deserted when we drove into town. Nothing moved across the streets and lawns except the cold desert wind. I looked in Rosita's as we drove by, half expecting to see Celinda and I laughing and talking together again, but the booths were empty and the counter glowed red in the light from the neon sign.

The porch light was on at my mom's house, as well as every other light inside. The house was a beacon, drawing me like a moth to a flame. The front door opened for us as we started up the steps, and I was surprised to see Al standing there in his pajamas.

"Hiya, Tony."

I looked past him into the house. "Hi, Al. Where's my mom?"

"She's in the kitchen waiting for you. Your dad's doin' a little better tonight."

"Thanks, Al. Al, this is my friend, Rachel."

"Pleased to meet'cha."

Al picked up our suitcases and set them inside the house. Mom was sitting at the kitchen table, sound asleep. A half-drunk cup of coffee was in front of her. We sat down quietly, and I reached over and gently shook her arm.

"Hey, Mom. It's Tony."

Mom opened her eyes and looked straight at Rachel. She jumped a little in her seat, closed her eyes and opened them again, like she wasn't sure what she'd just seen.

"This is Rachel," I told her.

Mom reached across the table and took Rachel's hand in hers. "Rachel. Such golden hair. I'm so glad you're here."

"Thank you, Mrs. Cassera. It's so nice to finally meet you."

"How's Dad doing?"

"Estefan tells me he's looking better, but they still don't quite know what's wrong."

"Estefan's my brother," I explained to Rachel. Mom then started in on Greta, my dad's wife. Mom liked her even less than I did.

"*She* won't let me see him. I'm not on the visitor's list. Why he ever married *her* is beyond me. *She* doesn't know that your father comes to see *me* every week."

I could hear the pride in her voice and see it in her face; and, for a brief moment, the pain that always hung around her eyes, haunting her face, disappeared. A shadow lifted, and I saw the face of the young woman standing next to my dad on her wedding day. She was still in love with my father after all these years.

My mother stood up and headed for the refrigerator.

"You two must be hungry. How about some spaghetti?"

"Mom, it's 4 a.m."

"I'd love some spaghetti," Rachel said. "Can I help?"

The two of them started on the tomato sauce. I was in charge of the noodles. I found the large pan under the counter next to a row of empty liquor bottles. She was still drinking. I looked over at her chattering away happily with Rachel.

"That's a beautiful necklace, Rachel." Mom lifted her glasses to get a better look. "It's a heart, isn't it?"

"Yes, Mrs. Cassera. Tony gave it to me."

Mom looked at me and winked.

My heart filled with love for her, and for the first time I didn't judge her for what she did. I was starting to understand how disappointments in life can affect us. I wasn't ashamed of her or her drinking, or saw them as faults anymore. I filled the pan with water and waited for it to boil. The sky was lightening by the time we finished eating.

Twin Oaks Hospital was barely a year old. They'd planted a few tiny trees and bushes to make it look friendlier. It was white everywhere, the floors were shiny, and it smelled like a hospital, pungently antiseptic. I was ten minutes early, so I walked up and down the hall. Framed prints of seashores and fields of daisies lined the walls between every door. They were there to make the place cheerier, but I found them depressing. The nurse came out of my dad's room and beckoned to me.

"You can go in now," she said. As I passed her, she spoke to me again. "You don't remember me, do you?"

My answer was a blank look.

"I'm Elena Morales," she said shyly. "You took me to the Homecoming Dance, freshman year. That was a long time ago now. I married Will Stockard. You remember Will, don't you? He's been very successful in real estate." I noticed she sighed when she said it. I'd bet money the guy wasn't home much.

"Of course. Elena. It's good to see you again. You look great." She blushed at my compliment, and I dug back in my memory for Elena Morales, but she wasn't there.

"You'd better go in. Your father's waiting for you." Elena headed for the nurse's station as I opened the door to the room.

The blinds had been drawn up, so my dad could look out at the mountains in the distance. He was lying in bed, propped on some pillows, gazing out the window. His arms lay limply at his sides. I stood rooted to the floor halfway between the door and the bed. He hadn't heard me come in.

"Hi, Dad."

"Antonio. You're here." His voice sounded weak. "Bring the chair over."

I carried the chair by the window over to the bed and sat down. He held out his hand to me, and I took it.

"How're you feeling?"

"A little better." He shifted in the bed, and a grimace crossed his face.

I adjusted his pillows. "Are you in pain? I can go get Elena."

"You're already on a first name basis with the nurses?" My dad was making a joke. That had to be a good sign. "I'm fine," he said, "besides I have this buzzer. I just push it, and they come running. How's your mother?"

"She's fine. Just upset that she can't get in to see you herself."

"That woman's been driving me crazy ever since I came to the hospital. I mean Greta, not your mom. Take care of your mother, Antonio."

He looked out the window. "I think that's an eagle circling the peak." I looked, but I couldn't see anything. "I should have never divorced your mom, Tony. Changing people doesn't change anything. I never knew how much pain your mother carried within her, the sadness and a million hurts from her childhood."

We sat there together, watching the clouds drift over the mountain range.

"That must be an eagle. Do you have any binoculars, Tony?"

"I think Mom does. I'll bring them tomorrow for you."

"Good. How's everything going, son?"

I looked down at my hands, and then I looked up into his eyes. I couldn't burden him with the truth.

"It's going great."

"You'll be successful. I know it. It's not easy. Things were not easy for me. Many times I wasn't sure how I'd make it through to the next week."

"But everything always seemed great. Mom never said anything."

"That's because I never told her. Antonio, sometimes there are things out of your control. Do you remember Pedro Cartegna?"

"Sure. He was your bookkeeper."

"For ten years, I trusted him with my payroll money. Then one Friday, he leaves, and we never see him again, and he's taken all the money. I mortgaged the house to pay everyone. I had to work twice as hard. That's when I went after new business, and we expanded. Best friends may turn into enemies, wives become bitter ex-wives. Things turn ugly when it all comes down to money. Don't let money rule you, Antonio. Be fair in your dealings with everyone, and stand by your word. Remember what we used to talk about when we were delivering tortillas in the old truck? *No te olvides de tus raices*, Antonio. Don't forget your roots or where you are from."

"I remember," I said. I'd heard my dad tell me these things before, about honesty and loyalty and integrity, but I seemed to have forgotten them once I started working in Washington. I suddenly realized how much more than a business I'd lost.

"You've accomplished so much in your life," Dad went on. "You're young. Your life is just beginning. Have confidence in yourself." He gripped my hand. "*Te amo.* I love you, Antonio."

"*Te amo, Papá.*"

"Now, tell me about this new girl in your life."

"Rachel? Who told you about Rachel?"

"Who do you think? I got a call this morning."

"Never tell Mom a secret," I said. "The whole world will know in ten minutes." I sat back, thinking about how to describe Rachel, searching for the right words. "Rachel is a miracle in my life. She's beautiful, with golden hair and eyes the color of the sea. Her nose is perfect, with a tiny bridge of freckles sprinkled across it. She's warm and funny, and I can just be myself with her. That's Rachel. I'll bring her to meet you. You'll love her, Dad."

"Sounds like you should marry her."

"Marry her!"

"Don't tell me you haven't thought about it?"

"Yes, I have, but taking care of a woman... I didn't do such a great job of it the first time."

My dad sighed. "You take care of each other. You choose each other. Did I ever tell you about your mother and Johnny Wiessmuller?"

"My mother and Tarzan?"

"We were at a party in Los Angeles, and Johnny Wiessmuller was there. He was real taken with your mom. Wanted her to stay there with him, but she chose me." He sighed and closed his eyes. "She chose me."

"Tired, Dad?"

"A little."

"Go to sleep. I'll come see you tomorrow."

"Okay," he said, so softly that I could barely hear him.

"Tony, what are you doing up in the attic? You're making a racket."

"I'm trying to find your binoculars, Mom."

Her head came through the opening in the floor.

"What do you want binoculars for?"

"For Dad. He wants to watch an eagle he can see from his room."

"Your father said that? Let me help you look." Mom came up the rest of the way. She had to walk bent over, as the ceiling was so low. "I don't think they're in there. There's another trunk down here, Tony."

Al poked his head up through the stair opening in the floor. "What the hell are you two doin' up here? You're stompin' on my head, and I can't hear the TV."

"I'm trying to find my binoculars, Al. We used them a couple of years ago."

"I packed 'em away." Al came up the rest of the way. "They're over in this here trunk." Al went over to another trunk and pulled it out from under the eaves. "What you wantin' the binoculars for?"

"My dad wants to watch an eagle he sees from his bed," I said excitedly.

Al stood up, bumping his head. "Ouch! He must be feelin' better." He rummaged around in the trunk. "Here they are. Lens caps have gone missin'," he apologized as he handed them to me, "so I wrapped 'em up in this old cloth."

"Thanks, Al." I hugged the binoculars to me.

We heard the front door slam, and someone called, "Hello. Anybody home? Hello?"

"We're up here, Rachel," I called back. I heard her steps on the attic stairway, and soon her head appeared.

"What are you all doing up here?"

I held up the binoculars. "Looking for these. Dad wants to watch an eagle he can see from his bed."

"Oh, Tony, that's wonderful." A smile lit up Rachel's face as she spoke. She knew how much that meant to me.

"I know. Let's all go get some Mexican food to celebrate," I said expansively.

Al looked shocked. I'd never invited him anywhere, but he and Mom decided to eat at home, so Rachel and I went by ourselves.

Don Frederico's real name was Jesus Luna. Somehow the name Luna just didn't seem grand enough for him. His restaurant had grown right along with my dad's tortilla business. The Don served only Tortilla King tortillas, and had for the past thirty years. I remember, as a kid, delivering tortillas to the Don when he was still calling himself Jesus, and his restaurant was little more than an old storefront. Now he was out on the Interstate in a stucco building with arches across the front. There was a tiled courtyard with a gurgling fountain, and the entry had huge wrought iron lanterns on either side. Hidden among the bushes were lights that splashed white, green, and red bands on the stuccoed walls. The place looked like a huge, illuminated Mexican flag.

"*Hola*, Antonio!"

It was definitely Jesus. He still had thick, black, wavy hair, but he'd gained about fifty pounds. He grabbed my hand in his fat, pudgy one, and squeezed it while hugging me with his free arm.

"You lookin' good, Antonio."

"*Gracias*, Don Frederico."

His eye caught Rachel. "*Precioso*, beautiful," he murmured in Spanish. "You eat tonight?"

"Yes, tonight we eat. Rachel has never had Mexican food, so I am counting on you to impress her."

He thrust out his chest and patted it with the palm of his hand. "It will be the best food the *señorita* has ever tasted."

He pulled two huge menus, covered in leather, from the pocket in the wall, and led us across the room to what he obviously considered his best booth.

"What's with the lights out front?" I said.

"Just plain old lights is boring. Too much like the *gringos*. *Señorita*." He opened Rachel's menu with a flourish and placed it gently in her hands. *Señor*." He handed me my menu with a precise, little bow.

"What do you recommend, Don Frederico?" I said.

"The chicken *molé* with perhaps some *chile relleños*. And to drink, Don Frederico's Margarita Grande."

"It sounds fine to me," said Rachel. "I don't know what any of this is. I can't even read the menu. I am sure if you have chosen it, it will be delicious, Don Frederico."

Don Frederico accepted the compliment, knowing in his heart it was well-justified. "Antonio, how is your father? We have been saying prayers for him. Pilar lights candles at the church."

"He's improving, but the doctors don't seem to know what's wrong."

"It was only Tuesday that we played golf, and he beat me. This growing old I cannot recommend. It is always some new ache and pain, but no one likes to hear an old man talk of his troubles." He glanced slyly at Rachel, but his question was directed at me. "Some *jalapeños*, Antonio?"

"Of course."

Don Frederico disappeared and came back with a bowl of *jalapeños*, a bottle of tequila, two glasses, salt, and lemon wedges. He stood by the table waiting for my invitation.

"Sit down, Don Frederico."

Rachel slid over in the booth, and the Don lowered himself into the seat next to her and rolled up his sleeves. He ate a *jalapeño*, then I ate one. Back and forth we went, *jalapeños*, then salt, tequila and a bite of lemon to cut the burn. Sweat beaded our foreheads. It was an ancient ritual that I'd seen my dad do many times until the tears fell from his eyes and rolled down his cheeks. It was the ultimate test. You were '*macho*,' a real man in the eyes of everyone. Dad swore it could cure anything, if it didn't kill you first. Rachel sat there, aghast, as the Don and I devoured the hot peppers and tossed back tequilas. When we were finished, the Don stood and slapped me on the back.

"*Macho*," he said, "just like your *papá*."

He went to see after our dinners, and I sat there and glowed. I'd just received the ultimate compliment.

"Why do you do that? It looks like torture."

"The nuns," I replied, teasing her.

"The nuns?"

"Everyone knows that you have to endure pain and suffering to get into heaven."

"You're not serious?" Rachel said.

"Sort of, I am. That's what the nuns taught us at catechism. We suffer here on earth to earn our place in heaven. Eating *jalapeños* is like a punishment for my sins. It proves I can withstand whatever pain comes my way. It makes a man strong."

"*Macho*," Rachel said.

"Yes." I smiled at her. "*Macho*."

Hours later found us sitting on Mom's front porch, in the old wooden swing. Rachel and I had eaten too much to even think about trying to sleep. We'd wrapped a blanket around our shoulders and one across our knees. The nights were still cold. Rachel curled her legs under her, while I kept one leg down on the porch to push us gently back and forth.

"So now I know what a '*Macho* Man' is," Rachel teased.

"Surprised?"

"A little. You know, you don't have to suffer through life to go to heaven. You can let yourself be successful."

"That's a funny thing to say."

"No more than it's a funny way to think."

I turned to her and pushed her hair back from her face. Even in the dark, I could see the sparkle in her eyes. "So how come you know so much?" I said.

"I just do." She pointed to the sky. "See that star? That's not really a star. It's a planet. Venus."

We sat there, staring at the night sky, while we rocked back and forth in the old swing. I remember my dad pointing out the constellations to me when I was a kid, but I could only find the Big Dipper by myself. An owl hooted nearby; the distant hum of the interstate replaced the crickets of summer.

The phone ringing inside the house broke the spell. Rachel and I locked eyes, and my heart filled with fear. I silently screamed "No!" to whomever or whatever could hear my one-word prayer.

Al came to the door. I heard my mom sobbing inside the house.

"Tony, your father's taken a turn for the worse. Can you drive your mom and I out to Twin Oaks?"

They were huddled in a small group outside the room, talking in whispers. Greta, my dad's wife, threw a baleful glance in Mom's direction. My brother, Estefan, was there, his arm around his wife, Eve. He had his pajama top on, an old pair of jeans, and work boots with the laces untied. My sister, Rosalie, stood off by herself, her arms wrapped around her in a hug. Her hair was braided in one single long braid that usually hung down her back, but tonight was draped over her shoulder.

Just as we reached them, a doctor came out of the room. I was relieved to see that it was Dr. Manrique, my father's doctor for the past fifteen years. Several technicians came out, wheeling some fancy machine. I tried to peek in the room, but all I could see was the end of the bed. Estefan spoke in a hushed voice, looking worriedly into the room.

"Dr. Manrique, how is he?"

"He's still unconscious. We're not sure exactly what happened. The nurse on duty saw the light come on for his room, so he'd evidently had time to buzz for her. When she got to him, he'd stopped breathing, and it was ten minutes before we could get his heart started again. We'd just about given up hope. We have him on a life-support system at this time. He's in a coma."

Greta gasped and started to weep hysterically. Dr. Manrique called a nurse for her, and had her helped to the lounge at the end of the hall. My mother clung to my arm, listening to every word the doctor said. He spoke slowly and kindly to us, rubbing his hand through his thick, gray hair. Only this gesture betrayed his emotion. He and my father had been friends for a long time.

"He was doing so much better," my sister Rosalie said. "How could this happen?"

The doctor shrugged his shoulders. He looked tired. "We don't know. He was in my office for a physical two weeks ago, and he was in excellent health for a man of his age." He shook his head. "There are just things we can't predict."

"Will he wake up?" I asked.

"I don't know that either. Maybe."

"Maybe?"

"Medicine is not an exact science, Tony. Anything is possible. We are doing all we can for him at this point. Now we have to wait. It's up to him. I must tell you, though, that the brain was starved of oxygen for quite some time. If he should wake up, there is the possibility of brain damage. I'm sorry."

Rosalie sobbed, and I put my arm around her.

"May we see him?" my mother asked.

"Yes, you may go in."

I was not prepared for what I was to see. There was only one light on in the room now, and a nurse I didn't know was sitting with him. She left when we came in. His eyes were closed, and he had tubes up his nose and something down his throat to help him breathe. Rosalie went over to the bed and ran her hand up and down over the bed cover near his right hand.

"Daddy?" she said, her voice trembling.

There was no response, and Rosalie turned to look at me with frightened eyes before she fled from the room. My mother started weeping at the foot of the bed. She touched my dad's foot like she was saying goodbye and left, too. I couldn't believe it was my father lying there with all these tubes in him. He'd been so vibrant, so strong, so in control of his life. I clenched and unclenched my fists in helplessness. Estefan and Eve slipped from the room, leaving me alone with him.

"Tony?"

I'd totally forgotten about Rachel. She came in quietly and stood next to me. The room seemed to brighten with her presence, and I felt my heart soar with hope. I was not giving up on him.

"Tony, Rosalie's standing out in the hall by herself. She's asking for you."

I looked at my dad and then at the door.

"It's okay. I'll stay with him."

I went out into the hall. Tears were streaming down Rosalie's face. She was twisting her braid with her hands, tying and untying it in a knot.

"I can't bear to see him like this, Tony," she wept.

"We can't give up on him, Rosie."

"I just can't bear it," she said, pulling away from me.

She ran off down the hall and out through the fire doors. I was torn between going after her and going back to my dad.

Rachel watched Tony go out into the hall, then walked quickly over to the bed. She bent her head close to Tony's father's face, and began talking quietly.

"There's something we need to do. I know you know what I mean, so if you can, give Tony a sign. It doesn't have to be anything big."

She heard footsteps coming into the room and moved to the foot of the bed. She felt Tony's hand on her shoulder.

"I wish you could have met him, Rachel. You would have liked him, and I know he would have liked you."

"Introduce me now, Tony."

He hesitated. "He probably can't hear us."

"You don't know that for sure."

He looked uncertainly at her, then he looked at his dad and then back at her. She gave him a little nod of encouragement. He went to the head of the bed and bent down close to his father's ear.

"Dad, I've brought someone to meet you. This is Rachel. Rachel, this is my dad."

They waited for something from him, some movement, but there was nothing. Rachel picked up one of his father's hands and held it in hers.

"Hi, Dad. I'm very happy to meet you," she said.

For the next week, I sat with my father every day. I brought the binoculars, and I talked to him. Maybe Rachel was right. Maybe he could hear me. Perhaps I could talk to him, wherever he'd gone, and bring him back.

"Remember the night you sat in the rain on the bleachers at my very first high school football game? It was me who put the dent in the side of your car with my bicycle. I let you think it was someone who parked next to you in town, but it was me. I'm not mad at you for throwing out my favorite dump truck, even though it was the best one and carried the most dirt and rocks. Remember the night I locked

Sammy in the garage by mistake, and he ate your favorite hat. I wish you'd come to Washington the time I'd invited you. You could have met the President. Your tortillas are the best in the whole world, Dad. Even Don Frederico agrees with me. Rachel and I ate at his restaurant the other night. Jesus and I did the *jalapeños*, just like you used to do. I stayed up with him, Dad, just like I used to see you do. I think Rachel thought we were a little nuts, but we know better, don't we?"

In the afternoons, I'd scan the mountaintops with the binoculars, trying to find the eagle my dad had seen. I even lifted his eyelids, looking for some movement, but his eyes remained fixed, staring off into space. He was still a strong, muscular man. I could feel the strength in his feet when I massaged them. And though his hand didn't grip mine when I held it, I could feel the power in it still. He didn't look sick. I told myself that he was only sleeping. Rachel sat with us sometimes, and Elena would sit with him a little when her shift ended. No one else in the family came. It hurt them too much to see him this way.

At the end of the week there was no sign of improvement, so Greta asked Dr. Manrique to discuss my dad's condition with all of us. Greta sat on one side of the table next to Dr. Manrique. Rosalie, Estefan and I sat across from them.

"Greta asked me to speak to all of you regarding your father's prognosis. She and I have discussed it privately, and it is with great sadness that I must tell you that I believe there is little hope of recovery. Greta has requested that the life support systems be stopped."

I glared at her. "Now wait a minute. You can't just give up on him. It's only been a week. Who are you to decide on my father's life?" I looked at my brother and sister for support, but they were both staring down at the table.

"That's the point, Tony," said the doctor. "She can't. Your father has a living will which stipulates that, if he is on life support and the doctors diagnose little chance of recovery, the life support systems be stopped. I cannot do that without all his children's consent, as well as his wife's."

"It's better this way, Tony," Estefan interjected. "Dad's not going to get any better."

"You don't know that," I said vehemently.

"Tony..."

Greta started to speak, but I stopped her.

"I don't want to talk to you," I spit back at her. "And what about you?"

Rosalie lifted her head and stuck her chin out. Her voice quavered, but it was firm. "I agree with Estefan. I can't stand to see him like this."

"But what about him?" I looked at the faces staring back to me, and knew their answer.

"No," I said. I pushed back my chair and stood up. "No. I do not give my consent."

That night, at the dinner table at my mom's house, I could hardly eat.

"How can they just sit around an ordinary old table and make a decision about taking someone's life like that?

"Tony," she said, "it was hard for Estefan and Rosalie. They've been over here afternoons, trying to come to a decision, while you've been at the hospital. It's not been easy for them."

"What about you, Mom?"

"I don't have a say any more. It's up to his children now."

"I said 'no.' Not yet. There's still a chance he may wake up."

Mom looked at me and smiled a crooked little smile. "You do what you think best, Tony."

"Where's Rachel?"

"She and Al are eating their supper on TV trays in the back room. Al's watching some old movie, and Rachel's keeping him company so we could have supper together, and you're not even eating. Look at your plate. You've hardly touched anything."

"I'm sorry, Mom. I'm just not hungry."

The phone rang, and we both jumped. Mom got up to answer it.

Every muscle in my body tensed, in dreaded anticipation of the message.

"Tony, it's a Mr. Buckman, calling you from Santa Fe."

"I'll get it in the front room," I said, relieved.

"Hiya, Tony. I called Washington and was surprised to hear you're in the Land of Enchantment. Thought you were out in L.A."

"I was, but my dad's been pretty sick."

"I'm sorry to hear that, Tony."

"Thanks, Hal. What's up?"

I could hear him hesitate on the other end. "More bad news, I'm afraid. Your accountant remembers those payments you made from the fifty thousand dollars, but we need the records to verify that they were actually made. The accountant fella says you had 'em at the house."

"Hell, Hal, Celinda's got everything from the house. You know that."

"Yeah, I know. I been talkin' to Celinda's lawyer, Ramirez, an' he says Celinda claims she doesn't have 'em, you do."

"Well, she's a liar, but so what else is new," I said wearily. "So where does that leave us?"

"So it leaves us with a problem, my friend."

I sighed inwardly. I could see Mom standing in the doorway, looking worried, and I didn't want to add to her worries right now.

"Hang on a second, Hal." I put my hand over the receiver. "Mom, how about making us some coffee?" She didn't move from the doorway. "Go ahead. This is just a business deal. Nothing major." She nodded her head and went back to the kitchen.

"Okay, Hal. Go on."

"Should I call back later, Tony? I hate to bother ya with your dad bein' sick an' all."

"No. Tell me."

"Well, the bankruptcy court's goin' to kick out your company bankruptcy protection, based on the allegations made by Celinda and Hightower. That means the creditors can go after you and collect." Hal paused.

"Go on," I said. I already knew what he was going to say next.

"You'll have to file for personal bankruptcy, Tony." Hal rushed on to the next sentence. "Now I've anticipated your response, and prepared the lawsuit against Celinda to get your furniture back like we'd discussed. It's not much, I know, but I'll have 'em..."

I cut Hal off. I kept my voice low so as not to alarm my mom, but my tone brought Hal up short.

"I don't want any of it."

"Whoa here, Tony, don' go givin' up. We still got options."

"Hal, you don't understand. I'll spell it out for you," I said, because, suddenly, it was real clear to me.

"She can have everything. If I have to file personal bankruptcy to start over, that's okay with me. I'm not putting any more time or money into this. Life's just too short. So, I guess what I'm saying is — thanks for all you've done, Hal, but you're out of a job."

There was dead silence on the other end of the line.

"But your furniture, you really wanted it," he finally said, sounding confused.

"I've changed my mind. I don't need it anymore."

"It's your call, Tony. Whatever ya want to do. I just never heard ya talk like this before. Tell you what, with the money left from your retainer, I'll file your personal bankruptcy papers and settle the IRS thing. You don' owe me a thing more, and good luck to ya, Tony."

"Thanks, Hal." I hung up.

I felt like something black and ugly that had been hanging around me for a long time was finally gone.

I continued to sit with my dad every day. I massaged his feet, and brought a cassette player to play his favorite music. I'd stand at the window with the binoculars, looking for the eagle, and describe the mountains and how the sun hit them. At the end of the second week, Dr. Manrique called another family meeting to discuss my dad's condition. I arrived early, but I couldn't bring myself to go into the hospital. I stood in the parking lot looking through the binoculars at the distant peaks, scanning the skies. That's where Rachel found me.

"They're waiting for you upstairs, Tony."

I kept looking through the binoculars. "I can't say, 'Let my dad die.' How can I live with myself if I do that? How can any of us make that decision?"

Rachel reached over and took the binoculars from me, so that I had to look at her. "None of you have to make the decision, Tony. Your dad made the decision for you. You just have to honor his wishes. You have to come now, Tony, they're waiting."

Reluctantly, I let her walk me up to the conference room. Greta was there, next to Dr. Manrique. She had dark circles under her eyes. I sat down between Estefan and Rosalie.

"I know how hard this is for all of you," Dr. Manrique began. "I regret to say that your father has shown no signs of improvement. It is still my professional opinion that there is, at this time, no hope of recovery. We can keep him alive indefinitely on life support, but I know that is against his wishes. I asked you all here again to discuss the situation. Greta has indicated that she still wants to have the life support stopped, in accord with your father's wishes. Estefan and Rosalie agree with her. What do you want us to do, Tony?"

They were all staring at me. Okay, Dad.

I nodded my head "yes."

"I have the papers here for everyone to sign." Dr. Manrique handed the papers to Greta first. We all signed in silence. Dr. Manrique collected the papers and stood. "I'll take care of everything," he said quietly. "I'm so very sorry."

"How long?" my brother asked.

"Two to three days at the most." Dr. Manrique left with Greta. Estefan and Rosalie and I hugged. Then they left, as well, and I put my head on the table.

The day my father died was a sunny one, with a blue sky and not one cloud in it. They'd taken the respirator from his throat, and he was breathing through his open mouth. The sound of each labored breath echoed in the room. I got out of the chair, went over to the bed, and held his hand while I spoke to him.

"I wish I knew you could hear me. I really love you, Dad, and I'm going to miss you. I'm sorry I wasn't successful, like you, but I hope you loved me anyway."

Then he squeezed my hand, just a little. I glanced at his face, waiting to see his eyes open. Instead his face totally relaxed, and I felt his grip loosen on my hand. Then his whole body let go, and the room was filled with his presence, vibrating with his energy. Ever so slowly, it faded from the room, and I knew he was gone from me forever. I laid his hand down gently on the bed. I reached for the buzzer by the bed and pressed it with all my might.

It couldn't have been more than three seconds when the door flew open, and Elena was there. The girl I took to the Homecoming Dance twenty years ago was with me, sharing one of the most important moments in my life, and I hardly knew her. She looked at me, then at my father. We stood together, and she held me while I cried.

Play CD Track 11
"Soaring with Eagles"
instrumental

The funeral was small and private, though the whole town acknowledged his passing in one way or another. He was an important man in Sanibel. The story of his life and death even ran in newspapers throughout the state. David and Sara flew in. David and I stood next to each other in the cemetery, and I liked the feel of his shoulder against mine. Greta was weeping at the graveside. My mom, pale and frightened, leaned on Al, who was actually wearing a suit, though it must have been borrowed, because it looked two sizes too big. Elena came, and Don Frederico was there. So was Rosita. Rachel held my hand, giving me her strength. When the priest gave the final benediction, I stared at my father's flower-draped casket, while everyone else bowed their heads in prayer.

"What will I be without my father?" I said to Rachel.

She linked her arm through mine and gave it a gentle squeeze.

"You won't be a child anymore," she said.

It was almost sunset when we left my dad's house that day, though I guess it was Greta's house now. Lots of people had come by to have something to eat and pay their respects to the family. Mom hadn't come, because she knew she wouldn't be welcome. As I was getting ready to leave, Greta came up to me.

"Tony, your father always told me he wanted you to have this."

I looked down. Lying in the palm of her hand was my dad's black onyx ring with the diamond in it, the one my mom had made for him. I never saw him without it. The smothering sadness I felt choked off my words.

"Thank you, Greta," I said brokenly. That moment was about as close as I ever felt to Greta. Death does that. It brings people together.

Mom had an Italian meal waiting for us when we got back home. After dark, we all gathered on the front porch to talk about Dad and tell stories. By ten o'clock, only Rachel, David and I were left. I pushed Rachel and myself on the porch swing; David sat on the front steps.

"Are you going back to Washington right away, Dad?"

"Probably the day after tomorrow, David. Rachel needs to get back to work, and so do I."

"Oh."

He sounded disappointed.

"What's the matter?"

"Well. I've got this gig. It's at a lodge in the mountains in northern California. I thought maybe you and Rachel would like to come and hear me and the band. It's only for one weekend. They're sort of trying us out. It's supposed to be a real pretty place."

"Oh, Tony, let's go," Rachel said.

"What about your patients, Rachel?"

"Oh, I rescheduled my appointments before we left for Los Angeles, to give me a good month free."

"Why didn't you tell me?"

"It didn't seem that important. I have some new clients I'm starting within a few weeks, so it's a good time for me to take a break."

"I wish you'd tell me these things," I said irritably.

"So what about it, Dad? Will you come?"

I looked over at Rachel.

"I'd love to go, Tony," she said.

"Okay, David, we'll come. I'll call the Ambassador, and let him know where I am. By the way, where *will* I be? What's the name of this place?"

"Elk Moon Lodge," David replied happily.

I put a call in to the Ambassador, who I hadn't talked to in over three weeks. It was good to hear his voice again.

"Hey, Cisco, I'm glad to hear from you. How's your father?"

"He passed away three days ago, Ambassador. The funeral was today."

"I'm sorry to hear that. Is there anything I can do for you?"

"Yes, there is, actually. We're going to the mountains for a few days, before heading back to Washington. I have some appointments I need to reschedule. Would you mind calling for me?"

"*No problema, amigo.*"

"They're in my desk calendar, in my room."

"I'll take care of it. I've got some great news for you. I've been wined and dined by this guy from California. He's invented a revolutionary new product that saves on energy consumption by as much as sixty percent. He's applied for a patent, so as of right now, it's patent pending status. He came to me, asking for help in getting a government grant and in marketing it to the federal government. He's willing to give us the rights to Maryland, D.C., and Virginia. I've looked at the promotional literature, and the device has some microchip inside a black box that attaches to your electric power panel."

The Ambassador stopped for breath and plunged on. "I know you're probably not ready to think about business, but he's got charts and testimonials from people, demonstrating a fifty to sixty percent cost savings when the device is mounted and plugged into the fuse box. This could be the Gold Rush of the next decade. With your connections at the Energy Department, Cisco, we could get a grant. Those congressmen might just mandate a federal requirement to reduce energy consumption at federal buildings, with just a little push from you. We'd have it made. What do you think? I've got a meeting set up with him in two weeks. We could work on this until we hear from Princess Sava."

"No thanks, Ambassador."

"What! You're joking."

"No, I'm not. It's all yours. Just be careful, Ambassador. This guy may have already sold his 'patent' a few times already."

"Tony, why don't you think it over before you decide? I haven't talked to anyone else about it. It'll be just you and me."

There was nothing for me to think over. "Ambassador, I'm just not interested."

"I'll tell you what. I'll leave the promotional material for you on your desk, Tony. No rush. You can look it over when you get back, and then decide."

He just wasn't hearing what I was saying. We hung up. I wished the Ambassador well on this one. Then maybe he could buy *me* lunch for a change.

Two days later, Rachel, David, Sara and I loaded up the rental car and started the drive to the airport in Albuquerque. We passed by Twin Oaks Hospital on the way out of town. I pulled off by the side of the road about a mile north of the hospital. The road curved a little closer to the mountains here, so I had a pretty good view.

"Rachel, grab the binoculars in the glove box."

Rachel handed them to me. We got out and stood by the road. David and Sara got out, as well, perplexed.

"Why're we stopping here, Dad?"

"I'm looking for something."

I put the binoculars to my eyes and scanned the peaks. The rocky face was deserted, glowing orange where the sun hit it, or hiding in deep purple shadows. He had to be there. He just had to be. I panned back to the right, and there he was. Soaring, his wings spread, swooping and circling right above the peak, where my dad said he'd seen him.

"I'll be damned." I lowered the binoculars. "He's there, Rachel. Why didn't I see him before?"

"Maybe you weren't ready to," she said.

I glanced at her, standing there, her eyes shaded by her hand. "What do you mean?"

She lowered her hand and turned towards me. "Sometimes we don't see things that have always been there until they're pointed out to us."

David interrupted us, impatient to look. "Let me see, Dad. What is it?"

I handed him the binoculars. He peered through them. "What kind of bird is that? A vulture?"

"It's an eagle, David."

"Is that the one Grandpa saw?"

"I think so," I said contentedly.

David continued peering through the binoculars. "That's weird. It looks like he's carrying a stick or something. You look." He handed the binoculars back to me.

"Maybe he's building a nest," Sara said.

I looked, but it wasn't a stick. The eagle had a snake clutched in its talons. "It's a snake he's got."

I passed the binoculars to Sara so she could see, and then Rachel looked through them, too. I thought back to the time my dad had told me about, when the Spanish Conquistadors were looking for a place to establish a fort in Old Mexico. They came upon an eagle sitting on a cactus, holding a snake. That's where they built their fort. Dad told me that's where Mexico City is now.

"The Mexican flag has an eagle with a snake on it," I said.

"No kidding," David replied. "That's neat."

Traffic was starting to slow as it passed. People were trying to figure out what we were looking at.

"Come on, you guys," I said. "Let's get going, before all these rubber-neckers cause an accident."

As we drove off, I realized I wasn't the failure I'd thought I was. My dad never saw me that way, and now I'd just seen what my dad always saw. Life has its ups and downs. Sometimes you're the eagle and sometimes you're the snake. That's just the way life is.

She sat at the zinc-topped bar and watched the flies crawl around the rim of her glass. She raised her hand and brushed them away. Carlos would be back soon. He wasn't a bad husband, but he wasn't an exciting one, either. The fish on the wall behind the bar was staring, laughing at her. She went behind the bar, grabbed an icepick and stuck it right in the center of its cold, dark eye.

The trees were thick on either side as we made our way up the mountain toward Elk Moon Lodge. The road wound like a creek, sometimes almost back onto itself, and it was narrow, just barely enough room for two vehicles. In some places the trees made a dark tunnel above and around us. In others, they made a wall stretching to the sunny sky above. Through darkness and light we drove, always climbing, for we were in the Sierras now, winding across the side of a mountain. The pine forest eventually gave way to walls of rock, with only a little pine sapling here and there growing out of a crevice or ledge. We curved with the road, and the rock wall on our left vanished, and below us lay a lake. It nestled between two folds of the mountain and shimmered like a mirror, reflecting tree and sky and snow-capped peak. The lake was full at one end; at the other end it curved to a point, like the horn of an animal. Elk Moon Lodge sat opposite us, on the fullest part of the lake. It was made entirely out of logs. I stopped the car by the side of the road, and we all climbed out.

"Wow," David said.

I took in a deep lungful of pine-scented air and let it out. I put my arm around Rachel's shoulders. "So, what do you think?"

"It looks like a little bit of heaven on earth to me. I'm so glad we came."

"So am I," I said. With my arm around her, I felt so lucky, so content, so loved. I thought about the women in my life — my first love, Julie, who gave me the gift of my son; sensual, ambitious Celinda, who taught me what love isn't; my mom, who gave me life itself; and Rachel, who showed me what love is really all about. How grateful I was to these women, and how little I had showed my gratitude or my love for them.

I brushed a strand of hair off Rachel's forehead, realizing how much I genuinely loved her, and cared about her happiness. Celinda and I had been using each other to achieve separate, manipulative ends. My hate and anger over what Celinda had done had vanished. I wished her well and felt sorry for her. I didn't want anything from Rachel except to share life with her. With her standing by my side, nothing was impossible. Even my mom I saw differently now. I was always criticizing her, judging her for her drinking and for catering to Al. Now I saw all the love and hugs she'd given me as a child, and I was happy for her that she had a companion. I stared down at the lake, at a new reflection of myself. I was the happiest I'd ever been in my life. Rachel laid her head on my shoulder, and I pressed my cheek against her hair.

David banged on the top of the car to get our attention.

"C'mon you two, we gotta go. I've got to hook up with the band." Sara was already back in the car, waiting. No romance in those two, I decided.

Elk Moon Lodge had a lobby that was two stories tall, with columns made of huge tree trunks holding up the roof. Faded Indian blankets draped the railings of the second floor balcony. Whoever had built the place, you knew they were his rugs that he'd hung up there himself, and he'd probably shot the elk whose head hung above the enormous stone fireplace, each stone put there with his own hands. Even though it wasn't cold, a fire crackled on the hearth. The brochure said the lodge had been built in the early 1920's, and it felt like we'd stepped back in time. The phone at the front desk was black with rotary dialing, and it was the only phone in the lodge. The desk clerk handed me skeleton keys with the room numbers burned into a worn leather disk. Our rooms were on the second floor, the doors opening onto the balcony overlooking the lobby.

I'd gotten two rooms, thinking David and I would bunk together, and Rachel and Sara would have the other. David set me straight on that as we carried the luggage up to our rooms.

"You're too old-fashioned, Dad," he whispered to me as he took one of the keys and carried his and Sara's luggage into one of the rooms. She followed him in. He stood with the door half-closed, trying to be polite and not shut it in my face.

"Catch you later for dinner?" he hinted and shut the door.

"Well, how about that?" I said to Rachel. She just smiled at me, and headed down the balcony, glancing at the doors looking for our room number.

While Rachel napped, I decided to do some exploring. I walked halfway round the lake to a timber gazebo that sat on the narrowest part of the water. From here, you could look back to the lodge or up the lake's horn. I decided this would do nicely. I headed back to the lodge, and the gift shop I'd seen off the lobby.

The old man behind the counter had two braids of iron-gray hair hanging alongside his face, which was weathered and worn, with small feathery creases. He wore a green-and-blue plaid shirt and jeans. There was a huge silver buckle, set with turquoise, on his belt. I asked to see some things in the case, and he pulled out a tray of rings. I was disappointed that there weren't any gold ones like I wanted, but I settled on a silver ring with turquoise bands set into it. Then I wasn't sure. I needed another man's opinion. I held the ring between two fingers, in front of the old Indian's face.

"What do you think?"

He squinted his eyes at it and shook his head "no."

"Better," he said, picking up a smaller ring in the back of the tray.

I had to admit the ring was lovely, with its circular chunk of turquoise flanked by two little pieces of coral.

"I'll take it," I said. "Do you have something to put it in?"

He found a faded old ring box for it, and I was pleased to see how pretty it looked wedged between two soft cushions of velvet. I slipped the little box into my pocket and headed to the Great Room, where I could hear David's band warming up for the night ahead. The polished wooden floor of the room extended out onto a balcony overlooking the water. I waved to David and headed outside.

Leaning on the railing, I looked out across the lake to the gazebo. Down below me, the old Indian from the shop was hauling the canoes out of the water. Elk Moon Lake was a beautiful place, and I wished my dad were here with me now to see it. The sun was getting low in the sky, and behind me I heard my son practicing. My life in Washington seemed so far away, further than mere miles. Somehow it didn't seem as important, anymore. Seeing my son as a man, and having a woman like Rachel in my life, made my life far richer than it had ever been before. I heard the band starting another song. This one I recognized. It was the poem I'd written, and David was singing it. I turned and watched him, glowing with love and pride in what we'd created together.

Play CD Track 12
"Sleeping With An Angel"

Lying here in my bed
Your image runs through my head,
And I dream about you all through night.
My heart's been searchin high and low,
And now that I've got you I can't let you go,
Cause what I'm feeling feels so right.

Sleeping with an Angel,
I do believe
That I'm sleeping with an Angel.
Who else could it be?

I use to be so afraid to let my feelings show,
My armor laced up good and tight.
But every time you come near,
The thunder clouds seem to disappear,
And the future looks bright and clear.

Sleeping with an Angel,
I do believe
That I'm sleeping with an Angel.
Who else could it be?

My love would part the sea
To be with you for eternity.
Oh, I'll do anything for you, girl,
You're the wonder of this world.
The wonder of this world
The wonder of this world
I'm sleeping with an Angel
I'm sleeping with an Angel
I'm sleeping with an Angel, yea, yea, yea
I'm sleeping with an Angel
I'm sleeping with an Angel
I'm sleeping with an Angel
Yea, yea, yea, yea, yea.

David's voice faded out. He lowered the mike and began to applaud. He was applauding me! Then the others in the band joined in. I walked toward him across the floor, clapping my hands for him. The song was beautiful. I couldn't wait for Rachel to hear it. David and I planned it all out. Rachel and I would go for a walk tonight, and when we came back in the room, David would start singing it to her.

That night, Rachel and I danced on the polished wooden floor of the Great Room at Elk Moon Lodge. Sara sat in a slip of a dress off to the side, watching David sing and play. It wasn't a big crowd, but they seemed to be appreciative, and they applauded loudly after every song. David took a break and joined us at a small table, where we were drinking cokes with Sara.

"I think he likes you, David," Sara said, nodding in the direction of the back wall. I turned to look.

"The old Indian?" I said. "He's the one who's thinking of booking you here?"

"Yeah, that's Richard Darkfoot. He made a killing in real estate, retired, and bought this place."

Real estate. That was an idea. I was definitely in the market for a new career. I looked over at the Indian. He gave me a little wave. The band started up again, and I asked Rachel if she'd like to go for a walk along the lake. Suddenly, I panicked. Had I remembered it when I changed clothes? I reached into my pocket and was relieved to find the little box there. I winked at David and glanced at my watch.

Rachel and I walked hand and hand along a little path that was lit every twenty yards or so with lanterns. Moths and night bugs swarmed around the lights, each insect making its own circular flight around the flames. We stopped to watch them.

"It's like a little dance, isn't it?" Rachel said.

"I wonder why they're so attracted to the light. They're so many of them."

We followed the path to a small bridge spanning a stream that fed into the lake. The lantern cast a flood of light onto the boards and branch railings, and all was dark beyond. The bark had peeled off the railings a long time ago. They felt smooth beneath our hands. I peered into the darkness, looking for the trees I knew were there, but I couldn't discern one tree from the night surrounding us.

The path led us into a clearing on the point of land where the timber gazebo sat. A lone lantern hung near the steps. Looking out across the lake from the gazebo, the lights blazed from Elk Moon Lodge and shimmered on the surface of the water. I was so nervous that I talked as fast as I could about whatever came into my mind first.

"Richard Darkfoot told me it's unusually warm for this time of the year. He was able to open up the lodge almost two months early. He said he bought four more canoes for this season. The people who come to stay really like to go canoeing on the lake."

"Really," Rachel said, but she didn't say anything more than that. She appeared enchanted with the scene before her, and hardly seemed to hear what I was saying.

"He's thinking about bringing elk back into these woods. The music's starting up again. Do you want to dance?"

"Yes," she said softly. "You know I'd love to dance."

I pulled her close and wrapped my arms around her, and we swayed slowly and gently to the music, barely moving more than a foot or two. I closed my eyes and leaned my cheek against her hair, smelling the familiar scent of roses. David's distant voice floated faintly out across the water towards us.

Play CD Track 13
"Sleeping With An Angel
(Reprise Solo)

Lying here in my bed,
Your image runs through my head,
And I dream about you all through the night.
Well, I've been searchin' high and low,
And now that I've got you I can't let you go,
Cause what I'm feeling feels so right.

Sleeping with an Angel,
I do believe
Sleeping with an Angel.
Who else could it be?

SLEEPING WITH AN ANGEL

Use to be so afraid
To let my feelings show.
My armor laced up good and tight.
But every time you come near,
The thunder clouds seem to disappear,
And the future looks so bright and clear.

Sleeping with an Angel,
I do believe
Sleeping with an Angel.
Who else could it be?

My love would part the sea
To be with you for eternity.
Oh, I'll do anything for you girl,
You're the wonder of this world.
The wonder of this world
The wonder of this world

Sleeping with an Angel,
I'm sleeping with an Angel,
Sleeping with an Angel, yea, yea, yea
Well, I'm sleeping with an Angel,
I'm sleeping with an Angel,
I'm sleeping with an Angel,
I do believe

"Rachel, I want to ask you something."

"Okay," she murmured dreamily.

"Rachel, will you marry me?"

She didn't say anything, but moved in closer to me. I wrapped my arms around her tighter. I was happy to think we'd be together.

"Tony, I can't marry you. I'm going to be leaving soon."

"Leaving? But where are you going?" I was hurt, confused. I stopped dancing and looked at her. "I thought...I love you, Rachel."

"And I love you, Tony," she said softly, "and always will. But I only come for a little while, and then I go."

I closed my eyes and hugged her to me, fighting the lump in my throat. "What are you talking about? You can't leave."

"You don't need me anymore," she whispered in my ear. "You have removed your armor. There is nothing that holds you back now."

"Of course I need you. You don't understand. I want to marry you."

"But I can't marry anyone, Tony."

"Stop saying that." I felt tears welling in my eyes as I opened them to look at her, but my arms were empty. Rachel was standing down by the water's edge. I looked down at my arms, trying to understand how I could have felt I was still holding her. When I looked up, her face was radiant and a faint glow of light emanated from her. My heart was flooded with a love that knew no bounds.

"But I love you, Rachel."

I started towards her, but she raised her hand to stop me.

"And I love you, Tony, always."

I watched as she bent down toward the water and made a sweeping motion with her arm. An arc of light rose from her hand. As she moved her arm, slowly and gracefully, a circle of light formed around her and grew brighter, and the Rachel I knew faded into a swirling sphere.

"Rachel!" I shouted.

I took a step forward and felt a crunch under my foot. Something glittered in the lamplight. I reached down and picked up the necklace with the gold heart and diamond that I'd given her at Christmas.

"Rachel? Where are you?" I called out, frightened.

"I'm here," her voice answered. I looked out over the lake, searching for her, but all I saw moving was the surface of the water, where the moon was reflected on it. But the moon hadn't risen yet. I watched the light dance on the water.

The wind began to blow straight and strong across Elk Moon Lake. I gripped the railing of the gazebo as its full force hit me, and I was a warrior on the prow of a ship slicing through a stormy sea. The tree limbs in the forest thundered and cracked around me.

I shouted once more into the wind.

"Rachel!"

The light on the surface of the water rose, hovered like beating wings, then slowly faded away. "I'm here," the wind whispered before dying to a gentle breeze. "Always."

I stood in silence, staring at the dark surface of the lake, hardly daring to believe what had just happened. God had not abandoned me. He had answered my prayers. He had sent me Rachel.

"Always..." I whispered to the moon rising slowly above Elk Moon Lake.

Contents of CD

1. **Zeptha's Theme**

Music: Jon Campos & Ron Turner
Vocals: Roger A. Campos & Laurie Kotter
Violin: Willem Elzevir
Cello: Ursula Encarnación
Viola: Catherine Frey

2. **Under Your Spell**

Words & music: Jon Campos
Vocal: Jon Campos
Hammond B-3: Dwayne Dupuy
Guitar: Greg Speed
Bass: Ronnie Ellis
Drums: John Graham

3. **Under The Sun**

Words & music: Jon Campos
Electric Guitar: Jon Catler
Vocal & Acoustic Guitar: Jon Campos
Classical: Jon Catler
Bass: James "Jimmy" Charlsen
Percussion & Drums: Tom Sabia

4. **La Vieja**

Music: Jon Campos & Gail Vogel
Violin: Willem Elzevir
Cello & Chant: Ursula Encarnación
Viola: Catherine Frey
Midi sequencing: Gail Vogel
Electric Guitar: Jon Catler
Acoustic Guitar: Jon Campos

5. **Prayer For My Angel**
   Words & music: Jon Campos
   Vocal: Jon Campos
   Keyboard & Drums: Chris Estes
   Guitars: Brian Lovely

6. **Depths of Despair**
   Words & music: Jon Campos
   Vocal: Jon Campos
   Guitars: Jon Catler
   Bass: James "Jimmy" Charlsen
   Drums: Tom Sabia

7. **She'll be Coming Soon**
   Words & music: Jon Campos & Eric Di Berardo
   Vocal: Jon Campos
   Acoustic Guitar: Billy McCoy
   Bass: Jason Rasberry
   Drums: John Graham
   Piano & Keyboard: Dwayne Dupuy

8. **I Wanna Know**
   Words & music: Jon Campos
   Vocal: Jon Campos
   Drums: Chris Estes
   Guitar: Dennis Hamlin
   Bass Guitar: Dallas Reed

9. **Dear Rachel**
   Words & music: Jon Campos
   Vocal & Acoustic Guitar: Jon Campos
   Electric Guitar: Jon Catler
   Bass: James "Jimmy" Charlsen
   Drums: Tom Sabia

10. **Search My Heart Search My Soul**
Words & music: Jon Campos
Vocal: Jon Campos
Hammond: Dwayne Dupuy
Acoustic & Electric Guitar: Greg Speed
Bass: Ronnie Ellis
Drums: John Graham

11. **Soaring With Eagles**
Music: Jon Campos & Ron Turner
Violin: Willem Elzevir
Viola: Catherine Frey
Cello: Ursula Encarnación
Guitars & String Arrangment: Ron Turner

12. **Sleeping With an Angel**
Words & music: Jon Campos
Vocal: Jon Campos
Classical, Electric & Acoustic Guitars: Ron Turner
Bass: James "Jimmy" Charlsen
Drums: Tom Sabia

13. **Sleeping With an Angel – Reprise Solo**
Words & music: Jon Campos
Vocal and Acoustic Guitar: Jon Campos

Tracks 2,7,10 recorded at Patrick McGuire Recording Studio, Arlington, Texas
Tracks 1,3,4,6,9,11,12,13 Recorded at MS PRO, Baltimore, Maryland
Tracks 5 and 8 recorded and mixed by Chris Estes, Cincinnati, Ohio
All other tracks mixed by Gary Charles at MS PRO
All tracks mastered by Gary Charles at MS PRO
Produced by Jon Campos & Roger A. Campos

Manufactured and Distributed by Inca Gold Records
P.O. Box 61362
Potomac, Maryland 20854